crime

Renfrewshire
Council

The library is always open at
renfrewshirelibraries.co.uk

Visit now for library news and
information,
to **renew and**
reserve online, and to
download
free eBooks.

Phone: 0300 300 1188
Email: libraries@renfrewshire.gov.uk

A
LIFE
TO
KILL

A LIFE TO KILL

MATTHEW HALL

MANTLE

First published 2017 by Mantle
an imprint of Pan Macmillan
20 New Wharf Road, London N1 9RR
Associated companies throughout the world
www.panmacmillan.com

ISBN 978-0-230-75238-2

1 3 5 7 9 8 6 4 2

A CIP catalogue record for this book is available from the British Library.

Typeset by Ellipsis Digital Limited, Glasgow
Printed and bound by CPI Group (UK) Ltd, Croydon, CR0 4YY

Visit **www.panmacmillan.com** to read more about all our books
and to buy them. You will also find features, author interviews and
news of any author events, and you can sign up for e-newsletters
so that you're always first to hear about our new releases.

For my mother, Rebecca.
Thanks for everything.

A
LIFE
TO
KILL

ONE

August 2014

Anna Roberts felt herself blushing as she handed the shop assistant the crumpled notes and assorted coins she had been carefully saving all summer. Her shame wasn't at buying a set of black silk lingerie, but at spending so much precious money on herself. Her husband, Lee, was a private soldier, and his meagre salary was barely enough to keep body and soul together. Most of Anna's clothes came from the town's weekly market or its many charity shops, and she relied on the second-hand stall run by the Regiment's Wives and Girlfriends Club to dress their three-year-old daughter, Leanne. The cash she had just parted with would have fed them for a fortnight.

Tucking her purchases into the plain carrier bag she had brought with her, Anna reassured herself with the thought that, when he shortly returned from a six-month tour in Afghanistan, the last thing Lee would be thinking of when he saw her new outfit was the expense. With a little luck, before too long they would be celebrating her getting pregnant again. Then they would be a proper family – the kind she had longed for throughout her short and lonely childhood.

As she set off on the mile-long walk back up the hill to

Highcliffe Camp, Anna felt her guilt dissolve and her spirits lift. She had nothing left for the bus fare and it would be yesterday's reheated leftovers for tea, but her agonizing wait was nearly over.

The men of C Company were due home in five days' time. The tension throughout the small garrison town of Highcliffe was increasing by the minute. Mixed with the collective sense of apprehension there was also great excitement. C Company was the last of the regiment and the very last of the British Army to be returning from front-line service in Helmand. After nearly thirteen years, the military campaign was over. For the first time since the end of the Second World War, there was no one left to fight. Another enemy in a foreign land would no doubt appear soon enough, but just for the moment the country was at peace and its servicemen safe.

Previous homecomings had been celebrated with a tea party in the officers' mess, but this time the occasion was going to be a little more lavish. The returning soldiers would parade along the High Street before joining their families for an outdoor picnic on the regimental playing field. After a rainy summer, everyone was praying for good weather.

As president of the WAGs Club, Melanie Norton was in charge of organizing the festivities. She had only recently turned thirty and her husband, now a major, was barely three years older, but she felt like a mother to the C Company wives and girlfriends, most of whom, like their partners, were in their early twenties or even younger. Melanie's headquarters were in the hall next to St Mary's, the regimental church that stood inside the front gates of Highcliffe Camp. It was chiefly used as a volunteer-run day nursery for preschoolers, but for the past week it had also doubled as an office, workshop and kitchen for Melanie and her team of helpers. Against a shrill background of crying babies and shrieking toddlers, they had painted banners and glued together endless yards of paper streamers that would decorate the marquee. Melanie had often thought that she would make a good army officer herself. With the help of a spreadsheet, she had allocated every member of her team a list of tasks to complete and dishes to make. Everything was planned down to the last sandwich. Besides everything else she had to do between now and the men arriving home, Melanie had also volunteered to produce three hundred cupcakes.

Melanie was no stranger to homecomings. She had never known a life away from the army. Her father had been an officer in the Paratroop Regiment, who through a combination of single-mindedness and exceptional bravery had risen to the rank of brigadier. His advancement had come at the cost of frequent moves and the family never being able to put down permanent roots. Melanie had hoped that her adult life would be more settled and that she wouldn't have to live with the constant fear that her husband might not come home. The opposite had happened. During the ten years of their marriage, Christopher had completed nine six-month tours of duty: five to Afghanistan and four to Iraq. Three and a half years in combat. Although she tried hard to convince herself otherwise, their two daughters, Emily and Hannah, aged nine and seven, hardly knew him.

This time, Melanie thought to herself as she painted the last 'E' on the welcome home banner, she would find the courage to tell Chris that she wanted things to change. Her brother-in-law had an opening at his insurance brokerage in Bristol and was prepared to offer a salary that would almost match what the army was paying. Plus, there was the opportunity for regular bonuses. If Christopher could go toe to toe with Al Qaeda in Iraq and the Taliban in Helmand, Melanie reasoned, selling a few insurance policies surely wouldn't pose him many problems.

Give him a day or two to adjust to home, then plant the seed. That was her plan, and this time she was determined to stick to it.

'Would you mind giving me a hand hanging this up to dry?' Melanie addressed her question to Sarah Tanner, a pretty nineteen-year-old, nearly eight months pregnant, who had spent the morning making elaborate table decorations out of coloured tissue paper. She was quite an artist.

'Sure,' Sarah said distractedly. Like most of the women working around the long row of trestle tables, she had been lost in thought.

'Are you all right?' Melanie asked as they each took hold of one end of the banner.

Sarah attempted a nod and a smile, but tears welled in her eyes.

Melanie knew exactly how she felt. The last few days of tour were almost the most painful.

'Why don't you come outside with me for a moment?'

They left the banner on the table and headed towards the door, Melanie looping her arm inside Sarah's as they stepped around two boisterous three-year-olds who had escaped from the roped-off nursery area in pursuit of a ball. An older woman, Kathleen Lyons, whose grandson was one of the youngest members of C Company, jumped up from her chair and came after them.

'Love . . .' Kathleen called out to Sarah. She dipped a hand into her cardigan pocket and brought out a small bundle of coupons. 'I was going to share these out later. Have some.'

Sarah sniffed a thank you and gratefully took a few.

Kathleen worked at a local supermarket and eagerly hoo-vered up the money-off vouchers that careless customers left at her till. She couldn't let them go to waste, so made a point of sharing them amongst the WAGs.

'Wedding plans going OK?' Kathleen inquired kindly.

'Great, thanks,' Sarah said, wiping away more tears. 'I just hope I'll fit into my dress. I won't at this rate.'

'You'll look beautiful,' Kathleen said.

Melanie agreed. Sarah turned heads everywhere she went, and her fiancé, Kenny Green, was the envy of his comrades.

Melanie and Kathleen exchanged a look as Sarah dried her eyes. Both knew how difficult things were at home for the young woman who was currently living with her future in-laws in their small house just outside the camp. Paul Green, her fiancé's father, had struggled with depression since being invalided out of the regiment a few years before, and Rachel, his mother, was a drama queen who broke all the unspoken rules by voicing her morbid fears over her son's safety at every opportunity. Neither Melanie nor Kath-leen could tolerate Rachel's company for more than a few minutes at a time. They didn't like to think what a strain it must be for Sarah. It was also no secret that Rachel Green wasn't looking forward to seeing her only son get married in a fortnight's time. There wasn't a young woman alive who would have been good enough for her precious Kenny.

'Problems at home?' Melanie asked, as they continued towards the exit.

Sarah nodded.

'I know it's tough, but I really think you ought to have it all out with Rachel before Kenny gets back. The last thing you want is him coming home to an atmosphere that'll spoil the wedding.'

'I'll try,' Sarah said.

As they neared the door it flew open and Anna Roberts burst in.

'Have you heard?' Anna said, her eyes wide with excitement, 'I just bumped into the padre—'

'Heard what?' Sarah asked with a note of alarm.

Anna could barely contain her excitement. She addressed all the women in the room at once. 'Listen, everyone.' She clapped her hands to gain their attention. 'I've got some news.' Concerned faces stared back at her. 'Don't worry – it's good news. Colonel Hastings has said they can skip decompression. They'll fly into Cyprus in forty-eight hours and come straight home from there with no delay. They'll be in Highcliffe on Thursday morning – two days early.'

As the spontaneous cheer went up, all Melanie could think of was how little time she had left to decorate the marquee and ice three hundred cupcakes.

TWO

Private Pete Lyons, or 'Skippy', as he was known to everyone, including Major Norton, felt like he'd taken more than his fair share of stick during the six-month tour. With only two days to go before they were airlifted out of this hellhole, it was adding insult to injury to pick on him *again*. The platoon had run out of the plastic bags that had to serve as latrines over a fortnight ago. Since then, they'd been using a hole in the ground, and it was Skippy's unpleasant job to fill in the old one and dig another two yards to the right.

It was nine o'clock at night but still hot as a furnace, and except for the men manning the guns on the four sangar towers, the platoon were under four big tarps – one for each section – at the far end of the post behind a screen of mosquito netting. Skippy had used up the last of his repellent during the first half of the tour, and since then his body had become a lunar landscape of livid, swollen bites that were being added to by the second. He would have traded his right arm for a squirt of DEET.

'Two days. Just two more lousy days,' he said out loud to himself as he hacked at the hard-baked earth.

Skippy's latest offence was fainting from exhaustion during that day's predawn patrol. What did Sergeant Bryant expect from a short-arse eighteen-year-old lad who had started the tour weighing less than ten stone? In forty degrees, even the big guys struggled under the weight of a rifle, ammo, med pack and bulletproof Kevlar vest. They'd already covered five miles when they came under fire from a couple of Tali fighters on the nearby hillside and had to sprint across a patch of open ground. He'd told the sergeant he could barely walk, let alone run, but Bryant's answer to everything was just to shout louder. It had served him right he was nearly shot. Maybe next time he'd take some notice.

Except hopefully there wasn't going to be a next time. The rumour that had been spreading throughout the platoon that afternoon was that Major Norton had issued the command that patrols were to cease. There was nothing more to be gained. The local villagers knew the British soldiers were moving out on Wednesday and the Tali up on the mountain probably did, too. Skippy didn't understand much about politics and cared even less, but he knew that the moment they left Helmand things would return to exactly the same as they had been before. Maybe some girls were going to school up in Kabul, but they certainly weren't being educated in the nearby village of Shalan-Gar. You saw them washing clothes at the stream some mornings, all covered up in their brown burkhas, but aside from that you never saw a female out of doors. Not even a face at the window of their mud houses.

In Skippy's opinion the whole place was a madhouse beyond any kind of help they could offer. When the platoon had arrived in February, Major Norton told them that they had received only two orders: befriend villagers to the north; kill or capture Taliban to the south. They'd done plenty of killing, but making friends had proved harder. Back in March they had received a truckload of potatoes with instructions to persuade the local farmers to plant them instead of opium poppies. The villagers put the potatoes in the ground but didn't waste a single drop of water trying to raise them. They just let them dry up and die. Meanwhile, their underground wells remained full of water ready for the poppy crop they would plant that autumn.

A madhouse. Flies, stink, bombs and bullets. Still, in a couple of days he'd be out of here and back at his nan's flat in Highcliffe. Compared with this place, those four small rooms were paradise.

From out of the darkness, Sergeant Bryant's booming voice hit him with the force of an exploding mortar round. 'Put your bloody back into it, lad! Scratching's no bloody good! Dig, you scabby little runt! Dig!'

Skippy redoubled his efforts. He was still hurting from the last time Bryant had cuffed him and didn't want to repeat the experience.

'Two more days, Skip. Two more lousy days.'

Bryant's yell jolted Private Kenny Green out of the doze into which he'd slipped while keeping watch from the north-east sangar. It must have been the slug of hooch that had made him sleepy. He had known it was a bad idea but the lads hadn't given him much choice. Half a cup after six months on the wagon had been enough to go straight to his head, and now he could barely keep his eyes open.

Discipline had started to slip as the end of the tour approached. Along with mobile phones, alcohol was strictly forbidden, but some of the boys had secretly managed to concoct some foul, mouldy-tasting brew by fermenting bits of fruit they had picked up on patrol in water bottles buried beneath their sleeping rolls. If Bryant were to find out, he wouldn't bother with official discipline: justice would be brutal and immediate. Kenny shuddered to think what form it would take. But although everyone complained about Bryant ruling with a rod of iron, at least you knew where you stood with him. And in a strange way, he made you feel secure. It was hard to be afraid of the enemy when your sergeant didn't know what fear was. Each day began with him shouting in your ear and ended pretty much the same way.

Nevertheless, Kenny had felt an almost mutinous atmosphere building all afternoon. It had kicked off when Lee Roberts let slip that he'd overheard Major Norton telling Bryant he didn't think they should bother with any more patrols. According to Lee, Bryant had objected violently. The twenty-eight-man platoon had carried out daily patrols for six months, suffering one fatality and losing several more to serious injuries. After each setback they'd kept on going as before. Even the day after Billy Dalton had been left screaming in the middle of the road with his guts spilling out while a firefight raged around him, they'd trudged out of the gate at four a.m. with Bryant in the lead as usual. Staying inside the dirt walls of their compound on the final day would have felt to Bryant like an admission of defeat.

The mood among the rest of the platoon couldn't have been more different. They had all had enough adventure for one tour. Thoughts of home had started creeping into their minds and taken the edge off their concentration. It had happened to Kenny while out on patrol that morning. He had been walking at the head of B Section following the wadi leading west from Shalan-Gar towards the next settlement across the valley. Some Tali had booby-trapped the dried-out river bed several times in recent months, but Kenny's thoughts had wandered off to Sarah and their wedding that was due to take place in just over a fortnight's time. Or more precisely, their wedding night. He could almost feel her soft skin and her breath on his neck.

Kenny had been less than ten feet away from the trigger wire when Lee spotted it. He had tried to tell himself that he would have seen it in time, but deep down, he knew that he wouldn't have. Following his near miss, his legs shook, his heart raced and he had started spotting imaginary gunmen behind every tree and rock. Later, when they came under fire and Skippy had collapsed out in the open, he had come close to freezing with panic. For once, Kenny had been grateful for Bryant's yelling. With incoming rounds spitting up the dirt all around them, the sergeant ordered them to take cover while he dragged the unconscious Skippy clear.

There was no question that Bryant was a bastard, but if he had learned one thing in Helmand, it was that bastards made good soldiers.

Kenny stifled another yawn and scanned the surrounding fields and orchards beyond the minefield that surrounded the camp's perimeter. The sky was moonless. With virtually no ambient light, his night-vision goggles allowed him to see only to a distance of approximately one hundred yards. All was still. Not even a rat crossed his line of sight. After several minutes his eyelids once again started to droop, but suddenly, and without immediately knowing why, he jolted awake. Then he saw it: at the edge of his range of sight, something moved behind a tree. Human or animal? He couldn't be sure. He crouched low over the sangar's heavy machine gun and trained the sights on the spot where he had seen whatever it was. It was happening again: his heart was beating faster and faster. Sweat trickled down his face. He waited, tensed, his finger trembling on the trigger. He felt sick and dizzy. An angry voice raged inside his head: *Pull yourself together. You're nearly home.* Nearly a minute passed. Then, in a split second, something streaked out from behind the tree. Kenny loosed off a burst of fire. White-hot streaks tore through the blackness. He refocused, breathing hard. Whatever it had been was now dead, lying in several pieces amidst the scrub.

'What the hell was that, Green?' Bryant shouted up from somewhere below.

'I think it was a dog, Sarge,' Kenny called back.

'Waste any more rounds on a dumb animal and you'll be scooping it up for breakfast. You got that?'

'Yes, Sarge.'

'*Yes, Sarge.*' Kenny heard several of the lads imitating him in exaggerated effeminate voices. Some of the others laughed. They sounded like they'd been drinking. It made Kenny uneasy. If Bryant found out, there would be hell to pay.

Private Lee Roberts stretched out on his thin sleeping mat and mentally ticked off another hour. Forty-six more until the Chinook would fly in and carry them back to Bastion. There they would board the RAF Tristar that would take them home. He scarcely dared believe the end was so close. Aside from seeing Anna and Leanne again, what he longed for most was a comfortable bed. That and some real food – he didn't care what kind, just so long as it didn't come out of a ration pack. Anna was always so careful about making sure they ate well at home – she would be horrified to learn that he'd eaten nothing but tinned and rehydrated food for six months. Not a single fresh carrot or lettuce leaf had passed his lips.

Running water. That was another thing he was looking forward to. He had almost forgotten what it was like to turn on a tap to fill a glass or step under a shower. At the post, each man was allocated two litres of water a day. This had to cover cooking, drinking and washing. Needless to say, most went without washing. Within days of arrival they had all smelt like tramps, but after a week or two they had stopped noticing. Everyone stank the same. Now and then they had sluiced down in one of the two springs that bubbled out of the ground to the north, but both of them had dried up in early July. The villagers had offered to sell them water but Major Norton hadn't allowed it. The risk of poisoning was too great. At one point during the height of summer they had run so short that they had set up evaporation stills to recycle their urine. It was just like the survival shows on TV. But that was the British Army for you. Everything cut to the bone. If an American soldier had turned up he'd have been appalled. Lee had heard that even at their most isolated posts, the Yanks had chemical latrines and refrigerated Coke dispensers.

As evening turned into night, the mood under the tarps was finally shifting from restless to subdued. Some of the lads were playing cards, and the ones who had been boisterous earlier were mostly drifting off to sleep or reading one of the battered paperbacks that got shared around the platoon by torchlight. The relentless banter had been replaced by the steady drum of crickets. Lee checked his watch. It was heading towards eleven p.m. If any of them were going on patrol tomorrow Bryant would have to announce it soon. He hadn't sounded a happy man when Lee heard him talking with Major Norton earlier that afternoon: 'The effing raggies will think they've bested us, sir.'

'There's no point taking unnecessary risks for pride alone,' Norton had said.

'It's not a matter of pride, sir. Surely it's our job? I wasn't aware we'd been given a holiday.'

His tone had come close to insubordinate, but Norton had chosen not to cross swords. 'I'll give it some thought,' he had said diplomatically, 'see what next door's planning.'

Next door was 3 Platoon, who was stationed four kilometres to their east. It was commanded by a young lieutenant, James Gallagher, who in any event would take his orders from Norton. Fully aware that he was being fobbed off, Bryant had marched away from the conversation with a face like thunder. Lee had taken care to scoot out of his way as he strode past. The man was obsessed. He seemed almost disappointed to be going home. Perhaps that was his problem, Lee speculated. Bryant was forty years old and had been in the army for more than half his life. As he often reminded them, he had completed more than a dozen tours of active duty in the Balkans, Sierra Leone, Afghanistan and Iraq. Combat was all he knew. All he lived for. It was like a drug.

The voices around him gradually fell silent. Torches switched off one by one. Lee felt his muscles slacken as he descended into the pleasant, hazy state between wakefulness and sleep. He pictured Anna and Leanne waiting for him on the parade ground. He imagined hurrying towards them, kissing Anna on the lips and scooping Leanne up in his arms. And at that moment he realized he couldn't bear the thought of leaving them again. He'd done his five years, proved all he had ever wanted to prove. After all he'd endured in Helmand he could hold his head up anywhere in Civvy Street. He had always known the time would come for a change of direction and this felt like the moment. When he got home, he promised himself that he'd look into training as a mechanic. Yes, that felt right. Something practical. A steady, hands-on job. Content that he had a plan, Lee drifted off to sleep.

'Right, you lazy sods! Attention!'

Lee jolted awake after what felt like only seconds after closing his eyes. A glance at his watch told him less than an hour had passed.

'Roberts! Get up!'

Bryant flicked a boot into Lee's ribs and doled out the

same treatment to several other malingerers. Lee scrambled to his feet grimacing in pain, but knowing not to show it. He stood to attention at the foot of his bedroll, arms pressed tight to his sides.

'Look at this bloody shambles,' Bryant yelled, kicking over mess tins and other stray possessions that lay scattered on the ground. 'Call yourselves soldiers? Dossers, that's what you are. A bunch of filthy, pikey dossers.' He stopped in front of Skippy and glared down at him. 'Are you looking forward to going home, son?'

'Yes, Sarge.' There was a tremor in the boy's voice.

'Why's that, then? So you can live like even more of a pig?' He nodded to Skippy's open pack, with its contents spilling onto the ground. 'Your nan likes living with pigs, does she?'

'No, Sarge.'

'Well, that's what she's got coming to her, hasn't she? A shitty little pig.'

'Yes, Sarge.'

Bryant picked the pack up in one hand and, while continuing to glare into Skippy's terrified face, shook its contents onto the floor.

'Kit inspection six a.m. All of you. One button out of place, you'll all be on a charge. Got it?'

The whole platoon answered in unison. 'Yes, Sarge.'

Without another word, Bryant turned on his heel and marched to the tarpaulin shelter he occupied next to Major Norton's at the end of the post.

'Thanks a lot, Skip,' Danny Marsh called across as the men returned grumbling to their beds.

Skippy didn't reply. It had been a long day. A long six months. As he knelt down to gather up his scattered possessions, he couldn't stop his eyes from welling up with tears.

*

Up on the sangar, Kenny Green was again losing his battle to stay awake. He was on guard duty until two a.m. Not long to go. For several minutes he dozed, slumped over his machine gun, until a mosquito bit him on the back of the neck. He jerked back to consciousness and crushed the insect under his palm. As he settled and refocused, he thought he saw something flit behind a tree out in the orchard. Another dog? Or was he imagining things? He peered out in the gloom, his finger tightening on the trigger. He waited to see it again.

All was quiet.

Nothing stirred.

THREE

Major Christopher Norton woke to the sound of his sergeant doing his vigorous morning exercises in the 'prison gym' they had set up a few yards from their primitive quarters. Lengths of wood lashed across empty oil drums served as push-up bars. Jerrycans filled with water served as weights. It was ten minutes before six a.m. Norton hadn't slept past five for the entire tour and the extra hour had left him feeling sluggish. He lay still for a moment, enjoying the strange and luxurious feeling of not having to ready himself for a patrol. The day ahead would be tedious, but at least it wouldn't involve stepping outside the walls. His thoughts drifted briefly to Melanie and the girls, but he hauled them back again and tried to decide how he would occupy the men during their final hours before departure. A football tournament, perhaps? It would soak up some of their nervous energy. Later on, he would give the talk he always delivered at the end of the tour. He would try to explain what he thought they had achieved here in their little corner of Helmand, then attempt to place it in the big picture, giving them something to go home feeling proud about.

Norton had pushed his platoon hard during the past six months and they had taken more casualties than he would have liked, but he couldn't fault their bravery or their loyalty. They had done as well as HQ could have expected of them. The company Norton commanded was leaving Helmand with the local Taliban severely if not fatally weakened. By their own admissions, the local communities felt far safer now than they had before the British arrived. And if all the reports he had heard were correct, the units of the Afghan National Army who would shortly be taking their place had been licked into decent shape by their British and American trainers. Barring disasters, the local population had every chance of enjoying a peaceful future.

Bryant's voice resounded around the post like a thunderclap. 'Right, you greasy little buggers, let see what you've got. "Ten – shun!'

The kit inspection. Norton had forgotten that Bryant had arranged to haul the men through the wringer one last time. Some mornings he felt as exasperated and bullied by his sergeant as they must. The man's energy and appetite for confrontation was superhuman.

Norton dragged himself to his feet and sought out a razor. Down to his last few cups of water, he couldn't afford to waste any on ablutions. He scraped the blade over his dry stubble while trying to blot out Bryant's yelling.

'Look at you, bloody shambles. And where the hell's the runt?' The sergeant's high-pitched yell made Norton wince.

'Don't know, Sarge,' answered a voice Norton recognized as belonging to Private Roberts.

'What do you mean you don't bloody know?' Bryant yelled at the top of his lungs: 'Ly-ons!' His voice grew even louder: 'You'd better show yourself, boy!'

Norton set down his razor and pulled back the flap of tarpaulin to see Bryant striding out into the centre of the post and scanning the sangars. Each of the sentries called down that they were alone. Apart from these four towers there was nowhere else in the post for a man to hide. The perimeter walls were twenty feet high and constructed of

Hesco bags – collapsible wire cages lined with tough fabric and filled with dirt – the only gap in which was the locked steel gate at the single entrance.

'Lyons!' Bryant's scream could have been heard on the far side of the valley.

There was no reply. The sergeant span round and shouted at the twenty-one men still standing stiffly to attention next to their beds. 'You bastards better not be taking the piss.' Without waiting for an answer, he decided they were. 'Where is he? You've got five seconds or I'll be sending every one of you little shits home in plaster.'

No one doubted that he meant it.

'We're not having you on, sir,' Lee Roberts piped up. 'Last time I saw him was at lights out. He was sorting out his kit.' He nodded towards Skippy's pack, which lay in its usual place at the end of the row. Its various straps and buckles were neatly fastened.

'Who saw him last?' Norton called out. He came towards them buttoning his shirt, anxious to calm the situation before it got any more heated. The mood Bryant had been in for the last few days, he didn't trust him not to crack a few skulls.

The men exchanged looks.

Norton threw his sergeant a disarming smile and assumed control. 'Look, boys, I don't mind if this is an end-of-term prank, and if it is, you got us fair and square. Well done.'

After a long moment of silence, Private Dean Paget spoke up. 'I don't think it is a joke, sir. At least, no one told me about it.'

'All right, if this is a joke, now's the time to fess up,' Norton said. 'No recriminations. No hard feelings.' He ignored Bryant's pained expression.

Again, silence. Norton studied the men's faces. No

smirks. No disguised smiles. No suppressed laughter. The only expressions he saw were of fear and concern.

'Lance Corporal, you bunk next to him – when did you see him last?'

'He was still getting his kit sorted when I went to sleep, sir,' Jim Warman said.

'In the dark?'

'With a head torch.'

'You didn't see him turn in?'

'No, sir.'

Norton looked down at Skippy's bedroll. There was no telling if it had been slept on or not. With the nights so hot, none of them used their sleeping bags. Skippy's was stowed in its compression bag and strapped to the side of his pack. There was no sign of his boots, though. An uneasy feeling stole over the major. He realized that all he knew about the youngest member of his platoon was that back home his only close relation was his grandmother. They had never had much in the way of a one-to-one: Skippy preferred to talk to his mates. What he did know was that he was a popular member of the platoon who more than made up in bravery for what he lacked in size. Skippy was always the one who volunteered to scout ahead while out on patrol and had never flinched in a skirmish. The collapse he had suffered the day before was the only minor blot on an otherwise pristine record.

'He didn't say anything to any of you?' Norton asked.

Heads shook.

'He was looking forward to going home?'

There were nods and mumbled confirmations. Expressions were growing more serious, confirming Norton's suspicion that this was no practical joke.

'He couldn't have got out, sir,' Bryant said. 'It's impossible. And why would he?'

'He's evidently not here,' Norton said gravely. 'Check his kit, Sergeant.'

'Sir?'

'His kit.'

Norton could think of nothing else to do. He was as confused by Skippy's absence as he was perplexed. Despite the unlikelihood of being able to scale the walls unseen, there was the problem of navigating the minefields that surrounded the post.

Bryant began by turning over Skippy's bedroll. There was nothing underneath. Next he unstrapped his pack and spread the contents on the ground. He poked through the spare clothes, water bottles, wash kit and mess tins and immediately spotted what was missing.

'No night-vision goggles, sir. No bayonet or pistol, either.'

'What about his rifle? Roberts—' Norton nodded to Lee Roberts, who stepped away from his bed and checked along the row of assault rifles stacked up against the Hesco wall at the rear of the sleeping area.

'Still here, sir,' Roberts replied.

'Everyone else's?'

Roberts counted. 'All there, sir.'

Norton nodded. 'Stand easy.'

Feet shuffled and muscles loosened, but the atmosphere among the platoon only grew more tense.

'Somehow or another, it appears that Private Lyons has left the post during the night,' Norton said. 'That can only mean one of you sentries must have seen him or been asleep on the job.'

Kenny Green felt the blood rush to his face. He had spent the second half of his watch from midnight until two a.m. losing an increasingly difficult battle to stay awake.

'We'll deal with that issue later,' Norton said. 'Now, has

anyone got any idea why Skippy would have run off into the night?'

No one spoke.

Norton squared up to the thought that had been lurking in the back of his mind and gave voice to it. 'I need to know – had anyone noticed him being depressed? Was there anything on his mind? You all know what I'm saying.'

After a long silence, Private Roberts spoke up. 'I know he felt bad about what happened yesterday, sir. But I don't see why that would send him over the wall.'

'Unless he thought he had something to prove,' Private Paget said.

'Such as?' Norton asked.

Paget shrugged his shoulders.

The image that came to Norton's mind was of the young man hanging from a tree, unable to cope with the humiliation of having collapsed on patrol. Was it possible that he was far more fragile than any of them had imagined, that they had all misread his cockiness for insecurity?

'What do you think, Sergeant?' Norton said quietly.

'I think someone here knows something, sir,' Bryant said.

Kenny Green couldn't hold it in any longer. 'I might have seen something, sir. I was up on the south-west sangar. Something moved out in the orchard. Must have been about one a.m.'

'A figure?'

'I couldn't be sure, sir. It might have been nothing.'

'Were you alert?'

Kenny Green hung his head. 'Not too brilliant, sir. I was struggling a bit, to be honest.'

Norton shot Bryant a look. 'I'll deal with him later, Sergeant. Proceed with the inspection. We'll have breakfast, then organize a search party. I'll put the word out on the radio.'

Norton left Bryant to it and retreated to his shelter from where he contacted the other platoons in the valley over the encrypted Bowman radio. They had a man missing. He was lightly armed and extremely vulnerable. Next he contacted HQ in faraway Camp Bastion and requested to speak to his commanding officer, Colonel Richard Hastings. He was not looking forward to delivering the news.

FOUR

At six forty-five, Norton was in his quarters studying a detailed map of the surrounding area when Bryant came to find him.

'Ready when you are, sir.'

Norton showed him the grid he had drawn on the map dividing the local terrain into sections each approximately two hundred metres square. 'We'll start close and move further out. I've spoken to Colonel Hastings at HQ – if we don't find him within the hour I'm to mobilize a full search the length of the valley. We want to avoid that if possible – no one wants to hand the enemy that sort of publicity on our last day.'

Bryant nodded in agreement.

'We'll begin here, to the south-west of the post, see if we can find any sign of him having crossed the orchard.'

'It's mined, sir. He'd never have got across.'

'He was on the party that laid them, as I recall.'

'So was I, but I wouldn't like to risk it.'

'Maybe he has a better memory than you do.' Norton reached for his Kevlar vest and pulled it on over his camouflage tunic, which even at this early hour was already glued to his back with sweat. 'I'll lead the first party. We'll take it in two-hour shifts. The rest of you can keep lookout from the sangars. I want eyes everywhere.'

'Sir.'

Norton stepped out into the bright sunlight before Bryant could raise any objections. He walked briskly towards the men, who were gathered listlessly, awaiting instructions.

'Right, I'll need six of you to come with me on the first search detail.' He singled out Kenny Green, 'Green, you'll be carrying the med pack.'

Kenny Green inwardly groaned at the thought of lugging the heavy pack straight after breakfast, but after falling asleep on the job he felt he was in no position to object.

'Any volunteers?' Norton inquired.

Two hands went up: they belonged to Privates Lee Roberts and Danny Marsh; both were from B Section.

'All right, we might as well have the rest of B Section while we're at it,' Norton said, 'as you were the ones who should have been keeping an eye on him.'

Dale Carter, Dean Paget, Mike Allerton and Lance Corporal Jim Warman let out a collective groan.

'Suit up. We move out in five minutes,' Norton barked.

While they grabbed their vests, helmets and weapons, Norton made his way quickly to the latrine. He had stomach ache and felt nauseous. He put it down to the previous evening's meal of rehydrated liver and onions. It was the same every tour: the food in the last few days comprised the inedible dregs.

'Stay there.' The order was shouted by Private Finlay from the north-west sangar. He was addressing someone out on the approach way to the post's entrance.

'Who is it?' Bryant yelled back.

Finlay checked through binoculars. 'Yusuf, sir.'

Norton stepped out from the latrine tent and squirted his hands with sanitizer. 'Is he alone?'

'As far as I can see.'

Yusuf was their primary local contact. A young man of

twenty-five and the grandson of the principal elder in the nearby village of Shalan-Gar. He had learned rudimentary English at school and picked up more from the soldiers who had been in the area for nearly eight years. Insofar as Norton trusted any of the locals, he trusted Yusuf the most. He had taken a big risk by acting as go-between with the British Army and Norton was keenly aware that the small amounts of money he had received in return was little compensation.

'Bring him up to the line. I'll talk to him from up there.'

Norton climbed the wooden ladder to the sangar where he joined Private Finlay. Yusuf was already standing at the white line spray-painted across the dirt road twenty yards from the gate. Close enough to talk, far away enough not to be able to kill anyone with hidden explosives. A quick glance reassured Norton that nothing was strapped to Yusuf's skinny frame, but now wasn't the time to take chances.

'Good morning, Yusuf. What can I do for you?'

'Good morning, Major Norton,' Yusuf gave a deferential nod. Something about his demeanour didn't seem right. His innocent smile had been replaced with a frown. 'I bring bad news.'

Norton felt his already queasy stomach churn.

'You have a man missing . . .'

'What about him?'

'Some fighters have him. They ask one hundred thousand dollars for his safe return.'

'He's alive?'

'Yes. He is alive.'

'Where are these people?'

'Near our village.' Yusuf glanced anxiously over his shoulder as if there might be someone listening. 'They talk to my grandfather. He send me here.'

Norton's head was filling with questions, but he stuck to the obvious ones: 'Are these people Taliban? Do we know them?'

'Yes. Taliban. Not from this valley – travelling through. If you want, I will talk to them, but it's dangerous . . .' He wrung his hands and stared at his feet. Norton guessed what was coming next. 'Very dangerous. Ten thousand dollars perhaps . . .'

'Sir—'

Norton glanced down and saw Bryant at the inside of the gate. He had heard every word of the exchange.

'It's all right, Sergeant. Bring Yusuf in, please. We need to talk business.'

Norton's subtlety of tone carried a message to Bryant which he hoped would have passed over Yusuf's head. He turned back to the go-between and called down to him in a friendly voice, 'We are so glad to hear he's alive. We'd like him back as soon as possible. Do I have your word that you won't be asking for any more than ten thousand dollars to make this happen?'

Yusuf looked hesitant and shot another glance over his shoulder. 'For me, yes. Ten thousand.'

He saw the gate opening ahead of him. A smiling Sergeant Bryant gestured him into the post.

'I'm coming down,' Norton called out, and clambered down the ladder.

Yusuf had never stepped inside the British Army post, but evidently the prospect of a large bundle of money overcame his fears. Norton arrived on the ground as Bryant closed and locked the gate behind him.

'Sorry about this, Yusuf.'

The young man's eyes widened in alarm at the sight of Norton's pistol levelled at his chest. Bryant took hold of him and strapped his wrists behind his back with nylon ties. 'No lies, Major. He is alive. He is alive.'

'And so are you. Let's try to keep it that way.'

According to Yusuf, the Taliban fighters had approached his grandfather's house shortly after dawn requesting food and water. They told the old man that they had been travelling across the valley by night when they found the young British soldier cowering in a ditch at the roadside. Seizing the chance to make some easy money, they ordered the village elder, Yusuf's grandfather, Musa Sarabi, to convey their ransom demand to the nearest military post.

Norton quickly concluded that the story failed to add up. Firstly, he questioned why Taliban fighters would run the risk of crossing the occupied valley only thirty-six hours before they knew the British would be departing, and, secondly, he didn't buy the idea of them having chanced on Skippy by accident. The more he thought about it, the more he became convinced that Skippy must have been the victim of an audacious kidnapping. The circumstances required to execute such a feat were improbable – two sentries would have to have been asleep at the same time – but not impossible. That meant that it had to be local Taliban who were responsible – men posing as farmers working the surrounding land who had kept the post under surveillance for weeks or even months waiting for such a moment.

It was scarcely credible, but the idea that one of his men left the post of his own free will was even more outlandish. There was a perfect motive, too: the capture of a British soldier on the final day of the occupation was propaganda of a sort money couldn't buy.

After talking round and round in circles with Yusuf, Norton once again consulted Colonel Hastings over the radio and settled on a plan of action. They agreed that kidnap was the most probable explanation. But while Norton remained concerned that the motive was chiefly political, Hastings insisted that it was more likely to be financial. The population of the Shalan-Gar valley was dirt poor and the opportunity to make even a few thousand dollars was one that men might risk their lives for. Unlike the French or Italians, the British were known for not paying ransom, but Hastings was convinced a local group had gambled on the rules being bent in the final hours of the occupation. The Shalan-Gar valley currently contained nearly 150 British troops and air support could be called in within minutes. The local Taliban had little in common with the new breed of jihadists Hastings and Norton had encountered in Iraq; they were shrewd and calculating men who remained interested in their personal survival. It all added up, in his opinion, to an attempt at extortion. And as Major Norton knew from long experience, when Colonel Hastings formed an opinion, there was no contradicting it.

It was agreed that Norton would lead a party to Shalan-Gar and attempt to achieve a peaceful conclusion. If whoever was holding him persisted in their demands for ransom, he was empowered to offer up to ten assault rifles and ammunition in lieu of cash – a tactic that had worked for the British in past hostage situations. If that failed, he was to withdraw and report back to Hastings. Meanwhile, Hastings would confer with General Browne to discuss the unprecedented possibility of meeting the kidnappers' demands. Hastings's gut told him that on this particular occasion, the rules might indeed be bent.

'It would stick in the craw,' Hastings said, 'but so would taking the shine off all your hard work.'

If the compliment was intended to make Major Norton feel better about the mission he had been ordered to lead, it failed to have the desired effect. He had realized that, like his men, he had lost his edge. Even a week ago he would have relished the challenge, but this morning he would gladly have crawled back to his bed.

'Softly, softly,' Hastings said. 'Let them know we're eager to leave quietly.'

'Yes, sir,' Norton answered, trying his best to sound compliant.

At the last moment, Major Norton made the decision to bring Sergeant Bryant on the expedition to Shalan-Gar. During a dozen years of combat tours Norton had dealt with numerous hostage negotiations and proved to himself that he possessed a cool head even under the most intense pressure, but he had never negotiated the release of a man for whom he felt quite so personally responsible as Skippy. Fearing that personal emotions were threatening to intrude on his judgement, he felt the need for his sergeant's unflappable presence.

Taking Yusuf with them, they travelled the kilometre to Shalan-Gar in the platoon's two armoured Land Rovers. It wasn't yet nine a.m. but the outside temperature was already thirty-five degrees and climbing. Sweat streamed from beneath Norton's helmet and trickled down his neck, yet as they drew up outside the rough dirt walls of the village compound, he felt a cold shiver travel the length of his spine.

'Paget, Allerton, Marsh, you three stay here with Yusuf. The rest of you will come inside with me.'

Requiring no further instruction, the men formed up and performed their routine radio and weapons checks. Seconds later they were ready to go. It was a procedure they had performed countless times before on their frequent visits to the village.

Norton approached the centuries-old rough-hewn gates

at the entrance to the compound and knocked three times. Almost immediately, a small shutter opened and a pair of vivid green eyes set in a face of almost Caucasian complexion stared back at him. They belonged to Ali-Mohammed Sarabi, one of Yusuf's many cousins and one of only a tiny handful of men in the village with a few words of English.

'Salaam, Ali-Mohammed,' Norton said. 'We would like to speak with Musa Sarabi.'

The young man nodded and drew back the heavy bolts securing the gates. They were clearly expected.

Norton stepped through into the village compound and led his party to the elder's residence. Several dozen single-storey dwellings and storage barns, all constructed of hard-packed mud, were scattered haphazardly inside the perimeter wall. The communal areas were quieter than usual. Only a few children were playing outdoors. Skinny goats scavenged the alleyways for scraps and chickens scratched hopefully in the dust. Here and there, clusters of sunburnt men crouched on their haunches sipping tea and casting furtive glances at the soldiers. There were no women to be seen.

Musa Sarabi's house was the biggest in the village and sited at its centre next to an open area that served as the village square, in the middle of which was a large, shady palm tree. Norton had spent many painful hours sitting cross-legged on its tiled floor, drinking tea and trying to explain the purpose and objectives of the British presence in the area. Musa Sarabi would nod inscrutably and offer the occasional smile from behind his thick grey whiskers, but how much notice he took of what was said, Norton had never been entirely sure. This morning they would cut straight to the chase. Norton was in no mood for lengthy discussions.

As they turned into the square, the major saw immediately

that things were different. Instead of waiting to receive them inside his house, Musa Sarabi was standing in the doorway. His usually unreadable face bore an anxious expression.

Norton handed his rifle to Private Kenny Green as they approached. He stepped forward alone to make the formal greeting. 'Salaam.'

They exchanged nods, but Sarabi was in a hurry to get down to business. He spoke quickly in Pashto to Ali, who relayed the message in faltering English to Norton.

'You have dollars?'

Norton answered patiently. 'First things first. Where is my man?'

Ali didn't bother with translating back to his grandfather. 'Dollars. You have dollars, or man dead.' He drew a finger swiftly across his throat.

'No dollars,' Norton said carefully. He shook his head. 'We have weapons.' He gestured to their rifles, then held up three fingers. 'Three rifles for my man.'

'No dollars?' Ali's eyes remained fixed on Norton.

'No.' He decided to up his offer. 'Five rifles – with ammunition.' He spread out his palms in a gesture of goodwill. 'We come as friends, Musa Sarabi. These rifles cost many thousands of dollars. Very valuable.'

Ali dipped his head and muttered in Pashto to his grandfather. The old man stared at Norton in bewilderment, then in fear, and without a further word retreated hastily behind the door, closing it behind him. In the same instant, Ali bolted.

'Sir!' Kenny Green pointed to an armed figure, his head swathed in a black turban, who had sprung up on a rooftop across the square.

Norton saw the flash of light from the muzzle of the gunman's AK-47 and heard the bullets slice the air inches from his body. As he and the others ran in separate directions in search of cover, two more figures popped up alongside the first and opened fire. A grenade exploded, hurling a cloud of thick red dust into the air. The last thing Norton remembered before he descended into hell was the sound of one of his men screaming.

FIVE

Sergeant Steve Price was looking forward to his comrades'
return. Highcliffe Camp had been like a ghost town during
his company's tour, and he had made few friends among the
professional desk-jockeys who worked alongside him in the
soulless regimental administration centre. It wasn't meant
to be like this. He hadn't joined the army to spend his days
shining the seat of his trousers. The life he had craved was
the one that had first fired his imagination on the TV
recruitment ads: all guns and adrenalin-fuelled action. He
had been lucky enough to experience it for five exhilarating
years, but now it was over and each day he struggled to
come to terms with the fact.

It had been nearly fifteen months since Lance Corporal
Steve Price, as he then was, drove over an IED that sent the
armoured Land Rover in which he was travelling spiralling
into the air. He remembered the noise of the explosion and
the blinding flash of light, but little else. The shock wave
knocked him out cold, which had turned out to be a bless-
ing. Mickey Turner, his only companion in the vehicle, had
somehow remained conscious throughout the whole ordeal.
Mickey's physical injuries had been less serious than Steve's
– only a couple of broken bones and a ruptured eardrum
– but his nerves were shredded. The army psychiatrist pronounced him a hopeless case and he was medically dis-

charged before his wounds were healed. Last time Price had seen him, Mickey's hands were shaking like an old man's. Price's mind was unaffected, but the loss of his right eye had permanently ruled him unfit for a combat role. It was nonsensical in his opinion – putting in six hard gym sessions a week, he was fitter now than he had ever been – but rules were rules and nowhere more so than in the army. He had been left with a choice between being tossed out into the world with precious few qualifications, or taking up the army's offer of alternative employment. He had taken the sensible option. The man of action now had a comfortable salary and a savings account. If he stuck it out, in about twenty years' time he could collect a decent pension. Except for the few wrinkles in his personal life that were yet to be fully ironed out, most people would say he had it made. Watching the office clock creep slowly towards five thirty, he tried to convince himself that he was one of the lucky ones.

Minutes later, Price was already heading across the parade ground en route to the gym. After a long day cooped up indoors he was ready for a tough ninety-minute workout before heading out for a few beers in the town. As he approached the PT block his phone sounded a message alert. He ignored it. Whoever it was would have to wait. He pushed through the door and made his way along the corridor. Another message sounded its arrival. There was only one person who would send him two texts the moment he left the office and he had no intention of speaking to her. It was over between them. Finished. He had made himself clear and there was nothing more to say. He shouldered open the door to the changing room, slung his bag on the bench and started to undress, eager to hit the weights and feel the rush of blood to his muscles. He was pulling on his trainers when his phone started to ring. Would she never give up? Sighing, he fetched it from his pocket ready to spell it out in words that she might just understand. But it wasn't her number on the screen. It was a work call, and the worst kind of all.

Anna Roberts paused to admire her handiwork. The kitchen in the little flat had never looked more spotless. Every surface was gleaming. She had even wiped the tops of the cupboards and pulled the fridge right out from under the counter to hunt out every last speck of grime. She wanted Lee to come back to a home as cheerful and bright as she could make it. Tomorrow would be taken up with all the frantic final preparations for the parade and picnic, so this evening was her last chance to apply the finishing touches. Leanne, however, wasn't impressed with being neglected and was starting to grizzle. It was past her meal time.

'I won't be a minute, love.'

As the grizzling rose to sporadic sobs, Anna hurried from room to room checking that she hadn't missed anything. Freshly ironed sheets and a new set of towels lay folded and waiting in the airing cupboard. Lee's casual clothes and shoes were neatly arranged in the wardrobe and, hanging on a separate section of the rail, his parade dress was pressed to perfection. Neatly arranged beneath, his boots gleamed like mirrors. In the bathroom, she had laid out fresh razors, soaps and toothbrush, and, knowing that the first thing Lee would want to do would be to take a long, deep bath, she had placed scented candles on the side of the tub. The only thing that needed attention now was her. After Leanne had settled for the night she would spend a self-indulgent hour or two making herself smooth and silky and polishing her nails. Tomorrow she would get up extra early to see to her hair. She hoped he liked her new style: she had let it grow past her shoulders and had tried for a sexy, tousled look copied from pictures of Cameron Diaz she had spotted in a magazine.

Leanne's sobs grew louder and more insistent. If she wasn't fed soon Anna knew she'd have a full-blown tantrum on her hands.

'I'm coming, Leanne! I'm coming!'

Not long now, Anna told herself as she dashed to scoop up her daughter. This time tomorrow the three of them would be back together again.

Leanne ate her macaroni cheese and broccoli with gusto, but Anna could barely manage a few mouthfuls. Nervous anticipation and excitement combined to tie her stomach in knots. She gave what she couldn't eat to Leanne and opened one of the bottles of beer she had bought on special offer. She wouldn't usually have dreamt of touching alcohol until after Leanne was in bed, but tonight was an exception. She needed it to calm down. After a few sips she began to feel more like herself again. The anxious feelings melted away. She decided that she would spend some of the evening phoning a few of her friends to offer some moral support. She was sure they would all be going through the same emotions, even Melanie Norton. Probably her more than most. Melanie worked so hard to put on a brave face for everyone else that she seldom got a chance to share what she must be feeling. Everyone knew that Major Norton had dodged so many bullets that the men joked that God must have mislaid the one with his name on it.

Having polished off a double portion of macaroni, Leanne devoured a large bowl of chocolate ice cream. Full and content, she happily succumbed to being bathed and changed into her pyjamas without any further protest. By seven thirty she was lying beneath the covers sucking her thumb while Anna read to her. Shortly afterwards, she was asleep.

Anna took a minute to savour the peace before heading out to tidy away the dinner plates. She loved her daughter dearly, but the moments after she had settled for the night always brought with them a sense of profound relief. There were still a few short precious hours left in the day to be something other than a mother. She eased Leanne's bedroom door shut, tiptoed across the corridor to change into her dressing gown, then retreated to the bathroom armed with a basket of creams, lotions, files and tweezers. With the radio playing quietly, she set to work.

The doorbell rang at a particularly bad moment. Anna was midway through showering the depilatory cream from her legs and her face was smothered in a thick, gooey mask. She hoped whoever it was would go away. No such luck. They rang again.

Damn! She rubbed the last of the cream from her calves, pulled on her dressing gown and ran along the passageway to the door, trailing wet footprints on the carpet. She lifted the receiver to the intercom and held it away from her face.

'Hello?'

'Mrs Roberts?'

'Yes.'

The intercom had been playing up for weeks and the caller's voice was contending with a loud crackle.

'It's Steven Price. Sergeant Price. Could we have a word, please?'

Price. The Notifications Officer. Anna felt her heart thump against her ribs. Her head span. She reached out a hand to stop herself from falling. She tried to speak but her tongue refused to move.

'Mrs Roberts? Are you there? I'm with a colleague. It's best if you buzz us in.'

'No.' She whispered. 'No . . .'

There was a pause. Then Price said, 'Lee's alive, but he's

been injured. There was a skirmish. He's been medevac'd to Bastion. I really think you should let us in.'

'No.' Anna gasped for air. 'How bad?'

Another pause. 'I really should be saying this to you in person . . .'

'Tell me,' Anna pleaded.

He hesitated, then seemed to accept this was how it would have to be done. 'I've been told he's lost both his legs. That's all I can tell you for now. Of course, I'll let you know the moment I hear anything else. I'm sorry. He's a good man.'

Anna stood in silence, staring emptily into space.

Sarah Tanner had followed Melanie's advice and attempted to clear the air with her future mother-in-law, Rachel, before Kenny's return home. In case things escalated she had wanted Kenny's dad, Paul, to be there when the moment came. Paul was working night shifts at a delivery depot a forty-minute drive away in Avonmouth, so the only opportunity Sarah had to catch them both together was after he arrived home at breakfast time. Unfortunately, Rachel was not a morning person, and with the added pressures of Kenny's homecoming and the imminent wedding, she was touchier than ever.

On most days, Sarah ate breakfast early and attempted to remove all traces of her presence in the kitchen before Rachel appeared to commence her daily search for things to grouse about. A few stray crumbs on the counter or grounds in the sink were all it took to start her off. This morning Sarah had made an extra effort to pass inspection, but even so, Rachel managed to convince herself that the milk had turned and that Sarah must have left it out overnight. It wasn't a good start. Things grew rapidly worse when, moments after Paul walked through the door, Sarah suggested that instead of complaining about perfectly good milk, Rachel should say what was really bothering her. In the brief silence that followed, Paul's already washed-out features grew even greyer.

Sarah braced herself for a string of objections ranging from her poor housekeeping to the tattoo on her shoulder bearing the name of her first boyfriend (she had promised Kenny she would get it lasered as soon as she could afford it) to the main issue, which was Rachel's belief that Sarah had deliberately become pregnant in order to trap her son into marrying her. 'Used goods,' was one of the more hurtful expressions she had overheard Rachel use to describe her.

Sarah would have been the first to admit that she had a chequered past. She had left school at sixteen and the home of her long-suffering foster parents in Taunton soon afterwards. In the two years before she and Kenny met at a nightclub in Bristol, she had led a chaotic life working behind bars and living in squats with a collection of colourful and unsavoury characters. But when the two of them got together, everything changed. Falling in love with a real man, a soldier, she realized how shallow and empty her life to date had been. It was true that the pregnancy was unplanned, but these things happen. And besides, it was just as much Kenny's responsibility as it was hers.

Rachel didn't take up Sarah's invitation to voice her churning emotions. Following a period of deathly silence there were melodramatic tears of hurt. Mopping her flooded cheeks with a square of kitchen roll, Rachel said to Paul that she didn't know what she had done to deserve such a suspicious and ungrateful daughter-in-law, and retreated upstairs to her bedroom, locking the door behind her. And there she remained, emanating toxic waves of self-pity that radiated throughout the house. Paul made a half-hearted effort to try to talk her out, but to no effect. He took his sleeping pill, drank a few beers in front of the TV and later in the morning made up a camp bed in the glazed lean-to at the back of the house which Rachel grandly referred to as 'the conservatory'.

Hours passed. Rachel refused to show herself. Sarah's frustration vied with guilt as she wondered if all families behaved this way or whether she was the problem.

When evening arrived and Rachel had still failed to emerge, Sarah concluded that her future mother-in-law must despise her even more than she had feared. The day-long sulk had, though, served one good purpose: it had made up Sarah's mind that if she and Kenny were to stand a chance, they would have to change their plans. Continuing to live with his parents while they saved for a deposit on a flat was no longer an option. After the wedding, preferably straight afterwards, they would have to move into rented married quarters in camp. Buying their own place would have to wait.

Paul woke shortly after six thirty in the early evening and trudged up to the shower. He looked tired and haggard and moved stiffly. Sleeping on the camp bed had done nothing to improve the sciatica which was the latest addition to his list of ailments. In an effort to make amends, Sarah quickly rustled up a microwave dinner, making sure there was enough for three.

She was setting the small table in the kitchen when she heard Paul come back downstairs.

'I've made us cod and chips. Would you like peas or beans with yours?'

'Peas would be nice.'

Sarah turned in surprise at the sound of Rachel's voice. She was dressed and made up and offered a friendly smile.

'Thanks for cooking, love – you've saved my life. I promised Melanie I'd pop down and help with setting up in the marquee this evening.'

'Oh,' Sarah was nonplussed. 'Do you think she'd like me to help, too?'

'I'm sure she wouldn't say no, if you feel up to it.'

Paul appeared dressed for work. He glanced apprehensively between the two women, as if expecting fireworks at any moment.

'Sarah's made dinner. Isn't that nice of her?' Rachel said, filling the water jug from the tap.

'Great.' Paul shot Sarah a nervous glance as he took his usual seat at the table. 'Thanks.'

'Sorry about this morning,' Rachel said breezily. 'I woke with one of my migraines. It's taken all day to shake it off.' She touched Sarah lightly on the arm, her eyes seeming to beg forgiveness.

'Poor you,' Sarah said.

Rachel mouthed a meaningful 'thank you' and ferried plates to the table.

Sarah ate in virtual silence, hiding her confusion at Rachel's dramatic turnaround and what it might mean for her carefully reconfigured plans. Rachel, meanwhile, chatted enthusiastically about the plans for the homecoming party. Apparently tensions in the WAGs Club were running high as they scrambled to get the picnic catering finished in time. Several women who had made promises of help had failed to deliver, heaping yet more burden on the shoulders of the same few who always bore the brunt on these occasions. Melanie had sent out a desperate email pleading for someone to produce half a dozen quiches before she resorted to buying them from the supermarket. It would mean slaving over the stove for half the night, but Rachel had volunteered. The very least the returning boys deserved was some proper home cooking. Paul nodded and agreed with everything she said. Bright, optimistic moods like this were rare, and he was not about to do anything to upset it.

Rachel was clearing plates and Sarah making Paul a final cup of tea before he headed out for his shift when the doorbell rang.

'I'll go,' Rachel said. 'You sit there.'

Sarah and Paul exchanged a look as she bustled out of the door. Paul shrugged and shook his head. Words failed him.

'I think I ought to go with her tonight,' Sarah said.

'Probably best,' Paul agreed. He brought his tea to the table and sat next to her. 'You've been great,' he said quietly. 'Really. I know it's not been, well, you know . . .'

It was as close to heartfelt emotion as he could manage, but Sarah appreciated it nonetheless. She had always liked him, despite his ups and downs. In his good moments he had the same mischievous sparkle in his eyes as Kenny.

The sound that emanated from the front hall was barely human. It was neither a wail nor a scream, but something far more horrible and shocking. Paul leapt up from the table and ran out to Rachel. Sarah felt the muscles in her stomach spasm. She forced herself to follow him to the door. There she came to a sudden halt. Standing on the front step at the far end of the hall was the unmistakable figure of Sergeant Price, and next to him a female corporal staring uncomfortably at the ground in front of her feet. Sergeant Price lifted his gaze from Rachel, who was weeping into Paul's shoulder, and met her eyes. He tried to speak, but his lips refused to move.

It was Paul who delivered the news to her. 'He's dead, love. Kenny's dead.'

Sergeant Price fought hard to get out the words. 'You all have my deepest condolences. All of you.'

It wasn't much, but it made all the difference. New curtains and a bedspread in matching blue transformed the tiny spare bedroom in Kathleen Lyons's flat into one that looked almost like it belonged to a young man. She hadn't been able to stretch to new wallpaper, but she hoped Pete might be persuaded to redecorate while he was on leave. In fact, she had a list of jobs that she'd been saving up while he was away, but she would try not to bother him for a day or two. The wives and mothers she knew all said that soldiers found it especially hard to adjust to home life after their first tour of duty. Melanie Norton had also warned her that she may take a while to get used to him herself. The boy who left Highcliffe only days after his eighteenth birthday would have transformed into a man.

Kathleen felt every one of her fifty-five years as she settled down for ten minutes in an armchair before thinking about heading out again to help at the WAGs Club. Her back and shoulders ached from a long day on the till and the arthritis in her fingers was causing them to throb. The pills the doctor had prescribed made little difference, so she dosed herself with cheap whisky. Two inches in the bottom of a tumbler and a few cubes of ice was enough to numb the pain and make her feel human again. As she sipped, she glanced over at the numerous photos of Pete that sat on the shelf behind the TV charting his growth from baby to soldier. Right from the moment of his birth, Kathleen had always been more of a mother to him than her daughter had ever managed to be. Since he was nine years old, he had lived with her more or less full time. Kathleen would have taken him on even sooner, but until then she had been living with Trevor, a jobbing builder who had no time for, or interest in kids. Looking back, it had been a mistake not to leave him sooner, but having suffered the pain of divorce she had been determined not to give up easily on another relationship. If only she had known how much better off she would have been living alone. No arguments. No complications.

No one keeping you awake at night snoring or pawing at you. Kathleen wasn't exactly happy with her life, but she was as close to content as she had ever been. Her only ambitions now were for her wayward daughter to re-emerge from wherever she had fetched up in London and for her to make her peace with her son.

There was a small picture of Holly nestled among the others – the only one Kathleen possessed that showed her and Pete together. It had been taken on the beach at Weston when Pete was six years old and Holly twenty-three. Her daughter looked young and pretty, though distinctly bored by motherhood. She had always refused to name Pete's father. Kathleen suspected that the truth was that she didn't know who it was. Still, it was probably better that way. There was a lot to be said for not having much in the way of family – fewer people to let you down or tell you how to live your life. Pete was free to become his own man and she would do her best to help him on his way.

Kathleen had finally started to get comfortable when the telephone rang. She sighed and pushed up from her chair, feeling a painful twinge in her lower spine. Hobbling slightly, she crossed the room and reached for the receiver.

'Hello?'

'Kath, it's Phil. Sorry to call you like this but Kayley's just rung in sick. Don't suppose you could stand in this evening?'

Despite the politeness of the inquiry from the store's deputy manager, Kathleen knew that she had no choice. It was no secret that management had been asked to trim the workforce and she didn't want to give them any excuse to cull her. Twenty years' service and the fastest till speed in the store weighed in her favour, but her age and sagging features didn't. Given the choice, supermarkets preferred their customer-facing staff as young and attractive as possible. She felt bad about letting Melanie Norton down but it couldn't be helped. Besides, Melanie had a husband bringing a wage in.

'Of course. I'll be there in ten minutes.' She tried to sound cheerful at the prospect.

'Thanks, Kath. See you in a while.' Her deputy manager sounded genuinely grateful, as if she had saved his neck.

Kathleen downed the rest of her whisky and steeled herself for another four hours on the till. It was the last thing she felt like.

The weather had turned stormy. Dark clouds had gathered and a damp, warm wind was blowing in across the Bristol Channel from the west. Kathleen felt the first spots of rain on her face as she hurried along the main road. She had forgotten her umbrella and had come too far to turn back. There was no choice but to speed up and hope she made it before the heavens opened. There was a low rumble followed by a crack of thunder and a chillier gust of wind. The spatters became a shower. Kathleen pulled her mac up over her head and broke into a run.

The car horn sounded behind her as she approached the junction with the main road. She glanced over her shoulder and saw two figures inside, one male, one female, both in military uniform. The driver was waving to her. It was a face she recognized but couldn't put a name to. He pulled up alongside her and climbed out, pulling on his cap. He was tall and muscular with one dead eye that didn't move. His colleague followed.

'Mrs Lyons?' he said.

'Yes . . .'

'Sergeant Price. This is Corporal Benson.'

The young woman gave an awkward nod.

'We need a word with you. Perhaps you'd like to get in the car – out of the rain?'

He reached for the door handle but Kathleen kept her distance. Something in his manner made her uneasy.

'Is something wrong?'

'Please, Mrs Lyons . . .'

Kathleen shook her head. The rain grew heavier.

'I'm sorry to approach you like this. We called at your home then spotted you as we were driving away.' He paused for a moment. His Adam's apple rose and fell in his throat. His colleague remained silent. 'You're Private Lyons's grandmother. I have you down as next-of-kin . . .'

'What about him?'

'I'm afraid he's missing. He disappeared from the forward command post where he was stationed yesterday night. We've been told he may have been taken hostage.' The young woman nodded in confirmation. 'Colonel Hastings would like to speak to you on the phone from Bastion as soon as possible. We can take you there now if you like.'

'I have to get to work.' The words fell mechanically from her mouth.

'Yes, but . . .'

'I finish at eleven.'

'Mrs Lyons, this is important.'

'So is my job. Or perhaps you can get me another?'

She hadn't meant to be rude but couldn't help herself. The two soldiers stared at her, unable to answer.

With her head filling with angry, ugly thoughts, Kathleen turned and hurried away into the rain before she said anything else.

SIX

Coroner Jenny Cooper took another mouthful of weak, lukewarm coffee and tried to concentrate on the pile of pathologists' reports and other long-neglected paperwork she had brought with her from the office in anticipation of a long wait for her jury. She had banked on them taking two or three hours to arrive at their verdict, but so far they had been deliberating for six. If they didn't make up their minds within the next few minutes, she would be forced to send them home and they would all be back to try again in the morning. She couldn't imagine what the dead woman's husband was going through. The poor man would be waiting on the hard seats in the public canteen drinking foul coffee and making awkward conversation with his lawyers. The Small Street Courts in the centre of Bristol were not the worst place to conduct an inquest – without a dedicated courtroom of her own, Jenny was often forced to conduct her proceedings in village halls in remote corners of the Gloucestershire countryside – but they were far from welcoming.

Jenny had grown used to such waits. The Thompson inquest was the last in a list of nine she had deliberately scheduled back-to-back throughout the months of July and August. Her eight weeks in court had been hot, exhausting and often tortuous work, but it had been the only way she could clear the backlog of cases that had stacked up throughout her busiest year yet. After a deceptively quiet winter, the unnatural death business had enjoyed an unprecedented boom during the spring and summer months. It seemed to happen that way: human tragedies were never evenly spaced but seemed to come in unpredictable waves. The reaper really did seem to cut people down in swathes. Thankfully, the end of her ordeal was finally in sight. The next hearing after this would be her last before she left for two weeks' holiday: the trip to Italy that she had been dreaming of for years but had never quite managed to pull off. Venice and Rome followed by a week on the beach. It would be her first ever holiday with Michael. She couldn't wait.

Of all the cases she had heard over the summer, that of Diana Thompson had been the most harrowing. The thirty-two-year-old primary schoolteacher and mother of three had been admitted to the Severn Vale District Hospital, which lay on the northern outskirts of Bristol, for a routine operation to remove a small benign lump from her left breast. The procedure was supposed to have taken forty minutes at most and, all being well, she was due to be discharged the following morning. Such was the unremarkable nature of the surgery that she had persuaded her husband not to take the day off work. He had said goodbye to her as he left the house at eight o'clock and spoken with her again at one thirty, just before she took her pre-med. At two forty-five he received a call from a member of the hospital's management team to say that his wife had died on the operating table. No further explanation was offered. The surgeon and other staff present in theatre were instructed not to speak to him.

The first post-mortem had been inconclusive. There was no doubt that Diana Thompson had suffered a cardiac arrest, but the locum pathologist who carried out the examination couldn't be sure why. A second post-mortem conducted by the hospital's senior pathologist concluded that there was a slight thickening of the heart muscle, probably due to a congenital condition, which, coupled with an unusual reaction to general anaesthesia, could have caused the arrest. In other words, Diana Thompson was the unlucky one in a million who dies on the table for no preventable reason.

The case had attracted huge attention on social media and the lawyers had swarmed all over it. Desperate to safeguard their reputation and to prevent a finding of negligence that would open the way to a huge claim for damages, the hospital trust had wheeled in the big guns. A leading QC headed up a team of four lawyers. A twenty-eight-year-old hotshot from London named Kelly Bradford represented the widower, Alan Thompson. One of the new breed of solicitor advocates who were cutting the ground from under the Bar, she had none of the stuffiness of the hospital's barristers and more than matched them in intellectual prowess. She was also attractive with a ready smile. Each time she rose to speak, the jury was reminded of the young woman who had died so tragically and suddenly.

The hospital's case was that Diana Thompson had suffered a cardiac arrest as the incision was being closed. Repeated attempts at resuscitation had failed to restart her heart. In response, Kelly Bradford had called an independent pathologist who claimed that Mrs Thompson's heart had been healthy, and that even if there were a slight thickening of the tissues, it wasn't enough to have caused a fatal arrest. Her case was that the young mother must have vomited and suffocated whilst lying unattended in the recovery room immediately after surgery. If this were true, it implied gross negligence and the most cynical and orchestrated of cover-ups. It meant Diana Thompson must have been left alone while still under anaesthetic, and that when she was discovered, a whole team of clinicians acted in concert to cover their tracks. If the jury believed that to be the case, the resulting shock waves would be huge. Clinicians and hospital managers would lose their jobs and criminal prosecutions would follow. Surgeons, nurses and their employers would find themselves in the dock charged with manslaughter and conspiracy to pervert the course of justice. Alan Thompson would receive seven-figure damages and Kelly Bradford's firm would collect 30 per cent.

Thanks to feverish press reporting, the ten men and women of the coroner's jury had been made acutely aware of the consequences of their verdict. It was a large responsibility to place on the shoulders of a collection of citizens among whom numbered a delivery driver, an office cleaner, a postman and at least two who were between jobs.

There was a knock at the door of her stuffy, windowless office. Without waiting for a reply, her officer, Alison Trent, burst through.

'They've got a note for you, Mrs Cooper,' she said excitedly, and handed Jenny a folded sheet of paper. 'I can guess what it says. They've spent the last hour shouting at each other. I can hear it along the corridor. It's that young lad—'

'I don't want to hear it, Alison,' Jenny cut in. 'Jury deliberations are confidential.'

Alison sighed impatiently. 'I've never understood the point of that. What if they're all idiots? More than a few of this lot are, in my opinion.'

Jenny ignored the remark. Two years after her car accident, Alison was still showing the after-effects of the head injury that had so nearly claimed her life. Sometimes she seemed to lack a filter between brain and mouth and her responses to normal social cues could, at times, be a little hit and miss. There were days on which Jenny seriously doubted the wisdom of having let her remain in post, but after seven years together, she simply didn't have the heart to let her go. Besides, at nearly sixty years old and with her medical history, Alison stood little chance of finding another job.

The note was short but clear.

Dear Madam,
    We reached a unanimous verdict as you instructed, but when it came to completing the Form of Inquisition, two of our number refused to sign. They claim they have changed their minds and no longer agree with the majority. What should we do?
    Colin Lewis (Foreman).

'Couple of troublemakers gumming up the works?' Alison said.

'I think we may have to settle for a majority verdict,' Jenny said, folding the note into her pocket. 'We'd better have them back in for a direction.' She got up from her desk and headed for the door.

'Oh, I should have warned you –' Alison added, as if by way of afterthought, 'you'll have a bit of an audience. A few more reporters turned up. Some of them seem to have got the wrong end of the stick – keep asking me how much Mr Thompson will get in damages. I told them this is a coroner's inquest and there's no money involved.'

Jenny's heart sank. A court filled with journalists meant she would have to watch every word she said. The recently appointed Chief Coroner was well known for beginning every working day by reading his press clippings. If he didn't like what he saw, he wouldn't hesitate to pick up the phone and make his feelings clear. Jenny had worked hard over the previous year to shed her reputation as a loose cannon and couldn't afford a backward step. She paused to collect her thoughts as she freshened up her lipstick.

'It's the one with the tattoos,' Alison said, ignoring Jenny's previous warnings, 'he's the fly in the ointment. I'll bet he's only doing this so he can drag us all back tomorrow and claim another subsistence.'

'He wouldn't be the first,' Jenny said, and stepped out of the door before she heard any more.

Alison was right. The court was crammed with reporters with pens poised. As Jenny took her seat beneath the royal crest, she noticed several other additions to the crowd. Seated between Alan Thompson and his lawyer, Kelly Bradford, on the front bench, was a tall, dark and expensively turned-out man in his forties whom Jenny assumed was one of the senior partners in Bradford's firm. Several rows behind him sat another man whose hand-stitched suit marked him out from the scruffy members of the media. Simon Moreton was the Chief Coroner's number two and his eyes and ears on the ground. Jenny hadn't seen him for more than six months and was amused to see that in addition to a deep suntan he was sporting a carefully trimmed salt-and-pepper beard. Always a late but enthusiastic follower of fashion, Simon no doubt imagined it made him look rather rugged and dashing. He met her gaze and gave her a warm, confidential smile.

Jenny informed the lawyers that she had received a note from the jury. She had Alison hand it to them for their inspection and also instructed her to bring the jury back from their retiring room. During the few moments in which they waited for the ten jurors to file back into court, Jenny noticed Kelly Bradford in urgent, whispered conversation with her boss. He appeared to be calling the shots.

'Thank you for your note, Mr Foreman—'

'If I may, ma'am.' Kelly Bradford rose to her feet, sweeping thick, auburn hair back from her face. 'I presume you intend to give a majority direction.'

Jenny remained patient. 'I was first intending to establish whether there remains any prospect of a unanimous verdict being reached.'

'The note says that two of them have changed their minds. Given time for more deliberation, what is to say that more won't change their minds?' Kelly Bradford struck a note of indignation: 'Surely you are not going to accept a verdict this evening?'

'If we are quick about it, there are still at least thirty minutes available. Thank you, Ms Bradford.'

The young lawyer refused to take the hint and remained on her feet. 'Ma'am, this really doesn't seem appropriate. The seriousness of this case surely requires that the jury be given all the time they need without any further pressure being placed on their shoulders.'

Jenny glanced at Alison, whose eyes slanted towards the heavily muscled and tattooed young man sitting at the edge of the jury box, his arms crossed defiantly across his chest. Next to him sat the twenty-three-year-old delivery driver who looked similarly detached from his colleagues. Neither of them looked like the kind who would be keen to spend a minute longer than was necessary inside a court building.

'The law is very clear, Ms Bradford,' Jenny said, more firmly now. 'If no more than two jurors disagree, I am entitled to accept the verdict reached by the others. If I may continue?'

Kelly Bradford reluctantly sat down and went back into a huddle with her newly arrived colleague.

'Mr Foreman, would you please stand.'

Colin Lewis, an employee in the city council's planning department, got nervously to his feet.

'I have read your note. Is it the case that you are unable to reach a unanimous decision?'

'Yes, ma'am.' He nodded to add emphasis and cast a disapproving glance at the two dissenters.

'And do you consider that at least eight of you might arrive at a verdict?'

'Eight of us have signed the form of inquisition, ma'am. We've already reached our verdict.' He pulled the document from his jacket pocket. 'There are just two of us who refused to do so – at the last minute.' Another glance at the two young men to his left suggested that relations had become rancorous.

Jenny instructed Alison to pass her the form on which the jury were required to certify their verdict. Eight signatures appeared at the foot of the page. In the box headed, *Conclusion of the jury as to cause of death*, only one word appeared: *Accidental*.

'Thank you, Mr Foreman. As eight out of ten of you have arrived at and certified your verdict, I am obliged to accept it. The form of inquisition reads as follows—'

'Ma'am—'

'That's not right.'

The simultaneous interruptions came from Kelly Bradford and the man with tattoos. His name was Craig Walters, and he had stated his profession as 'job seeker'. Before Jenny had a chance to respond to either of them, Walters leaned forward, angrily waving a finger. 'I don't agree with any of this, and nor does he.' He pointed to the delivery driver seated next to him, who nodded. 'And I know she only signed because she was letting herself be bullied into it.' He jabbed his finger towards Fay O'Connell, the fifty-year-old office cleaner. The blood drained from O'Connell's face and she stared hard at the floor as if wishing it would swallow her up.

'Ma'am, this is completely irregular,' Kelly Bradford butted in. 'You can't possibly accept the verdict of this jury now.' Her colleague nodded his agreement.

'It's a joke,' Walters added for emphasis.

'Sit down, Ms Bradford.' Jenny felt her heart start to pump hard. An angry yelling juror with no respect for the dignity of the court was not something she had had to deal with before. 'Mr Walters, isn't it?'

'Yeah.'

Stay calm, Jenny, she told herself. *You can handle this.* 'Firstly, it's not appropriate to call out. As you were instructed, if you have something to say, you should write me a note.'

Walters responded with a surly grunt.

'And secondly, the correct procedure is for me to note the names of those jurors who dissent from the majority decision, which I will do as soon as I have presented the verdict to the court. Do you understand?'

'What I don't understand is how anyone can say a healthy woman can die by accident. Something went wrong – stands to reason. That's probably why they left her on her own. They thought, she's young, she's fit, nothing'll go wrong with her—'

'Mr Walters. I won't tell you again.'

'They wouldn't hear it. Wouldn't even discuss it.' He pointed his accusing finger at his fellow jurors.

Jenny turned to Alison. 'Would you please escort Mr Walters from the court?'

He shot up from his seat. 'It's all right, I'm going.' He turned to Alan Thompson. 'Sorry, pal. You and your kids deserve better. This isn't justice.' With that, he marched out of the electrified courtroom. The journalists had their money quote and were tapping it into their phones and broadcasting it over the social networks even before the door closed after him.

Jenny took a breath in a bid to steady her jangling nerves. Simon Moreton's eyes were raised to the ceiling as if hoping that by some miracle the last two minutes could be erased from history.

She forced a smile she hoped might give the impression that she had taken the disruption in her stride. 'Well, I have the name of the first dissenter.' She addressed the man who had been sitting to Walters's right and once again checked her list. 'Adrian Mallinson?'

He nodded.

'And you also dissent?'

'Yes. I agree with him.' He nodded towards the door through which Walters had made his theatrical exit.

'Noted,' Jenny said.

'When you thought there was something in it for you.' The whispered comment from the jury box was almost inaudible, so quiet in fact that Jenny doubted whether she had heard it or merely imagined it.

Kelly Bradford rose to her feet yet again. 'Ma'am, having heard directly from a juror that substantive issues were not properly discussed, I would urge you to set this so-called verdict aside. This inquest has to be heard again in front of a fresh jury. And if you choose not to do so, on behalf of Mr Thompson we will immediately apply to the High Court seeking a fresh inquest.'

Her impertinence deserved a firm riposte, but Jenny's mind was momentarily elsewhere. She glanced along the two rows of jurors in search of the whisperer. She thought about asking the lawyers if they had heard it, too: *When you thought there was something in it for you.* Was the voice suggesting that Walters and Mallinson had deliberately sought to sabotage the proceedings? Had all the talk of hefty damages given these two uneducated men the idea that they could somehow get a slice of the action by siding against the hospital? Or worse, could someone have sought to influence them? She looked at Kelly Bradford's boss. A gold Rolex poked out from beneath his shirt cuff. Thirty thousand pounds sitting casually on his wrist. Clearly a man who cared about money and made plenty of it. She made an educated guess that the magic number his firm would be chasing was £3 million. Two for the client, one for them. The scene with Walters was just the sort of stunt she could imagine an arrogant fee-hungry London lawyer like him arranging, but she didn't have a scrap of evidence, only a gut instinct.

'Ma'am, as I see it, having been duly signed by eight of the jurors there is no possible ground for objection.' The intervention came from Richard Cotterell QC, the smoothly understated lead counsel for the hospital trust. 'Mr Walters's outburst was unwarranted and intemperate, but hardly undermines the conclusion of the others.'

'I agree, Mr Cotterell,' Jenny said, her eyes still fixed mistrustfully on the silent lawyer next to Kelly Bradford. 'The verdict will stand.'

As Bradford opened her mouth to renew her objections, her colleague held up a hand to stop her. They had fought and lost and it was time to throw in the towel with dignity. He patted Alan Thompson's arm and whispered words of condolence in his ear.

'I will overlook your rudeness on this one occasion, Ms Bradford,' Jenny said, 'but don't expect me to be so forgiving in future.'

The young lawyer's face reddened in anger and embarrassment. Behind her, reporters smirked.

Jenny once again began to read out the completed form of inquisition signed by eight members of the jury. It stated that Diana Thompson had died from a cardiac arrest during surgery and that her death was accidental. There were muted smiles and looks of relief on the faces of the hospital team. Simon Moreton, too, visibly relaxed. Alan Thompson, who had remained stoical throughout, broke down.

Jenny hastily concluded the formalities and dismissed the jury against the sound of a grown man sobbing like a child.

SEVEN

'Well done, Jenny. Very deftly handled.'

Simon Moreton had invited himself backstage and insisted on taking Jenny for tea in the judges' dining room. It was a place Jenny usually avoided. Judges, in her experience, formed a tight clique and tended to view coroners as their poorer, intellectually inferior cousins. Perhaps it was just a lack of confidence on her part, but when she was at Small Street, she tended to keep her own company.

'Thank you.' She took a sip of the lapsang souchong Simon had specially requested and tried not to wince at the unpleasant, smoky flavour. She preferred her tea strong, white and ordinary.

'You don't sound altogether convinced.'

He was right. She wasn't. 'I felt obliged to accept the verdict, but I suppose in an ideal world I would like them to have spent another hour or two making sure they were certain.'

'But if you hadn't taken their verdict immediately, they would have assumed that you weren't happy with it.'

'Which was one of several reasons I did what I did.' She gave the tea a second chance. It hadn't improved. 'Just one of those cases, I suppose.'

Moreton gave her what he must have assumed was a

reassuring smile. 'You might as well share it with me, Jenny. Strictly entre nous.'

'The one who stormed out, Walters – he had a point. The surgical team would have assumed her to be fit and healthy. It's entirely possible they did cut a few corners.'

'You can't tell me that between you, you and Ms Bradford didn't cross-examine every one of them to within an inch of their lives.'

Jenny had to concede that he was right. She had interrogated the evidence rigorously. The surgeon had spent nearly half a day in the witness box and the anaesthetist even longer. Their accounts and those of the nurses had been thoroughly consistent and never altered: Diana Thompson had died from a sudden, unexpected and catastrophic cardiac arrest that had defied all attempts at resuscitation.

'Well then,' Moreton said, 'you're merely suffering from an entirely understandable bout of excess sympathy.' He took an appreciative sip of tea. 'You're a good person, Jenny. You've done an excellent job in a sticky situation, and for the sake of your continued sanity, you have to move on – and with a clear conscience.'

It was easy for Simon to say. He hadn't spent the previous five days sitting opposite a thirty-four-year-old widower and father of three motherless children. But she kept these protestations to herself. Simon prided himself on never becoming emotionally involved in the work of the coroners he oversaw. Jenny also had another reason to keep her feelings private. She had strived hard over recent months to prove that she wasn't the erratic, oversensitive female that Simon and, no doubt, the Chief Coroner, had previously assumed her to be. In fact, she had made a determined effort to appear as capable and responsible as she could. Perhaps it was something to do with being in a steady relationship for the first time since her divorce, or a function of slowly

creeping away from forty-five towards the next unmention-
able milestone, but from somewhere unexpected, she had
developed a desire to survive in her career as the Severn Vale
District Coroner. In future, she did not intend to risk her
tenure, livelihood and sanity with every hard case.

'You're right,' Jenny said, trying to appear cheerful. 'Eight
to two is an unequivocal verdict. My conscience should be
clear.' She corrected the note of ambiguity: 'It is clear.'

Simon smiled gently and seemed to appraise her for a
moment before satisfying himself that her sentiments were
genuine. 'Glad to hear it. Now then, you may not be surprised to learn that I didn't cancel my tennis match with the
Cabinet Secretary this afternoon just to watch you in
action, however much of a privilege that always is.'

Sitting in the judges' dining room wasn't good for Simon.
It encouraged his florid tendencies. Over a drink in a pub
he was capable of being perfectly human.

'I'm not in trouble, am I?' Jenny hastily ran through a
mental list of her recent inquests. Some had been knotty, but
so far as she knew, none was controversial enough to bring
Simon running all the way from London.

'Quite the opposite.' Simon's eyes brightened as he leant
forward and knitted his fingers on the starched white table-
cloth. 'We received very complimentary reports from your
performance on the training course back in the spring. I
don't think we've had a chance to discuss it. So, what did
you think?'

'I enjoyed it,' Jenny lied politely. 'I met some very interesting people and learned a lot I didn't know.' She hoped to
sound enthusiastic without overdoing it. The fact was, she
had found the whole experience slightly sinister. She had
been chosen to be one of the dozen or so coroners who were
to receive special instruction to qualify them to conduct
military inquests. Given her past reputation as a headstrong

boat-rocker, she was astonished to have been selected at all. She had assumed that she had been included to make up the female quotient.

The course had taken place over an intensive eight days at Magdalen College, Oxford during the student vacation. Quite literally cloistered in splendid medieval surroundings, the trainees had been subjected to an intensive series of lectures and seminars given by various military bigwigs, government lawyers and shadowy officials from the Ministry of Defence along with a handful of tame coroners who had managed to conduct inquests into the deaths of military personnel without making political waves or awkward headlines. A few relatives of young men and women killed in action had made brief walk-on appearances, but Jenny had gained the impression that their contributions had been carefully stage-managed to give the best possible spin. If they were to be believed, they all trusted the military authorities to be nothing less than entirely truthful at all times. Their only complaint was that the coroners they had dealt with seemed to lack understanding of life in the armed services. The principal lesson Jenny had learned was not one the organizers had intended to convey: the military didn't much care for its business being pried into by civilians. In fact, it was positively hostile to the idea.

'How would you like to put it into practice?' Simon asked delicately.

The way he posed the question without referring to specifics told her there must be a catch. But as one of the chosen twelve, she could hardly turn him down.

'I'd be glad to.'

'Excellent. That's what I hoped you'd say.'

'Do you know Highcliffe? North Somerset. Don't you hail from that neck of the woods?'

He had clearly been digging deep into her file.

'I know it a bit,' Jenny answered, 'not that there's much to know – apart from the camp and a couple of streets.'

'A garrison town. And a tight-knit one at that,' Simon pronounced. 'There was a young man killed in Helmand yesterday, twenty-four hours before his company was due to fly home. We thought someone with a touch of the local burr might be what's called for.'

'The "local burr"?'

'You'll be trusted, Jenny. Feet firmly rooted in Somerset soil and all that. We'd like the family to feel as if they're being looked after by one of their own. They'll be terribly traumatized.'

Jenny had never thought of herself as rustic, or even real-ized that she still carried more than the merest hint of her childhood accent. But evidently to Simon's sophisticated London ears, there was no doubting that she was a West Country girl. It was a revelation. She wasn't sure whether to feel insulted or oddly proud.

'As I said, I'm happy to take the case, but I can't help feeling there's something you're not telling me.'

'Not really.' His obfuscation was transparent. 'The only slight wrinkle is the time issue. We'd like it all tidied up within the next few weeks.'

'Any particular reason?'

'We're wrapping up our operations in Afghanistan. The Secretary of State wants it all to end on a high note. No sour aftertastes. Quite right, too, given all the sacrifices our people have made.'

'I'm going on holiday next week. My first in years.'

'Oh? Where?'

'Italy.'

'Splendid. But far nicer in the autumn. No mosquitoes or bad smells. Still warm enough for cocktails on the terrace.' His expression became serious. 'Jenny, please. We'll meet the

expense. I'm asking you as a friend as well as a colleague
– I really would appreciate you taking this one for the
team.'

She knew that she was being given no choice.

Five minutes later, Jenny found herself in her office with
Simon and Alison, being handed a fait accompli. She was to
adjourn the one remaining inquest on her current list and
start the military case immediately. A file of highly confidential documents would be couriered to her office shortly. Her
initial point of contact was to be Sergeant Steven Price. He
was the regiment's Notifications Officer and had been
appointed official Army Liaison Officer to the Coroner. The
idea seemed to be that he would operate as a sort of second
coroner's officer alongside Alison. This wasn't the only
novel aspect of the procedure – she was to be based not at
her Bristol office, but at Highcliffe Camp itself. She and
Alison would be provided with rooms in the administration
block and the hearing would take place in the regimental
hall.

Simon seemed thoroughly satisfied by these arrangements but Alison was not. The moment he left to be whisked
back to London in a chauffeur-driven government car, she
delivered her verdict: 'It's not an inquest they want, Mrs
Cooper, it's a whitewash. And if you're the one who delivers
it, it'll look whiter than white, won't it? The whole thing
stinks, if you ask me.'

'You're not looking forward to having a colleague, are
you?'

'Don't worry about me,' Alison said. 'No one tells me
what to do.'

Jenny believed her.

It was oppressively hot and the traffic was heaving. Jenny
wound up the air conditioning and endured an agonizing

forty-minute crawl along the Portway as she tried to escape the city. The sight of the softly swaying trees that lined the Avon Gorge and the glints of sunlight off the river made her confinement in the car even more painful. She was longing for fresh air, loose clothes and the feel of grass beneath her feet. She finally left the traffic behind as she left the northern outskirts of Bristol and headed along the motorway towards the Severn Bridge. Ten miles further on, its twin supporting towers soared against a clear blue sky. Striking out across the mile span of the estuary, Jenny felt the weight of the previous weeks' work lifting from her shoulders. She would be starting a new and no doubt harrowing case in the morning, but at least it involved a change of scene and she would no longer be cooped up in the stuffy court building.

The final stage of her evening commute took her beyond the Welsh border town of Chepstow that sat at the foot of the hills on the far side of the bridge, and northwards along the Wye Valley. This was her favourite part of the journey: the winding road beneath the forest canopy felt like a tunnel connecting her workaday world to a brighter one beyond. Since the burnout seven years ago that had prompted her to gather up the fragments of her life and move from Bristol over the water to Wales, Jenny had come to think of this valley as her refuge, her sacred wilderness. Each morning she drew on its beauty as she made her way to work, and each evening it soothed away her tension as she returned. Five miles further on, she emerged from the trees into the riverside village of Tintern, from where she made her way up the steep, narrow lane that led to her home. By the time she arrived at Melin Bach, her stone slate-roofed cottage set amongst meadows and woods, she felt almost whole again. Her only immediate problem was how to break the news to Michael that Italy would have to wait.

Michael's car was parked on what remained of the old cart track at the side of the house but there was no sign of him indoors or outside in the garden. Jenny guessed he had taken off into the woods for one of his walks. A former RAF pilot, he now worked long hours for a small airline that specialized in high-value and time-critical freight. Because of his military background, his employers expected him to keep flying when others wouldn't. A series of fierce summer storms over continental Europe during the past fortnight had not prevented Michael from continuing to ferry cargoes of rare pharmaceuticals and specialist medical equipment from Zurich to destinations as far apart as Athens and Oslo. Jenny had frequently woken in the night to imagine him bumping through thunder clouds, the instrument panel a blur in front of his tired eyes.

She quickly showered, changed into a cotton dress and took a cool drink to the rough pine table in the garden together with the file that Simon had had sent to her office. It was a glorious summer's evening. Warm sun, a clover-scented breeze, sheep grazing in the meadow that surrounded her half-acre of garden and tiny trout making ripples in the stream at the end of the lawn. Almost too perfect to spoil by thinking about work.

The documents in the file were thankfully few and brief. There was a short dispatch from the company commander, Colonel Hastings, an official confirmation of death issued by a military surgeon at Camp Bastion and a copy of the army's slender personnel file on the dead soldier, Private Kenny Green. Skimming through the details, Jenny learned that Kenny had recently turned twenty-one, that he had joined the army at seventeen and that at the date of his death he was at the end of his third tour in Afghanistan. He was single, but the next-of-kin was nevertheless recorded as, 'Sarah Tanner, fiancée'. In terse, military prose, Colonel

Hastings described the circumstances of the fatal incident as he understood them:

Following the suspected kidnap of Pte Lyons (23135627), Pte Green (21913408) was one of a multiple led by Maj Norton (542461) which attempted to secure his release. The patrol travelled 2 km from the PB to the village of Shalan-Gar where intelligence suggested Pte Lyons was being held.
The objective was to negotiate with kidnappers through the village elder, Musa Sarabi. Once inside the compound the multiple was engaged by small-arms fire and grenades. Pte Green sustained a single fatal GSW to the head. Ptes Roberts (31134626) and Carter (33245726) also sustained serious injuries assessed as T2. All casualties were extracted by MERT within 20 mins of initial contact. Lessons learned report to follow.

The military surgeon had inspected Green's body some two hours after the incident in the hospital at Bastion. He stated that the medical officers who arrived at the scene found Green already dead from a single bullet wound to the head. Death was judged to have been instantaneous. An official note added at the foot of the document confirmed that the body had been cleared for immediate repatriation.

'There you are.'

Jenny looked up with a start. She had been so absorbed that she hadn't heard Michael approach.

'Still working? I thought you were getting a verdict today?' He leaned over to kiss her cheek.

'We got there in the end. Accidental death.'

'That's what you were expecting, wasn't it?'

'Yes . . .'

Michael sat in the other lawn chair next to her and tilted

backwards, soaking up the sun. 'I can't tell you how good it feels knowing I'm off the hook for another couple of weeks.'

Jenny felt a painful pang of guilt. She knew she should get the bad news over with but didn't like to spoil the moment. He looked so content. So at peace with himself.

Michael reached over and touched her hand. His skin was warm from the exertion of his walk over Barbadoes Hill. 'When we hit the beach I was thinking of hiring a boat. Have you ever sailed?'

'Once or twice.'

'You'll love it. Skim over the waves for a while. Drop anchor in a little secluded bay. Sip a cold beer watching the sun go down.' He seemed to sense her rising tension. 'I didn't see "MOD" on that file of yours, did I?'

'Well spotted.' She closed the file and set it on the ground.

'Which service?'

'Don't worry, it's not the RAF. It's the army. Some poor lad on the last day of his tour.'

'Let me guess – roadside device?'

'No. A firefight. They were attempting to recover a hostage. Can we talk about something else?'

'A civilian hostage?'

'Another soldier. Please? I think I'm ready for a glass of wine. How about you?'

'Sure.'

Jenny got up from her chair and reached for the file, but Michael's hand got to it first.

'Mind if I have a quick look? Just curious.'

There were several reasons she would like to have said no, not least of which was that Michael had finally shaken free of the symptoms of post-combat stress that had dogged him for the years since his retirement from the RAF and he had been warned to avoid any triggers. Close behind was the fact that her files were strictly confidential, and while she trusted him completely, the rules were there for a good reason.

She let out a sigh. 'If you promise—'

'I know.' He smiled and shook his head, as if the very idea that he might breathe a word was preposterous.

Against her better judgement, Jenny went through the stable door into the kitchen and fetched a bottle of Sauvignon Blanc from the fridge. She poured two glasses, took a large mouthful from one of them, then topped it up again before carrying them outside.

Michael set the file aside. 'Thanks.' He took his glass and clinked it against hers. 'To happy times.'

Jenny smiled, 'Happy times.'

They drank in silence for a moment watching the sun slowly dip towards the tops of the trees. House martins flitted busily, chasing the insects that rose out of their hiding places as the air began to cool. Jenny sensed a dip in Michael's mood. Had he guessed already?

She glanced across with a look that invited him to say what was on his mind.

'Your case looks like trouble,' Michael said quietly. 'Worried about it?'

'Reads like a typical military case to me,' Jenny said. 'Not much different from all the others I studied on the course back in April.'

'You'd expect an incident like that to make the news. I didn't hear anything.'

'I haven't caught up with it yet today,' Jenny said.

'There's a hostage, it says. Taken the day before they're due to pull out. Sounds like a pretty big coup for the enemy. Not one the army's going to publicize, if it can help it.'

Jenny had feared that reading the file would ignite all the feelings he had worked so hard to leave behind. Two decades in a fighter cockpit had taken a heavy toll. He had ultimately proved too sensitive a soul for the work he had to do. And the more troubled he had become by it, the more frightened he had been to resign his commission and venture out into the real world, where people weren't trying to blow each other up. She regretted ever having let him read it.

'I'll try to keep it simple,' Jenny said briskly. 'The cause of death shouldn't be hard to ascertain. It may only take a day or two. And I want you to know this now – I shan't be bringing this one home with me. That's a promise.'

Michael forced a smile and took a sip of wine.

Jenny shuffled her chair closer and hooked her arm under his. The physical connection between them broke down the invisible barrier. She felt the tension in his muscles slowly abate. The expression of contentment returned. She hated to spoil the mood yet again, but if she left it any longer it would only be worse.

Michael beat her to it. 'We're not going away next week, are we? You've been asked to clean this mess up first.'

Jenny threaded her fingers between his. 'Simon Moreton turned up this afternoon. He didn't exactly present me with a choice. We'll go straight after. It might even be nicer. The beaches will be quieter.'

'There's always that.' Michael nodded with an air of resignation. 'I like September in Italy.' His expression changed to one of concern. 'So long as you know what you're getting into, Jenny. You think you've had a tough time in the past, wait till you come up against the MOD.'

'I'll just follow the protocols. It'll be fine.'

Michael stared into his wine glass. 'It's interesting they chose you. The coroner who must have caused them more trouble and embarrassment than all the others put together.'

'Simon said it was because of my local connections.'

'Sounds to me like this is it, Jenny. The powers-that-be

are putting you to the test. Jenny Cooper is facing her Waterloo.'

'I think you're being a little overdramatic.' She leaned over to give him a reassuring kiss. She had intended a quick peck, but the moment their lips touched it became something else entirely. They hadn't kissed like this in days, probably not in weeks.

Jenny broke off to catch her breath. 'It's getting a bit chilly out here. Shall we . . . ?'

She didn't need to finish the question. They disappeared inside the house, and for the rest of the evening she managed to forget all about Private Kenny Green and his missing comrade, Pete 'Skippy' Lyons.

EIGHT

The tragic events at Shalan-Gar caused the homecoming to be delayed for three further days. It wasn't until the following Sunday that the RAF Tristar carrying the three returning platoons of C Company touched down at RAF Brize Norton in Oxfordshire. Kenny Green's body was on board. There were no members of his family present to witness it being transferred to the hearse that would deliver it to the mortuary at the John Radcliffe Hospital in Oxford. The men stood to attention in two ranks as six pall-bearers in full dress uniform carried the coffin draped in a Union flag across the tarmac. The watching soldiers saluted to their fallen comrade as the hearse crawled past, each of them sharing the same thought: it was only through the grace of God that it wasn't them coming home in a box.

The atmosphere in the buses that carried them across country to Highcliffe was muted. A fine drizzle smeared the windows, obscuring the view of what to their unaccustomed eyes was the almost oppressively green Wiltshire countryside. Some men slept, others were plugged into headphones, the rest retreated deep into their own private thoughts. At the front of the lead bus, Major Christopher Norton was seated next to Colonel Richard Hastings. The two men had done their talking the previous day in Hastings's air-conditioned office in Bastion. Unlike most of the soldiers they commanded, they had made this return trip more times than they cared to remember. Each had developed his own way of managing the traumatic adjustment from theatre to home, and today, each was privately struggling more than they had on any other occasion. On top of all that had happened, the end of the Afghan campaign felt like the end of an era. A full stop. The peaceful future was a dark, forbidding country.

Major Norton had become skilled at blanking out unpleasant events. He even had a mental image for it: a wave washing over sandcastles and leaving smooth, unsullied sand in its wake. In his mind's eye he pictured the beach at Ilfracombe, close to where he had spent his carefree, somewhat sheltered childhood playing among the dunes. It was the place to which his imagination inevitably transported him during moments in which there was something he wished to forget. He was there now.

'Mel's got things organized as usual, I hear,' Hastings said, looking up from a crumpled copy of the *Daily Mail* he had borrowed from the bus driver.

'Yes,' Norton answered.

He and Melanie had managed to exchange a few stilted emails once he had arrived back in Bastion from the post. She had told him about the arrangements for the afternoon.

'Can't wait to see her, I bet,' Hastings added unnecessarily.

Norton nodded, hoping to avoid any discussion of his family life with his CO. Hastings was married to a jolly, practical, rather unglamorous woman named Lizzie. They had no children but numerous dogs and two horses to whom Lizzie devoted most of her considerable energies. Norton suspected that theirs had been a marriage of habit and convenience for some time and that Hastings was growing tired of the arrangement. His mention of Melanie carried an uncomfortable subtext – *spare a thought for me while you're lying next to your beautiful young wife.*

'You'll have a few house calls to make, though,' Hastings remarked, as if Norton needed reminding. 'Always better coming from the horse's mouth, and as soon as possible.'

'I'll be visiting this evening,' Norton assured him, 'straight after the picnic.'

'I'd get straight to it, if I were you,' Hastings said. 'I'm sure Mel will save you some sandwiches.'

'Of course, sir.' Norton realized that he wasn't merely being offered avuncular advice; he was being issued with a formal order.

Hastings lowered his voice and leaned across between their seats. 'And if you could please stress that they shouldn't talk to any press? You might tell them that Lyons's life may depend on it.'

'I had intended to, sir. They'll obviously want to know what we're doing to get him back, and why we left without him.'

'His next-of-kin – grandmother, isn't it?'

Norton nodded.

'Can we trust her with the truth?'

'I'll gauge it when we meet, sir. I'm not sure I've ever met her.'

'Well, mind how you go,' Hastings said, returning his attention to the newspaper. 'Maybe give me a bell when you're done. Let me know how you got along.'

With that, the conversation was over and Hastings once again engrossed himself in the sex lives of various minor celebrities he had probably never heard of. Still, Norton thought, it might provide him with something to talk to Lizzie about over dinner.

*

Highcliffe town centre had been closed off to traffic. The three buses carrying the troops came to a halt and parked on the small cobbled square outside the town hall. Their weary occupants looked out in surprise to see crowds lining the High Street all the way down to the front. Young and old stood side by side cheering enthusiastically. Flags waved, bunting and balloons fluttered. The effect on the men was immediate. Soldiers who had endured six months of un-relenting hardship without displaying a flicker of emotion suddenly found their eyes filling with tears. As they emerged onto the square, the sun even managed to break out from behind the clouds. A school band, which had been practis-ing for weeks, struck up and led the crowd in a spontaneous rendering of 'For He's a Jolly Good Fellow'.

Fearful that his men were in danger of making an ex-hibition of themselves, Sergeant Bryant yelled at the top of his lungs. 'C Company, fall in!'

Like trained animals, they responded on reflex and within seconds had formed two long rows.

When the band reached the end of the chorus, the crowd fell silent. The only sound was that of a single seagull circling overhead.

'Atten-shun!' Sergeant Bryant's order echoed down the street like a rifle crack.

In response, 120 boots struck the ground in unison.

The silence settled again. Then, from around the side of the town hall, came the thunderous beat of bass drums.

Boom. Boom. Boom-boom, boom.

The regimental band struck up with a peal of trumpets and their signature march. The bandsmen appeared from behind the building, led out by three mounted police officers on gleaming horses.

'Left, turn!'

The two ranks swivelled to form two sixty-man columns.

With a swagger stick tucked smartly under his elbow, Colonel Hastings assumed his place at their head. When the band had passed by, Bryant gave the order: 'By the left – quick march!'

With their hearts swelling and eyes fixed straight ahead, the soldiers marched in step to the music. They were young and handsome, and their sunburned faces belonged to men who had seen and done things that the crowds applauding them could only guess at. Alongside the relief and joy they also felt sadness for those who had not come home or who were lying in hospital beds, but this was chiefly a moment to celebrate. They had done their duty. They had survived. And they were back in the bosom of those who loved them.

Major Norton slipped away from the festivities unnoticed and sent Melanie a text promising to catch up with her shortly. He knew that Emily and Hannah would be bitterly disappointed not to see their father walking through the town with his men, but their feelings had to come second to more important business.

His first call was to a modest semi-detached house a quarter of a mile from the entrance to Highcliffe Camp – the home of the Green family. Paul Green had been a sergeant in the regiment and their paths had crossed many times during Norton's early years as a newly commissioned lieutenant during several tours in Iraq. He had met Paul's wife, Rachel, on a few occasions but hadn't to his knowledge met Sarah Tanner, Kenny's fiancée. He had, however, heard members of the platoon telling Kenny what a lucky man he was to be marrying her. She was evidently considered quite a catch.

As Norton had anticipated, it was Paul Green who answered the front door. He had dressed in a regimental tie and blazer in expectation of the visit. They exchanged formal greetings and a stiff handshake before Paul ushered him into the small sitting room at the front of the house.

'Sorry we didn't make it to Brize Norton,' Paul said. 'Things have been a little, you know – difficult.'

'Of course.'

The two soldiers understood each other perfectly.

Norton removed his beret and took a seat while Paul went to fetch the others. The Greens' home was like that of so many military families Norton had known throughout his career. There was little money in evidence, but a deep sense of pride. The walls and shelves were decorated with photographs charting both Paul and Kenny's army careers. Paul's campaign medals were displayed in a small glass case. Pride of place was taken by a photo of him speaking to the Queen as she inspected his platoon. It had been taken more than twenty years ago and the young Paul looked almost identical to his son. Norton imagined Kenny growing up in this house looking at that picture and feeling the weight of expectation on his shoulders.

Paul returned a short while later with Sarah. She was deathly pale and very obviously pregnant. She wore a dark dress and minimal make-up and looked as if she might burst into tears at any moment. Norton stood to greet her. She shook his hand weakly and sat with her head bowed on the sofa opposite him alongside Paul.

'I'm afraid my wife doesn't feel up to meeting just yet,' Paul said. His voice was quiet but steady, the soldier in him firmly in control of his emotions. Norton was grateful for this.

'I understand,' Norton said. 'Whenever Mrs Green wishes to speak with me, I will make myself available.'

'Thank you.'

Norton steeled himself. There was no easy way to do this. He would just keep it brief and factual.

'Kenny died in action doing the job he loved. I didn't see exactly what happened, but I was present at the scene and involved in the exchange of fire in which he was fatally injured.'

Sarah began to sob. Paul reached for a box of tissues and handed it to her, grateful for the momentary distraction.

'As you may already have been told, Private Peter Lyons had somehow been captured during the night by insurgents. The following morning, with the assistance of a local go-between, I led a section to a nearby village intending to negotiate his release. This party was comprised entirely of men who had volunteered for the task. Kenny was the first to put himself forward.'

Paul nodded. Norton knew that although this wasn't the unvarnished truth, it would sustain the dead soldier's father until his dying day. Sarah continued to weep.

'Unfortunately, once inside the village compound – a place which, I should say, had always been friendly to us and grateful for our assistance – we came under attack from insurgents who had been lying in wait. It was all very quick, probably less than two or three minutes from start to finish. We inflicted casualties but also received them. Kenny, was, I believe, shot once and died instantly. Two others were badly injured by shrapnel from a grenade. Private Carter remains unconscious with severe head injuries and Private Roberts has unfortunately lost his legs. Both are currently in the specialist ward at Queen Elizabeth Hospital in Birmingham. If it's any consolation, I believe the man who fired the round at Private Green was killed in the subsequent exchange. I am told there will be a coroner's inquiry. The details of the incident will be closely examined.'

Norton knew that Paul would have either a host of questions or none at all. In his experience, bereaved families either felt the need to pick over every detail or contented themselves with the thought that their loved one had died with honour.

Paul considered what he had heard for a moment then gently took Sarah's hand between his. 'We can all be proud of him, love,' he said. 'Anyone can be a hero when it comes to saving their own skin, but laying down your life for a mate, that's something else. There's a special place for men like that.' He met Norton's gaze, 'Isn't that right, Major?'

'Yes. Indeed.' He addressed Sarah directly: 'It was an honour and a pleasure to have worked with him, Miss Tanner. He was much respected. His loss will leave a hole in many lives.'

Sarah was unable to speak except to mouth 'Thank you'.

'Is there anything else you'd like to ask me?' said Norton.

'No,' Paul said, then appeared to change his mind. 'Well, I suppose I do have one question.' His voice quavered with emotion for the first time during their encounter. 'I suspected that Kenny was out on the front line in Helmand because we heard nothing from him, but in the last email he sent us, back in February, he said he was going to be spending the tour in Bastion.'

'Some of the men do that,' Norton said. 'It's not something I necessarily advise.'

'My wife thinks he was told . . .' Paul swallowed, his words sticking in his throat.

'Let me reassure you, Mr Green,' Norton said. 'Before they left here in February, each member of the company knew where they were being posted. If your son tried to sweeten the pill for his family, that was his decision alone.'

'Of course,' Paul said.

Norton repeated his sincere condolences and left them to their grief.

The visit had proved far less troubling than Norton had feared but the image of Sarah's stricken, tear-stained face stayed with him. She looked barely more than a girl. In a few weeks' time she would give birth to a child who would never know its father. She was living with her intended in-laws, but in due course she would doubtless make a life with someone else and Paul and Rachel Green would suffer another form of bereavement as their grandchild grew up thinking of another man as its father. It was a sequence he had witnessed many times before. He hadn't managed to be much of a father himself, but as soon as each of his two daughters was able to understand, he had told them in no uncertain terms that they must never marry a soldier.

On leaving the house, Norton checked his phone and found a text message from Sergeant Price informing him that Private Lee Roberts's wife, Anna, and Private Dale Carter's girlfriend, were both en-route to the Queen Elizabeth Hospital in Selly Oak, where they would be met by one of the regiment's two visiting officers. It was a relief. Dealing with the relatives of the badly injured could often prove more difficult than dealing with those of the dead. Few young families could cope with the relentless struggle, financial hardship and emotional fallout that ensued when a previously strong, fit man found himself incapacitated for life. It left him with only one further house call to make. He checked the address he had entered in a notebook and headed for a similar street a short distance away.

Norton arrived outside a nondescript block of flats built in the years after the war, and rang the bell. While he waited for an answer, he noticed that the front door and window frames were in need of paint. Like many of the buildings in the neighbourhood surrounding the camp, it had a faintly depressing air of neglect.

Kathleen Lyons was a tired-looking woman with a face older than her years. Her first-floor flat smelled vaguely of cigarette smoke and the sickly lemon-scented air freshener she used to disguise it. After living in the open air for six months, Norton's sense of smell was finely tuned and the mixture of odours in the stuffy room made him want to throw open a window and let in some fresh air.

They sat at the table in the small kitchen with a window that overlooked a garage on the neighbouring trading estate. Kathleen's view from the sink was of piles of tyres and a collection of old cars in various states of dismemberment.

'I'm not sure how much Sergeant Price told you . . .' Norton began.

'Very little,' Kathleen said. 'He's phoned every day, but I'm still none the wiser.'

'To be fair to him, he has only had the barest details,' Norton said, trying to sound as conciliatory as he could. 'But the fact is, the circumstances of your grandson's disappearance or abduction are rather baffling.'

Kathleen listened with an expression that bordered on the sceptical as Norton outlined the events of the evening of the previous Tuesday and the following Wednesday morning. He emphasized that the post was fortified, permanently guarded and surrounded by mines, and that to leave it unnoticed was a virtual impossibility. Nevertheless, it appeared that Pete had either been skilfully abducted or had found a way of leaving which had caught them all unawares.

Kathleen absorbed every word. Norton sensed that her downtrodden exterior disguised a shrewd mind. Her eyes were sad, but she never once gave the impression that she might break down.

'How could he be abducted with all the other men bedded down next to him?' she asked, when he had completed his explanation.

'It's hard to comprehend, Mrs Lyons,' he replied, aware of how unsatisfactory it sounded.

'And how do you know that they're all telling the truth?'

'All I can say is that I trust my men with my life. They have no reason to lie.'

Kathleen folded her arms, keeping her thoughts about that to herself. 'And so you've all come home and left him?'

'Our Special Forces are still on the ground and are pulling out all the stops looking for him. Units of the Afghan National Army have already taken over the company's former positions and are employing their intelligence network to try to make contact with whoever is holding him.'

'Sergeant Price said it's all an official secret – is that right?'

'Not exactly. We haven't informed the press in case it jeopardizes his safety. We would advise you to back us up in this until we have some more definite news.'

'Because it looks bad, doesn't it? The army losing an eighteen-year-old lad the day before he's meant to come home.' Her tone grew more defiant still. 'I'd like to believe you, Major, I really would, but I've listened to all you've said and none of it makes any sense at all. I'm not even sure I can believe he did go missing like you say.'

'I appreciate it must be very difficult. I'll ask some of the platoon to make themselves available for you to talk to if it would help.'

'Thank you. Maybe I'll do that.'

It felt like time to draw the conversation to a close. Norton felt that whatever he said would, for the moment at least, only make matters worse. There was one last question he had to ask, however. 'Before I go, Mrs Lyons, I hope you don't mind my asking if you can think of any reason why your grandson might have had misgivings about coming home?'

'What do you mean?'

'He was always a very cheerful young man. The life and soul. Immensely brave, too. But I'm also aware that his family circumstances might not have been the happiest.'

'Is there something you're not telling me, Major?'

'I beg your pardon?'

'You're talking about him like he's dead.'

Norton floundered for a moment. 'I apologize. That really wasn't my intention.' He pulled out his notebook and wrote down his number. 'I'll call you every day even if there's no news. You must feel free to call me, too. I can assure you, the search will not end until he's found.'

Kathleen took the number and tucked it into her cardigan pocket. The wave of anger that had briefly surged through her had subsided, but having kept her feelings so tightly contained, her sadness had now escaped to fill the room. Norton experienced it with her: a sense not so much of grief as desolation.

As she rose from her chair to show him out, she said, 'I don't need to be sold a story, Major. I know he was just a kid. And a skinny little kid at that. If something else happened to him, even if he disgraced himself, I won't hold it against you. Believe me, whatever the truth, it's far better than not knowing.'

'Your grandson never failed to do his duty to the utmost of his ability, Mrs Lyons. He was out on patrol several times a week like every other man. He more than held his own.'

She gave a silent nod and led him to the door.

Norton arrived to find the homecoming picnic in full swing on the playing field at the camp. The clouds had dispersed, the sides of the marquee had been rolled up and the late-afternoon sun shone on the happy scene. The regimental band was playing a medley of familiar tunes, excited children were bounding on several large inflatables and queues of smiling soldiers and relieved women were converging on a buffet set out on a long row of decorated trestles. Melanie was right at the centre of things, overseeing an efficient team of helpers dressed in matching blue aprons. Norton watched her from a distance, a disconcerting although not unexpected feeling of dislocation welling up inside him. He seemed to experience it a little more keenly each time he returned from a tour. His work in Afghanistan had been dangerous and fraught with difficult life-or-death decisions, yet all of that felt somehow straightforward compared with the complexities of marriage and family life. The rules had become unfamiliar. He hadn't spoken to Melanie since February, yet tonight they would be sharing a bed. As if responding to a sixth sense, she glanced up as she served large scoops of summer pudding. Her pretty face lit up.

'I'll be with you in a minute, darling,' she called out, as if no time at all had passed. 'I think the girls are on the bouncy castle.'

'No hurry,' he called back. 'I'll see you shortly.'

He made his way invisibly through the crowd. Everywhere he looked people were laughing and embracing. He reminded himself that this was what he had been fighting for. Here it was in front of his eyes: peace and freedom. He emerged from the crush of the marquee and headed across the grass in search of his girls. He picked out Emily amidst the squealing melee and waved. He remembered to smile.

Anna Roberts and a girl named Susan, whom she hadn't met before, had been collected from Highcliffe by taxi and driven to the hospital in Birmingham. Apart from exchanging names, neither said a word during their journey along the M5 motorway. Instead, they silently endured the football commentary the driver was listening to on the radio. The previous four days had become a blur in Anna's mind. If it hadn't been for Melanie Norton stepping in so quickly she wasn't sure that she would have coped. She had immediately offered to mind Leanne and had arranged for members of the WAGs Club to deliver hot food to the flat twice a day. Thanks to Melanie, there had been people in and out all the time, several visits from the padre and even a house call from the GP, who had given her some tablets to help her sleep. In fact, until the car journey she had barely had a moment to be alone with her thoughts.

Now that she did, the thought that had kept returning to her was that she was now all that Lee really had. His mum was in her second marriage and his father had gone through so many relationships they had lost count. Between them, Lee's parents had produced seven children, with Lee the eldest at twenty-one, stretching all the way down to a two-year-old. They had both phoned to say they would be visiting as soon as they could get away, but Anna knew that both were tied down with their young families and would be of no practical help. Lee had once let slip that his mother had warned him that if he insisted on joining the army he would have to take the consequences without any help from her. When he left school, she had tried to persuade him to go to work with his uncle as a trainee plumber. That prospect had been enough to send him straight to the recruitment office.

Anna and Susan were met in the hospital's reception area by two of the regiment's visiting officers, whose job was to oversee the rehabilitation of the injured and to liaise with their families. Corporal Terry Matthews, a wiry terrier of a man in his early forties, took care of Anna, Corporal Hanson was attached to Susan. They were frank, brisk and brutally honest from the outset. Following polite but cursory introductions, the two women were taken upstairs to the ward dedicated to military casualties. En route, Corporal Matthews explained that Lee had lost the lower part of both legs as a result of a grenade blast. The explosion had also ruptured his left eardrum leaving him with the possibility of permanent hearing damage. He had been under heavy sedation since incurring his injuries, but the doctors had allowed him to return to consciousness earlier that day. His situation had been explained to him and, according to Matthews, he had taken it well.

Corporal Hanson followed several paces behind with Susan. Anna couldn't help but overhear what he was saying to her. Dale Carter had been hit in the head by shrapnel which had penetrated his helmet. He was unconscious and, following an MRI scan, was awaiting surgery. The neurosurgeon gave him a 50 per cent chance of surviving the initial procedure, and even if he came through it he would suffer permanent physical and mental impairment. As he led Susan towards the intensive care unit where Dale was being monitored, Anna realized for the first time how much worse her situation could have been.

Anna followed Corporal Matthews into the ward where Lee was being treated. He was in a curtained-off bay at the far end. On the way they passed beds containing men with missing limbs and faces grossly disfigured by burns. Yet despite the horrific nature of their wounds, the atmosphere was purposeful and optimistic. The nurses greeted her cheerfully. It was the brightest, cleanest hospital ward Anna had ever seen.

'Visitor for you, Private Roberts,' Matthews announced, and pulled back the curtain.

Anna closed her eyes for a moment and uttered a short prayer the padre had used. She opened them again to see something she hadn't been expecting. Lee was propped up in bed, clean shaven and dressed in a fresh hospital gown. A frame positioned under the immaculate bedclothes kept them from touching his legs. He looked a little pale and tired, and a lot thinner than she remembered, but he greeted her with a smile.

'I'll leave the two of you alone for ten minutes, then I'll be back to run through your programme for the next two weeks.'

'Yes, Corp,' Lee replied.

'Your husband will be kept busy, Mrs Roberts,' Corporal Matthews said. 'Rehabilitation is hard work and it gets harder. Every soldier is expected to put his shoulder to the wheel. All right. Carry on.'

He marched off along the ward.

Anna stood and stared at her husband, not knowing where to begin or how to behave.

She reached for his hand and clasped it. She wanted to kiss him but felt strangely inhibited by the formal military atmosphere.

'I want you to know, I'll be with you every step of the way,' Anna said bravely.

'They say they can get you walking again in a few months. I'll try to be as quick as I can.' He forced a smile.

'That's great. Fantastic. If anyone can do it, it's you.'

He squeezed her hand, his fingers rough against her skin.

There was a long silence as Lee seemed to disappear inside himself. To Anna it seemed almost as if he had forgotten she was there. She felt helpless.

'Are you all right?' she asked eventually. 'Is there anything I can do for you?'

Lee shook his head.

'Do you want to talk about how it happened?'

He looked up sharply. 'Actually, there is one thing you can do for me, Anna – never, ever ask me that again.'

88

'Sorry, love,' she whispered. She wanted to cry but managed to stop herself.

'It was just dumb luck,' Lee said. 'Dumb, stupid bad luck.'

NINE

Jenny drove towards Highcliffe with Alison following behind her. The familiar, undulating patchwork fields of north Somerset unleashed a host of buried memories. Although it was less than twenty miles from the house in which she had grown up, the small town sitting almost directly on the imaginary point at which the Severn Estuary became the Bristol Channel had seemed a world away. It had been the place to which her family escaped on sunny weekends. She recalled day trips in her father's open-topped Triumph Herald. Blue skies, warm breezes, her mother in a headscarf and Jackie Onassis sunglasses, her father with one hand on the wheel, a cigarette between his lips and his other arm around her shoulder. Jenny had thought they looked like film stars.

As they approached the outskirts of the town, she remembered the two sharp bends that her dad would delight in taking at high speed, throwing her across the back seat and pinning her against the door. Just like the waltzers at the fairground. And here they still were, every bit as perilous as she remembered them. She navigated them slowly, then as the road straightened and widened she found herself on a tree-lined avenue that led all the way down to the front. It hadn't changed in thirty-five years. The same Victorian villas with jaunty names – Montego Bay,

Westward-Ho; the same faded vacancy signs in the guest-house windows, and here and there, sprouting from fussy front gardens, an exotic palm or two. It felt like coming home. But the comforting sights sat strangely with the purpose of her visit. This harmless, quaint little town that she had associated only with carefree family picnics and splashing in the chilly sea, had become the stage for the most daunting assignment of her career.

Highcliffe Camp was situated on high ground nearly a mile from the centre of town on its poorer, eastern edge. A short distance up the hill, the elegant houses gave way to council-built, post-war semis interspersed with blocks of flats and a scruffy, none-too-prosperous parade of shops. Across the street from it, a group of bored teenagers loitered at the edge of a rubbish-strewn playground.

Jenny turned into a road named Cliffside and followed it for a short distance past more grey homes until it terminated at the heavily fortified camp entrance. A sandbagged checkpoint manned by several sentries was flanked by high fences topped with coiled razor wire. A soldier stepped out of a booth. He held himself confidently and exuded authority, but he had the smooth face and clear eyes of a boy. Jenny gave him her details. He noted them down, then retreated into the booth, from which he emerged shortly afterwards with security badges for both her and Alison. As she clipped hers to her jacket, Jenny noticed that it read, HER MAJESTY'S CORONER, MRS JENNIFER COOPER. No one had ever referred to her as Jennifer. To her knowledge, the only document which referred to her by that name was her birth certificate, and then only because a bureaucratic registrar had insisted on it. Her name was plain 'Jenny' – even the tax man agreed. Passing through the raised barrier and following the signs to the administration block, she pondered whether it was simply a mistake or whether she had been subjected to a detailed security vetting. And if so, who would have ordered it?

Two parking spaces had been set aside for them outside the red brick building that was as attractive as its name suggested. There it was again, on the laminated sign: RESERVED FOR HM CORONER, MRS JENNIFER COOPER. It was as if someone was trying to tell her something.

Jenny and Alison had barely set foot outside their cars when another soldier appeared to meet them. He politely introduced himself as Sergeant Steven Price and led the way to the main entrance. He was over six feet tall with shoulders that looked as if they had been carved from granite. His uniform was immaculate, his boots and brass buttons shone. The only imperfection in his handsome features was an unmoving right eye with a deep scar at its outer corner.

Alison cast Jenny a sly glance as they followed him inside. Too loudly for Jenny's comfort, she whispered, 'I wouldn't say no.'

Jenny ignored the remark, hoping there would be no more. Alison smirked. Unrepentant.

Sergeant Price led the way along a corridor painted in a shade of institutional green that had disappeared from the outside world during the previous three decades. Regimental photographs were displayed at evenly spaced intervals and at the foot of the main stairs was a glass case containing medals and other mementos from glorious battles long in the past.

Colonel Hastings's office was at the far end of the building on the first floor. Sergeant Price knocked twice on the heavy door then ushered them into a large, airy room with a view over the parade ground and the playing field beyond.

'Good morning.' Hastings stepped out from behind his desk to greet them. Jenny guessed his age at about fifty. He had greying sandy hair and the lean physique of a man who had kept himself fit. His smile was disarmingly soft and welcoming.

'Mrs Cooper. Mrs Trent. Pleased to meet you. Richard Hastings.' He shook them both by the hand.

'Good morning, Colonel,' Jenny said, resisting his implicit invitation to call him by his Christian name.

He motioned them to four chairs set around a low table on which coffee was already waiting. Sergeant Price filled their cups as they exchanged introductory pleasantries.

Hastings exuded charm and urbanity, which was quite a feat given that he had returned to the UK from Afghanistan only the previous day. He explained that while the men would have a period of leave after their tour, his would have to wait. There were personnel matters to deal with and a lot of newly returned equipment that needed servicing and repairing. Drudge work, he called it. Jenny suspected that this was an excuse to delay the transition to the slower pace of life at home. She sensed that beneath the controlled exterior, he was still operating with the same keyed-up energy that had sustained him throughout the tour.

After a decent interval, Jenny steered the conversation away from small talk towards the incident in Helmand. Hastings explained that he had been managing operations from Brigade HQ in Bastion, the temporary mini-city erected piecemeal by US and British forces over the long years of the occupation. The men of C Company were distributed among five forward command posts. Major Norton was the senior officer on the ground and based with 2 Platoon of which Private Green was a member. It was, he said, probably no accident that the incident occurred during the final hours of the occupation. It bore all the hallmarks of an operation timed and planned for maximum publicity. A Taliban coup: the British sent running with their tails between their legs.

'On that issue . . .' Hastings said, changing the subject

slightly, 'I had a call shortly before you arrived indicating that a DA-notice is in the offing.'

'DA' was the acronym for Defence Advisory. A DA-notice could be issued by the government's Defence, Press and Broadcasting Committee requesting news outlets not to report on a story if it risked endangering national security or the lives of individuals. Compliance was voluntary, although in practice orders were seldom breached. Jenny instinctively rebelled against official secrecy of any sort, but in this instance she reluctantly saw the argument in favour.

'Because Private Lyons is still missing?'

'Yes,' Hastings said. 'Whether there's any chance of finding him, we don't yet know, but between you and me it's one of the most comprehensive searches the army has ever launched. Drones, satellites, Special Forces. If he's alive, we'll find him.'

'I've only had sketchy information, but it seems odd that he was abducted from under the noses of his colleagues.'

'Strange things and unexpected things happen in war,' Hastings said. Price nodded his agreement.

'Presumably you've discussed the incident with Major Norton in some detail?'

'We had a session together before we embarked for home.'

'I've read your short report. Is that all there is?'

'As far as I can ascertain, there was an ambush, the whole thing was over very quickly and Private Green was unfortunate enough to catch a bullet in the wrong place. Frankly, there's not much more to it than that. Thankfully, he didn't suffer. Not much of a comfort, but it's something.'

'He was a sound lad,' Sergeant Price said, unprompted. 'I knew him well.'

The two men exchanged a look. Jenny sensed a deep

bond between them. It surprised her. She had expected more distance and formality between officers and other ranks.

'In your report of the incident you said that there would be a detailed lessons-learned inquiry to follow,' Jenny said. 'Has that already taken place?'

'That would be an internal matter,' Colonel Hastings said. His tone and expression were diplomatic but Jenny sensed she had hit a significant obstacle.

'If a formal inquiry has taken place and evidence gathered, that would be something that I would need to know about. Whether or not your findings would be made public, I would certainly expect them to form part of the evidence at the inquest.'

Colonel Hastings gave a polite but non-committal smile that said that it was not a discussion he was prepared to enter into. 'Sergeant Price will be serving as your liaison officer. He'll be on hand to assist you in whatever way he can,' he continued, attempting to brush the issue aside. 'All the men and their families know him, so his presence should help oil the wheels, as it were.'

'I'm sure it will,' Alison said, having apparently forgotten her previous objections to having to share her role as coroner's officer.

'We've set two offices aside for you along the corridor here. Sergeant Price will show you to them in a moment, and then he'll take you over to have a look at the regimental hall, where Mr Moreton suggested you conduct your inquest.'

Jenny had decided overnight that Simon's suggestion that she hold her hearing at the camp was a step too far. 'The offices will be very useful, thank you,' she replied, 'but I've decided that the inquest itself will be conducted elsewhere in the town. It's an independent inquiry and has to appear to be so.'

Hastings was unfazed. 'Of course. I thought you might take that view. Sergeant Price tells me that the local magistrates' court was mothballed a few years ago – if we grease the right palms I believe we might be able to bring it out of retirement.'

'It sounds ideal,' Jenny said. She resisted the urge to return to the issue of Hastings's internal inquiry. She wanted to leave him in no doubt that she would insist on seeing every relevant piece of information, but at the same time she had the sense that this was what he wanted of her; that he would have welcomed the opportunity to lock horns and assert himself at the outset. She wouldn't do that. Better to keep him guessing.

Hastings seemed to sense something of Jenny's thoughts. Behind the benign smile that carried a vague hint of amusement, his eyes were constantly assessing. He seemed to enjoy the game of silently jousting with her.

'Have you spoken with Green's family?' Hastings asked. 'The father used to be a sergeant in the regiment. Served with him in Iraq. He's a good man.'

'We haven't yet,' Jenny confessed. 'We intend to make contact today. Doubtless they'll want to know about the body, perhaps wish to view it. I'll talk with the pathologist at the John Radcliffe and see what the position is before we meet. Hopefully we can get the post-mortem out of the way today.'

Another glance passed between Hastings and Sergeant Price. 'That's already happened, as far as I know,' the colonel said cautiously.

'The post-mortem?'

'The body was transferred to the mortuary at the Severn Vale Hospital late last night. We like to bring them back close to home as soon as possible.'

Jenny failed to conceal her surprise. 'On whose instruction was this post-mortem carried out?'

'Mine,' Hastings said. 'I thought you'd want to get things ticking along.'

Jenny's first instinct was to tell him that she considered this a gross intrusion on her authority, but she stopped herself. Starting off on a sour note would only hinder her. If she was going to mount an effective inquiry, she was going to need the army's cooperation.

She did her best to strike a conciliatory tone, 'Well, it's not how things are normally done, but I'm sure you were operating from the best of motives. Has there been a report from the pathologist?'

'Her name is Dr Langham. Fiona Langham. She has your details. I'm sure she'll be in touch.' Hastings glanced at his wristwatch, suddenly keen to bring the meeting to an end. 'Is there anything else I can do for you, Mrs Cooper?'

'No, I don't think so.'

'Call me any time or have a word with Sergeant Price. Anything we can do to help. I'm told this may only take a matter of days if all proceeds smoothly.'

'Really? By whom?' This time Jenny couldn't conceal her annoyance.

'Moreton? Is that his name?'

'Coroners' inquests take as long as they take, Colonel. When I'm satisfied that we have statements from all relevant witnesses we'll proceed to a hearing, but not until then.'

Hastings flashed another of his disarming smiles. 'Understood, Mrs Cooper. I'm sure we both suffer with men in grey suits telling us how to do our jobs.' He stood up from his chair, bringing the meeting to an end. 'Sorry about the post-mortem. I must have got a bit too used to barking orders.'

Jenny responded with a smile of her own. As they parted company she decided that on balance she liked him, but would have to be on her guard. He was a hard man not to trust.

Sergeant Price led them out of the office and along the corridor to the far end. Two adjacent doors had fresh name cards in their polished brass holders. For a third time, Jenny's name appeared as Jennifer. The second bore Sergeant Price's name alongside Alison's.

'The two offices are interconnecting,' Sergeant Price explained.

He showed them through the first door into the large office that Alison and he would share. It was fully equipped with phones, computers and photocopier. Besides the two desks, there was a table and chairs they could use when speaking to witnesses or relatives.

'I feel very privileged,' Alison said. It was considerably roomier that the small set of ground-floor offices from which she and Jenny operated in central Bristol.

Sergeant Price opened the connecting door into the smaller but rather more plushly furnished office reserved for Jenny. A large, important-looking desk was equipped with a sleek new computer. A pair of leather armchairs was arranged in one corner. A glass-fronted cabinet contained several decanters and a selection of crystal glasses.

'If you require coffee or any other refreshments, dial nine on the desk phone and inform the batman what you require. You're invited to lunch in the officers' mess any time between midday and two p.m. Would you like me to show you where it is?'

'In a moment,' Jenny said. 'If you wouldn't mind, I've a quick call to make.'

'Certainly.' He turned to the door.

'Maybe you can show me how to use the computers?'
Alison suggested.

'Of course.'

Sergeant Price took her through and closed the door
behind him.

Jenny took a moment to orientate herself in her new
surroundings. The office could have belonged to a general,
except now that she observed a little more closely she detected some feminine touches: a discreetly positioned vase
of flowers, tissues in a decorative silver box, a framed
mirror hanging on the wall that looked suspiciously new.
Someone had gone out of their way to make her feel comfortable. But who? It was an intriguing question. She very
much doubted that Simon Moreton would have had an eye
to such detail.

Deciding not to trust the switchboard-routed landline for
sensitive communication, she called through to the John
Radcliffe Hospital on her mobile phone and asked to be put
through to Dr Langham as a matter of urgency.

It took several minutes before the pathologist came on
the line. She was terse, bordering on the irritable, and immediately let Jenny know that she was in the middle of a very
tricky post-mortem.

Jenny ignored her rudeness and got straight to business.
'I understand you carried out an autopsy on the body of
Private Kenneth Green, yesterday? Can I inquire why you
went ahead without my instruction?'

'I assumed it was on your instruction. I was told you
needed a report by the end of today.'

'Colonel Hastings told you this?'

'The first call came from the MOD, even before the body
had been repatriated. I was told this was a matter of
urgency.'

'May I ask what you found?'

'A single bullet wound. It entered behind the right ear, exited through the left temple. A few other cuts and bruises, but that was it.'

'Are there any personal effects?'

'There were a few items of uniform. They were transported along with the body. It's very straightforward. There's no doubt it was a fatal shot. You'll get the paperwork this afternoon. Is that it?'

'Yes. Thank you.'

Jenny rang off, tapped the internet icon on her phone screen and ran a search on Dr Fiona Langham. It took only a few moments to learn that she had appeared as an expert witness on behalf of the MOD in several high-profile inquests and civil actions. Her name occurred repeatedly in newspaper reports of the case of two young British helicopter pilots who had crashed while flying a mission at night in the latter part of the Iraq War. The pilots' families claimed they had repeatedly complained that poor maintenance was putting their lives at risk. Dr Langham testified that she had detected small but significant traces of an antidepressant drug in the pilot's body which suggested he was suffering from an undeclared condition that would have rendered him unfit to fly. The court found for the MOD and decided that the pilot had contributed directly to his death and that of his colleague. His widow was left with nothing but a hefty legal bill.

Having read enough, Jenny called the mortuary at the Severn Vale and established that Private Green's body had indeed arrived very late the previous night. She informed the mortuary technician that she would be along to view it shortly and that it was not to be touched until she arrived.

Jenny found Alison sitting at a computer with Sergeant Price leaning over her shoulder looking less than entirely comfortable as he guided her through the system.

'I've told the Vale we're on our way to view the body.'

She had addressed her remark to Alison, but it was Sergeant Price who answered first, 'I can drive, if you like.'

'Thank you, but that won't be necessary,' Jenny said firmly. 'Alison?'

Alison prised herself away, thanking the sergeant for being so patient.

'It's really no trouble to drive you, Mrs Cooper.' Price wasn't to be easily deterred.

'We'll see you later, Sergeant.'

Jenny shepherded Alison out of the office and headed for the stairs.

'What's the hurry?' Alison said. 'I was just getting to grips with it all.'

Jenny's patience was wearing thin. 'If you're not careful, he's going to think . . .' She paused briefly to rephrase a sentence that was at risk of sounding cruel. 'Well, let's just say he may not take you as seriously as he ought to.'

Alison gave a mischievous grin. 'Isn't that what we want, Mrs Cooper?'

Colonel Hastings looked up impatiently from the pile of paperwork that had landed on his desk to see Sergeant Price stepping through the door. He seemed preoccupied.

'Yes, Sergeant?'

'Mrs Cooper and her officer have gone to view the body, sir. They preferred to go alone.'

'What about the family? Has she spoken to them yet?'

'Not as far as I know, sir.'

'Well, you'd better phone them. And if Mrs Cooper hasn't already been in touch, you probably ought to apologize on her behalf. And let them know that we're eager to get things resolved as soon as possible.'

'Will do, sir.'

Hastings gazed distractedly out of the window for a moment. 'What do you make of the blonde one – the officer? Bit batty, don't you think?'

'Mrs Trent. She's harmless enough. She told me she'd been in a car accident a couple of years ago – hit her head.'

'Sounds like you're getting on famously.' He gave an amused smile. 'Try and stay close to her – well, within reasonable limits. And make sure to keep me regularly informed. I don't want any unpleasant surprises.'

'Yes, sir. Understood.'

Hastings returned to his paperwork and Price turned to go with a weary sense of resignation. Being lumbered with a desk job was bad enough, but being asked to cosy up to a sixty-year-old woman with a penchant for young men in uniform was definitely not his idea of soldiering. The only speck of light was Colonel Hastings's promise that if he performed well he would put in a good word with the Promotions Board. With a bit of luck he would quickly make staff sergeant, and with a fair wind, warrant officer not long after that. A crown on his sleeve instead of stripes.

Hastings called after him as he was leaving. 'Actually, Sergeant, I'd like you to offer to drive the family to the Vale yourself. I'm sure they'll want to go.'

'Now, sir?'

'Yes. You can take my car. I want them to feel looked after. And I want Mrs Cooper to understand that the army looks after its own.'

'I'll do my best, sir.'

As he pulled the door closed behind him, Sergeant Price began to wonder what it was about the circumstances of Kenny's death that was making the colonel jumpy. Price had already seen the body at the John Radcliffe when he had arrived to oversee its transfer. It was obvious what had happened – he'd taken a shot in the wrong place. All he could think of was that Kenny hadn't died the way you were meant to – bravely, facing down the enemy. If Price had been forced to predict which members of 2 Platoon might not come home, Kenny would have been near the top of his list. He was a nice lad, sweet natured, but lacked the killer instinct. To survive, a soldier needed a ruthless streak. Whatever had happened to him out there, Price doubted very much that Kenny had died in a way to make the regiment proud.

TEN

Jenny had trained herself to tolerate the sight of bodies laid out on trolleys packed end to end along the corridors of the overstretched mortuary, but she had never become used to the gut-churning smell or to the high-pitched whine of the buzz saws that emanated from behind the doors of the autopsy room. The foul odour of decay and disinfectant was particularly pungent on this warm August afternoon and she was forced to cover her mouth as she and Alison followed Joe, the senior mortuary technician, to the refrigeration unit.

The cool air on the far side of the insulated doors at the end of the corridor came as relief.

Joe checked the names scribbled on the whiteboard next to the bank of identical steel drawers, then exchanged a glance with Alison – they were both enjoying Jenny's obvious discomfort.

'Don't worry, Mrs Cooper,' Joe said, in his thick Somerset accent. 'They cleaned him up pretty good, far as I could tell. Patched up his head, they did.'

He pulled open the drawer and drew back the overlapping flaps of white plastic encasing the corpse to reveal the head and shoulders of a very young man. After the shock of first sight had passed, Jenny observed – as she had done so many times before – that the body looked more like an alabaster statue or a waxwork than an object that had once been animated. There was nothing so dead, so unlifelike, as human remains drained of all colour and chilled to four degrees.

The dead soldier had a military crew cut leaving nothing to disguise the post-mortem scar which ran full-circle from the top of the forehead to the back of the skull. A large exit wound was immediately visible on the left temple. As Joe had said, the technicians at the John Radcliffe had used mortician's wax to plug the jagged hole that was about three inches in diameter, but the wax was a little pinker than the surrounding skin, giving the impression of a large, strawberry-coloured birthmark. Jenny crouched down to see if she could get sight of where the bullet had entered.

'You only have to ask, you know.'

Joe used both hands to lift the head up as far from the bed of the drawer as rigor mortis would allow. It took considerable effort. A real corpse, unlike those that featured in films, was about as flexible as a sheet of board.

The bullet hole was, as she would have expected, roughly half an inch wide and situated just below and behind the right ear.

'Must have got in under his helmet,' Alison observed.

Jenny noticed the clear polythene bag containing various items of clothing that was stowed at the foot of the drawer.

'I don't suppose his helmet's with his things.'

Joe lifted the bag out and checked the contents that were itemized on a tag attached to it. 'Boots, socks, underwear, trousers, T-shirt, tunic, wristwatch, dog tag and gold crucifix.'

'It would've been the first thing to come off,' Alison said. 'Probably went straight back to stores.' She leant forward and tugged the plastic back from the rest of the body. 'Hardly a scratch on him.'

Jenny forced herself to take a long and detailed look. There were, as Dr Langham had said, several lacerations and various cuts and bruises on the upper arms significant enough to have been caused by flying shrapnel. But there were no further bullet wounds. Private Green had indeed, it seemed, been killed by a single shot. He had been unlucky. An inch or two higher and the round would have bounced harmlessly off his Kevlar helmet.

Joe was covering the body back up when Dr Kerr, the Vale's senior pathologist, joined them. Fresh from conducting a post-mortem, he was dressed in green surgical scrubs and smelled strongly of the medicated soap he had used to sluice down his muscular forearms. Since his recent marriage, the taciturn Ulsterman had taken to smiling occasionally. He greeted Jenny with uncharacteristic warmth, 'Good to see you, Jenny. But according to my diary, you're meant to be on leave.'

'That was the plan. Then this came along.'

'They want it dealt with yesterday,' Alison butted in.

Dr Kerr nodded. 'I've already had the call.'

'From Simon Moreton?' Jenny asked.

He shook his head. 'From someone upstairs here. I'm to give this case top priority, apparently. It gets to jump the queue.'

'Did they give any explanation?'

'No,' he said, matter-of-factly, 'and I've learned not to ask.'

Jenny left it there. She suspected Moreton's hand, but was beginning to appreciate that he was only a small part of the machine that had swung into operation to ensure her inquiry concluded swiftly and beneath the public's radar.

'Have you had a look?'

'A quick glance,' Dr Kerr said. 'Cause of death seems

obvious enough. I haven't had the Radcliffe's report yet, but I can't imagine I'll be able to add much to it.'

'Maybe not, but I need you to conduct a second post-mortem – as a matter of principle as much as anything else. And it needs to be thorough – everything you can discern about cause of and circumstances of death.'

The conversation was briefly interrupted by the sound of Alison's phone ringing. She ducked outside the door to take the call.

'Circumstances . . . ?'

'Was he standing up, lying down, inside, outside? Did it really happen when they said it did? Anything you can find.'

He nodded in the inscrutable way he had when he was keeping his thoughts to himself.

'Treat it as a top priority, and if you come under any pressure, let me know. I'll happily deal with the hospital management.'

Alison reappeared, her phone cupped in her hands. 'It's Sergeant Price. He's on his way over with Private Green's parents and fiancée. They'd like to talk to you.'

'Now?'

'They'll be with us in half an hour.'

Jenny had intended to make contact with the family later that afternoon. Meeting bereaved relatives was something she liked to prepare for, and she tried at all costs to avoid meeting for the first time in the emotionally charged surroundings of a mortuary. She couldn't help feeling that Price had done this deliberately; that, having been left behind, he was trying to muscle his way in on the action.

'Shall I tell him we'll wait?'

'He hasn't given us much choice.'

There was a small family room off the entrance lobby – the only place in the mortuary you could go without bumping into a body. Jenny ushered Paul and Rachel Green and Kenny's fiancée, Sarah Tanner, straight inside then promised to join them in a moment. She closed the door after them and turned to Sergeant Price.

'May I ask why you spoke with them before clearing it with me?'

'I was acting in my capacity as Notifications Officer, ma'am,' he answered politely. 'It's usual procedure for me to inform relatives of a body's return as soon as possible. I always offer to accompany them to the mortuary for a viewing. It was a convenient moment for everybody.'

'Well, it's less than ideal for me. This is the last place I would choose to meet next-of-kin for the first time.'

'My apologies, ma'am. Force of habit.'

'Some of those habits are going to have to change, Sergeant. This is my inquiry, and I determine procedure. Is that understood?'

'Yes, ma'am.'

Dreading the meeting she now had to face, Jenny left Price with Alison and went through to join the family.

All three were formally dressed. Paul Green was ashen-faced but able to cope with introductions. Except for a muttered 'Hello', Sarah Tanner said nothing more. Unable to meet Jenny's gaze, she stared at her feet, her hands crossed over her pregnant belly. Rachel Green was by far the most visibly traumatized of the three. Her eyes were glazed and staring with slivers of white visible beneath the pupils. Her grey features were pallid and lifeless. She looked as if, after several days and nights in the full throes of grief, she had collapsed into exhaustion.

Jenny began by explaining that her role as a coroner was to discern precisely when, where and how Kenny had died. She stressed that although she was being given the assistance of the army in conducting her inquiry, she was completely independent. She would be holding an inquest as soon as she could, and that as matters stood it was unlikely to be reported in the media. Next, she gently inquired what they had already been told about the circumstances of Kenny's death.

Paul Green told her about the visit from Major Norton. 'He said he volunteered to help bring back his mate. Sounds like Kenny.' Paul spoke with pride. Jenny could tell that he had been a soldier.

There was a brief lull in conversation. With no more information to impart, all that remained was for Jenny to arrange for them to make the short walk along the corridor to view the body. The only question in her mind was whether to send all three at once, or to suggest that Sarah go separately. She responded to an instinct which told her that sending Sarah alone was indeed the right thing to do. A mother and a lover's grief were very different things.

Jenny was on the cusp of making the suggestion when Rachel broke her silence.

'It shouldn't have happened. He shouldn't be here.' She spoke not to Jenny but as if in casual conversation with a disembodied presence. 'He told us he was in Bastion.'

'The major explained that, love,' Paul said patiently. 'Lots of the boys say that to their folks. They don't like to scare them.' He turned to Jenny: 'He emailed back in February to say that he would be spending the tour in Bastion. It was the last we heard from him. The moment he went two weeks without being in touch it was obvious where he was. The major told us – they all knew where they were going before they left home.'

Jenny turned her gaze to Sarah. 'What did you think, Miss Tanner?'

She shrugged. 'Same as Paul, I suppose.' She spoke

quietly, but evenly. 'You try not to think about it. You put it out of your mind.'

'They knew it was the last tour. They knew they were leaving no matter what. Why do you put boys like that in harm's way when there's no need?' Rachel said, continuing her dialogue with thin air. 'Boys. That's all they were. Young lads who didn't know any better. The major came home, didn't he? And his sergeant. They aren't lying dead. Too cute for that. They had all those boys to take the flak.'

Paul glanced at Jenny with sad, apologetic eyes. His despairing expression said that he feared that his wife had come apart at the seams.

'It's my job to make sure that we all learn exactly what happened, Mrs Green,' Jenny said gently. She left it there, aware that Rachel was barely hearing her. 'Would now be a good moment for you to go through? I was going to suggest that you might not all want to go at once—'

Rachel cut across her. 'You know what I want to know? What was it for? What was it all bloody for? Can anyone tell me?'

Caught off guard, Jenny found herself at a loss for an answer.

'That's not the issue here, love.' Paul patted the back of her wrist. 'Come on, now.'

Rachel snatched her hand away and plunged it into her lap. 'I asked Kenny that. He couldn't tell me. You know why? They don't want soldiers thinking. They just want them obeying orders. They're not human beings to them, they're just . . . they're just *things*.'

Paul took a deep breath. Jenny could see that his patience was wearing thin. 'When I was in uniform, I knew exactly what I was doing. So did Kenny.'

Rachel shook her head. 'They're taking us for fools. What

about Pete Lyons? A man can't get snatched from inside his own camp. Not without someone knowing. Even I know that.'

Paul shrugged, but seemed in his expression to acknowledge that she had a point. 'That's what all this business is about,' he said, as if to convince himself. 'To find out.'

Rachel turned to address Jenny directly for the first time. Her eyes had come alive with fury. 'It's not though, is it, Mrs Cooper? The army didn't have to send a car and driver to the family of a private soldier for me to smell a rat. I knew as soon as I heard their story.' She pushed up from her chair and turned her back on her husband. 'I'd like to see him now, please. Alone.'

Paul Green shrugged, relieved to be spared the ordeal of going with her.

Jenny took Rachel to the door and handed her over to the care of Sergeant Price. He led her away with the minimum of fuss.

'How about you, Miss Tanner?' Jenny asked.

'I'll go with Paul.'

Jenny wondered what it must be like to be nineteen, pregnant and widowed. Sarah seemed bewildered and overwhelmed, unsure how to behave or even how to feel. Jenny sensed that having been cooped up with Rachel, she had had few opportunities to express her own grief.

'Do you have anyone to talk to?' Jenny knew the question crossed the invisible line that marked the boundary of appropriateness, but couldn't help herself. She didn't like to think of this young woman suffering in silence.

Sarah looked up, and for a moment seemed to react as if she had been offered a lifeline, but then a wail – a dreadful, primal, rending howl of grief – sounded along the corridor and travelled through the door. It cut through them all and sent Sarah's eyes plunging back to the floor. It carried on and on, and Jenny knew that they were all sharing the same thought: *Please, God, make it stop.*

ELEVEN

Rachel Green's cries continued to echo inside Jenny's head throughout the forty-minute drive back to Highcliffe. Just as firmly imprinted were images of the pregnant Sarah's pale, slender features and the grave, resigned expression with which Paul Green went with her to view his son's body. Jenny had felt their grief seep inside her until she carried the full, dull weight of their loss coupled with their sense of impotent rage at Kenny being among the unlucky few. Similarly affected, Alison sat unmoving in the passenger seat, her usual flow of chatter replaced by silence.

They arrived at the entrance to the camp. The guard checked their passes and waved them through. Moments later they came to a halt as two ranks of young soldiers marched across the road in front of them on their way to the parade ground. Straight-backed, clear-eyed young men. Jenny tried to imagine holding responsibility for their young lives. What must it be like to be an officer tasked with ordering the fathers of infants and unborn babies into the line of fire? Try as she might, she couldn't conceive of it. All she could summon was the hollow, uncomprehending sensation she experienced whenever she stood at a cenotaph on a cold November morning struggling to comprehend the paradox of sacrifice. Professional soldiers offered their lives willingly, but with the complicity of loved ones and the encouragement of those who knew far better than they the horrors that awaited them. Death and loss and the yearning for honour and glory, all tangled hopelessly together. The waste of unlived lives as inevitable as the setting of the sun.

'You just want to mother them, don't you?' Alison said.

Jenny had to agree.

Jenny left Alison to set up operations in her shared office and went through to her own room to find a handwritten note from Colonel Hastings inviting her to tea in the officers' mess. No doubt it was kindly meant, but it placed her in a dilemma. How far should she allow herself to be drawn in? Would shunning all social contact raise hackles and prove counter-productive? No doubt it would. But engaging on a personal level carried the risk of being drawn into the heart of an establishment that would demand her loyalty; one in which comfortable compromises were arrived at against the civilized sound of tinkling tea cups.

There were six messages on her voicemail. The first five were from journalists requesting interviews about the circumstances of Kenny Green's death. Despite the communications blackout, several had heard rumours about Private Lyons's abduction and were asking her to confirm that Kenny died in a failed rescue mission. They phrased their questions so as to give themselves a guaranteed headline if Jenny were to be foolish enough to offer an answer: *Coroner Denies British Soldier Killed in Botched Rescue*, or *Soldier, 21, Killed in Botched Rescue, Coroner Confirms*. She couldn't win. The sixth was from Simon Moreton: 'Jenny, call me. Pronto. I've been trying to get you on your mobile. I suppose you're hiding out in darkest Wales?'

What was it about a certain type of Englishman who thought civilization ended at the Severn Bridge, she wondered. The Celtic half of her railed against his casual prejudice. She pulled the phone from her pocket and saw that she had failed to switch it on. Just as well. She had needed the quiet time in the car to process the morning's events and clear her head. She told herself to remain calm and dialled his number.

'Jenny – at last. I thought you'd gone to ground,' Moreton said, as if he possessed the authority to dictate her every movement.

'I was with the bereaved family. And before that with Colonel Hastings. I hear the two of you have been chatting.'

'Briefly,' Moreton said dismissively. 'Only to let him know what you were up to.'

'And the post-mortem at the John Radcliffe . . . ?'

Moreton stalled for a moment. 'What of it?'

'It happened without my say-so.'

'You know what the army's like – it runs on rails.' He pressed on. 'Now listen – the hope was there'd be a DA-notice on this. The last thing any of us wants is the press piling innuendo on top of rumour, but I'm afraid it didn't clear the hurdle. The committee weren't satisfied that news silence would help the missing soldier. Quite the opposite, in fact. They seemed to think a bit of brouhaha might satisfy his captors enough to let him go. They've got what they wanted, after all – we're off their patch.'

'And the British don't pay ransom . . .'

'We most certainly do not. We leave that sort of grubbiness to the garlic-loving nations.'

Jenny experienced another wave of the feeling that had consumed her in the car: the chill reality of sacrifice. A boy soldier abandoned to his fate.

'So the point is,' Moreton continued, 'you can expect your every last word broadcast to the four corners of the earth the moment they've left your lips.'

Jenny detected a note of panic in his voice. 'I have conducted one or two sensitive inquests in my time, Simon.'

'Yes, well . . .'

'Well, what?'

'No discourtesy intended, Jenny, but you can rather shoot from the hip occasionally.'

'Which makes me wonder – why me? No one seems to have registered my "Somerset burr" yet, by the way.'

'They're slippery fish, these military types. A bit of robustness won't go amiss in dealing with them, but for God's sake don't give them any ammunition. You know what I'm saying.'

'Not entirely, no.'

Moreton changed the subject. 'How's the office?'

'Rather civilized. Why?'

'I asked that you be well looked after.'

'Thank you, I think.'

'I also insisted on privacy, but even so, mind how you go.'

Jenny detected genuine concern in his voice. Even when he was being deadly serious, Moreton invariably delivered his lines with at least a hint of playful irreverence.

'Has something happened, Simon?'

'No. Why?'

'You make it sound as if I've been inadvertently tossed into a shark pool.'

He was briefly silent. She heard him give a short, strained sigh. 'Beware the rolling snowball, Jenny, that's all. We want a quick, clean, conclusive inquiry. No hostages to fortune.'

'You've been ticked off for appointing me, haven't you?'

'Leave the politics to me, Jenny. And make sure to keep me posted.'

'I will,' Jenny said, choosing to mollify him.

'Thank you. And don't be shy of that accent – it suits you.'

'Goodbye, Simon.'

She sat back in her large, reclining chair and tried to make sense of the call. Office politics had never been her strong suit, but she was beginning to have an inkling why Simon had sounded so anxious. She knew that his boss, the new Chief Coroner, considered her lucky to be still in position after her many run-ins with the authorities over the years – no matter that her instincts had invariably been proved right. She owed her career to Simon – since her earliest days in the job he had consistently backed her when others were calling for her head. Now nearing retirement and with the looming prospect of the knighthood he so desperately yearned for, he had to prove that his judgement had been sound. Jenny had, until now, naively assumed that his keenness for her to conduct military inquests had been a show of confidence in her abilities. In fact, it had simply been an attempt to neuter her awkward tendencies.

Simon had flirted with her tirelessly ever since she was appointed. Fortunately, he had been too timid to make a determined pass, even when she had been at her most vulnerable, but it was transparently obvious that he secretly entertained the thought that if he did, just maybe, she might respond. She never would, of course – married, emotionally arrested public schoolboys weren't her type – but nevertheless, she couldn't help being fond of him. Poor old Simon. She could only imagine how anxious he must feel with his fate in her hands.

The officers' mess was a short walk from the administration block and situated in one of the many anonymous, solidly rectangular buildings that dotted the camp. The unpromising exterior proved misleading. Once inside the doors Jenny found herself in surroundings that mimicked those of a smart London club: thick, crimson carpets, elaborate candelabras and polished oak panelling decorated with portraits of the regiment's great and glorious. To her left was a large dining room almost entirely filled by a vast mahogany table that was being set for dinner by a small team of staff in starched white jackets. To her right, a gentle babble of voices sounded from behind a door marked SMOKING ROOM. She suppressed a flutter of nerves and went through.

Jenny entered a spacious, comfortable lounge in which twenty or so officers, nearly all of whom were men, were mingling in small groups, some standing, others seated on deep leather sofas.

Colonel Hastings emerged from a cluster to her right.

'Mrs Cooper. So glad you could come.' He smiled warmly and led her to a highly polished walnut table on which several large silver teapots were set out on a tray. 'We've never believed in keeping things for best in this regiment,' he said as he filled a delicate china cup. 'Milk?'

'Just a little. Thank you. Does this happen every day?'

'On the stroke of four,' Hastings said, handing her the cup and saucer. 'You mustn't be shy – I can assure you, we're far friendlier than we look. You'll want to meet Major Norton.'

'Well . . .' She was about to object that meeting with witnesses was seldom a good idea, but he gave her no choice in the matter.

Hastings steered her towards a tall, angular, dark-haired man with sunburned skin who was talking to one of the few female officers present.

'Chris, I'd like you to meet Mrs Cooper, the coroner.'

Major Norton's companion quickly excused herself and moved off, leaving the three of them together.

'Pleased to meet you,' Norton said, stiffly.

'And you.' Jenny felt the dry calluses on his palm as they shook hands. His face was gaunt after six months in

Helmand and his dark eyes, set in bony hollows, appeared oddly lifeless. With more flesh on his bones Jenny imagined that he would be a strikingly good-looking man, but fresh from theatre he looked badly depleted.

'I appreciate we mustn't discuss the case,' Hastings said, 'but you ought to know that Chris has more battlefield experience that any officer in the regiment. Nine tours now, isn't it?'

'Is that all?' Norton said, with a faint smile. 'It feels like twice that.'

'You'll have heard a lot about Helmand, but frankly Iraq was livelier. At least the Taliban was a single entity, but in Iraq the problem was knowing who the enemy was. It felt like we were fighting the many-headed Hydra.'

'Would you count your operations a success?' Jenny asked.

The two men exchanged a glance. 'I would,' Hastings said. 'We've left both countries with a sporting chance of getting their houses in order. Whether they choose to see it through or go back to their old bloodletting ways, is up to them.'

'We did the job that was asked of us,' Norton said. 'Ultimately we're just soldiers. If I were interested in politics, I'd stand for Parliament.'

His comment raised a wry smile from Hastings.

'I'm curious to know what the reward is,' Jenny said. 'Surely, if you're risking your life, you have to feel that you're making a difference?'

'That's certainly true up to a point,' Norton said. He glanced at his wrist watch. 'I'm sorry. Would you excuse me? I've a meeting to get to. Very nice meeting you, Mrs Cooper. Doubtless we'll see each other soon.'

'We will.'

Norton left them and made his way to the door.

'Top man,' Hastings said. 'One of the most effective soldiers I've ever known.'

'And what's his secret?' Jenny asked.

'It's a gift,' Hastings said. 'He's a born warrior. He's just agreed to go off to Kenya next month to help train them for their operations against Al Shabaab.'

Hastings's eyes flitted to a distinguished, grey-haired officer who had crossed with Norton in the doorway and was now looking expectantly in his direction.

'Ah, that's General Browne. I'd better see what he wants. Would you excuse me a moment?'

'Certainly,' Jenny said, although she didn't relish the prospect of being marooned amidst a sea of unfamiliar faces.

She stood self-consciously alone for a short while pretending interest in an extravagant Victorian portrait of *Captain Belfont and Thunder*: a gallant young officer astride his white charger. Two more minutes and she could slip away unnoticed. She turned her gaze to the picture hanging next to it: *The Battle of Abu Klea, 17 January 1885*. It depicted a bloody scene of red-coated British soldiers plunging their bayonets into the wild-eyed fanatics of the Mahdi's army.

'Not a lot's changed in a hundred and thirty years, has it?'

Jenny glanced left to see a young officer refilling his cup. He looked no more than twenty-five at the most, but his wise brown eyes could have belonged to a much older man. Like Major Norton, he was thin to the point of gauntness and darkly tanned.

'James Gallagher. You must be the coroner I've heard about?'

'Yes.' Jenny accepted his handshake and noted the two pips on his shoulder. He was a lieutenant. 'Jenny Cooper.'

'Hastings left you in the lurch, did he? That doesn't surprise me.' He smiled as if at a private joke. 'What have you done to deserve this gig?'

'Luck of the draw, I guess,' Jenny lied.

'Ever had much to do with the army?'

'No. Nothing.'

'Lucky you,' Gallagher said, and took an unhurried sip of tea. There was no trace of tension or urgency about him. He exuded an aura of faintly amused resignation.

'You look like you might just have come back from tour?' Jenny said.

He nodded. 'Next post along from Major Norton's. Quite an experience.'

'Had you been to Afghanistan before?'

'First time and last time.' He gave a rueful smile. 'I certainly got what I wished for.'

Jenny was unsure if his answer was an invitation to pry further or not. She decided that he had a friendly face and wasn't posturing in quite the same way as his colleagues in the room. 'Do you mind if I ask what made you join the army?'

'Good question.'

He met her gaze and seemed to be deciding whether she was someone he could trust.

'Sorry. I'm being nosy,' Jenny said.

'Not at all. The short version is I was studying for a theology degree when the light went out. Lost one vocation and thought I'd found another.'

'Had you?'

Gallagher was silent for a moment. 'Your cup's empty. Would you like some more?'

'Thank you.'

He took it from her and pointed out a nearby sofa that

had come free. 'Why don't you have a seat? I'll bring it to you.'

Deciding that she could do with taking the weight off feet that were beginning to feel the strain of being wedged into tight heels, she took him up on the offer and crossed to the large and well-worn Chesterfield.

From her new vantage point, she looked out across the room. Hastings was deep in discussion with the general over some urgent matter. The other officers, too, all gave the appearance of being engaged in conversations of deep significance. She realized that far from being merely a social event, the tea room was an arena for impressing and posturing. Gallagher, though, moved among the others with an air of detached indifference. Whatever game was being played, he didn't appear to be taking part.

He returned with their tea and took a seat next to her. The bones of his crossed legs showed through the fabric of his trousers. Beneath his uniform he was painfully thin.

Gallagher registered her glance. 'We all look like POWs, don't we?' he joked.

'Don't they feed you?'

'After a fashion. I wouldn't say the food was a highlight.'

'What was it like – the forward command post? I've tried looking online – there's not much out there.'

'There's nothing much to it. Just an open compound made from dirt-filled Hesco bags, a few sheets of tarp and, if you're lucky, your very own plastic bag to crap in.'

'Why so basic?'

'Keeps you on your mettle, I suppose. I always thought it's a bit like being a monk: the fewer the distractions, the more concentrated the mind. Life stripped down to its essentials. Gets to be weirdly relaxing after a while. Almost Zen-like.'

It felt like a description that had been waiting, ready

formed in his mind, until he found an appropriate audience. Despite his reserved manner, he seemed happy to share his experience.

'So, tell me, what's the daily routine?'

'Up before dawn. Most days I'd lead a patrol. Sometimes close in, sometimes out across the valley. Nearly everything we did was on foot.' He paused. 'It was left almost entirely up to me, to be honest. All the platoon commanders in C Company had the same two orders: kill or capture Taliban to the south, befriend villagers to the north. The first problem was how to tell them apart.' He gave a smile of vague amusement. 'We took a few casualties – only one dead, thank goodness – but I had a sergeant who taught me to shave the odds. His view was, if no one's making you step outside the gate, why do it? Poor guy lost his leg to an IED, but that was just bad luck. Could have been any of us.'

Jenny saw Hastings glancing her way while the general continued to bend his ear. Something told her he didn't entirely approve of Lieutenant Gallagher.

'I confess I'm having a little trouble understanding what happened to Private Lyons,' Jenny said. 'I read that he was abducted from the post, but how likely is that?'

'Not very. But no one's going to say he went off his rocker and disappeared on a one-man suicide mission.'

'Do you think that's what he did?'

'I've no idea,' Gallagher said.

'You must have a theory?'

'Well, put it this way – the nearest I came to getting my head blown off was when I went to fetch a football we'd kicked over the wall.'

'If it was something like that, why not just admit it?'

Gallagher laughed. 'Can you imagine? Good morning, Mrs Cooper. I'm sorry to have to tell you that your son has been killed in action. Well, not *in action* exactly—' He nodded to the portrait of Captain Belfont. 'Image is everything in this business. Courage. Efficiency. Valour. And of course, all buffed up with just the right dose of grace and good manners. Not that I'm saying there's a better way . . .' He shrugged. 'That's life, I suppose.'

'James giving you the benefit of his wisdom, is he?' Hastings made a sudden reappearance, his business with the general concluded. 'I keep telling him that he'd have been right at home in the pulpit.'

Gallagher gave a tolerant smile. 'I ought to be getting on.' He rose to his feet, transformed in an instant into a brisk, energetic young officer. 'Nice to have met you, Mrs Cooper. Sir.' He moved off quickly to the door.

'One of my prodigies,' Hastings said. 'Still only twenty-three, if you can believe it.'

'In sole command of a platoon?'

'Certainly. I've had them at twenty-one,' Hastings said. 'We grow up quickly in the army. Now, who else should you meet?'

Alison's first task was to arrange interviews with all possible witnesses. Two of them were lying seriously injured in hospital at Selly Oak. She spoke with a nursing sister on the phone and established that Private Carter had survived surgery but was in a coma from which he showed no sign of emerging. An MRI had been conducted which revealed serious and permanent brain damage. He would be lucky to live, let alone make a statement. Private Lee Roberts was stable, but on large doses of morphine. He was lucid, but the sister wouldn't commit to saying that he was ready to give a statement. She promised to get his consultant to call later.

If twenty-five years in the police and nearly a dozen more as a coroner's officer had taught Alison one thing, it was that memory faded and warped with alarming speed. In particular, the imagination tended to fill gaps in recollection. The human mind craved a complete narrative, preferring a false but coherent story to disjointed truth. For this reason, she liked to catch a witness while events were still raw; while she could record the gaps as well as the remembered parts. Unable to speak to Roberts himself, she tried calling his next-of-kin in the hope that she might have had a conversation with him about the events of the previous week. Anna Roberts's phone rang, but she failed to answer.

Frustrated in her attempts and already growing impatient with the lurking presence of Sergeant Price at the other desk, Alison gave up and went in search of a snack from the NAAFI shop she had spotted on her drive across the camp.

It was less than a five-minute walk to the small convenience store sited close to a group of accommodation blocks. Alison entered to find the aisles almost deserted. Her search for something healthy folded when she spotted a tray of freshly baked doughnuts. She grabbed one, and then, lured by a two-for-one deal, added a pair of chocolate bars to her basket.

'So much for my good intentions,' she said to the homely looking woman behind the till.

'You've nothing to worry about,' the woman said warmly. 'You've still got your figure.'

'Thank you,' Alison said, more than happy to accept the compliment.

'I've not seen you before, have I?' the cashier said. 'It's a small world up here – I always notice a new face.'

'I'm the coroner's officer,' Alison said. 'You probably know all about Private Green?'

'Lovely lad. I've known his mum and dad for years, too. Terrible.' She handed Alison her change.

'You must have worked here a long time?'

'More than twenty years. Some of these boys get to feel like family.'

'I'll bet.'

'I feel almost as bad for the girls left behind,' the woman said. 'Poor things. Half the time when the lads are away, they don't know where to put themselves. I'm Jacqui by the way – with a q.'

'Alison. Pleased to meet you.'

They exchanged a friendly smile.

With the ice broken, they lapsed easily into several minutes of chitchat about life at the camp. Alison learned about the rumours of redundancies sweeping through the Regiment and how hard some of the soldiers' families were finding it to get by. Jacqui was a fount of information, full of gossip and not short on opinions about the government's willingness to send young men off to fight in other people's wars.

Along the way, Alison picked up the fact that many of the wives and partners of the soldiers looked out for each other through the WAGs Club, which operated from the regimental church hall. For the last week they had been concentrating their efforts on looking after the families of the two critically injured soldiers, Lee Roberts and Dale Carter.

'If we all looked out for each other like that, the world would be a much better place,' Jacqui said regretfully. 'Then I suppose it takes a bit of hardship to bring people together.'

On that they were both agreed.

The mid-afternoon lull ended with the arrival of several other customers and Alison took her cue to leave. Heading back towards the administration block, she spotted a sign to St Mary's church. She took a detour and went to investigate. It wouldn't do any harm to look in at the WAGs Club, if only to let them know she was a friendly face before any gossip started. And if she could manage to meet a few people without Sergeant Price in tow, so much the better.

WAGs DROP-IN – 2 TILL 4. The handwritten sign festooned with painted flowers provided a welcome dash of colour amidst the drab military buildings that surrounded the hall and the modern church building next door. Alison stepped through the doors and found herself in a large, airy room filled with the sounds of excited young children and the babble of female conversation. Part nursery, part impromptu cafe and social club, twenty or so young women were seated at tables arranged at the near end of the hall while a host of preschool children played in a roped-off area at the other. Many of the women had babies and young infants on their knees.

A woman with tied-back blonde hair and an air of polite authority appeared almost immediately to greet her.

'Hi. I'm Melanie Norton.'

Alison introduced herself as the coroner's officer and told Melanie that she was happy to explain to anyone who might be interested what she and the coroner, Mrs Cooper, were doing at the camp.

Melanie seemed a little unsure how to respond, then mentioned that she was the wife of Major Christopher Norton, Kenny Green's commanding officer.

'I thought you might be,' Alison said. 'Don't worry about that, I'm not here to ask questions, only to answer them. I don't suppose I could get a cup of coffee – I'm parched.'

'Of course.'

Melanie found them a space at the end of a table and watched politely as Alison wolfed her doughnut. A tendency to eat too quickly and messily was one of several unfortunate consequences of her accident. Sometimes she was even aware that she was doing it, but if she was hungry enough, somehow it didn't seem to matter. Between mouthfuls, and sometimes, during them, Alison explained to Melanie that, with the help of Sergeant Price, she would be spending the next few days gathering statements from members of Kenny Green's platoon. There were obviously only a small number of witnesses to the incident that had resulted in his death, so it shouldn't take long. Melanie said that, sadly, she was familiar with the process. There had been three fatalities in the regiment during the past year. It had been the worst period she could remember.

Alison wiped the last crumbs of sugar from her lips with the back of her hand. 'That's better. I was famished.'

Melanie smiled, glad she didn't have to watch any more.

'I can't imagine Chris will be in any state to talk for a while yet. It takes a while. Even my husband . . .' She hesitated. 'Coming home's such a shock. Everything's different. It takes a good while.'

'I'm sure,' Alison said. It dawned on her that Melanie was probably only a little over thirty, yet apart from her, she was the oldest woman in the room. She seemed to be carrying a heavy weight of responsibility on her slim shoulders. 'How's Mrs Roberts coping? How do you cope in her situation?'

Melanie shrugged. 'You just do your best. We do what we can. Her little girl's over there – Leanne. I'm minding her this afternoon.'

Alison followed her gaze to a little girl shooting down a plastic slide.

'We haven't told her yet,' Melanie said. 'Anna's waiting for the right moment.' She forced herself to look away. 'So, who would you like to meet? There are a couple of women here with husbands in 2 Platoon. Shall I introduce you?'

'Do you mind if I ask you about Kenny Green first? I suppose you must have known him?'

Melanie nodded. The sadness that had been lingering beneath the surface forced its way into her eyes. 'He was always smiling. Kind. One of those you knew you could rely on completely. That was my impression and I've heard Christopher say it, too. I'm sure that's why he had him in his platoon.'

'But tough? The sort you'd imagine could handle himself in a tight spot?'

'I'm sure,' Melanie said. 'They're all tough, and brave. Too brave for their own good, sometimes. The problem is . . . the problem is that it's always the nice ones. I don't know . . .' She shook her head. Whatever it was she was about to say, she stopped herself. She pushed a hand through her hair. 'I'm not making a lot of sense, am I? Bit tired, I'm afraid. Things have been rather hectic.' She stood up from her chair. 'You must come and say hello.'

Without waiting for an answer, Melanie set off towards a group of women seated at a far table. Alison followed her wondering what it was that she hadn't been able to share. Something her husband had told her? Or maybe just a suspicion based on all the subtle signs only a wife could read? There had definitely been something.

Alison decided to bide her time. Earn her trust. She put on a smile and went to meet the WAGs of 2 Platoon.

TWELVE

Sarah lay on her bed staring at the screen of her cheap tablet computer and tried to make sense of the confusing jumble of long words. The email from one of the regiment's admin officers began with the sentence: '*Dear Ms Tanner, I am writing to explain the procedure for administering financial support to the dependants of a deceased serviceman.*' She understood that it was a letter about money, but there was no mention of how much. The only other part she understood was at the end: '*While Mr Green's salary will no longer be paid, you may well be eligible upon application to a Survivors' Guaranteed Payment and Bereavement Grant. You will be contacted by the Service Personnel and Veterans' Agency within the next few days who will process your application shortly.*' Again, no numbers. Just a vague promise.

She switched the tablet off and placed it on the bedside table next to the photo of her and Kenny taken at their engagement party, a fortnight before he left for Helmand. He was wearing a black, muscle-hugging Hugo Boss T-shirt she had bought him for Christmas. She was dressed in the Free People bardot top and matching skirt they had chosen in Bristol. Her outfit had a gipsy feel and she had styled her hair to match. Two long, loose plaits, the rest teased into what the hairdresser had called 'designer scruff'. God, they looked happy. She even remembered how he smelt that night, and the feel of his arms around her waist. The touch of his cheek against hers as they danced had been delicious. The softness and the smoothness and the gentle way he had held her had brought them closer than they had ever been. She had almost forgotten they were boy and girl. It was just skin on skin, body against body.

The thought of it made her ache. Tears dripped down her cheeks. She didn't even try to wipe them away. She wanted to feel them. Holding an image of him in her mind, feeling him close, she closed her eyes and sank back into the pillow.

Sarah blinked awake feeling the now familiar stirring in her belly. The baby was on the move again. It felt like it was kicking at an imaginary football. It always happened around this time in the early evening, just when she should be thinking about eating. But tonight, food was the last thing on her mind. An image of Kenny's body lingered behind her eyes. Rachel had kept calling the body 'him', but it wasn't him, it was an empty shell. She wished she hadn't seen it. She had only gone with Paul because she knew how much it would have upset Rachel if she hadn't.

The baby kicked again, sharply. Sarah rolled onto her side wishing it would stop. She just wanted to sleep. To blot everything out. No chance. Moments later she heard footsteps outside her bedroom door and a cautious knock.

'Sarah?' It was Paul. 'There are a couple of people downstairs who'd like to talk to you. Solicitors or something.'

'Solicitors?'

'Yeah. They're in the sitting room. Look, I've got to go to work in a minute . . .'

'It's OK. I'll come.' She hauled herself out of bed. Her limbs felt like lead. And she had heartburn. She grabbed a hairbrush but gave up after a few strokes. It was a hopeless, tangled mess. She pushed it back from her face and forced it into an elastic. The spots would show on her forehead, but it couldn't be helped. She was past caring.

Sarah came downstairs clutching her tablet computer, assuming that whoever had come to see her was something to do with the letter.

Paul was hovering nervously at the foot of the stairs. The door to the sitting room was closed. 'Rachel's still in her room. She took a sleeping pill earlier. I thought it best not to wake her.'

'OK.' Sarah didn't know what she was meant to do with this information.

'I've got to shoot off in five minutes . . .' He cast an anxious glance up the stairs and seemed to change his mind. 'You go on in and talk to them. I'll go and have a word with her.' He patted Sarah on the shoulder and went on up.

Something was wrong, but with Rachel there always was. Sarah couldn't remember a day without a mood or a drama. She carried on into the sitting room.

The two lawyers stood to greet her. One was a man of about Paul's age dressed in a dark suit and tie with streaks of silver in his swept-back black hair, and the other a woman of about thirty, blonde and slim. Both were tall and imposing and loomed over her. She could tell at once that they were rich. Seriously rich. She caught a flash of gold Rolex as the man extended his hand.

'Claydon White. Pleased to meet you, Miss Tanner. You have my deepest sympathies. This is my colleague, Carrie Rhodes.'

Carrie offered her perfectly manicured hand. She smelt of delicate perfume and was wearing a diamond engagement ring that made Sarah's look like something from the Saturday market. 'Good to meet you, Sarah. I'm so sorry for your loss.'

'I apologize for calling on you without warning,' the man

said, 'but we felt it was important to make contact as soon as possible. Do you mind if we sit?'

Sarah shook her head and took a seat in an armchair while the two strangers seated themselves on the sofa. Their beautiful clothes made the room feel shabby.

'Is this about the letter?'

'The letter?' The man glanced at the woman, then back at Sarah. 'Which letter is that?'

Sarah fumbled with the tablet and brought it up on the screen. 'This one.' She handed it to the woman, who glanced at it briefly, then showed it to her colleague.

'I see. No. This is a letter from the army letting you know that you are going to be eligible for some compensation for Kenny's death as well as a sum of money every month. We're nothing to do with the army. We're independent solicitors.' He reached into his inside pocket and handed her a business card bearing a London address. 'Samson, Masters and White – that's the name of our firm. Those are my details on the bottom right – Claydon White, email and direct line. You can call me Claydon, by the way. Claydon and Carrie. We should have our own TV show.'

Sarah nodded. He seemed nice. Friendlier than most of the rich people she had met.

'What we do, what Carrie and I do in particular, is represent people who have suffered serious injuries through no fault of their own, or the families of those who have been killed as a result of negligence. You must have heard of people suing for compensation . . . ?'

'Like on the ads?'

'That's the lower end of things. We only handle big claims. High Court actions. Cases with large sums of money involved. And we especially like to represent people who can't afford lawyers' fees. We don't believe that justice should only be for those who can afford it. We don't charge people a penny for what we do. We take all the risk, and if we win, we take thirty per cent of whatever the court awards. Look us up on the internet. Have a look at the sort of cases we've fought and won. You'll see that most often I deal with people who have suffered medical accidents. Yours would be the first case of a serviceman killed in action, but it's a challenge I would relish, I can assure you.'

Carrie took over. 'The way it works, Sarah, is that when a soldier dies in action, his dependants – that's wives, partners, children – are entitled to a modest amount of money from the Ministry of Defence. Besides the bereavement grant you might end up with something like a thousand pounds a month.'

At last, a figure. Twelve thousand. Just enough to get by, but it would be a struggle to manage in a place of her own.

'The grant could be up to thirty-seven thousand. It sounds like a lot, but it doesn't go far.'

Sarah had no idea it was that much. That was two years' wages in one go. Enough for a deposit on a flat.

'I presume you're pregnant?' Carrie said.

'Eight months.'

'It's expensive bringing up a child. Especially by yourself. Clothes, cots, buggies, nappies. It all adds up. I'm sure I'm not telling you anything you don't already know.'

All the things she and Kenny were going to buy together when he came home. She already knew which car seat, carry cot and buggy she wanted. They weren't even expensive ones, but they would still cost more than £500.

'That's why it's important to make sure you get the maximum you're entitled to,' Carrie continued. 'That's what we want to make sure of.'

'We certainly do,' Claydon said. He leaned forward and gestured with his hands as he spoke. 'I appreciate this is a difficult time and I don't want to load you with information, but I'm going to try to explain exactly why we are here today. It's really quite simple. If a soldier dies in action simply doing his job and the army is not at fault – just doing its job – then all you are entitled to is that bereavement grant and the thousand pounds a month. But if there's evidence that shows the army was negligent in some way, and that a man was put in harm's way when he shouldn't have been, then you have a case that can go to court and you can argue for a lot more money. Money that your fiancée would have earned over a working lifetime. Now, nobody says the army has an easy job, and we all know that soldiers are paid to take risks, but if an officer knowingly leads his men into a situation where there's a risk of death, and that is not a risk that it's reasonable to take, then we can argue that he was negligent. Do you follow?'

'I think so.'

'Good. So the question is, how do we know if there is such evidence? Well, the first place it might emerge from is the coroner's inquest. The men who were with Kenny when he was killed will all be giving evidence. We would like to represent you at that inquest – free of charge. Firstly, because we would like you to know as much as you can about how and why Kenny was killed, and secondly, because if there is evidence that unreasonable and unnecessary risks were taken with his life, I want to take that before a court and get you what you deserve. How does that sound? Would you like us to represent you, free of charge, Sarah?'

Claydon sat back and waited for her to reply.

Sarah thought about what he had said. There were many questions she knew she ought to ask, but she didn't know where to begin.

'You can ask us anything,' Carrie said. 'Anything at all.'

Sarah brought her hand to her belly as the baby kicked

again. She was starting to feel faint as well as sick and even more upset and confused. 'What do you mean by "unreasonable risks"? How do you know what happened?'

'We don't,' Carrie said.

'You must know something otherwise you wouldn't be here.' Sarah had never passed any exams, but she did understand money. She knew that these two wouldn't have come all this way if there wasn't plenty in it for them. 'Do you know something I don't? Who told you about Kenny, anyway?'

Claydon and Carrie exchanged a glance.

'I'll be honest with you,' Claydon said, 'I had a phone call from a journalist who's been covering the war in Afghanistan almost since it began. I have asked this woman to let me know about any cases like Kenny's. She called me to say that he was killed and two others seriously injured while attempting to rescue a colleague who was being held hostage by Taliban fighters. She had heard a rumour that the hostage was taken from out of the forward command post where Kenny's platoon was based. From what she tells me, there's something not quite right about that. Those posts have permanently manned watchtowers and are surrounded by minefields. There may be a rational explanation, but the army aren't offering one. In fact, they're refusing to make any comment at all. She's hit a stone wall which, understandably, makes her suspicious.'

Sarah heard voices on the stairs. Paul was speaking to Rachel in the quiet, pleading tones he used when he was trying to calm her down. She was having none of it. A moment later she burst through the door.

'I'm Kenny's mother. Would someone please tell me what's going on?'

White touched Carrie's arm, letting her know he would handle it, and rose to his feet.

'Claydon White. Solicitor. Pleased to meet you, Mrs Green.'

Rachel refused his offer of a handshake. 'It didn't take you vultures long, did it? We're a grieving family. If we need a solicitor, we'll get one. Now, please go and leave us in peace.'

'I appreciate you're Kenny's mother, Mrs Green, and you have my deepest sympathies for your loss, but the person we actually came to see was Ms Tanner, his legal dependant and mother of his child.'

Rachel shot Sarah an accusing glance.

'I don't care who you came to see. This is my house and I didn't invite you into it. My husband thought you were something to do with the inquest. Now will you please get out before I lose my temper.'

Claydon glanced at Sarah. 'If this isn't convenient, perhaps you'd like to continue our conversation elsewhere?'

'She's going nowhere,' Rachel said. 'I said, leave.' She stood aside waiting for them to go.

'Love, if Sarah wants to talk . . .' Paul said weakly.

'To a pair of chancers who turn up out of the blue? Were you born yesterday?'

'I'm OK,' Sarah objected.

Rachel ignored her. 'Out. Now.'

White smiled graciously and motioned Carrie to come with him. 'I'm sorry to have disturbed you, Mrs Green,' he said, then turned to Sarah, 'If you'd like to call me tomorrow I'll be happy to answer any further questions. Goodbye.'

Rachel remained standing in the sitting-room doorway while Paul showed the two lawyers to the front door. When they had gone, she turned her anger on Sarah. 'Do you honestly think those people are out for anyone other than themselves? They don't care about us.'

'You didn't hear what they had to say.'

'I'm sure they're full of it. I'm sure they'll promise you the world if they think there's something in it for them. And even if they could make you a few quid, what then? The army don't take these things lying down. They'll drag Kenny's name through the mud. They'll drag you and us with it and we'll end up without a friend in this town. Is that what you want?'

'You said Kenny shouldn't have died. If that's what you think, why wouldn't you want to do everything you can to make sure his child gets looked after?'

Rachel's face went through a carousel of emotions that ended with an expression of tortured bitterness.

'Money counts for nothing. Nothing.'

'Love. They've gone. You're letting yourself get worked up over nothing.' Paul put a tentative hand on her arm. 'Maybe I should call in sick tonight?'

Rachel batted him away and stamped through to the kitchen, where she started noisily clanking the pans Paul had left to dry on the drainer.

Paul stood helplessly, stifling a desire to yell in frustration. He took a breath and tried to stay calm. 'You look pale, love. You haven't even eaten, have you?'

Sarah hauled herself out of the chair. Her head was swimming. 'I think I'll go out for a bit. Get something in town.'

They exchanged a look, both sharing the same unspoken thought. If it had been Rachel the lawyers were coming to see, it might have been a different story. Now it was official: Kenny wasn't her boy any more. He was first and foremost Sarah's – her partner, the father of her child.

'I'll support you,' Paul said quietly. 'You know that. But just be careful, hey?'

The house resounded to the sound of Rachel slamming a cupboard door. It sliced through Sarah like a knife and made the baby startle. That was it. She had to get out. 'See you tomorrow.' She fetched her phone and her bag and left the house.

Her call connected before the front gate had closed behind her.

'Is that Mr White? It's Sarah Tanner. You said we could talk elsewhere . . . ?'

Claydon said he and Carrie were just on their way to a restaurant in the centre of town. He would send his driver back to pick her up straight away.

Anna Roberts tried to sleep in the back of the taxi driving her back along the M5 motorway from Birmingham to Highcliffe, but her racing mind wouldn't let her. She had hoped for a quiet afternoon with Lee, a chance to talk, but instead they had barely had a moment alone. Although it was an NHS unit, the patients were all soldiers and it was run in military style. Anna learned that Lee was woken before seven a.m. and told to shave himself, even though his hands shook and the whole procedure took him nearly half an hour. Then he was washed and changed by nurses, and after breakfast inspected by a sergeant, who would make him shave again if he hadn't done it properly. A nurse explained to Anna that the discipline helped the men recover. They were expected to get themselves well, mentally and physically, and as soon as possible. It was part of their job as soldiers.

Dr Thurlow, the surgeon who had operated on Lee, met with them both to discuss his injuries. The good news was that there had been enough leg left on both sides for him to amputate through the knee. This meant Lee had been left with longer stumps and would eventually be able to walk with relative ease on prosthetic legs. He then produced a photograph album and took them through the stories of many soldiers who had passed through the unit, plenty with injuries far more severe than his. They had all had similar journeys: from wounded, traumatized patients struggling to see a future for themselves, to smiling, confident men with new lives and careers. By the end of their session with Dr Thurlow, Anna had almost been left believing that having his legs blown off was one of the best things that Lee had ever had happen to him.

Shortly afterwards, they were visited by one of the men who had featured in the album. Corporal Sam Taylor was a handsome, mixed-race man with eyes that sparkled with life. A former paratrooper, he was now a military liaison officer at the hospital. He told them how he had lost his legs when a rocket-propelled grenade aimed at a nearby armoured personnel carrier had literally knocked them both off on the way to its target. The impact with his body had been enough to steer the grenade off course with the result that it missed the vehicle and the lives of three soldiers inside were saved.

'I give thanks for my injuries every day,' he said. 'And everything I've seen in this place convinces me that it's the strongest who are called on to make this sacrifice. The way I see it, your life is a gift to you, and the way you live it is your gift back. Make up your mind to be an inspiration right now, and you will be. You have the opportunity and the power to make everyone who knows you proud. That's some privilege, Lee. Treasure it.'

Corporal Taylor's words had made Anna cry. He had made her feel as if she and Lee had been chosen to do something special. She could see a future in which they raised money for charity and devoted their lives to the sick and poor. Suddenly she had felt like someone with a purpose in life. A mission.

Several nurses arrived to lift Lee out of bed and into a wheelchair for the very first time. Corporal Taylor then took them to see the physio facilities. There, they met two other soldiers who had lost legs. One had been a patient for two months, the other had been there for nearly four and was about to be discharged. Both were strong and healthy and optimistic for their futures. One was remaining in the army, the other was going to train to become a PE teacher. They promised Lee he would get better and more confident every day. They were living examples of what Corporal Taylor had been talking about and Anna had found herself yet again shedding tears. It was strange: they were almost tears of happiness. She had never met people filled with so much positivity and hope.

The only down note had come towards the end of her visit when they had finally had a few minutes together. Lee had become quiet and pale. Anna could tell there was something he wasn't saying, but he insisted he was fine. When the nurses came to take bloods and carry out their observations, she went to have a word with the sister, a motherly woman named Angela. She told Anna that Lee was going to be seen by the psychiatric nurse in the morning as they had a few concerns about him. He insisted he had little or no memory of the incident in which he'd lost his legs, yet he was shouting a lot in his sleep and suffering nightmares despite heavy medication. Angela thought that he could remember the incident very clearly, but couldn't yet bring himself to talk about it. He would have to learn to do so, though. Talking was a vital part of getting well.

Before she left, Anna whispered to Lee that she thought he could remember more than he was admitting and that he had to speak to the doctors about it.

Lee had looked at her with dead eyes, and said, 'I remember nothing. And that's how it's going to stay.'

She knew it was early days, but that look he had given her left her with a deeply uneasy feeling. She wanted to believe that he would soon be as cheerful as Corporal Taylor and the others, but there was something dark and self-destructive in his expression that frightened her.

The other thing playing on Anna's mind was the message from the woman at the coroner's office saying that she wanted to speak to Lee about what had happened in Helmand. She wasn't sure exactly what a coroner did, but it sounded official, like the police, and she was scared that Lee would get into trouble if he didn't tell them what he knew. Anna was fond of Sarah Tanner. She and Kenny had looked so happy together at their engagement party. A dream couple. The thought that Lee might not do everything to help troubled her. She would have to work on him. He had a phone now – she would send him an email as soon as Leanne was in bed.

Melanie Norton was as kind as always when she handed Leanne over, but seeing her nice clothes and glimpsing through the living room window her two daughters sprawled on a cream-coloured sofa watching a huge, cinema-style TV, Anna felt as if she were trapped in a colder, crueller world.

'She's had plenty to eat,' Melanie said. 'Lasagne, salad, French bread.'

'And chocolate ice cream,' Leanne chimed in.

'Plenty of that, too.' Melanie smiled. 'Any time. You know she's always welcome.' She touched Anna comfortingly on the arm. 'If you ever need to talk, just call. Any time.'

'Thank you.'

As the taxi drove them the final few minutes to home, Anna felt Leanne's disappointment at leaving the leafy streets and Melanie's cosy, comfortable house behind. It pained her that she would never be able to compete, that Leanne would grow up feeling jealous of the kids who had more. But that was just how it was. You got what you were given and had to make the most of it.

It was almost nine o'clock when they pulled up outside their block of flats. Anna thanked the driver and helped a sleepy Leanne out of the booster seat. She was scooping her up in her arms ready to carry her to the front door, when she noticed the big, sleek BMW parked nearby. The rear doors opened and Sarah Tanner climbed out along with a man and woman who looked as if they had stepped off the cover of a magazine.

Sarah came towards her. 'Hi, Anna. How are you?'

'OK . . .' She glanced past Sarah to the two approaching behind her.

'These are my lawyers,' Sarah said. 'They want to get me compensation for what happened to Kenny. I told them about Lee. They'd like to talk to you.'

'What for?'

'If I'm entitled, you might be, too. Can we come up?'

'I don't know . . .' Anna felt panicky. She didn't feel able to handle this by herself. 'Maybe I should talk to Lee first? Leanne needs to go to bed . . .'

Sarah stepped in closer and put a hand on her arm.

'Please. You and Lee need this as much as I do . . . Look, I know money's just—' She glanced away and wiped tears from her eyes. 'Don't take this the wrong way, Anna, but this is huge. They're talking about a million pounds.'

Anna glanced again at the two strangers, noticing their expensive suits and the chauffeur-driven car.

'OK,' Anna said, nervously. 'You'd better come up.'

THIRTEEN

Melanie was becoming anxious. It was getting late, the girls were in bed and Chris still wasn't home. She had given up any hope of them having dinner together and gone ahead and eaten her lasagne alone. He had been home for nearly five days and they had hardly spoken. He always had an excuse. He was too busy. Too tired. Too caught up with compiling all the reports and inventories that had to be filed following a return from tour. He had spent the entire weekend in his office at the camp and most of his time at home hunched over a laptop. It was a familiar pattern, but this time it seemed worse. She knew the reason: for the first time since he had joined the army there were no more wars to fight.

The kitchen clock ticked past ten p.m. Melanie tidied the last stray items and polished the worktops until they shone, all the while trying to fend off the irrational fear that something had happened to Chris. He had a mobile phone, but she didn't like to call him in case he thought her foolish. Over the years they had developed an unspoken agreement not to indulge in unnecessary communication. It had developed as a sort of superstition – no news is good news – and taken hold. Phoning him except in an emergency would be a show of weakness that would violate the rules that underpinned their marriage. Even so, she felt he was leaving her little choice. It had gone half-past.

Melanie was reaching guiltily for the phone when she heard the key in the lock. She hurried to the doorway feeling a rush of relief.

It was him.

'There you are. I was getting worried.'

'Sorry about that,' he answered in clipped tones. He hung his cap on the peg. 'Mountain of paperwork. Actually, I wish it were paper – nothing worse than staring at a screen all day. Have we got any aspirin?'

'I'll find you some.'

She had hoped for a kiss, or at least some small show of affection, but he just smiled stiffly and kept his hands firmly at his sides. She went to rummage in a kitchen drawer and told herself not to worry about the fact that he had hardly touched her since he'd arrived home. It was only to be expected. He had been camped out, living on his wits for six months. It was still early days.

She filled a glass with water and handed him two pills.

'There's some lasagne left if you're hungry.'

'I had sandwiches at the office. Sorry.'

'It'll keep.'

She watched him swallow the aspirin. His face was so thin. Even bone visible beneath tightly stretched skin. He invariably came back from tour several stone lighter than he'd left, but she had never known him quite so skeletal. It scared her.

'I was minding Leanne Roberts all day,' Melanie said. 'She's ever so sweet.'

'I'm sure,' Chris said distractedly. He slotted the empty glass carefully into the dishwasher.

'No one's told her what's happened to Lee yet. I heard her saying to the girls that her mum had gone to see him in hospital, but she doesn't know what's wrong.'

'Difficult,' Chris said. 'No easy answer to that. I expect she'll be all right. Children adapt.'

They looked at each other, their eyes meeting almost by accident. He managed another awkward smile.

'Drink?' Melanie asked. 'There's some white wine open in the fridge.' Chris had never been much of a drinker, but when he was at home he had always joined her in a glass at the end of a long day.

'I think I'm about ready to turn in. I'm sure you must be exhausted.' He sensed her disappointment. 'You go ahead. Don't let me stop you. Just a bit out of the habit.'

'I'm really not bothered, either,' Melanie said, although if the bottle had been in front of her she could have drunk it all. 'You're right. I am tired. Still, only another week and the girls will be back at school. I might manage a few moments to myself again.'

There was an uncomfortable pause. Chris met her gaze, then dropped his eyes to the floor.

'Don't think I take any of your efforts for granted, Melanie . . . I really don't. Truly.'

He reached out a hand, and without looking at her, clasped her shoulder. The nearest he had come to an intimate gesture since his return.

Melanie put her hand on top of his. 'I know this bit's difficult for you. I understand . . . And you know that if there's anything you want to talk about—'

'Yes. Of course,' he said, cutting her off. 'Thank you.' He closed his eyes briefly as if consciously curbing his abruptness. 'Shall we go up?'

They climbed the stairs without speaking. The silence stretched into the bedroom as they each undressed on opposite sides of the room. Melanie couldn't tell if it was the silence of emotional paralysis or of anticipation. They took it in turns to visit the bathroom and climbed woodenly into bed, she dressed in loose pyjamas and he in a white T-shirt and boxers. They lay still for a moment, a foot of empty space between them as there had been every night. Melanie agonized over whether to reach out and touch him, if only to reassure him that she wasn't being chilly, that she was there as a comfort if he needed her.

She glanced over and saw that he was staring at the ceiling. The novel he had been reading lay closed on the bedside table. The dim light exaggerated the taut lines and hollows in his face. Despite the dark suntan he looked a ghost of himself.

'Shall I turn out the light?' she whispered.

He didn't answer. His eyes remained fixed and unfocused, staring into empty space.

'Chris? Are you all right?'

After a moment, he said, 'It's a bit like being a polar explorer. You get used to being cold. Sensation takes a while to return.'

'I understand . . . I do.'

He turned his head towards her. 'Shall we . . . ?' The words stuck in his throat. 'Shall—'

'Sshh.' Melanie pressed a finger to his lips, then dared to kiss him.

Her hand travelled over his body. He was nothing but taut knots of muscle, sinew and bone. She stroked his skin, gently massaging his shoulders and back. Slowly, ever so slowly, she felt him begin to unwind. His dry lips softened and moved against hers. His hands – cold, despite the warm evening – sought out her flesh. He was clumsy and nervous but she felt the passion rise in him and the heat slowly return to his skin.

In a moment, the walls that had held him in seemed to fall away. He tore off his clothes, knelt over her, tugged off her top and pulled down her pyjama bottoms using both hands. He stared at her nakedness as if surprised and frightened by it. For a moment she feared he might recoil, but driven by impulses she could no longer control, she pulled him towards her and drew him in.

Afterwards, they lay breathless side by side, their fingers touching, their bodies slick with perspiration. For a long while neither spoke, both of them happy to bask in the afterglow. Melanie felt like a prisoner released from heavy shackles. Her fearful thoughts had melted, leaving her hopeful and relaxed.

'Feel better?' she whispered.

'Much,' Chris said gently.

She slid her fingers between his. 'You haven't told me what happens next – after you've tidied everything up from the tour. You are going to take some leave?'

'We've got this inquest. Maybe after that.'

'How long will that take?'

'They want it done next week.'

'And you'll be a witness?'

'Yes.' He offered nothing more.

Melanie probed gently, 'If you want to talk about it? . . . I know you thought highly of Kenny.'

'I'd rather not,' he said dismissively. 'One of those things. Can't be helped.'

They lapsed into silence. Chris seemed content to stare at the ceiling but Melanie was bursting with questions.

'Chris . . . ?'

'What?'

'We need to talk – about the future.'

'What about it?'

'There have been lots of rumours while you were away. Talk of cut-backs. Redundancies. If you believed half of it you'd think there wouldn't be any infantry left this time next year.'

She felt him tense. He wanted her to change the subject, but she knew there may not be another moment like this for days or even weeks.

'If the worst were to happen, my brother's always asking after you.' She tried to say it casually, as if responding to an idle thought, but Chris wasn't fooled.

'Insurance salesman.' He gave a dismissive grunt.

'At least we know there's an option.'

'You married a soldier, I'm afraid.' He extracted his hand from hers. 'I've been asked to go to Kenya – training their army in counter-insurgency.'

'Kenya? When?'

'In a month or so.'

'You never said anything. When did this come up?'

'I was waiting for the right moment. Thought we might all go.'

'Take the girls to Kenya?'

'You followed your father abroad. It's what army families do.' He climbed out of bed and pulled on a bathrobe.

'Where are you going now?'

'Can't sleep. I'll be up shortly.'

Melanie listened to him go down the stairs. There was something wrong. Badly wrong. She didn't know whether to go after him or leave him alone. She pulled on her pyjamas and decided to read for a while before going down to check on him. In the morning she would call Lizzie Hastings and ask her to have a quiet word with Richard. He was bound to know what was troubling him.

Melanie woke suddenly in darkness. The bed next to her was empty. The alarm clock glowed dimly: three forty-five. A jolt of panic shocked her fully awake and propelled her out of bed.

She found Chris lying on his back on the living room

floor. For a cold and desolate moment she thought he might be dead, but then she heard him mumbling and groaning beneath his breath. 'Don't . . . No. Don't . . . No. No . . .'

Too nervous to wake him, she stood watching from the doorway hoping his dream would pass, but it continued on and on in a seemingly continuous loop. Eventually, she left him where he lay and went guiltily back to bed. As dawn broke, her sense of foreboding grew deeper and crystallized into a thought she had been trying to hold at bay: the man asleep downstairs on the floor wasn't the one who had left for Helmand last February. Chris had returned a stranger, and he was frightening her.

Jenny had spent the early evening at her desk making frustratingly little progress. Her encounter with Sarah Tanner and Kenny Green's parents at the mortuary had left her with an even heavier sense of her responsibility to unearth the whole truth of the young soldier's death, but she had so little to go on. There would be few documents, the forensic evidence would be limited to whatever Dr Kerr turned up during the post-mortem, and the only witnesses to events would be members of 2 Platoon. She could certainly deliver a swift verdict, but without objective evidence, there was little chance of it being conclusive.

There was nothing more she could do tonight. She decided to go outside and catch the sunset. With a little luck, she might forget about the case for a while.

Jenny stepped out of the back door into warm, sultry air. The sheep grazing the meadows either side of her garden were repeating their daily ritual of calling lazily to one another in the twilight. When, still reeling from her divorce, she had transplanted herself here from Bristol, the timeless landscape of fields and forest had slowly helped to heal her wounds. Her transient problems and all the human crises that occupied her working days faded like the mist amid the steady, unbroken and unyielding rhythms of nature. She kicked off her shoes and walked barefoot over the dewy grass to the millstream that separated her patch of land from the field beyond. There, beneath the ash trees, she paddled, childlike, in the ankle-deep pool, squashing the sandy silt between her toes while she watched the sun dip towards the brow of the hill.

Her reverie was short-lived. A brilliant orange crescent was still hovering above the tree tops when she heard the familiar sound of Michael's ageing Saab climbing up the lane. She stepped out of the water and went to meet him.

Michael had accepted the postponement of their holiday with more grace than Jenny had a right to expect. Stoically, he had gone straight back to work and had spent the day flying a round-trip to Geneva. He was weary but relaxed, and after dinner they sprawled on the sofa, Jenny with her legs resting across his lap. If he was thinking that they should now be having dinner on a Venetian piazza, he was hiding it well. He sipped from a bottle of beer and listened patiently as Jenny regaled him with the events of the day.

Almost without realizing she was doing it, Jenny soon found herself talking about the details of the case. 'I asked Colonel Hastings about his lessons-learned inquiry . . .' Jenny said. 'He insisted it was a strictly internal matter.'

'He would.' Michael shrugged. 'It is.'

'You must have been involved in a few – what does it amount to?'

'Could be anything from a quick heads-together to a full board of inquiry with evidence taken from all those involved.'

'He won't have had time for anything detailed.'

'I'd be surprised if your colonel didn't want all the facts – given the circumstances.'

'How do you think that would work?'

'He probably had the major and relevant members of the platoon into his office at Bastion before they left for home.'

'Would he have kept a record?'

'Oh, there'll be a record. Whether he'll admit to it is something else. And whether you'll ever get to see it, well . . .' he paused for another sip of beer, 'that's a matter of politics. And military politics is something I spent twenty long years of my life failing to get my head round.'

Jenny thought back to her training course in the spring and tried to recall if they had discussed the disclosure of the results of informal inquiries. It didn't ring any bells, and if the subject had been mentioned, it had been passed over quickly.

'I can't *not* ask for it,' Jenny said. 'If there's a record, it's a relevant document. Perhaps the most relevant document there'll be.'

Michael looked at her in a kindly, concerned way. 'I know you have to ask, but if you want my advice, Jenny, pin your hopes on the squaddies telling the truth. They'll be good lads. You don't want to go to war with a colonel unless you have to, still less with the MOD. It's not an outfit that forgives.'

'Meaning?'

Michael let out a sigh – the first sign he had shown of impatience. 'Ask yourself why you took this on, Jenny. Was it really to make trouble for yourself? Or was it to show them you could be trusted?' He waited for her to answer, but the question had hit her in a vulnerable spot. 'Anyway, the boy's gone. He knew the risks. And he certainly wasn't going to war for the money. You've got to accept this isn't like your other cases. No one's interested in the truth. What if he disgraced himself? What if he was a coward? His family want to know he died like a man so they can look at his picture with pride, that's all.'

An uncomfortable silence settled between them. Jenny lifted her feet from Michael's lap and sat upright. The room felt suddenly colder.

'I think I'm ready for bed,' Michael said, and got up from the sofa. 'I might be flying to Hamburg tomorrow. I'm expecting an early call.'

'I'll be up in a minute,' Jenny said, and retreated to her study.

For several minutes she sat in front of her laptop with the feeling that she was at a crossroads. Michael's words had struck home, but she was a coroner, and her duty was to the truth, not to the feelings of a handful of relatives. And if she failed to seek it, what would that make her?

Twice she began an email, and twice she deleted it. On the third attempt she completed it, flagged it as urgent, and pressed send. It was to Colonel Hastings, requesting that he disclose all records of his lessons-learned inquiry to her immediately. So that he was not left in any doubt, she stressed that it was evidence vital to her inquiry which she would take all necessary steps to obtain.

The bedroom lights were already off when she pushed open the door. The sound of steady breathing told her that Michael was deeply asleep. A glance at the alarm clock told her that she had been at her desk for more than an hour. She slipped under the duvet and lay awake in the darkness with her mind churning and her heart pounding. It was a feeling she had experienced before when she'd chosen the difficult path: she was afraid. Of what and of whom she couldn't say, but she was in no doubt that she would find out soon.

FOURTEEN

Jenny woke in an empty bed to the sound of heavy rain drumming on the roof. She plodded downstairs, still half-asleep, and found Michael's hastily scribbled note on the kitchen table. He'd been asked to make the Hamburg trip followed by a hop to Stockholm before flying home, but weather reports weren't good and there was a chance his return would be delayed until the following morning. He had signed off simply 'M'. No kiss. He'd left toast crumbs scattered over the counter as well as his dirty dishes and last night's empty beer bottle. The T-shirt and boxers he'd slept in lay on the floor by the washing machine, which he had failed to empty. On rare occasions she felt a hint of nostalgia for her ex-husband's meticulous cleanliness. This was one of them. David had kept their smart suburban home as spotless and ordered as his operating theatre. He never left so much as a stray sock on the bedroom floor; the hangers in his wardrobe were positioned precisely three finger widths apart.

Jenny dealt with the laundry, dosed herself with strong coffee, wiped up the crumbs and was left with no time to do anything else but to bolt a piece of toast, hastily shower and run for the car.

*

Jenny arrived at the administration block in Highcliffe only a few minutes after nine, but already the corridors were busy with uniformed staff who looked as if they'd been hard at work for hours. She found herself climbing the stairs alongside Lieutenant Gallagher. He was carrying an armful of files and, in marked contrast to his colleagues, couldn't have looked less enthusiastic about his day.

'You look busy,' Jenny said, feeling obliged to make small talk.

'Shit rolls downhill,' was his dry response. 'Have a good one.' He continued on up to the second floor.

Jenny turned to her office and saw that there were four or five young soldiers waiting on a row of chairs. Sergeant Price appeared through the door to his office.

'Private Davies, please.'

One of the young men answered with a smart, 'Sir', and followed him inside.

Jenny glanced at them as she passed, realizing that these were Kenny Green's comrades, the men who less than a week before had been in a bloody firefight in a dusty corner of far-off Helmand. She smelt their sweat mixed with the scent of cheap deodorant. They were tense and nervous, their wiry, undernourished bodies taut and alert. She smiled and offered a cheerful good morning. They mumbled greetings in return, their eyes feral and suspicious. She entered her office feeling strangely affected by the fleeting encounter, as if she had absorbed something of the violence still coiled inside them.

The voices of Sergeant Price and Alison travelled through the connecting door with sufficient clarity for her to make out the gist of their questions, but Private Davies' muttered replies were inaudible. It was evident that he was a less than forthcoming witness. Every answer was having to be dragged out of him.

Jenny flicked on her computer and checked her emails. There was no reply yet from Colonel Hastings. There was, however, a message from Simon Moreton asking her to call him as soon as possible. Could news of her request for the results of the lessons-learned inquiry have reached him so quickly? It was possible. She took a deep breath and dialled the number she knew by heart. He answered on the first ring, which was never a good sign.

'Good morning, Jenny. Keeping country hours, I see.'

'I make it nine fifteen. Why, what time did you get in?'

'Seen the papers?' he said, dodging the question.

'No . . .'

'I should start with the *Telegraph* – at least they've found a flattering photograph.'

She tapped on her keyboard and brought up the paper's website. Kenny Green's face and that of the still-missing Pete Lyons stared straight back at her. The headline read, *One Dead, One Missing: The Mystery of the Last Post.* She clicked on the link and opened the full article. Halfway down the page was a photograph of her taken outside the Small Street Courts earlier that summer. No doubt it had been chosen because she wasn't wearing a jacket and her open-necked shirt inadvertently revealed rather more cleavage than was seemly. The caption beneath described her as *Maverick, anti-establishment coroner, Jenny Cooper.* Even from a quick scan she could see that someone had been briefing in detail, and not from within the army. One paragraph in particular instantly leapt off the page:

Sources close to the inquiry describe the official explanation for Private Lyons's suspected abduction as being incredible. They also point out that the appointment of Mrs Cooper, a coroner with a long track record of unearthing inconvenient truths, to conduct the hastily convened inquest, indicates that unease with the army's account is being shared at the highest levels.

'Who are these sources?' Jenny said. 'I can't think of anyone involved with this case who would know a thing about me.'

'How's Alison doing these days? Still taking the tablets?'

'No . . . She wouldn't. I'm sure. She hates all journalists . . .'

'Hmm.' Simon didn't sound all together convinced. 'Well, my next best guess is that it's a lawyer. Anyone on the record yet?'

'No . . .' Jenny ran her eye down her list of unread emails. 'Oh. Hold on . . .'

The subject line of the message read: *Notice of instruction.* She opened it and found a brief message from a London-based firm of solicitors whose name she vaguely recognized: Sampson, Masters and White.

'Yes. It seems Private Green's next-of-kin is being represented by someone named Claydon White.'

'Claydon White . . .' Simon pronounced the name as if it were that of some ancient nemesis. 'Well, that explains it. You've got to admire him – straight into the minds of the jury before you've even begun. You do know who he is?'

'I think I may already have met him,' Jenny said. She had already searched his name and was looking at a photograph on her computer screen of the senior lawyer who had appeared alongside Kelly Bradford on the final afternoon of her recent inquest into the post-operative death of Diana Thompson. Listed below were numerous news stories reporting on a string of high-profile negligence actions of the sort that provoked popular outrage.

Claydon White wasn't picky about his causes. Among his past clients there numbered a radical Islamist preacher who had exploited every legal loophole to successfully avoid deportation, a prisoner who had sued the Prison Service for denying him access to pornography, and a morbidly obese woman who had been awarded £500,000 damages against the fast-food chain she blamed for her predicament. There had been worthy causes, too: a group action against a pharmacy chain that had supplied toxic, grey-market drugs, and a case against a former government minister accused of conspiring in the illegal rendition of innocent terrorist suspects. But above all else, Claydon White's CV was testament to the fact that he was principally a lawyer who sought the limelight.

Simon was going through the same exercise at the other end of the line. 'Looks like you've got your hands full, Jenny. A man like him only turns up when he smells money, and lots of it.'

'Fortunately, I don't award damages.'

'But you deliver verdicts. He's going to move heaven and earth to prove the army negligent or worse. And if he succeeds, any civil action he mounts on the back of it will be a formality.'

'I hope you're not suggesting I'll allow myself to be compromised, Simon?'

'Of course not. I'm just thinking aloud.' He sighed. 'Claydon White,' he repeated the words as if the name itself held the key. 'What a shark like him likes is cases that open the floodgates, ones that cut new ground and bring him a whole slew of work. *That's* why he's here. We've already got the European courts saying that the Human Rights Act applies on the battlefield. OK, our courts have tried to limit its scope, but after the Smith case we're in uncharted waters. An injured soldier or a dead soldier's family can technically bring an action for negligence or for violation of the right to life. But there are no rules established. The Supreme

Court left it all hanging. It's all down to individual circumstances – was this or that decision grossly negligent? Did the officer take reasonable steps in all the circumstances to ensure his men weren't heading into certain death? What White's after is a clear precedent. He wants to be the man who knocks out the doctrine of combat immunity and makes every life and decision taken on the battlefield one with a potential price tag attached.'

'Simon – are you genuinely having these thoughts for the first time, because something tells me you must have anticipated just this scenario. In which case, my involvement makes even less sense. I am the "maverick", after all.'

'Yes, you are,' he said, with palpable regret. 'I suppose I had better write a press release to reassure them that you haven't been appointed to do a hatchet job on the army.'

'You're sure about that? It really is just my Somerset burr?'

'Would I lie to you, Jenny? After all we've been through?'

She thought carefully before answering and decided to give him the benefit of the doubt. 'No, Simon.'

They ended the conversation on amicable terms. Only when she had put down the phone did Jenny realize that she had failed to mention her request to Colonel Hastings. No matter. Technically, it was no concern of Simon's. The privilege and burden of being a coroner was being allowed to make one's own decisions without reference to a higher authority. Ultimately, it was up to her alone to decide how far to go in pursuit of the truth.

Jenny turned back to her ever-increasing stack of emails and started to sort through them. Minutes passed and there was still no sign of a reply from Hastings. Witnesses came and went in the office next door. From the little that Jenny could make out through the connecting door, all the men of 2 Platoon were reluctant talkers. Shortly after ten, Alison knocked and came through.

'Steve's popped out for a minute,' she said quietly. 'They're not telling us much.'

'I guessed.'

'There's only one man who was there with Kenny when it happened – Lance Corporal Jim Warman. Sergeant Bryant should be coming in later, and we're hoping Major Norton can find time, though he's playing a bit hard to get.'

'What does Warman have to say?'

'Not a lot. Norton was about to talk to the village elder when some Taliban popped up on a roof and started firing at them. They all ran for cover. A couple of grenades went off. There was gunfire and smoke for a few minutes, and when it was all over they had three men down – Lee Roberts, Dale Carter and Kenny Green. Roberts was conscious. Carter had a heartbeat, but Kenny was clearly dead. They did their best to keep the two of them alive while they waited for a helicopter to turn up.'

'What do they say about Private Lyons?'

'They all say the same – he vanished while they were asleep.'

'Have they got any idea how?'

'All I've got so far is the names of the four on the sangar towers. Lee Roberts and Dean Paget were two of them. We'll be talking to Paget in a minute.'

'Well, push him hard.'

'I'm trying, Mrs Cooper, but Steve's doing his best to steer clear of the subject. He's clearly been told that whatever happened to Skippy is outside our remit.'

'*Skippy?*'

'That's what they all call Pete Lyons. He was a little lad apparently. Barely more than a kid. Looked like one, too.'

She cocked her ear to the door. 'That's Steve coming back. I'll see you later.' She hurried out.

Another half-hour went by. Jenny had cleared her correspondence and there was still not so much as an acknowledgement from Hastings. His silence had started to feel like a deliberate act of defiance. Decent people replied to awkward emails, even if just to explain their dilemma. Silence, in her experience, was either a sign of cowardice or the first weapon of a bully. Hastings was certainly no coward. Perhaps he had convinced himself that a woman would be an easy touch. Well, if that really is what he thinks, Jenny said to herself, he's got another thing coming.

She arrived at the door to Hastings's office and knocked firmly. There was no reply. She knocked again, even louder, and when there was still no response she tried the handle. It was locked. She pulled out her phone and tried to reach him on his mobile number. Her call connected to his terse voicemail message. She declined to leave one of her own.

Hastings knew that she was running against the clock. He must also have calculated that if he chose to avoid and frustrate her, even for a day or two, she would come under pressure to complete her inquest with or without his documents.

Not prepared to let him avoid her for a minute longer than she could help, Jenny went in search of the one person she suspected might give her an insight into what the colonel truly thought of her: Lieutenant Gallagher.

Jenny worked her way up and down the corridors of the second and third floors, searching the names on office doors. There was no sign of Gallagher's. Having drawn a blank on the lower floors, she made her way up a narrow set of stairs to the fourth at the top of the building. The rooms leading off the passageways seemed mostly to be repositories for archived files and redundant office equipment. No one seemed actually to work up here. She was ready to abandon her search when she heard music coming from behind a door down a side corridor. She made her way towards it. There was no name card in the brass holder. She knocked anyway.

'Come in,' Gallagher called out, at the same time killing the music.

Jenny entered the small, plain room, that resembled an attic den more than it did an office, to find Gallagher hastily scrambling to his feet as if in anticipation of a visit from a superior officer.

'Oh, it's you, Mrs Cooper.' He visibly relaxed. There was a pile of files on his desk, but little evidence that he had been working. A paperback lay open beside them.

'Have you got a moment?'

'Sure. Have a seat.' He dropped back into his chair.

She glanced at his book – a popular treatise on the illusion of religion. 'Any good? It's one of those I probably should have read.'

Gallagher shrugged. 'I'd say he knows about as much theology as I do evolutionary biology. Still, the man's entitled to his opinions.'

Among the several rows of volumes on the shelf to the side of his desk, Jenny noticed several translations of the Bible and a copy of the Koran. And in amongst them, many obscure and searching titles on philosophical and religious themes.

'That's quite a library.'

'If you want answers, you've first got to isolate the questions,' Gallagher said. 'That bit's still a work in progress. Anyway, you look like you've got questions of your own.'

She detected a hint of warmth in his still, distant eyes, along with a suggestion of complex and contradictory layers not far beneath the surface. Her instinct was to trust him, but she told herself to proceed with caution. Her instincts hadn't always served her well.

'I'm trying to get a handle on what a lessons-learned inquiry amounts to. There was one after the incident at Shalan-Gar.'

'That's pretty standard. What about it?'

'As I understand it, Colonel Hastings would have asked each man involved for his account of what happened. Is that correct?'

'More or less. Though I doubt he talked to all the men. He probably just made do with Major Norton and his sergeant.'

'Because?'

'Because he's a fucking colonel. Sorry—'

Jenny waved his apology away, letting him know that she wasn't one to take offence at a little bad language. 'But in a sensitive case like this one?'

Gallagher smiled, this time with a touch of mischief. 'Like I told you, shit rolls downhill. The man at the top is not going to break sweat shovelling it back up again.'

'Meaning what, exactly? He doesn't want to know what happened? It's just a cosmetic exercise?'

Gallagher glanced at the door, then back at Jenny. He studied her cautiously for a moment. 'There's no danger of you trying to tie me up in any of this, is there? I was several kilometres away. I didn't even catch any of it on the radio.'

'No,' Jenny assured him. 'I'm just trying to understand how it works. And why Hastings doesn't want to share the results of his inquiry with me – even though it may be the best evidence there is.'

'This is the army. It runs on trust. Fundamentally, it's all we have. If you want a man to risk his skin for a cause he barely understands and, if he did, he probably wouldn't support anyway, you either have to put a gun to his head or win his complete trust. The men trust their sergeant. The sergeant trusts the officer and the officer trusts his CO. With their lives.'

'And if someone makes a mistake?'

'The army doesn't make mistakes. It can't afford to. Or at least that's the myth we all buy into. How else could we function? The trust would be broken. If something goes wrong, it must be an accident.'

Jenny struggled to follow Gallagher's logic. She asked if he was telling her that Hastings wouldn't have wanted to hear that his subordinates had made a mistake, or that if he did hear that they had, he would have made it his business to ensure that any blame would be dumped on the lowest man in the pecking order.

'Probably both,' Gallagher said. He swivelled his chair and gazed through the open window at the scudding clouds. 'I lost my sergeant in a roadside ambush back in March. We'd been in theatre less than a fortnight. We'd misread the maps and got lost. We were wandering around like idiots for more than an hour before we got our bearings and headed back to the post. It happens. It shouldn't, but it did. I told Norton exactly what happened – chiefly because I didn't know any better – he reported to Hastings and little more was said.'

'What about the inquest?'

'I wrote a statement and was never called on again.'

'A truthful one?'

'In as far as it went.'

'Norton told you to tone it down?'

Gallagher gave her a sideways glance. His expression seemed to say he had already said far more than he had intended.

'You stuck to the facts of the incident,' Jenny ventured. 'Perhaps you were told that was all that was necessary?'

'What was the alternative? Let his family know he died as a result of a cock-up? In whose interests would that have been, exactly? I'm a professional soldier, Mrs Cooper, and I went to war wanting action, not a scrupulous and possibly humiliating inquiry were my guts to be spilt on the ground.'

'I see,' Jenny said, with a note of doubt.

Conversation lapsed. The fact that Gallagher tolerated silence between them without embarrassment told Jenny that they were already on the way to forming their own bond of trust.

It was he who spoke first. 'All right. This is probably what happened. Norton will have briefed Hastings fully on the incident, and depending on how delicate he considered the situation to be, Hastings might have a heads-together with the men present. He'll have written a confidential report which he will have passed up to General Browne. One of the several reasons he won't be keen on releasing it to you is that it will have dealt with the circumstances of Private Lyons's disappearance. And as I understand it, that's outside your terms of reference.'

'Moot point,' Jenny said.

Gallagher's eyes slid questioningly towards her.

'I decide my terms of reference,' Jenny explained, 'not your colonel.'

'Well, you should know, Mrs Cooper – he's a warrior. A real cold bastard when he needs to be.'

'I'm used to those,' Jenny said, touched by his concern. 'Now, you don't have to answer this, Lieutenant, but I've one last question before I leave you in peace. How plausible is it that Private Lyons was kidnapped from inside the post?'

Gallagher smiled faintly. 'You realize you're asking me to disobey an order? I've been told not to say a word to you on that subject.'

Jenny tried to read his expression. Had she pushed him too far? Had she destroyed their trust already?

'I'm sorry . . .'

'But if I were to be reckless enough to give you an answer, how about you being stupid enough to meet up for a drink?'

Jenny felt the blood rise to the surface of her cheeks.

'I get the feeling we might find a lot to talk about,' Gallagher said, perfectly relaxed. 'I'd like to hear more about your work. It sounds interesting.'

Jenny didn't know whether to be flattered or insulted. He was half her age, only a year older than her son, and asking her out on a date. She struggled for an appropriate response, but failed to find one.

'Good. Let me know when you're free,' Gallagher said. 'I'm not doing much outside office hours, or inside them, for that matter. 'Now, Lyons –' he carried on, seemingly oblivious to her embarrassment, 'short of the gate being left wide open and the men on watch being unconscious, I can't see how that could have happened. Is that what you want to know?'

'Thanks,' Jenny said mutedly and got up from her chair. She turned to go, but paused at the door. She had to say *something*, but the words that came out only dug her in deeper: 'I'll see you around.'

'Any time,' Gallagher said.

Jenny smiled awkwardly and hurried from the room.

The statements of Sergeant Bryant and the men who had accompanied Major Norton on the ill-fated mission to Shalan-Gar were even sketchier than Jenny had feared. They contained only the barest details of events leading up to Private Lyons's disappearance and their description of events in the village were monotonous and identical. They entered the village with their local interpreter and fixer, Yusuf, who had told them that he had information that Taliban in the area were holding a British soldier hostage. Their intention, as far as she could make out, was to use the village elder, Musa Sarabi, as a go-between with the hostage takers. A few moments after arriving outside his house, they came under fire. None of the soldiers claimed to have seen Private Green being hit.

Jenny reached for her phone to call Alison through. She needed to prime her before she met with Major Norton. Whether he liked it or not, she was going to insist that he provide her with a full and detailed account. If he refused to part with the facts now, she needed him to know that they would be wrung out of him in court.

There was a knock at the door as she was lifting the receiver. Jenny set it down again and called her visitor in. It was Hastings. His sudden appearance caught her off guard. He was in a hurry – dashing between back-to-back meetings, he said – and apologized for not having answered her request earlier.

'I could have written you an email, but I always think face-to-face is better.' He sat on one of the smart green leather chairs. 'I'll get straight to the point, Mrs Cooper. The material you have requested, even if it exists – and I am not even prepared to confirm or deny the fact – is out of bounds. My private discussions are private. They are what enable me and every other officer in the army to do our jobs. Have I made myself clear?'

He tried to draw the sting from his words with a disarming smile.

'Perfectly,' Jenny said. 'But you know where this leaves me?'

'I'm afraid I don't.'

'I'll have to ask the High Court to make the order for

disclosure. Given the circumstances, I can probably get before a judge this week, but it will be a public hearing.'

Colonel Hastings stared at the floor and tapped the tips of his fingers together. Jenny felt his impatience like a malevolent force.

'If you insist on playing hardball, Mrs Cooper, I can assure you, you will soon wish you hadn't.' The lines in his face stretched tight like strings of tensioned catgut.

'That sounds rather like a threat, Colonel.'

'Merely a statement of fact.' He stood up. 'Take my advice – don't pick fights you don't have to. It never ends well.' He managed to bring his agitation under control and offered a smile that lifted the corners of his eyes. 'Good day.'

Jenny could have let him leave the room unchallenged, but succumbed to a surge of anger. 'I'll instruct counsel this afternoon. You have until close of business to reconsider.'

Colonel Hastings turned slowly to face her. In a clear and level voice, he said, 'My job is ultimately to kill people, Mrs Cooper. To kill them so that you and everyone else in this island gets to visit the supermarket and go about your business in safety. The banal, everyday reality we all take for granted depends on bullets, on blood and on good young men and women laying down their lives. But whatever way you cut it, killing is a foul and ugly business and it's our job. We are the butchers and the slaughtermen who keep you fed. If you don't like our bloody aprons, then you've no business eating our meat.'

He turned and left the room.

Without missing a beat, Jenny picked up the phone and dialled the number of her most trusted lawyer. Ellen Goodson answered from an echoing corridor in the Royal Courts of Justice.

'Ellen, it's Jenny. Is there anyone you'd gladly kill right now?'

'Several. I've just spent a week in the Family Division failing to stop a seven-year-old boy and his younger sister being sent to different foster homes.'

'Well, bottle that rage. I need it. Right now.'

FIFTEEN

Jenny had banked on it taking at least a week before a High Court judge could be found to hear her application, but by some mysterious back-room process, an appointment before Mrs Justice Talbot, who was currently hearing a murder trial in Bristol Crown Court, was found for nine a.m. on Thursday morning – thirty-six hours away. She had expected the Ministry of Defence to object vociferously to being given so little notice, but to her great surprise they proceeded without protest. Before close of business on Wednesday afternoon, Jenny's barrister, Ellen Goodson, and her opposite number, Robert Heaton QC, counsel for the Ministry of Defence, had exchanged skeleton arguments together with lists of the legal authorities on which they sought to base their presentations. In truth, there was very little dispute over the law and none over the facts. The judge's task was to perform a simple balancing exercise: did the interests of justice outweigh the threat to national security that the Ministry of Defence claimed would occur if army officers were forced to disclose their personal notes and records of lessons-learned inquiries?

From the moment the application was filed with the court late on Tuesday afternoon, Jenny had been on edge, expecting Simon Moreton to turn up in her office at any moment. The hours ticked by and he didn't put in so much as a phone call or email. His silence began to spook her. Surely he must have known the case was being heard? She had toyed with the idea of phoning him as a courtesy, but decided against it. If he really was white with fury there was little to be gained by talking to him.

She arrived at the court building as the doors opened at eight o'clock on Thursday morning. Save for a handful of cleaners and the odd harried-looking barrister landed with a last-minute brief, she had the building virtually to herself. Although her hearing was scheduled for nine, most of the courts wouldn't sit until ten or ten thirty. In the hour before-hand, lawyers, clients and witnesses would stream through the doors and the Victorian atrium at the centre of the building would be filled with the hubbub of horse-trading and plea-bargaining which was the way in which much of what passed for justice was conducted.

Savouring the moments of quiet before the storm, Jenny went in search of breakfast in the nearly empty canteen. Ellen had texted to say she was running a little late, but not to worry, she was on top of her brief and feeling confident. Alone and jittery, Jenny sipped her coffee and picked at a croissant while nervously checking the newspaper websites on her phone for any reports of the morning's hearing. She could find no mention of it. That much was a relief. There was nothing that would annoy the Chief Coroner and his officials more than a media circus before her inquest had even begun.

'Mrs Cooper?'

Jenny turned to see a lean, slightly stooped, grey-haired man wearing the distinctive QC's waistcoat which lawyers referred to as a 'monkey jacket'.

He set down his cup and offered his hand. 'Robert Heaton. Counsel for the MOD.' He glanced at the vacant chair opposite hers, 'May I?'

'Of course.'

He took a seat. 'No Mrs Goodson yet?'

'She'll be here shortly. Is there anything I can help you with?'

Heaton moved straight to the point, though with impeccable politeness. 'I was simply going to suggest that you might want to think again. It's not as if you've a lot to gain – you'll have the testimony of all the relevant witnesses at your inquest. What difference will a few notes made a few days earlier make?'

His mild and reasonable manner had the instant and unnerving effect of making Jenny immediately question her motives. Was she simply being belligerent and indulging in petty point scoring? *Was* she wasting everybody's time?

She reminded herself how angry and threatening Hastings had been when she asked to see his notes. 'I have no idea what difference they'll make until I see them. I appreciate the MOD is upset at my insistence, but my job involves upsetting people. Today your clients, tomorrow someone else's.'

Heaton nodded patiently. 'This is a bit of an odd one for you, though, isn't it? I mean, for a coroner of your pedigree.'

'A troublemaker, you mean?'

'Your word, not mine.' He gave a meaningful look and took a sip of coffee.

Jenny couldn't resist taking the bait. 'You're driving at something, Mr Heaton – what?'

'Robert, please. May I call you Jenny?'

'Feel free.' She could hardly object.

'Yes, well, maybe I am,' Heaton continued. 'The thing is, Jenny, I'll admit to being something of an admirer. I remember that first big case of yours – the young boy murdered in custody. I'm not sure anyone else would have got anywhere close to the truth.'

'The internet's a wonderful thing,' she said with a trace of sarcasm. 'You can dig out a whole life history in seconds.'

'I can assure you my esteem is genuine. Hence my concern.' He glanced around the deserted tables. They were still the only customers, but he nevertheless lowered his voice. 'This war in Afghanistan has not been a success. In fact, there are plenty of insiders who'll tell you that our presence there has done no discernible good since 2003. Now it's over, we're left with a cash-strapped government eager to slash the army to the bone and replace professional soldiers with reservists and joystick-twiddling geeks. And ranged against it is an MOD determined to fight tooth and nail to cling on to its empire. And both sides know they've got to carry the public with them.'

'And your point is?'

Heaton's manner became even more conspiratorial. 'This may just be a wild guess, Jenny, but it occurs to me you might just be the human equivalent of a guided missile aimed at the military high command.'

Jenny tried to conceal her surprise. Could this be the real reason she had been asked to handle the case? Had Simon Moreton selected her because he *wanted* her to make waves and face-off against the MOD?

Despite her best efforts, Heaton read her perfectly. 'I sense you agree. Someone, somewhere is exploiting your noble instincts. Press ahead, by all means, but I just thought I should warn you.' He offered a sympathetic smile. 'I can't help feeling that your position isn't dissimilar to the proverbial goat tethered in the desert. In which case, my advice is to slip your collar and run.'

Jenny made no reply.

Heaton sipped the last of his coffee, told her that he was happy to talk again, and went on his way.

*

The encounter left Jenny feeling rattled and betrayed. She tried dialling Simon Moreton's office landline and mobile numbers but both went straight to voicemail. He was avoiding her. What a coward and a disappointment he was. Any charitable feelings she had held for him vanished.

There were thirty minutes to go before the hearing. Jenny went in search of Ellen, hoping to find her in the women's robing room. Emerging from the canteen and entering the cavernous lobby, she was greeted by the sight of an excited scrum of reporters surrounding a tall, confident man who was accompanied by a head-turningly attractive younger woman. As she drew closer, she recognized him as the lawyer who had made a brief, non-speaking appearance in her court the previous week. This was the famous Claydon White.

'It is my privilege to be conducting this case for no fee. Private Green left a fiancée and an unborn child who deserve answers. It may come as a surprise to many people, but while the taxpayer foots the bill for almost every criminal who comes before the courts, there is no legal aid for a family needing representation at a coroner's inquest. So, it's left to people like me to give up their time and expertise in the belief that justice is worth more than money. That's why I'm here. I want to see justice for Kenny Green – and for all the other young soldiers who have lost their lives in this needless war.'

He was strangely mesmerizing, and Jenny found herself still staring when Ellen appeared, clutching an armful of papers. 'Sorry I'm late.' She followed Jenny's gaze to White. 'He's quite the showman, isn't he?'

'I'll say. But what's he doing here? He's not even a party to this hearing.'

'I guess it's all about the photo opportunity. You've heard

he's scooped up the families of the two injured soldiers, as well?'

'No. Where did you get that?'

'He put out a press release. I got a copy by email. You probably had it, too,' Ellen said. 'Has Heaton leant on you to fold your hand, yet? I'll admit, part of the reason I cut it fine was to avoid him. He's got a way of making you feel guilty.'

'He tried,' Jenny said. 'And part of me wishes he'd succeeded.'

There was a sudden rush of reporters as they turned and hurried back across the lobby away from the two lawyers. Sarah Tanner had just come through the main door in what felt like a choreographed entrance.

'Her as well,' Jenny said, experiencing a sinking feeling in the pit of her stomach. 'And I was hoping this morning would be low key. Some chance of that.'

Court hearings consisting of dry legal arguments over the disclosure of documents weren't usually a public spectacle, but Claydon White had managed to conjure one. Mrs Justice Talbot's face registered surprise and disapproval in equal measure as she entered her courtroom. She would have been expecting no more than a handful of participants, but instead found herself confronted by at least twenty reporters on the public benches and by Claydon White, his colleague Carrie Rhodes and their client Sarah Tanner in the well of the court.

Ellen Goodson and Robert Heaton QC sat several seats apart on the advocates' bench at the front of the court. Seated directly behind Heaton was his junior counsel along with two senior and humourless-looking solicitors from the Ministry of Defence – both balding and equally anonymous middle-aged men in grey suits. Colonel Hastings had wisely stayed away.

Mrs Justice Talbot was a recent appointment to the High Court and had already earned a fearsome reputation. 'Yes?' she said, crisply.

Ellen Goodson bobbed up. This was her application, which made her master of ceremonies. 'May it please Your Ladyship, I appear for the Severn Vale District Coroner and my learned friends, Mr Heaton and Mr Jarvis appear for the Ministry of Defence. As Your Ladyship will have gathered—'

'If I may, Your Ladyship . . .' Claydon White rose majestically from his seat. My name is Claydon White, I am the solicitor advocate representing Private Green's fiancée, Sarah Tanner, and I would like to become a party to these proceedings.'

'Have you lodged the appropriate documents, Mr White?'

'I have them here, My Lady. Unfortunately, the quite incredible speed with which this hearing was called left me with no time to lodge them in the usual way.'

The judge let out an impatient sigh. The High Court was not a place where rules of procedure were easily bent. 'Ms Goodson – was Mr White informed of these proceedings in a timely fashion?'

'Tuesday afternoon,' Jenny whispered.

'Yes, my Lady. Tuesday afternoon.'

'Is that right, Mr White?'

'I knew nothing of this matter until three o'clock yesterday,' Claydon White said with a straight face.

It was a bare-faced lie. Jenny had sent the email to his office herself. It was a straightforward ploy to paint him and his client as victims of a conspiracy to deny them due process. But it wasn't a lie she could prove: White could easily claim that her email had got lost in the ether before arriving nearly twenty-four hours after it was sent. Jenny was also aware that it would be of no concern to White whether he won or lost this particular skirmish. All that mattered to him was having his brave stand reported in the hope that it might find its way into the minds of some of those who would become jurors in her inquest. It was known in the business as 'building a narrative' – a technique created by the PR industry, eagerly adopted by politicians and now, late to the party but every bit as enthusiastically, lawyers.

The court usher carried Claydon White's documents forward to the judge and distributed copies to both lead counsel. Mrs Justice Talbot flicked through them with a laser-like eye and looked up, unimpressed.

'I'm familiar with these authorities, Mr White, and you know as well as I do that they don't entitle you to a voice in this application. Now I've no objection to you listening in, and I can't possibly have any objection to your conferring with any of the counsel involved here, but I am not at this late stage prepared to admit you as a party.'

'You're not even prepared to hear argument on the point?'

'Mr White, this is an urgent application for which I have set aside a brief appointment before I resume my trial. If you wish to appeal my decision elsewhere, you may try, but there will be no stay of these proceedings in the meantime. Do I make myself clear?'

Claydon White was undeterred. 'With Your Ladyship's permission, might I ask counsel for both parties whether they have any objection to my being heard?'

'I've no objection,' Ellen Goodson said, 'as long as we can conclude this matter quickly.'

'My sentiments also,' Heaton added, impatient with Claydon White's impertinent interruption.

Mrs Justice Talbot sighed and sucked in her cheeks. 'I am not admitting you formally as a party, Mr White. If you have something material and constructive to add I may, at my discretion, be prepared to hear it.' She moved on quickly before he could object, 'Carry on, Ms Goodson. And let's hope you have no more interruptions.'

Claydon White returned to his seat and exchanged satisfied smiles with his colleague, Carrie Rhodes. They had scored their first, albeit minor, victory.

Ellen Goodson took the judge quickly and adroitly through her best arguments. Despite having little time to prepare, she had all the facts and every detail of the law at her fingertips. Her principal point was that Hastings's notes were potentially the best and most untainted evidence available to the inquest. It was a well-known fact that witnesses' recollections altered in subtle ways over time. If there were differences between what the soldiers present at the time of Kenny Green's death had reported only twenty-four hours after the incident and what they told the inquest jury, these were matters that required examination. On the big issue of whether a commanding officer had a right to keep his notes confidential, she argued skilfully that recent decisions of the Supreme Court had established the principle that human rights laws could potentially apply to the battlefield. That being so, the established right to have an unnatural death thoroughly investigated required the best evidence to be examined.

Robert Heaton QC remained respectfully quiet throughout his opponent's submissions. His composed expression and occasional nod told Jenny that nothing that he was hearing was coming as a surprise. When his turn came to address the judge, he began by saying, 'I agree with almost every word my learned friend has said. Who among us would not want every last scrap of evidence examined if it were our loved one who had died in a foreign field? But, My Lady, this is a case in which the interests of the individual and his family must be weighed against the interests of a nation and its security. To function at all, the army and its officers must have freedom to manoeuvre, and, most importantly, freedom to make mistakes. War is an imprecise science. Risks are unknown and unweighable. Any attempt to make army officers accountable for each and every decision made under pressure will lead to the avoidance of risk, paralysis and the neutering of our armed forces.

'When a man or woman joins the army, they know that they are placing their lives on the line. But they also know that they will be commanded by officers who will do all in their power to safeguard their lives while achieving their military objectives. This is the person-to-person, man-to-man, woman-to-woman trust on which our soldiers operate. No written laws, no matter how comprehensive, can ever serve as a substitute.

'The question for you, My Lady, is what will be lost if Colonel Hastings is required to release his private notes. The answer is simple: the bond of trust will be lost. If he is not free to record his thoughts privately, there are two alternatives. He will either record nothing at all, or, far more likely, a strict and bureaucratic procedure will be applied to every incident, the inevitable objective of which will be to absolve those in authority from blame. The first casualty of bureaucracy, My Lady, is always the truth.'

Heaton continued in a similar vein for a further fifteen minutes, at the end of which Jenny found herself feeling almost persuaded that the army was an institution built on precious and intangible commodities which the intrusion of the law would only serve to destroy. But in her response, Mrs Justice Talbot neatly nailed the problem: noble principles are fine until someone breaks them. Then what? Who holds the officers to account?

Claydon White couldn't resist an intervention. 'My Lady, it may interest you to know that over the course of the last ten years, men under Colonel Hastings's command have suffered casualty rates that run at almost twice the average. He is known as an officer unafraid to take risks with soldiers' lives. In Iraq, twenty-eight men under his command were killed. In Afghanistan the figure is close to forty.'

'Casualties have to be weighed against the effectiveness of the operations in which they are incurred,' Heaton countered, 'quoting mere numbers is meaningless.'

Claydon White glanced at the journalists seated to his right. 'Tell that to the families of the dead.'

'Mr White – would you kindly desist,' Mrs Justice Talbot said sharply.

'My Lady, Mr Heaton asked what would be lost by forcing Colonel Hastings to disclose. I have a simple answer: what he stands to lose is the licence that the army has given him to waste young lives while he sits safely behind a desk.'

Mrs Justice Talbot tapped her pen ominously on her desk as reporters eagerly recorded the sound bite.

Claydon White had got his headline and that should have been enough, but now he was pushing his luck. He remained on his feet, waiting for the judge to shoot back.

She obliged him. 'You will either withdraw that remark and express your regret at having used such an intemperate phrase having advanced no evidence whatever to substantiate it, or I will hold you in contempt, Mr White. And what is more, I will impose reporting restrictions on this hearing.'

She waited for his answer.

Claydon White allowed several seconds to pass as he weighed his options. Eventually, he said, 'I apologize for allowing my profound concern for my client to cause me to make remarks which should not have been made until formal evidence of Colonel Hastings's military record is produced before a court.'

'I asked you to withdraw them, Mr White.'

Claydon White folded his hands behind his back. 'Very well, My Lady. I withdraw them.'

'Thank you.'

Jenny glanced at the reporters and noticed that many of them were openly smirking.

'He had his fingers crossed behind his back, didn't he?' Ellen Goodson whispered over her shoulder. 'What a pathetic little rat.'

Jenny reserved judgement. Claydon White wasn't a man you would trust to mind your handbag, but he certainly had guts. Perhaps a little too much for his own good.

He at least had the good sense to sit tight while Goodson and Heaton concluded their arguments. A little more than an hour after they began, Mrs Justice Talbot announced that she had arrived at her decision. In a brief *ex tempore* judgment she performed a neat judicial side-step and declared that she didn't consider that the case involved substantial issues of national security, nor did it raise the question of whether Private Kenny Green had been protected by the Human Rights Act during the fatal operation. It was a case that could be decided on its facts alone. A coroner was entitled to access to all relevant evidence except in the most exceptional circumstances. The results of Colonel Hastings's lessons-learned inquiry were, she concluded, relevant to the coroner's inquest.

For a moment, Jenny felt her heart skip, but then came the sting in the tail: 'But only those parts which relate directly to the immediate circumstances of Private Kenny Green's death. All other material may be redacted.'

Something was better than nothing, but the smile on

Robert Heaton's face as they filed out of the courtroom was proof, if any were needed, that it was a hollow victory and not the dangerous precedent the MOD had feared.

Ellen Goodson offered her commiserations but her attention had already moved on to the next hearing in her frantic schedule. Such was the life of a busy barrister: cases came and went like anaesthetized bodies on the surgeon's table. Jenny threaded her way through the now crowded lobby, envious of the lawyers and judges who could treat their cases like crossword puzzles – mere intellectual challenges with no emotional strings attached. All the years she had struggled as a family lawyer dealing with kids in and out of care, she had longed for just a few days when she wasn't haunted by visions of suffering and unhappy children. It never came. When she took up her post as a coroner, she had secretly hoped that dead clients wouldn't pull as strongly at her heart strings. It had been a vain wish. At one time she had considered her tendency to feel deeply about her cases to be a strength. A few years further on, she wondered if it might not be a weakness. *The heart of a true professional lies in her head*. The little epithet, picked up from her first female boss, sprang into her mind. *Care a little less, think a little more*, is what she had actually meant.

As she emerged from the court building into the bright morning sunlight, she told herself that she would try to approach her inquest with a level of detachment she had never quite managed in the past. Cool. Objective. Dispassionate. These would be her watch words. She repeated them like a mantra.

Jenny found herself tested less than a minute later. She turned a corner and saw Sarah Tanner standing alone on the pavement. She looked tired and troubled. One hand was supporting her swollen belly, the other was pressed to the painful small of her back. She glanced towards Jenny and inadvertently caught her eye. Jenny could simply have smiled and carried on her way, but Sarah seemed lost and she felt compelled to stop and ask if she was all right.

'I thought they were giving me a lift home,' Sarah answered, grateful to see a familiar face, 'but they said they had to get back to London.'

So much for Claydon White's overwhelming concern for his client.

'Oh,' Jenny said. 'How did you get here?'

'I didn't even know I was meant to be coming till they called this morning.' She pushed her hair back from her face. 'Didn't even bring my bag. How stupid's that?' She shook her head. 'Sorry. It's not your problem.' She turned away.

'Would you like to borrow my phone? Here . . .'

Jenny offered her handset but Sarah just looked at it.

'I thought you might want to call someone,' Jenny said.

'I didn't tell them I was coming,' Sarah said guiltily. 'They don't trust these lawyers . . .' She hesitated, a catch in her voice. 'It's almost like she blames me, like she's forgotten that she was the one who was so proud of him being a soldier. I didn't even want him to go on this tour. Part of me *knew* this would happen. I should have told him. I should have told him to ignore all her crap and stop trying to be a hero.' She rubbed away a tear with the heel of her palm. 'You couldn't lend me a tenner for the bus? I'll pay you back.'

'I'm heading back to Highcliffe. Why don't I give you a lift? But we can't discuss Kenny or the case, OK?'

Sarah nodded, grateful to be rescued.

Jenny switched on the car radio in an attempt to lighten the atmosphere, but as hard as she tried to place her thoughts elsewhere, all she could think of was the quietly sobbing girl in the passenger seat. She would have offered some words of comfort, but it took all of her strength not to cry with her.

SIXTEEN

Alison decided that while Sergeant Price was nice to look at, she couldn't face another entire day cooped up with him in the office. She was also concerned that as the inquest drew nearer, she had yet to gain a real insight into what had been going on inside 2 Platoon in the hours and days before Kenny Green's death. Her career in the police force had taught her more than a thing or two about the tensions and rivalries that develop between members of a close-knit team. If the statements they had were to be believed, all the men were the best of friends. The fact that Sergeant Price seemed content with that only added to her sense of suspicion and unease.

She ducked out of the office shortly before eleven with the excuse that she had errands to run in the town. What she didn't tell him was that she intended to revisit one of their witnesses – the one who had caused her antennae to twitch most violently: Private Danny Marsh. Alison had studied each of the soldiers closely during their interviews. Employing a mixture of instinct and a feeling for body language which she had picked up during her career as a detective, she had concluded that all of them were talking from a script and that the soldier most tempted to veer from it was Private Danny Marsh. Marsh had been among the group who had gone to Shalan-Gar with Major Norton, and was one of the three who had been stationed outside the village gate while Norton led the others in. She wanted to talk to him again. Off the record.

Alison arrived at the front door of the single person's accommodation block where Marsh was quartered, but there was no reply to his bell. She was reaching for her phone when she spotted Jacqui, the cashier from the camp shop, who had stepped outside for a cigarette. She crossed over the road and joined her.

'No customers?'

'Quietest day of the month. Then it's all change to-morrow – when everyone gets paid.' She offered Alison a Silk Cut.

'I'd love to,' Alison said, 'but I daren't. Took me too many years to give up. Thanks all the same.'

'You look like you're looking for someone?'

'Danny Marsh – do you know him?'

'I know Danny. I know where you'll find him, too – either in the bookies' or next door in the King's Head. He's a gambler, that boy. Love him, but he's always coming in asking for credit.'

'He seemed quite a serious lad, when I spoke to him.'

Jacqui looked astonished. 'Are we talking about the same one?'

'Maybe I made him nervous,' Alison joked, 'I tend to have that effect on young men.'

Jacqui smiled and dobbed her ash carefully into an open matchbox. 'Shall I tell him you were looking for him?'

'Better not – he might get the wrong idea. I'll find him.'

She left Jacqui chuckling and hurried to her car.

The Broadway sported a mixture of betting shops, fast-food outlets and pound stores. The ironmongers, grocers and family owned department stores, some of whose names were still ghosted on the brickwork of the grand Victorian buildings, were a distant memory. At some point in recent decades, someone had thought it a good idea to pave the entire street over, with the result that it had become a place for kids to skateboard and bored and unemployed youths to congregate in menacing groups and drink cheap cider. A typical British seaside town. The sole survivor from Highcliffe's heyday, it seemed, was the King's Head – a wide-fronted, Jacobean building that had been a social hub for centuries. Having drawn a blank in all the betting shops, this was where Alison finally spotted Danny Marsh pumping coins into a fruit machine.

Pretending not to have seen him, she made her way to the bar and ordered a coffee. While she waited, she heard him curse colourfully as the machine gleefully swallowed the last of his money. He turned and slouched over to the bar, where he sipped at the dregs of his beer. Alison waited for him to notice her. Eventually, he glanced her way with a look of dim recognition.

'Oh, hello,' she said brightly.

He took a moment to place her.

'We met the other day. I'm the coroner's officer. Alison Trent. I remember now – you're Danny. Danny Marsh – is that right?'

'Yeah.' He didn't seem anxious to talk.

'Can I get you another drink?'

He hesitated, but not for long. 'Thanks. Lager.'

He made his way towards her as she placed the order, the promise of a drink overcoming his reserve.

'On leave, are you?'

'Supposed to be. With all this business going on, we've been told to stick close to camp.'

Alison cast her eyes around the bar. 'Are you on your own?'

'Yeah,' Danny said with a shrug.

They fell into silence while the barman finished pulling his pint and handed it across the bar.

'Don't feel you have to stay and talk to me if there's somewhere you'd rather be,' Alison said.

'It's all right. All my mates are off with their other halves. I'm the only saddo with no one to go to.'

He lifted his glass and spilt a drop on the shiny wooden counter. His hand was trembling. He noticed Alison spot it.

'Post-tour shakes,' he said, a little embarrassed. 'It'll go after a couple of days and a few more beers. It's like some part of your brain still thinks someone's going to loose a round off at you.'

'I know the feeling. See that?' She pushed her hair back from her temple to reveal the flattened area of skull. 'Two years ago. A bloke in a Range Rover drove at me. Tried to kill me. I should be dead.'

'Yeah? What was he trying to kill you for?'

'It's a long story – one of our inquiries. We ran into some dangerous people. Still, we bagged them in the end.'

'Wow.' Danny was impressed.

'They gave me some pills and a bit of therapy. It all helped. Does the army do anything for you?'

'No.' Danny shook his head. 'I can handle it, though. This was my third tour.'

'You've been lucky.'

He nodded. 'I guess 2 Platoon's had more than its share. Had a few mates killed or had lumps blown off them.'

'Is that usual? For one platoon to have so many casualties, I mean?'

'Some officers keep their heads down and stay out of harm's way, others like to get out there and show them who's boss. Mine was the kind who liked to keep busy. We dealt with a lot of Tali, but we paid for it.' He took a large gulp of lager, clenching his fist hard around the glass to stop it shaking. 'Still, no point being out there if you're sitting in the post all day.'

'You're going to need another. Go on – drink up. Don't tell anyone – I'll put it through expenses.'

She smiled and Danny smiled back. He looked lonely, poor lad, and far too thin. She felt like taking him home and giving him a proper meal.

The alcohol soon brought him out of his shell. He joked about the way in which his mates in the platoon had changed from macho warriors to cooing dads in the few days since they'd been home. He couldn't switch on his phone or look at his laptop without being bombarded with pictures of snotty-nosed kids. Alison guessed that behind the bravado there was more than a hint of envy.

'It seems funny, such young lads having kids. Most of you don't look old enough.'

'Human instinct, isn't it? Have them while you can. You never know what's coming.' His mood took a sudden dip. He stared sullenly into his glass.

'It must have been tough coming home without Lyons?'

Danny looked up. His blue eyes, clouded with drink, nevertheless saw straight through her.

'What are you after?'

'Nothing. I just—'

'No one knows what happened to Skip. Little fucker just vanished.'

'You sound angry with him.'

'Not with him . . .' He sighed. 'Six months out there would mess anyone up. Especially the way Norton runs the show.'

'How do you mean?'

'Trigger-happy bastard, isn't he? Never happier than shooting some raggy's head off. I'll tell you, when you wake up every day thinking it might be your last, it does things to you. Sounds crazy, but you end up almost wanting it to happen. It's like, let's get it over with. It's the waiting, not knowing what's coming at you – that's the hardest part.'

Alison saw that his hand was now shaking so violently that beer was spilling over the edges of his glass. She dipped into her handbag and reached out her purse.

'Enjoy the rest of your leave, love.' She placed a ten-pound note on the bar. 'Have another couple on me.'

Jenny entered her office in Highcliffe less than two hours after Mrs Justice Talbot had delivered her judgment. Already waiting in her email inbox was a message from Colonel Hastings marked 'Strictly Private and Confidential'. A brief, curt message announced that a copy of the requested item was enclosed. The attachment amounted to a two-page document headed simply, *Fatal Incident, Shalan-Gar*. It was dated 23 August, the day after the skirmish, but there was no way of proving that was in fact the date when it was written – the judge's order had not included the requirement that all relevant electronic trails be revealed.

It took Jenny less than a minute to read. In now familiar terse, military prose, Hastings set out the barest facts:

06.00 Pte Lyons reported missing. Post searched. Neighbouring platoons contacted by radio.

06.45 Local interpreter Yusuf Sarabi reported Pte Lyons held by Taliban and relayed ransom request of $100,000.

07.30 Mjr Norton led detail to Shalan-Gar. Objective: negotiate Pte Lyons's release.

07.45 Mjr Norton led detail into Shalan-Gar village: Sgt Bryant, Lnce Crpl Warman, Roberts, Carter, Green. Ptes

Marsh, Allerton, Paget posted at gate. Objective: negotiate with hostage takers through village elder, Musa Sarabi.

07.46 Detail came under fire from surrounding rooftops. Pte Green shot in head (died at scene), Ptes Carter and Roberts injured in grenade blast.

Est. 4 Taliban killed in exchange. Village searched – Pte Lyons not found

08.15 Medevac to Bastion – 1x fatality, 2x casualty

At the foot of the document was a short concluding paragraph:

Reason for Private Lyons's absence from post remain unclear. Abduction by enemy unlikely, not impossible. Guards on sangars claim nothing suspicious observed and 'alert at all times'. Possible lapse in vigilance and/or concentration, though no similar incidents reported during tour. Mjr Norton's decision to negotiate release face-to-face reasonable in circumstances – Musa Sarabi an established conduit to Taliban; relations well-established. Risks to Pte Lyons judged serious and requiring immediate action. Conclusion: fatality and injuries incurred in proper exercise of operational duties.

In other words, no lessons learned, Jenny said to herself. She sat back in her chair and wondered if she'd been played for a fool; whether Hastings had skilfully sold her a dummy with the express intention of sucking up her precious time and energy in the few days available to her before the inquest. The most frustrating thing about the cursory document was how little it said about what was shaping up as the most critical issue of all, yet one that was technically beyond the scope of her inquest: how on earth Private Lyons could have gone missing from the post with no one noticing? *Possible lapse in vigilance.* Was that code for everyone being asleep on the job? The fact that Hastings's observations went no further was baffling. One way or another it was a question she was going to have to probe.

Her train of thought was interrupted by her phone. She retrieved it from the depths of her handbag and saw that it was Dr Andy Kerr calling from the mortuary.

'Andy. How's it going?'

'I've had a look at your soldier. Alison mentioned you weren't getting much in the way of privacy out there in Highcliffe. I wasn't sure how you'd want my report de-livered.'

'You've got my private email?'

'I'll send it right over.'

Jenny lowered her voice, unsure if Sergeant Price was still the other side of the connecting door or if he was still out at lunch. 'What have you found?'

'Well, for one thing he had traces of alcohol in his system. He'd also been struck by at least three other rounds which were repelled by his Kevlar vest – all of them hit his chest.'

'How much alcohol?' Jenny said.

'Not a lot. I'd say it was residual from the night before. I'm guessing booze was strictly off-limits?'

'I'll say. Do you know what kind?'

'Afraid not. Could have been anything from Dom Pérignon to scrumpy. No telling.'

'Champagne in Helmand – I doubt it. You've certainly given me something to think about.'

'There's more . . .'

'Oh?' Whatever it was, it didn't sound like good news.

'You asked for the full suite – that's what you've got. I requested hair analysis and it registered a positive for can-nabinoid THC. A tiny amount, probably some weeks in the past.'

Cannabis. The implications were huge.

'On the upside, it was only three picograms per microgram. Almost negligible, and right at the margins of reliability.'

Jenny read in his tone the unspoken offer to omit this finding from his report. It was tempting, but she didn't succumb. The truth was always ugly at first sight.

'Thanks, Andy. I'll look forward to reading it. See you in court.'

'Always an experience.'

Alcohol and cannabis. Jenny wondered whether, if he had known what his soldiers had consumed, Colonel Hastings would have included it in his lessons-learned exercise. Somehow she doubted it.

Jenny winced as she opened the lengthy document Dr Kerr had sent her. It included a full set of autopsy photographs. The first showed Kenny Green's body laid out naked on the stainless-steel table. The last showed his brain in a kidney dish – two flagged pins marked the entry and exit wounds. In between were pictures of each of his vital organs as they were weighed, examined and cut into sections. Post-mortem was a brutal procedure, as close to butchery as it was to surgery.

Skipping quickly to the substance of the report, Jenny noticed that Kenny Green weighed only 65.2 kilos – not quite 10st 4lb. It was very low for a young man over six feet tall. The alcohol finding was included in the *Histology* section: 15mg/100ml of blood. The legal limit for driving a car was 80mg, suggesting that this was indeed a morning-after residue. It wasn't much, but added to the finding under *Hair Analysis* that recorded THC Metabolites detected at 3pg/mg. It painted a picture that Major Norton would have great difficulty explaining away. Her eye was then caught by a short sentence in the penultimate section of the report, headed, *Other Comments and Observations*. It read: *Small amount of broken glass found in left breast pocket of tunic – approx. 12g.* She checked back and saw that two of the three bullets that didn't make it through Kenny Green's Kevlar vest had struck the left side of his chest. She scribbled a note to investigate further.

Jenny turned at the sound of the door to the corridor being opened from the outside. She felt her hackles rise as she braced herself for an intruder, but it was Alison who tiptoed in. She pointed to the connecting door.

'It's all right, he's still out,' Jenny said.

'Sure?' Alison mouthed.

'Yes. What's going on?'

'I went to have a word with Danny Marsh,' Alison said in barely more than a whisper, just to be on the safe side. 'Tracked him down at the pub. He'd had a couple, but he started to talk about Norton – said he's trigger-happy, loves a fight. It sounds like he pushed them so hard some of them ended up with a bit of a screw loose.'

'What do you mean?'

'He seemed to be saying that if you're involved in that much action, you can end up with a death wish. He's not in a great way himself. I suppose there's only so much one lad can take.'

'Do you think he'll say it again on oath?'

'Maybe if you feed him three or four pints first. But I wouldn't bank on it.'

'Oh, well, it's good to know, I suppose.'

'How was court?' Alison asked.

'We won.'

'Fantastic!'

'Not really, as it turns out. Hastings released his document but it doesn't tell us anything we haven't already learned. The only explanation he gives for Private Lyons's disappearance is "possible lapse in vigilance". Kenny Green's post-mortem is more interesting, though – he had traces of alcohol in his blood and his hair sample tested positive for THC.'

Alison's misaligned eyes stared back at her in disbelief. 'You're sure about that?'

'I've never known Andy Kerr to be wrong.'

'No wonder taking their statements was like pulling teeth. They could be court martialled.'

Jenny nodded, and felt herself shudder at the prospect of the press getting hold of this information.

'What are we going to do about Sergeant Price?' Alison said. 'You don't want him seeing this report yet, do you?'

Deception went against the grain, but in this case Jenny didn't see much alternative.

'I'll produce an edited version. He can see that. I also want to hold a preliminary hearing first thing on Monday morning. There are some directions I need to give.'

'I can guess,' Alison said.

They both fell silent at the sound of Sergeant Price returning to the next-door office.

His chair scraped on the polished wood floor as he sat at his desk.

'Set the wheels in motion,' Jenny said.

They exchanged another look, understanding each other perfectly.

Chris was upstairs in the bath. He had been in there for an age. Melanie Norton eyed the unopened bottle of wine on the counter as she peeled potatoes. Her rule was, and always had been, nothing to drink before dinner. She tried to keep to one glass, only occasionally allowing herself a second on a Friday or a Saturday night, but Sundays and Mondays were strictly dry. It was a rigid system she had adopted to prevent herself ever going the way of her mother, whose sudden death aged forty-six came after years of secret, heavy drinking. Like her, her mother had suffered during the lonely months when her husband was away. But unlike her daughter, she had sought the company of other men. Now and then, at unprompted moments, Melanie would recall the crippling shame of coming home unexpectedly from school one afternoon, to hear her mother upstairs with a lover.

Somehow her father had managed never to see beyond the pretty frocks and pasted-on smiles. The two of them had seemingly inhabited parallel realities. Military couples could do that. For the ones that stayed the course, it was their distinguishing feature.

The wine was beckoning. Just a single glass would dissolve the pain and give her all the artificial cheer she would need to steer Chris and the girls through dinner. She felt her willpower dissolve. She pulled herself back from the brink. *No.* It wasn't the answer. She needed to deal with the problem. Talk to him straight. Tell him that he was clearly traumatized and in need of help. If he wouldn't take steps to get it for himself, she would arrange it. She quartered the last potato, placed the pan on the stove and steeled herself to confront him.

Melanie tapped on the bathroom door. 'Chris? Can I come in?'

'Hold on.' She heard him lean over and slide back the bolt. 'It's open.'

She stepped inside and closed the door behind her. He was lying chest-deep in the tub. Even after a week of home-cooked food there was no flesh on his bones. His skin was stretched tight across his ribs. His eyes seemed unnaturally large in his hollowed-out face.

'Are you sure you're feeling all right, Chris?' Melanie said with concern. 'You really don't look well to me.'

'Just a little tired.' He seemed impatient at her presence.

She sat on the side of the bath and realized that she was still wearing the blue striped apron she wore around the kitchen. 'Not my best look – sorry.'

'I'll be out in just a moment. Must have got lost in thought. A lot on my mind.'

Melanie tried not to look too closely at his emaciated body, but she couldn't help noticing that he was a mass of goose flesh. She dipped her fingers in the water. 'It's cold. What are you doing in a cold bath?'

'Is it? I hadn't noticed.'

'It's stone cold. How could you not notice?' She touched his arm. 'And so are you.'

'It was hot in Helmand,' he said. 'Forty degrees through the night. You dream of being cool.'

She took hold of the chain and pulled the plug. 'Well, it's certainly come true. Come on. Get out before you catch your death.' She reached for a towel but felt his icy fingers snatch hold of her wrist. 'I am perfectly capable of bathing myself.'

'Ow! You're hurting me.'

He let go. 'Sorry . . .'

Melanie rubbed at her sore skin. She saw that he was breathing rapidly. His pupils were wide, like black saucers.

'You need to see someone, Chris – to help you unwind. I've never seen you this way after a tour. You need to talk about it with someone professional before it turns into anything worse.'

'You want me to see a shrink?'

'Or a counsellor. *Someone*. Yes, I do.'

He inhaled deeply and brought his rapid breathing under control. 'If that was what I needed, darling, believe me, I would have no objection.' He smiled, as if the very thought of it were absurd.

'What happened, Chris? You can tell me. I'm your wife.'

'Mel, I can assure you – apart from feeling a little under-nourished, I feel absolutely fine. If I've seemed a little distant, I apologize. Frankly, I'm exhausted.' He stood up and stepped out of the bath. He reached for a towel with a look that said he would now like to be left alone.

It was no good. There was no getting through to him.

Melanie went back downstairs to check on dinner. She poured herself a large glass of Merlot, swallowed it in three mouthfuls, then poured another. Then, ashamed of herself, she stowed the open bottle out of sight at the back of the cupboard under the sink.

SEVENTEEN

Jenny drove to work on Monday morning in the afterglow of an unexpectedly romantic weekend. Michael had prised her from her study, led her on a long meandering walk, cooked dinner on the outdoor barbeque he had built earlier that summer and told her she was the only woman he had ever truly loved. Lolling on the warm grass, watching the sun go down, they had both agreed that Italy wasn't a patch on the Wye Valley and almost convinced themselves that they had forgotten the disappointment of missing their holiday. She arrived energized and rejuvenated outside Highcliffe's old magistrates' court.

'I'm glad someone's smiling,' Alison said, as they met on the front steps of the building. 'There won't be many on the faces of the lawyers this morning. They don't take kindly to being dragged down from London at short notice – especially when they don't know what for.'

'They'll find out soon enough.'

She followed Alison through the large oak doors into an impressive lobby. 'Wow – is this a court or a museum?'

A statue of a long-forgotten dignitary stood in the centre of the marble floor. An elaborate oak staircase with ornately turned balustrades wound up to the courtroom on the floor above. The building had been erected in the early 1800s when Highcliffe had been a prosperous trading port and crime was sufficiently rife for the town to hold quarterly assizes. For hosts of smugglers, roistering sailors, prostitutes and petty thieves, this would have been the last stop before the gallows or a creaking, stinking prison ship bound for the colonies.

'We've had worse, Mrs Cooper,' Alison said.

It was certainly in a different league from the draughty church halls in which Jenny had held many of her more challenging inquests. She continued up the stairs, passing beneath a vast and splendid portrait of Admiral Horatio Nelson.

Jenny gave Alison strict instructions that she was not prepared to meet with any of the lawyers before the hearing and retreated to the office that had been the original judge's chambers. A polished mahogany table with four chairs occupied the centre of the high-ceilinged room. A portable gas fire sat incongruously in an elaborate, now redundant, marble fireplace. A set of glazed bookcases contained a set of All England Law Reports and an extensive set of volumes, bound with tooled leather, containing the annual records of the Highcliffe Assizes beginning in 1810 and ending in 1939.

It was odd to think that this was the room to which judges had retired before delivering sentences of death. She wondered what some of the old boys would have made of her. Not much, she guessed.

As she unloaded her files from her briefcase, her phone buzzed in her pocket. She drew it out to find a text from Michael: '*No fear! Love you. M x.*' She was touched. She could count the number of spontaneous messages he had sent her. Then she remembered he was attending a biannual medical that morning. He was probably sitting in a doctor's reception with only his phone to amuse him. Still, she appreciated the sentiment.

It was scheduled as a brief hearing formally opening the inquest, but with five minutes to go, Jenny felt a familiar flutter of anxiety. She could hear the voices in the court-room from across the passage. She felt irrationally self-conscious and empty-headed. In the past, she had tried dosing herself with pills to counter this stage fright. It had proved a poor sticking plaster. Experience had taught her that the only effective method of overcoming it was to let the fear flow freely and to allow the imagination its full rein. For several minutes before entering court, her mind would flood with increasingly disastrous scenarios of public humiliation; her heart would pound, her palms sweat, and then, as the crescendo of panic threatened to overwhelm her, it would recede as quickly as it had arrived.

Alison chose the moment shortly before this turning point to knock on the door and announce that everyone was ready for her.

'Just a second.' Jenny pretended to be searching for some-thing amongst her papers. Beneath her calm exterior, her heart was still thrashing.

'There's quite a crowd,' Alison commented. 'Even Colonel Hastings turned up. I wasn't expecting that. I left Sergeant Price looking after him – thought it was the best way to keep them both out of your hair.'

None of this made Jenny feel any better.

'All right?' Alison prompted.

No, was the truthful answer, but there was no point cowering. Jenny gathered up her file with trembling fingers and told Alison she was ready.

They crossed the narrow corridor and, for a tense moment, Jenny waited like an actor in the wings while Alison went ahead and issued the instruction: 'All rise.'

Jenny entered, her legs wanting to buckle beneath her, and took her seat at the head of a full courtroom. Among the sea of faces she immediately picked out those of Paul and Rachel Green and, several seats away from them, Sarah Tanner. In the rows behind them were numerous young soldiers with their wives and partners. Seated at the rear of the room were half a dozen or so senior officers. Jenny spotted Hastings at the end of the row next to Major Norton, but there was no sign of Lieutenant Gallagher. In amongst the crowd there would be a number of reporters, some of whom, she could be sure, would be relaying proceedings in real time over social media.

A silence descended. Jenny felt the weight of expectation on her shoulders.

'Good morning, everybody,' she began, then paused to swallow. 'This is a short hearing, the purpose of which is formally to open my inquest into the death of Private Kenneth Green, aged twenty-one years and three months, who died in Shalan-Gar, Helmand, Afghanistan, on the morning of 22 August this year. He was, of course, on active service at the time. I propose to begin the full hearing later this week once some preliminary matters have been dealt with.' She turned to address the lawyers. 'Could the legal representatives please introduce themselves.'

Robert Heaton QC was their nominated spokesman. 'Ma'am, I, together with my junior, Mr Cameron Clark, represent the Ministry of Defence. Mr Claydon White and Ms Carrie Rhodes appear for Private Green's fiancée, Miss Sarah Tanner.'

Claydon White rose to his feet. 'Ma'am, before we go any further – if indeed we are going any further – there are two urgent matters I wish to raise.'

'If you're quick, Mr White.'

'Firstly, this . . .' He snatched up a thin document from the desk and held it at arm's length. 'A young soldier dies. Two more sustain life-threatening injuries. A colonel holds a lessons-learned inquiry, and we are expected to believe that this is all he comes up with. I don't know whether it's true or not, or which alternative is more shocking.'

Jenny held up a hand urging Robert Heaton to remain in his seat. 'Mr White, I'm sure we've all got questions about that document and the discussions that preceded its writing. I suggest we deal with those at the next hearing.'

'Ma'am, the order of Mrs Justice Talbot was for full discovery. If that has not been complied with, it is a serious matter of contempt, and a potentially imprisonable offence. I need my opponents and Colonel Hastings to be aware of that fact.'

Robert Heaton rolled his eyes wearily. Colonel Hastings, and next to him Major Norton, remained impassive.

'Point taken, Mr White. We'll deal with this later in the week. And please, although you may be in the habit of issuing sound bites in other courts, please try to keep them to a minimum in mine. They don't impress me, and they certainly won't help us get to the facts.'

Claydon White took the blow on the chin and responded with a disarming smile. Jenny refused to soften. 'Your second point?'

'We are all still waiting for the post-mortem report, ma'am. I'm sure there can be no disagreement that it is customary to release the pathologist's findings before an inquest begins.'

'If you'll be patient, Mr White, I'm coming to that.' From her file, she produced copies of Dr Kerr's full report, though with the photographs omitted for the time being. She nodded to Sergeant Price, who was seated next to Alison on the court clerks' bench, and asked him to distribute them to the lawyers and family members. 'You will see that much of what the report contains is relatively straightforward and uncontroversial, however the histology and hair analysis findings are not.'

The lawyers hurriedly scanned the report's pages. There was a long moment of silence as they read, reread and digested the salient information. Then Claydon White and Robert Heaton leaned towards one another and engaged in an intense whispered conference. Meanwhile, the officers at the back of the court exchanged puzzled glances. Jenny saw Colonel Hastings turn to Major Norton, who shrugged.

Jenny pressed on. 'The report's findings are matters for exploration later this week, but in the meantime I am making the following order—'

Robert Heaton shot to his feet. 'Ma'am, on behalf of my client I make formal application for a further post-mortem examination by a pathologist of my client's choosing.'

'Likewise,' Claydon White added.

'And in the meantime, we would be grateful if the contents of this report were to remain undisclosed until the substantive hearing.'

It was precisely the request Jenny had anticipated. Both parties had their own powerful reasons for wanting to rubbish Dr Kerr's findings, and if she gave them long enough, she was in no doubt that a small army of highly qualified experts would be produced to do just that.

'I am making the following order: all members of 2 Platoon including Major Christopher Norton will provide hair and blood samples for the purposes of drugs and alcohol testing. I have made arrangements for the samples to be collected this afternoon in the gymnasium at Highcliffe Camp. Any men unable to attend will be visited at home this evening. I will have results within forty-eight hours and will make them available to all parties immediately.'

Heaton and White found themselves momentarily at a loss for words.

'And for the avoidance of doubt, I have no intention of suppressing the findings in this report. Very small traces of both alcohol and cannabinoid THC were found in samples taken from Private Green's body. Whether any of this is significant to ultimate cause of death is something we will explore at the inquest. My officer will provide details of where and when the testing is to take place. I shall see you all again here on Thursday morning.'

Before anyone could respond, Jenny had risen from her seat and exited the courtroom. As she closed the door behind her she heard an eruption of outraged voices. The loudest was Claydon White's: 'What the hell does the mad bitch think she's doing?'

Jenny knew precisely what she was doing. She was refusing to be pushed around.

Alison ignored Claydon White's haranguing and demands to see the coroner in private and told him to communicate via email. Promising dire consequences for 'the most shoddy and amateurish behaviour I have ever witnessed', he swept out of the room with Carrie Rhodes and a bewildered Sarah Tanner. Paul Green attempted to offer soothing words to his wife, but they did nothing to stem Rachel's anguished tears. 'They're trying to rubbish him! How could they?' she repeated over and over. Meanwhile, Robert Heaton and his team of grey-suited MOD lawyers formed a sombre huddle that included several senior officers including Hastings and Norton.

Sergeant Price collared Alison as she made her way to the door of the court with a bundle of printed leaflets detailing the time and location of the testing. Every soldier would be required to provide hair samples that would disclose whether drugs had been taken at any stage within the previous few months.

'Did you know about this?' he asked accusingly.

'I just do what the coroner tells me to,' Alison said, 'I'm the coroner's officer. And as our liaison officer, it's your job to round up all the men in the platoon and make sure they're at the camp gymnasium this afternoon. Here, have some leaflets.'

'Sergeant Price!' Colonel Hastings was calling him over to join the conference.

'I'm busy,' Price said, and left her to it.

Alison stood at the door offering a leaflet to every man who left the room. There were no takers. She still had the full pile in her hand ten minutes later when Major Norton approached her. Save for one or two stragglers, he was the last to leave.

'Please accept my apologies,' he said politely. 'If you give them to me, I'll make sure they're distributed. You can assure the coroner that we will all be there.'

Jenny and Alison spent a tense few hours in their respective offices making preparations for the start of the full inquest later in the week. But the expected phone calls and emails failed to materialize. There was no furious communication from Claydon White, no threats of appeals to the High Court and no requests to send in teams of highly paid pathologists to overturn Dr Kerr's findings. The silence was as unnerving as it was unexpected. Sergeant Price excused himself after the morning hearing and said he would be occupied for the rest of the day on other duties. He gave no indication what they might be.

During her lunch break, Jenny performed a rapid sweep of the principal online newspapers and found several early reports of her inquest's opening session. All led with the information that traces of alcohol and cannabis had been found in Private Green's body, but each also went to considerable lengths to explain that the amounts involved were at the threshold of testing tolerance. One article went so far as to suggest that the alcohol residue could have been caused by as little as a teaspoon of cough medicine or by eating fruit that had fermented in the heat. Someone had evidently been working the phones and twisting arms. Whether it had been the MOD, Claydon White or a combination of both, she could only speculate.

A team of four nurses, provided by the private laboratory Jenny had engaged at great expense to carry out the tests, arrived at the camp shortly after three o'clock. A fifth nurse had been dispatched to Selly Oak to collect samples from Privates Dale Carter and Lee Roberts. Usual protocol would have dictated that Alison oversee the procedure, but she agreed with Jenny that they would need as many pairs of eyes as possible to ensure that there could be no possible tampering with samples. Any question mark over the process – the merest possibility of samples having been mishandled, mislabelled or mislaid – would open the door to a legal argument claiming a break in the evidential chain.

They joined the nurses – two male, two female – twenty minutes before the doors to the gymnasium were due to open. Prelabelled sample bags had been set out on a registration table. Nearby, two screened-off cubicles had been set up in which hair samples would be taken from each man's head and body. As far as Jenny could ascertain, the system appeared foolproof.

She withdrew to a seat at the far corner of the gym and left Alison to oversee the practicalities. A low babble of voices outside the main door indicated that her main fear – that she would have to enlist the civilian police, and perhaps even the military police, to round up unwilling participants – had proved unfounded. Alison unlocked the doors as the bell of St Mary's church struck four. The men of 2 Platoon, all dressed in identical regimental PT kit of black vests and white shorts, filed in. Major Norton was at their head, Sergeant Bryant at the rear. On Bryant's order, they formed into two rows.

Every single man had shaved his head.

After a moment's silence, Jenny got up from her chair and walked across the wooden floor, her footsteps echoing off the bare walls. She stopped several feet in front of Major Norton and looked along the row. She could see that it wasn't just the men's heads. Arms, legs and chests were all freshly shaved. It was safe to assume the rest of their bodies had been similarly depilated. The twenty-four underweight and hairless men made a disturbing sight: like convicts in a prison camp.

'Who ordered this?' Jenny said.

'No one,' Major Norton said.

'Then who suggested it?' She was dangerously close to losing her temper.

'We received legal advice to the effect that we were entitled not to incriminate ourselves or run the risk of doing so.'

'From Colonel Hastings?'

'I don't feel at liberty to say. Nor do I believe that it's required of me.'

'That may be so, Major, but the fact that this happened at all will be evidence at the inquest. What the jury will make of it, I've no idea.'

Norton was unmoved. 'Will that be all, Mrs Cooper?'

'For now, yes.'

'All right, lads, off we go.' The informal order was issued by Sergeant Bryant, who herded them out of the door.

Jenny apologized to the medical team for their wasted afternoon while silently fuming at the connivance of the lawyers and officers who had hatched the plan to frustrate her attempts to collect critical evidence. Meanwhile, Alison was making a phone call to see how the nurse dispatched to Selly Oak had fared. She rang off and shook her head.

'Same story there with Carter and Roberts.'

'Isn't Carter in a coma?'

'He won't have been able to object, then, will he?' Alison said with a shrug. 'What happens next?'

Jenny had reached the end of her tether. She knew that if she stayed in Highcliffe a moment longer, she would be in danger of doing something she would later regret. 'I'm going home,' she said to Alison. 'I'll see you tomorrow.'

Jenny's temples were still throbbing as she sped across the Severn Bridge. It was only when she had fully plunged into the green folds of the valley beyond that she felt the pressure begin to subside and the angry words that had filled her head give way to softer voices. The late-afternoon sunlight filtered through the branches of the trees that formed an unbroken canopy over the road. Here and there, a glimpse of the river winding through the gorge. The warm air flowing through her open windows carried the musky, mossy scent of the woods. On the last leg of her journey she passed a small meadow that was being mown for a late crop of hay and the car filled with the smell of freshly cut grass. Summer was gently ripening into autumn.

Michael's car was parked outside the cottage but there was no sign of him in the house. Jenny changed and showered and took some tea out into the garden. She was determined to savour a few minutes' peace before daring to look at her emails and deal with the fallout of the day.

He appeared a few minutes later. He'd been out for a walk, he said, but seemed preoccupied. There was no trace of the smile that he had worn all weekend.

'Thanks for the text,' Jenny said, sensing there was something amiss. 'It came just at the right moment. You'll never guess what happened, though.'

He sat in the chair alongside her. 'They were never going to do what you asked.'

'They shaved themselves. Every last one of them.'

Michael smiled. 'What did you expect? Anyway, so what if they had the odd joint? Would you really hold that against them? You'd want something to take the edge off if you were stuck out there.'

'No one made them. They are volunteers.'

'Moot point. I never felt I had much choice. My dad had me signed up from birth.'

Jenny reached for his hand. 'Are you all right?'

'I feel fine,' Michael said. He sighed. 'But apparently there were "possible anomalies" in my ECG that require "further investigation".'

'Anomalies? What does that mean?'

'Couldn't – or wouldn't – tell me. I had a phone call this afternoon – not from the doctor, from some receptionist or other. Apparently, my licence is suspended until further notice. I'm to see a consultant sometime in the next few weeks.'

'Have you told the company? What do they say?'

'They're making all the right noises for the moment, but when you're on a monthly contract you're as easy to let go as the window cleaner.'

'It's bound to be all right. You've never had anything wrong before.'

Michael nodded as if trying to convince himself. He gazed out at the garden, keeping his thoughts locked inside.

'There's something you're not saying,' Jenny said.

'You have to admit – there's something odd about the timing.'

'You think your medical is connected with my inquest? I know how pressure can be brought to bear, but it's a bit of a stretch to interfere with your medical, don't you think?'

'You'll know better than most, Jenny.'

'Can't you see another doctor – get this sorted out?'

'There's a procedure. It could take weeks.'

They looked at each other, sharing the same irrational but nevertheless potent fear.

'If you can make your opponents doubt their sanity, you're most of the way to winning,' Michael said matter-of-factly.

Inside the house, the phone rang.

'I'll go,' Jenny said.

The pressure inside her skull had returned, and more powerfully than before. For once she answered the phone begging for it to be a sales pitch.

'Jenny? It's Simon.'

She braced herself for a rebuke and wondered why it hadn't come sooner. But he made no mention of the abortive drugs test.

'There's been a development,' he said. 'This isn't yet for public consumption, but the body of the missing soldier, Private Peter Lyons, has turned up. Dumped at some crossroads. In several pieces, from what I can gather.'

'I see,' was all Jenny could find to say. It wasn't unexpected news, but she realized that she had held a picture of Lyons in her head – assembled from fragments of information she had gathered over the previous ten days – as a cheerful, mischievous boy. The thought of another young life snuffed out, another grieving family, filled her with despair.

'It obviously changes things somewhat. It would make sense to combine the inquests, of course. We can't think of any good reason not to. The Chief would like a word with you in the morning. The earlier the better. Maybe you could jump on a train tonight? We'll stand you a room at the Langham. I might even join you for a nightcap.'

Standing barefoot in her cottage kitchen, Jenny couldn't have felt less like embarking on an evening dash to London, less still like enduring an awkward date with Simon Moreton. But however politely it had been put, she realized this wasn't a request she was at liberty to turn down.

'I could probably make the eight o'clock train,' Jenny said. 'And just about be on parade at ten.'

'I'll be in the bar at five past. See you later.'

She set down the phone and turned to see Michael in the doorway.

'The body of the missing soldier's been found,' Jenny said. 'It looks like I'll be conducting a double inquest.'

'And you're willing to take it on? You're shooting off to London the moment they snap their fingers? I thought you were meant to be independent. Why don't you say no?'

Jenny couldn't answer.

'I'll tell you why – you don't think you could trust anyone else,' Michael said. 'And they know that.'

'Michael, we've both had difficult days. Now's not the time.'

'You think today's been difficult? If my medical was a shot across the bows, I don't like to think what the main event is going to look like.'

'You're reading too much into it,' Jenny said. 'You're upset. Of course you are.'

'Well, you've clearly made up your mind,' Michael said. He shrugged. 'Let's hope I'm wrong.'

EIGHTEEN

Anna Roberts was in no mood to be told that visiting hours were over. It had taken her nearly five hours to travel a hundred miles: a local bus from Highcliffe to Bristol, a National Express coach to Birmingham and another bus to Selly Oak. She would have half an hour with Lee at most before having to do it all again in reverse. If she missed the last coach, her bed for the night would be a bench somewhere in Birmingham city centre. The nurse listened to her story but repeated the line that relatives weren't admitted after seven thirty. She was very sorry, but if they bent the rules for everybody the patients would never have any peace.

Anna tried explaining that she wasn't asking for the rules to be bent for everybody, just for her, and just this once, but her words fell on deaf ears. Anger and frustration overwhelmed her. She gave up trying to be reasonable and simply walked on past her towards the ward.

'Madam—' the nurse called after her.

Anna ignored her and pushed through the door.

There were eight beds in the room. Lee's was at the far end on the left. Anna headed for it, then stopped halfway across the floor, not recognizing the shaven-headed man propped up on pillows. Only when he turned to look at her did she realize that it was him. Everything was gone – even his eyebrows.

She hurried over and pulled the curtain to give them some privacy. 'What the hell happened to you?' she whispered, unable to disguise her shock.

Lee looked at her with absent eyes.

'It was an order,' he said. 'Something to do with the inquest and tests.'

'She wants every man in the platoon tested for drugs. I was there. Something showed up in Kenny's body – alcohol and cannabis.'

Lee gave a slight shake of his head. He looked strange. Not all there. Anna wondered if he might be heavily drugged.

'That's why I came,' Anna said. 'I knew something was going on. Melanie Norton looks stressed out and no one down in the WAGs Club is talking about Kenny or what happened. It's like a taboo.' She noticed a wheelchair parked at the far side of the bed. 'Is that yours?'

'Yeah.'

'You've been out of bed again?'

He nodded, but his mind – if it was working at all – was elsewhere.

The nurse thrust her head between the curtains. 'You can have ten minutes,' she hissed. 'There are people in here trying to sleep.'

'OK. Thanks.' Anna struggled to remain civil.

The nurse finally left them alone.

'They treat you like kids. It's worse than the army,' Anna said.

Lee hadn't seemed to notice.

'You look sleepy. Is it the morphine?'

'I suppose.'

Anna took his hand and squeezed it. He made a feeble attempt to squeeze hers back.

They sat in silence. Anna's mind was racing, churning

over why a man who had had his legs blown off would have been treated this way. What were they trying to hide? Something was badly wrong. Lee seemed more depressed now than he had days ago. She could see it in his face. He looked like the life had been sucked out of him, as if he had given in. He hadn't even asked after Leanne.

'Leanne's over at Sue and Mike's,' Anna prompted. 'She's staying the night.'

No response.

'What's going on, Lee? You've got to talk to me. It took hours to get here and they're kicking me out any minute.'

'Skippy's dead. The sergeant here told me they found him on the road.'

Anna absorbed the news and tried to use it to remind herself that things could have been so much worse. Then she thought of Kathleen alone in her flat. As far as she knew, she was Skippy's only family.

'You knew though, didn't you?' she said. 'You knew he was dead.'

Lee nodded.

She decided to ask the question that had been weighing on her mind for days. 'How did it happen, Lee? How did he get snatched from under your noses?'

He remained still and silent, then shrugged.

'You do know something. I know you do. Why can't you tell me? . . . Lee? . . . Please?'

He turned to her, his empty eyes looking at her and through her at the same time. 'I shouldn't be here. I should be dead.'

'No, don't say that. It'll get better. Everyone says so. You'll be starting physio soon . . .'

Lee sank back into the pillows and stared at the ceiling. 'If you don't want to come back here, you don't have to.'

Anna tried hard not to cry. 'You've lost a friend. You're

bound to be feeling down.' She gripped his hand tighter, but got nothing back. 'Look, there's something else I want to tell you.' She dropped her voice to a whisper, 'I had a visit from some lawyers – the ones who are looking after Sarah – Kenny's fiancée. They said if the army have been negligent, you'll be in line for some money. A lot of money. Enough that we won't have to worry.'

She waited for his reaction, but none came. He didn't even turn his eyes to her.

'Lee, did you hear me? . . . Lee? If they're hiding something you need to tell me. It's important – for all of us.'

He sank further into the pillow with a soft groan. His lack of hair and eyebrows made him look like a corpse.

'We'll talk again, hey? I'll come again soon. I'll manage it somehow.' He didn't react. Anna felt herself start to panic. She could hardly bear to see him like this. She leant over and kissed his cheek. 'Sleep tight, babe. Be strong. We're going to get through this.'

He didn't answer.

It had been a mistake coming this late in the day: they gave him more drugs at night to help him sleep through. No one could be themselves on that much medication. She would probably behave the same way in his position. Give it another week and he'd be smiling again and turning his mind to the future like the other men in the ward.

These were the thoughts with which Anna consoled herself as the nurse ushered her out and she began her long journey home.

Kathleen was fetching her coat from the staff rest room when Phil Peters, the deputy manager, popped out of his office and asked for a quick word. It was past eight o'clock. She'd been working the till since midday and her back was as stiff as a board, but she obeyed without complaint. She left the whining to the young staff.

'Have a seat, you look a bit tired,' Phil said as she stepped into his office. He was around thirty, but his hair was already thinning at the temples and he was showing the beginnings of a paunch.

'I'm fine,' Kathleen said. She sat on the chair in front of the cheap desk. The air in the windowless room was stale and smelt vaguely of souring milk.

'I keep meaning to ask – any news of your grandson?'

'Not yet.' She hadn't mentioned Pete at work and preferred to keep it that way.

Phil seemed to take the hint and glanced at his computer monitor. 'I was just checking to see the last time you took any leave. You've had none since Christmas. You've even worked two bank holidays.'

'Really? Time goes by so quickly,' Kathleen said, and for a moment allowed herself to believe that she'd been called in to be congratulated, or perhaps even rewarded.

'I know you've had a lot of worries, but it's not a good idea to push yourself so hard. We all need balance.'

'Of course,' Kathleen said, while at the same time asking herself what right this boy had to lecture her.

Phil laced his fingers together on the desk, wearing a serious expression. 'At least having seen this I've got an idea of what might have caused the recent problems.'

'Problems?' Kathleen said, feeling her face flush with alarm.

'Your last few shifts – the till hasn't reconciled. Twenty-three pounds off on Friday, thirty-four pounds adrift on Saturday.'

Kathleen shook her head. She'd been known to be a pound or two out occasionally, but never by this much. 'They were busy days. You were here – you saw it.' She heard the defensive note in her voice and wished she could start again. 'It shouldn't have happened. I don't know how it did,' – with every word she seemed to dig herself in deeper – 'I'll make it up in extra hours if you like.'

Phil gave a sympathetic smile. 'Maybe you should take a few days off, Kathleen? Recharge the batteries.'

'No, I don't need to do that. Really. I prefer to keep working.'

It wasn't true. She was exhausted, but at the same time she knew that if she were to stop, even for a day, she'd come down with something and be off her feet for a week. She longed to ask for a guarantee that she wouldn't be one of the names considered for the redundancies they all knew were coming, but was too afraid. At the very least she knew that once she raised the issue he would turn it around and invite her to think of it as a positive step. She could hear him saying it: 'a breathing space while you consider new opportunities'.

In their exchange of looks Phil seemed to read all of this and more. He may have been young, but there was a reason why they had made him assistant manager: he handled staff in the same way a shrewd farmer did cattle. Outward fondness was matched with a ruthless acceptance of the facts of life. He could measure the health of his stock with a glance. And he knew to get a tiring beast out of the yard before it became a liability.

'I'll tell you what we'll have to do then, Kathleen,' he said, spreading the responsibility amongst invisible associates. 'Seeing as you're quite sure tiredness isn't to blame, we'll have to give you a warning and continue to keep a close eye. I'm sorry, but you know how it is. It's the same for everybody.'

Kathleen nodded. 'I'll be certain to take extra care.'

'But don't feel you have to slow down,' Phil added.

'Remember that in this war we're in with the discounters, till speed is everything. If we can make it even two per cent more convenient here, this is where the punters will spend their cash.'

Two per cent. He'd let it slip – perhaps on purpose, perhaps not. All the staff knew that their performance could be measured to within a fraction of a second. Somewhere on his computer there would be charts that would tell him how many items she had scanned in any given minute during the last ten years. Other charts would show her performance day to day, week to week, month to month. The worsening arthritis in her fingers would show up as the slightest downward movement in the line on the graph, and on the days when her back had played up there would be V-shaped dips that would drag her average lower. Meanwhile, the young girls, for all their gossiping and complaining, were moving gradually in the opposite direction. Two per cent: every extra half-second it took to turn a tin of soup in aching fingers in search of its bar code was another step closer to the end.

'Well, have a nice evening,' Phil said. He opened the door for her and sent her on her way with a smile.

Kathleen walked home along pavements speckled with drizzle and tried not to brood on her encounter with Phil. She didn't have much of a faith, but what she did have, aside from some snatches of hymns and a handful of Bible verses, was a belief that everything happens for a reason. Life had always seemed to her to be a series of tests and trials. Why some had to suffer more than others was the only mystery, but the older she got, the more she accepted that there could never be an answer to that in this world. You could only do your best with what you were given. Compared with many others, she was lucky.

It was only as she approached the gateway to her block

that she lifted her gaze from the ground in front of her. She saw the shiny boots and dress trousers first, and knew before she arrived at the soldier's face that it was Sergeant Price. He was standing with his hands clasped in front of him like an undertaker. The silent young Corporal Benson stood at his side. Although Kathleen had been expecting this moment, she felt her legs wobble beneath her. She steadied herself on the gatepost.

'It's not good news, I'm afraid, Mrs Lyons. Would you like us to come inside?'

She shook her head.

'Would you like me to—'

'Yes. Please be quick.'

'A soldier's body was found at a crossroads near the village of Shalan-Gar this morning. The identity tag is that of your grandson. According to the limited information we have so far received,' Sergeant Price faltered briefly, 'Private Lyons was murdered by his captors. I'm afraid that's all we can tell you at the moment. Please call at any time.'

He offered her a card. She took it from his hand, but immediately dropped it. His colleague picked it up from the ground and placed it in her hand, unable to meet her gaze.

'I'd like you to know that all his comrades consider him a hero, Mrs Lyons. I'll be in touch.'

Kathleen walked slowly through the silent flat and stopped in the centre of her living room. It was quiet. The only sound, that of the breeze gently rattling the window. She looked at the row of framed photographs arranged along the mantel over the gas fire. Her life in pictures: her long-dead parents, a cheating husband, the daughter he drove away, the grandson conceived by accident, now dead at eighteen. She had wanted to care for him, to set him along a straight road, but it had taken all she had merely to keep him clothed and fed. His inexhaustible, restless energy would have sapped a strong man, let alone a woman of her age.

She wished she could weep, but all she felt was a cold, hard rage at the waste of the beautiful boy she had let slip through her fingers.

NINETEEN

Jenny awoke from the semi-doze in which she had passed the ninety-minute train journey to the faintly bitter ammonia smell that invariably seeped into the carriage as soon as the fields of Berkshire gave way to the outer sprawl of the city. It was the signature of the London railways and existed nowhere else. The air grew staler and more humid the closer they drew to Paddington. There, she stepped on to the platform into the sultry heat of the late evening and all the unwelcome odours of a busy station in the dog days of summer. Her fellow passengers jostled impatiently in their race for the ticket barriers and most sped on across the concourse to the Tube station as if fleeing from some threatening catastrophe.

Recoiling from the prospect of travelling underground, Jenny swallowed the expense of a taxi. The journey across the West End to Portland Place was short, but took in enough of the capital's wealthy heart for her to wonder at the extravagance on display, while at the same time giving thanks that her life wasn't confined to its skyless streets. London, she felt, had a high conceit of itself that bordered on the ridiculous. Cars that cost as much as houses sat in traffic with no audience to admire them; bars and restaurants that strained to outdo each other in fashionable chic merged into an indistinguishable blur. It was somewhere and nowhere; a city that in its bewildering collision of cultures and styles defined itself by offering something of the exotic essence of everywhere else. You can have anything you desire all at once, it seemed to say. A place for restive, rootless spirits and dream chasers.

But even as she had these uncharitable thoughts Jenny was aware of their source. She had had to go to ground in the country to find her equilibrium. The moment she was cut off from the steady pulse of nature she began to lose her bearings and become, by slowly ratcheting degrees, ever more anxious. The streets that held so much excitement and promise for some were, in the depths of her subconscious imagination, a labyrinth, the walls of which were steadily closing in. She supposed this made her something of a 'city-phobe', if such a word existed. To maintain her balance, Jenny needed anchors, a sense of place, of permanence, a viewpoint from which to establish her bearings. Some years before, the psychiatrist who had helped her regroup after her 'episode' had explained to her how much of the brain's efforts go into editing out what the senses relay. It had struck a chord and she had learned to lower her input, to focus her attention on the elemental things her work required: life and death; truth and lies. She needed to exist apart from the chaotic rush in order to see clearly. She couldn't afford to be dazzled.

Avoiding the lift in the Langham (another of her many inconvenient phobias), Jenny climbed the six flights of stairs to her room where she performed a quick change into a pair of tight, uncomfortable heels and the one black dress she possessed. In her haste, she had forgotten to bring any jewellery or make-up. She had to make do with the lip gloss and a stub of eyeliner pencil that lived permanently in the pocket of her handbag. She went downstairs feeling respectable rather than glamorous, but nevertheless distinctly underdressed as she stepped into the Langham's famous cocktail bar, the Artesian. It was a busy evening and the patrons were conspicuously wealthy and international: the kind who travelled in limousines and first-class cabins and seemed only to acknowledge those who were members of their caste. Jenny anxiously scanned the room and finally spotted Simon lolling comfortably on one of the scallop-backed purple leather sofas at the far end of the bar. He looked very content to be among the moneyed elite, passing himself off as one of their number.

As she crossed the floor, Jenny felt the subtle evaluating glances of women glad to see that their diamonds hadn't been outshone or their slender waists upstaged. It was a strange place to be talking about death in the Afghan desert, but she had grown used to such incongruities in her deal-ings with Simon. The more thorny the subject, the more refined the location he would choose in which to discuss it. He relied on her being too embarrassed to make a public scene.

Simon rose to greet her with a warm, soft handshake and a presumptuous kiss on the cheek. 'Jenny – so sorry to call you in at such short notice.' He smelt faintly of gin. 'Will you join me in a Martini? They mix the best in the world, apparently.'

'Why not?' She couldn't recall the last time she had drunk cocktails. She couldn't even be sure what a Martini consisted of.

Simon nodded to the barman and made a circling gesture with his index finger. Apparently this sufficed to order two more of what he was already drinking.

'The Chief sends his apologies,' Simon said, as they set-tled into seats opposite one another. 'He would like to have been here this evening but he's a lot on his plate – that ghastly business in Lincolnshire last week.'

He was referring to a warehouse fire that had incinerated nearly a dozen illegal migrant workers. Allegations were flying that the employers had failed to inform fire crews that they were inside. It was a nasty situation that had sparked a minor riot in a nearby market town and embarrassed the junior government minister who served as the local MP. Jenny could understand that the incident was a high priority for Peter Etherton, the Chief Coroner, but she doubted whether it came close in importance to her inquest at High-cliffe.

'Yes, he had to go up there for a couple of days,' Simon continued, 'so I'm afraid you'll just have to put up with me.'

The Chief's motives became clearer still: there would be no face-to-face meeting between them. No possibility of her blaming whatever might transpire on a steer from above.

Jenny felt justifiably annoyed and couldn't contain the fact. 'I thought the whole point of my coming was to meet with him. Has he had second thoughts?'

'Not at all. Why ever would you say that?' Simon appeared genuinely bemused. 'He knows we have an under-standing. I assured him I would be able to convey his sentiments.'

'Informally, away from the office – without the inconveni-ence of someone keeping a note?'

'Oh, Jenny . . .' Simon gave a look of faux exasperation. 'You're not in one of those moods, are you? We are all trying to do the same job, you know.'

A waiter arrived with their drinks. Jenny noticed Simon steal a glance at her neckline as she was momentarily dis-tracted by the task of lifting the delicate, top-heavy glass to her lips. He never changed.

'Delicious, isn't it?' he said, with a glowing smile. 'Makes one nostalgic for the days of curling smoke and tinkling pianos.'

He was right: it was an exquisite drink. Gin and vermouth mixed with a wisp of lemon peel. Since she'd missed dinner, the first sip went straight to her head.

It was lazy of her, but she allowed Simon to drift off into his usual routine of mildly flirtatious small talk while she drank. The alcohol relieved her tension along with the niggling worry she had carried with her all evening about Michael's medical. By the end of her first Martini she was in the moment, her earlier self-consciousness forgotten.

Another round of drinks had arrived by the time Simon steered the conversation back to the purpose of their meeting. 'We heard about the shaven heads this afternoon. The press haven't got hold of it yet, but I'm sure it'll only be a matter of time.'

'Who told you?' Jenny asked.

'I called your officer for an update. I had a suspicion Hastings wasn't going to let you get your way.'

'You're not in communication with him?'

'Of course not. He'll be under strict instructions not to speak to anyone outside the army, in any event. He's just a colonel, after all. The real tussle here's going on right up at Chief of Staff level.'

'Tussle for what, precisely?'

'Power. Leverage. Influence.'

'I suppose I should be grateful for your honesty. At least I know where I stand – in the middle of a battle zone, from the sound of it.'

'The army's feeling got at. Of course, it is – its reward for thirteen years of attritional war is having its budget and personnel cut to the bone. The last thing it wants is criticism for incompetency on top of all that.'

'And you expect me to do what, precisely?'

'Your usual, very thorough job, of course.'

'And you've brought me all the way here for that?'

Moreton smiled and touched his hand lightly to the bare flesh of her arm. 'I wanted you to hear from me in person – we'll back you to the hilt – just try not to fall into any more bear traps.'

'That sounds like qualified support . . .'

'Not at all, Jenny. Trust me.' He squeezed her wrist. 'Now – Private Lyons. Are you happy to hear the case together with that of Green?'

'A cynic might say that lands me with a lot of responsibility others might be eager to avoid.'

'Can you think of anyone who would do it better?'

Jenny took a large sip of Martini. 'It's a peculiar feeling, Simon – on every other occasion I've found myself with a contentious case, you've been the one trying to put the brakes on me.'

'In a way I am, Jenny. They'll want to trip you up, discredit you. All the Chief and I want is for you to do your best and protect the reputation of the Coroner's Service. We have every faith in you.'

Jenny eyed him suspiciously. 'I still don't see why you brought me here.'

Simon stared thoughtfully into his glass, then glanced up with what Jenny supposed was meant to be an enigmatic smile, but which several cocktails had made a little crooked. 'Think about it – you *are* being trusted with a big responsibility. Good jobs don't go unnoticed – or unrewarded.'

'I'm not sure I follow.'

Simon gave a sigh of mild exasperation. 'Do you really want to be Severn Vale District Coroner for twenty more years? Peter won't be doing his job forever. And you know you'll always have a champion in me.'

'Oh,' was all Jenny could find to say. She wasn't sure whether to be flattered or unnerved. It was at moments like this, she suspected, that people like her were invited to step

over that invisible line into the realm marked 'Establishment'. It was a place where understandings were tacit and
trust implicit, where outcomes were arranged by silent nods
and only if required, by the most cryptic and oblique
exchanges. It made her uncomfortable.

'Robert Heaton tried to tell me I'd been given the Green
case because the government wants to embarrass the army.
He thinks this case is being fought as a proxy war in the
scrap over military cuts.'

'Nonsense. Honestly, Jenny – he's just playing mind
games. I asked you because I trust you like no one else.' He
clapped a hand to his chest. 'Have I ever lied to you?'

She thought about it. Then gave the honest answer: 'No.'

'Thank you. You see, you and I, we have an understanding, don't we? We've been through the mill together. We
trust each other. And this case, it's so, so sensitive. I need a
coroner who can handle it with kid gloves but who doesn't
look like a placeman.' He slowly sidled up to the point: 'And
with the political atmosphere being so febrile . . . I need a
coroner I can talk to, who'll keep the lines of communication open.'

The penny dropped. Jenny finally realized what this
evening was all about.

'Simon, are you by any chance being held personally
responsible for what happens at these inquests?'

He looked at her over his glass, but didn't venture an
answer.

'The Chief's got you carrying the can, hasn't he? I
thought he liked you. What have you done to deserve that?'
She sensed she had hit the nail on the head. Simon was
suddenly pensive. 'There must be something?'

'I'm afraid loyalty isn't the valued commodity it once
was,' he said regretfully.

In all the seven years she had known him, Jenny had

never known Simon as anything less than effortlessly confident. Now she saw it for what it was: a confidence that
stemmed from having a safe and guaranteed sinecure in the
civil service. With his security threatened, she was glimpsing
the frightened creature beneath.

Jenny offered a sympathetic smile and tried to resist revel-
ling in a sense of schadenfreude. 'Do you want to tell me?'

Simon stared disconsolately into space. 'It's a long story.
Not one for this evening.'

'Fair enough. I can't say I'm that interested in your machin-
ations, anyway.' She drank the last of her cocktail. 'I'll deal
with Private Lyons's case – it makes sense to hear them
together – but I'm no one's puppet. I'll play it how I see it.
Are we clear on that?'

'Yes. Thank you.'

'Well, if that's it, I'll say goodnight. The cocktails were
delicious.'

Simon looked at her pleadingly. 'Won't you stay a while,
Jenny? We're off the leash, for goodness' sake. Let's have a
cognac.'

She considered the offer. It wasn't yet late, but Simon had
the vaguely desperate air of a man daring himself to do
something he might regret. 'Promise to behave yourself?'

'I can only try my best.' He got unsteadily to his feet and
headed to the bar. 'We'd better make it large ones.'

Anna Roberts sat alone in the corner of the WAGs Club
with a splitting headache that several aspirin had failed to
shift. The excited screams of the kids on the other side of
the hall cut through her like knives. It had been nearly
three a.m. by the time she'd crawled home from her round-
trip to Selly Oak and she had lain restlessly awake until
dawn. An hour later she'd been up and making breakfast
for Leanne and the teenage babysitter who had spent the

night on the sofa. An image of Lee's forcibly shaven head had stuck stubbornly in her mind and refused to leave. It added insult to injury. He had seemed humiliated. Defeated.

The atmosphere amongst the other women in the hall was subdued, too. There were fewer here than usual, and those who were scattered among the tables were mostly keeping to themselves or talking in pairs. Talking – from what Anna could overhear – about anything other than what had happened in the gym the previous afternoon or the news about Pete Lyons. It was the survival instinct at work: she could see it in their guarded looks and occasional twitchy glances in her direction. If their menfolk were under threat, so were they and their children. Anna was a living reminder of how quickly their lives could be turned upside-down, and they were giving her a wide berth.

She went to fetch more coffee from the urn that stood on the counter of the serving hatch. Inside the kitchen behind it, Melanie Norton was washing up at the sink. She looked fraught and preoccupied. Her shoulders were hunched and she was crashing the crockery as she stacked it. Like the others, Melanie had been avoiding her. Anna took her coffee through the open door to the kitchen and closed it behind her.

'Would you like a hand with that?'

'I can manage,' Melanie said, with none of her usual warmth.

Anna knew this was her cue to leave her alone, but instead she reached for a tea towel and started to dry the wet cups and saucers. Melanie barely tolerated her presence. They worked silently for a while before Anna plucked up the courage to speak.

'I saw Lee in hospital last night. They shaved him, too. And Dale Carter.'

Melanie didn't reply.

'You must have heard about Pete Lyons?'

'Yes,' Melanie said, in scarcely more than a whisper. 'Awful. Kathleen didn't answer her door when I called this morning.'

'Knowing her, she'll have gone to work this morning. That's how she copes.'

'I'll try to find her as soon as we've finished here.' She reached for the last saucer. 'Leanne seems bright this morning.'

Anna resisted her attempt to change the subject. She struggled to find her voice and thought she might burst into tears. She forced out the words. 'What's going on, Melanie? Why did Chris make them do that? Were they drunk – is that why it all went wrong?'

'No!' The force of Melanie's reply made Anna start. She dropped the cup she was drying and it smashed on the linoleum-covered floor.

For a long moment, neither said a word.

'This all stinks, Melanie,' Anna said. 'You've still got your husband. Mine's had his legs blown off and wishes he was dead.'

Melanie swallowed and glanced away. 'I don't know what happened.'

'Why don't you ask him?'

'He won't talk to me . . .' Her voice was shaky. 'He's not the same . . . He's changed.'

'You've got to try. For all of us. Please.'

Melanie turned to look at her with a tragic expression that rendered her usually cheerful face unrecognizable.

'Chris is a good man,' Anna said. 'He'll do what's right.'

Stifling tears, Melanie tugged off her apron, threw it onto the counter and hurried out of the door.

TWENTY

Jenny had arranged that Private Lyons's body would be taken straight from RAF Brize Norton in Oxfordshire to the mortuary at the Severn Vale Hospital. She had been assured by a medical officer in Camp Bastion that there had been no autopsy or medical inspection in Afghanistan and that the body would be arriving exactly as it had been found. To make absolutely certain that it was conveyed without a hitch, she drove the seventy miles across country to the airfield late the following afternoon to observe the repatriation.

Jenny was directed by a young airman to park next to a hangar, a short distance away from where the formal proceedings would take place. Already lined up at the edge of the empty runway were more than a dozen officers and men from the regiment dressed in immaculate parade uniform. Both Major Norton and Colonel Hastings were among them. At the end of the row, next to Sergeant Price, stood a diminutive but composed female figure dressed in black, whom Jenny assumed to be Private Lyons's next-of-kin: his grandmother, Kathleen. Several paces in front of them a bearer party of six privates and a sergeant stood at ease. To their right was a bugler and an army chaplain dressed in a crisp white vestment and purple surplice which flapped gently in the light wind. All were silent. A single vehicle was parked off to the left: a black, windowless van bearing the incongruous words, 'Private Ambulance'. Jenny stepped out of the car and stood on the tarmac alongside it.

The low, deep drone of the Hercules's four turbo-prop engines could be heard for close to a minute before its dark grey bulk appeared like a vast, dark angel through the clouds. It slowly descended and touched down with puffs of smoke from its tyres at the far end of the runway. It came smoothly to a halt and taxied towards them. The sergeant called the bearer party to attention. As the aircraft drew closer, Jenny felt a lump form at the base of her throat. Kathleen Lyons retained her upright posture and dignified expression.

The Hercules turned through ninety degrees and came to a halt. The engines fell silent and the propellers were still. The loading ramp descended and came to rest on the ground. The sergeant gave the order and the bearer party marched forward in two columns of three. Marching with short strides, they ascended the ramp and disappeared into the belly of the plane. There followed an agonizing wait, then, on some invisible cue, the lone bugler lifted his instrument to his lips and sounded the first two long notes of the 'The Last Post'. As he continued to play, the bearer party made their way down the ramp in perfect step. First their feet, then their legs, then their bodies appeared, until finally their burden came into view: a coffin draped with the Union flag. Jenny saw the watching soldiers stiffen at the sight of it. Kathleen held her poise, though finally dabbed the corner of her eye as the coffin passed in front of her before being solemnly loaded into the van. The doors closed. The bearer party formed up and, on the sergeant's order, saluted. The van moved off and started on its journey homewards.

Jenny waited while the assembled company dispersed. As Major Norton and Colonel Hastings steered Kathleen

Lyons towards a waiting car, she stepped forward and intercepted Sergeant Price.

'How is Mrs Lyons coping?' Jenny asked.

'Extremely well, all things considered,' Price answered. 'She's a resilient woman. She was at work on the supermarket till this morning.'

'Do you ever get used to these occasions?'

'Never,' Price held his handsome features in a frown. Jenny could see that behind the mask his emotions were churning. It was the first time she had seen this human side of him.

'I was wondering about Private Lyons's kit.'

'What about it?'

'His personal effects – all that. Presumably it was bagged up and shipped home at some point?'

'It'll have come home with the company. I'll make inquiries.' He glanced over at the car. The driver was gesturing to him. 'You'll have to excuse me – I'm travelling back with them to Highcliffe.'

'Would you tell Mrs Lyons that I'll come and see her tomorrow. Perhaps you could arrange a convenient time?'

'Certainly.'

He gave a stiff nod and marched off to the car.

Jenny watched it drive away. Colonel Hastings had a comforting hand placed on Kathleen Lyons's shoulder. She was accepting the gesture, but from what Jenny had seen of her that morning, she was sure that she was as tough as any soldier, if not tougher.

Andy Kerr had agreed to reschedule his day in order to conduct the post-mortem on Private Lyons's body during the late evening. It was a little after nine p.m. when Jenny pulled up outside the mortuary. As they had arranged, she oversaw the unloading of the coffin onto a gurney and its transfer through the rear entrance. They were met inside by Joe, the technician, who had stayed late specially, and the coffin was opened to reveal a zipped-up army-issue body bag. There was little enough room in the overcrowded mortuary as it was, so the body bag was transferred to one of the mortuary trolleys and the undertakers took the empty coffin away.

Determined to ensure the complete integrity of the evidence, Jenny remained alone with the body in the mortuary's refrigeration unit while Joe went to assist Dr Kerr in tidying up their previous autopsy. She tried to distract herself by checking the messages on her phone, but her eyes were inexorably drawn to the bag on the trolley. The dark green plastic revealed contours beneath. Private Lyons had been short and very slim – the undertakers had lifted the bag with virtually no effort – but she scarcely noticed these details. All Jenny could focus on was the fact that the spherical bulge of the skull was a third of the way from the top of the bag and pressed against its outer edge.

'You look pale, Mrs Cooper,' Andy Kerr said, when he eventually pushed through the door. 'Are you all right?'

'I've felt better.'

Andy followed her gaze and evidently saw what the problem was. He gave her a sympathetic smile. 'Why don't you go and make yourself a coffee in my office while I take a look?'

'I'd rather be there. But thanks for the offer.'

Andy nodded, knowing better than to argue with her once she had made up her mind. He grabbed the rail of the trolley and backed out through the swing doors.

Jenny followed behind along the corridor and into the autopsy room, where she immediately reached for a paper mask from the dispenser just inside the entrance. She hastily fastened it over her face as Andy and Joe unzipped the bag.

Inside, there was a second bag. The reason for this soon became clear. Almost the moment the second zip was drawn, an overpowering stench of decomposing flesh overwhelmed the room. Andy and Joe both recoiled. Joe hurriedly drew the zip back up.

'Respirators, I think,' Andy said, wiping tears from his eyes. 'Are you sure you want to be in here, Jenny?'

She nodded and prepared herself for what was to come as Joe crossed to the store cupboard and brought out three respirators.

Jenny pressed the rubber mask tight to her face to form a seal and tried to get used to the feeling of having to make an effort to suck in every breath. Meanwhile, Joe unzipped the inner bag a second time. He exchanged a glance with Andy, who nodded. The respirators were doing their job. Jenny glanced away as they lifted the body onto the stainless-steel table.

'It's not too awful – badly decomposed, of course,' Andy said, his voice muffled by the mask. 'He's been dead for a while.'

Jenny forced herself to look. He was right: the sight that met her eyes was of human remains rather than a recognizable body. She stepped closer, trusting the respirator now, gradually acclimatizing herself to the spectacle on the table. The head had been separated from the body but thankfully Andy had placed it more or less in its correct position. The flesh was gangrenous and bore no relation to living tissue. Her gaze travelled from the feet upwards: heavy army boots rising to the lower calf into which were tucked camouflage trousers. The only clothing on the upper body was a khaki T-shirt. She noticed that the shirt was riddled with what appeared to be bullet holes but there was little in the way of blood stains. Lastly, she noticed the wrists. Dangling from each was the remains of rough hemp twine. It appeared that his hands had been bound together but cut loose at some point.

Andy drew down the magnifier suspended over the table and peered through it at the torso.

'What do you think?' Jenny asked.

Andy was counting the bullet wounds. He finished the task before answering her.

'Twenty-three shots. All fired from the back – these are exit wounds. He'd clearly bled out before they were fired, so I think we can assume that the most likely cause of death was decapitation.'

Jenny shuddered, not in response to any thought, but purely as a visceral reaction. Her overwhelming sensation was of disgust, closely followed by a sense of despair that one human being could do this to another. To a boy.

'He's been dead some time. A week to ten days. It'll be hard to pinpoint exactly.'

'Can we make sure to have plenty of photographs, please,' Jenny said. 'Every stage. And if we can bag and tag every item of clothing?'

'Sure,' Andy said. He looked at her with concern. 'You really don't look well. Sit this one out. Trust me. Do yourself a favour.'

Jenny nodded. Despite her determination to tough it out she was beginning to feel faint. She left Andy to it and retreated to his office to await the results.

The examination took a little over an hour, by which time Jenny had steadied herself with several cups of coffee and managed to catch up with her emails on her phone. Andy entered smelling strongly of antiseptic soap along with the lingering odour of the autopsy room.

'I was as quick as I could be – left Joe bagging up.' He

dropped into the chair behind his desk and slid down in the seat. It had been a long day.

'Did you learn anything else?' Jenny asked.

'I had a look at the stomach contents – there was some undigested rice and vegetables in there along with what I'd guess were dates. Doesn't strike me as typical army rations.'

'So he ate after he went missing?'

'I think that's a fair assumption. But whatever's in the small intestine is different – not much in the way of fibre. Tinned meat, maybe. He hadn't gone hungry for long, is what it amounts to.'

'So he hadn't gone what – more than a few hours between meals? – and he was killed shortly after eating something that could have been fed to him by his captors?'

'That's not an unreasonable conclusion.'

'Cause of death?'

'Decapitated. Struck at the back of the neck with a sword or more likely a machete. Several blows – three or four. At least it wasn't done with a knife.'

The feeling of weakness swept back through Jenny's body.

'As I understand it, these folks are sometimes kind enough to drug their victims before they kill them, so I'll check the bloods for opiates. It may be some consolation.'

Not much, Jenny thought.

'What else?'

'He was very light. The body weighed just over forty-five kilos. That's a hundred pounds, or little more than seven stone. Add fifteen to twenty pounds to make up for lost fluid and he's still a featherweight. Borderline emaciated.'

'All the men come back skin and bone.'

'There are also signs of a recently healed fracture on his fifth left rib. Looks like it might have been quite painful for a while.'

'How painful, do you think?'

'He was obviously able to function, but he would certainly have complained about it. It's the sort of injury that makes it difficult to sleep at night, especially on hard ground.'

'Any idea what could have caused it?'

'There's no way of telling. One for his colleagues, I would have thought.'

Jenny considered what she now knew: however he had gone missing, Private Lyons was wearing at least the clothes he was found in – boots, trousers and a T-shirt. He had been fed something by his captors shortly before his death, and not many hours before that he had consumed a meal of army rations. The evidence, such as it was, tallied with him having been killed the same day that Major Norton led his rescue party into Shalan-Gar. What made less and less sense was how Private Lyons had come to be captured. The fractured rib troubled her. In none of the statements Alison and Sergeant Price had taken from other members of the platoon had there been any mention of it.

Usual protocol was for the pathologist to include all findings in the coroner's post-mortem report, and for the report to be distributed to all interested parties at the earliest opportunity before the inquest. Jenny was always scrupulous about this procedure, but her gut told her that this was an occasion on which she might have to make an exception.

'Can you do me a big favour, Andy?'

'Sure. What?'

'Bury the information about the rib somehow. Maybe hide it away in a list of general observations – make it ambiguous. But meanwhile take a close look at it. I want to know when it happened, how it might have happened, and exactly how it would have affected him.'

'I'll do my best.' He gave a concerned smile. 'You seem

like you could do with a holiday, Jenny – you're all wound up and twitchy.'

'I'm OK.'

He shook his head. 'I haven't seen you like this in a long time. You need to look after yourself.' He leant over and patted the back of her hand. 'Remember – it's just a job.'

Andy's parting words stayed with her as she drove back through the night, along with a mental image of Private Pete Lyons's decomposing remains. They were kindly meant, but couldn't have been more wrong. It was not *just* a job.

Melanie had washed up, wiped every surface until it shone, polished the stove top and bleached every last stain from the sink. Her kitchen was immaculate, as was the rest of the house. She had been cleaning for nearly eight hours, pausing only to feed the girls dinner and later to shoo them to bed. At regular intervals she had paused to pour herself a glass of wine, and through the course of the day had worked her way through two bottles. The rinsed-out empties were now safely hidden outside, deep in the recycling bin. The alcohol had sustained her in a relatively painless haze from which she had managed to smile and chat to the girls and go about her chores. They hadn't noticed that their mother was pleasantly drunk. She hadn't even let them see her drinking.

The kitchen clock, which she kept permanently set five minutes fast, tipped past eleven. She had had no word from Chris since he left home early that morning. All she knew from the few stilted words they had exchanged at breakfast, was that he was going to Brize Norton to meet the body of Private Lyons. They had barely spoken since he emerged from the bathroom the previous afternoon without a hair on his body. He had crossed the landing naked, a skeletal apparition. He had given her such a fright that she spilled the contents of her laundry basket she was carrying down the stairs. Thankfully, the girls had been in the garden and hadn't seen him. When Melanie had asked him what he was doing, he'd said, 'Protecting my men.' No apology. No further explanation. He had simply dressed and left the house.

It was only later in the afternoon that Melanie learned what had happened. The wives of two privates in the platoon had approached her in the street to ask if there was any danger their husbands would be in trouble for what Chris had ordered them to do. She hadn't known what to say, so had fobbed them off with an assurance that no one got in trouble for obeying orders. She had felt herself cringing with embarrassment even as she spoke. She had always been the one they could rely on, the one who put the false rumours to bed. But in that moment she knew that she had lost the right to their trust. And then there was Anna. She could hardly bear to think of her. But how could she not? She had said what Melanie had barely dared think.

The painful memory of Anna's accusing eyes propelled Melanie to the corner cupboard, where, behind the neatly stacked bottles and jars, she kept a bottle of cheap cooking brandy. She grabbed a tumbler and filled it two inches deep. A knockout dose to send her to sleep. She heard the key turn in the front door as she rinsed the empty glass under the tap. Chris appeared in the kitchen doorway and removed his cap.

'Late again. You'll be sick of me saying sorry,' he said woodenly. 'A lot of red tape to tie up after the repatriation.'

'You didn't think to call?'

'I wasn't sure when I'd be finished.'

Melanie looked at him standing there stiffly, a stranger in his own home. His bald head jutted from a collar too large for his neck.

'Why are you avoiding me, Chris?'

'Avoiding you?'

'What is it you're afraid I'll find out?'

'I really have no idea what you're talking about.'

'Do you think I don't know what happened yesterday? Do you think people aren't talking about it all over the camp?'

His shoulders grew even more rigid. 'There are some people who would like to discredit my men. I won't allow that to happen.'

'Anna Roberts came to me today. She knows something went wrong in Helmand. After yesterday, we all do. What is it, Chris? What happened?'

After a short pause, he said, 'I think you may have been drinking. I'll go to bed.'

He turned to the door.

'No.'

Melanie stepped in front of him and barred his way, her back pressed to the door. 'Look at you, for goodness' sake! What do you expect me to do – pretend everything's normal? It isn't. You've never come back from a tour like this. You don't speak, you don't smile, you don't show any feeling. It's not fair, Chris. You're part of a family – you're not entitled to hide away inside your own head. Your first duty is to us, not to the men.'

'Could you step away from the door, please, Melanie. We'll discuss this tomorrow.'

'Now.'

'Please, step away from the door.'

'Or what?'

He looked at her with unmoving eyes.

'You know what you're being, Chris? You know what refusing to talk to me makes you? A coward.'

There. She had finally hit a nerve. The muscles in his jaw twitched. His hairless brow creased into a frown.

'A brave man does not shut out his family and retreat into silence.'

He stared back at her. Speechless. Paralysed. Infuriating.

Melanie was hardly aware of what she was doing as she raised her hand and hit him hard across the cheek. He barely flinched. He seemed to feel nothing. She hit him again and again. He absorbed each blow without a sound; without a flicker. It was like beating a brick wall.

Her eyes flooded with tears. She felt her body convulse as she sobbed. She tried to speak, to say sorry, but the words choked in her throat.

Chris stood impassively, watching her, then, as if his absent soul had returned to his body, he opened his arms and folded them around her. He held her close, cradling her head against his shoulder and stroking her hair.

'I love you, Melanie,' he said softly. 'I don't know why I chose this life. I don't know why it had to be this way. It just did . . .'

He kissed her forehead and tilted her face so he could look at her. He wiped away her tears. She saw the pain and melancholy in his eyes and felt eaten up with guilt and shame for having hurt him, for having been so weak.

'I deserved it,' Chris said, seeming to read her thoughts. 'I've not been any sort of husband or father since I've been back. Please, try to forgive me.'

Melanie felt more tears spill down her cheeks as he kissed her. She didn't deserve to be kissed, but the feel of his body pressed against hers and the urgency of his need forced her guilty thoughts aside. She felt a dam burst inside her and months of bottled up emotion erupt and crash up against the flow cascading out of Chris. They clung to one another, their pasts, their futures and their presents combining into a sensation that seemed in that moment, to encapsulate all the pain they had endured, and all the love that they had ever shared. She knew then that there was no life without him; that they were indivisible.

TWENTY-ONE

Jenny came downstairs, her hair still damp from the shower, to find Michael at the kitchen table dressed in his T-shirt and underwear, reading a letter. The post arrived early at Melin Bach – seldom later than seven a.m. The postman liked to start his round at the farthest point from town and Jenny's house was it. Michael didn't have to say a word for her to know that what he was reading wasn't good news. She glanced at the open envelope as she reached for the coffee pot and saw the Civil Aviation Authority stamp.

'Is it about your medical?'

'They want to investigate the possibility of intermittent arrhythmia, whatever that is.'

'Have you had palpitations?'

'No.'

'Then you probably haven't got it. Why not go to the GP and get a second opinion? I could probably organize something at the Vale if you like – a full-body MRI, if needs be.'

Michael set the letter down on the table. 'There's nothing wrong with my heart. The point is they want me tested once a week for six weeks. Six weeks without a licence. What message does that send to my boss? No smoke without fire, that's what.'

It was too early in the morning to be dealing with Michael's drama. Jenny felt barely awake and was still raw from her visit to the mortuary the previous evening. 'Why don't we have some breakfast and talk about this calmly. There's a way through. There must be.'

Michael pushed his hands back through hair that was beginning to need a cut and seemed to be showing more greys all of a sudden. 'It's not only this. I had a call yesterday – from the RAF.'

'The RAF? How many years has it been?'

'Six. They want to know if I'm free for a "chat" in the next few days.'

'About what?'

'They didn't say.'

Jenny took a slug of coffee and finally felt her blood start to pump. It had been late when she got home. She had sensed Michael was preoccupied but had avoided asking him why. She had had a feeling it would be a difficult discussion.

'But you've an idea. I can tell you have.'

'I expect it's about some incident from the past someone wants to rake over.'

'A combat operation?'

'Can't think what else it would be.'

'Any idea which one?'

He shrugged. 'They've got several hundred to choose from. Them, or whoever it is.'

Jenny grabbed some bread and slotted it into the toaster. 'Can I make you some?'

Michael shook his head. 'I'll eat later.' He screwed up the letter and tossed it into the bin beneath the sink. 'I'm going to shower.' He tried to smile. 'You look nice, by the way.' He kissed her cheek.

'It might just be coincidence,' Jenny said, as he turned to the door.

He nodded. 'Just so we're clear about this, Jenny – I love

you and I respect you, and whatever this is, I promise not to hold it against you.'

She was touched. And not a little surprised. 'You've every right to be cross. We could be in Italy right now.'

'Well, put it this way – if someone's prepared to go to this much trouble, you must be on to something.' He ran a finger down her arm and traced it across the back of her hand. 'You're a fighter. A better one than me. Stick it to the bastards.'

Alison woke early and slipped quietly from under the duvet leaving her partner, Paul, snoring gently. Like her, he was a former detective, but unlike her, didn't have a full-time job to haul him from bed every morning. With the single exception of having married his ex-wife, he had always had the luck of the devil. Through a network of old police contacts, he had managed to secure lucrative part-time work as an insurance investigator which earned him almost as much as Alison's salary. He also managed to schedule his visits so that eight a.m. was the earliest he ever saw daylight. So, as usual, she breakfasted alone in the kitchen of their neat suburban flat in leafy Stoke Bishop.

Over coffee and muesli she toyed with her iPad. She flicked from emails to news sites to Facebook. Scrolling down through her feed she felt the familiar contradictory mixture of boredom and curiosity that accompanied the endless photographs of friends' grandchildren and middle-aged holidaymakers. An old schoolfriend was about to be admitted for cancer surgery – that was bad news. But on the bright side, one of her former colleagues was all set to run a marathon aged fifty-eight and had never felt fitter. There was a moral in there somewhere. She was about to switch off and head into the shower when an electronic chime that she had never managed to cancel signalled the arrival of a message. Curiosity got the better of her. It took her a moment to work out that what she had received was a direct message in Facebook. The sender was Danny Marsh, the young soldier she had tracked down to the pub.

> Hi. Need to know what's all this about Kenny being drunk and stoned on watch? I thought it was just 'traces'. There's ugly rumours going round that Kenny's name is being protected because of his dad. Someone needs to say something before it gets out of hand. People are really angry about Skip. Just a heads-up. Danny.

Alison typed back.

> Hi, Danny – you're right, it was tiny traces. No suggestion he was drunk or anything else. Will talk to Mrs Cooper and see if we can put out a statement. Please feel free to pass this on.

As soon as the message went, Alison picked up the phone and dialled Jenny. She answered from her car with the impatient tone she struck when there was something weighing on her mind.

'Hi Alison, everything OK?'

'More or less. How was the post-mortem?'

'I'll fill you in as soon as I get back to the office. I'm seeing Kathleen Lyons first. If any reporters call, just promise them a press release later this morning. Otherwise, no comment.' She sounded anxious to bring the call to an end.

'I had a DM from Danny Marsh.'

'A what?'

'A direct message. Never mind. He's telling me there are rumours flying around the camp that Kenny Green was drunk on watch and that's what caused Lyons's abduction. He thinks we should put an end to it before it gets nasty.'

Jenny sighed. 'What does that mean?'

'I'm not sure. It doesn't sound good, though.'

'I suppose I'll have to talk to Hastings when I get back. If anything was sure to start rumours it was that performance yesterday afternoon. And as far as I'm concerned, it's on him.'

'Maybe I should draft something – see if we can get it emailed around the regiment. That's the sort of thing Sergeant Price could be doing to make himself useful.'

'He's coming with me to see Mrs Lyons. We'll deal with it when we get back.' She paused, then sighed again. 'Seeing as this Marsh lad trusts you, there's something you could usefully do – ask him to make a statement about Lyons. See if he remembers him suffering any injuries in the weeks before his death.'

'What kind?'

'It's probably best you don't know. See what he comes up with. I'll catch you later.'

Alison put down the phone with an uneasy feeling. She was turning back to the iPad with the intention of sending another message to Danny Marsh when Paul appeared in the doorway. He was dressed in a pair of white Calvin Klein's that showed off the trim waistline he'd been working so hard for in the gym. Not quite George Clooney, but slowly getting there. He smiled and struck a jokey pose.

'What do you think?'

'You don't look a day over forty-five.'

'You wait – another three months of working out, I'll be turning heads.' He smiled, with the same glint in his blue-grey eyes that she had first fallen in love with.

Alison smiled back. She knew how lucky she was to have found a man who was both kind and looked after himself.

Her ex, Terry, had let his stomach flop over his waist almost the moment they left the church. No amount of prompting had ever made him take himself in hand. There was never a thought as to how being married to a man who cared so little for himself made *her* feel.

Paul glanced at the clock. 'You don't have to dash out just yet, do you?'

She hesitated just long enough for her resistance to crumble. Leaving the message to Danny unsent, she followed him back to the bedroom.

Jenny approached the entrance to Kathleen Lyons's block to find Sergeant Price standing looking at the dozens of bunches of flowers and numerous cards heaped either side of the front door. Price looked up with a sombre, pained expression. He had briefly allowed the military mask to slip.

'Good morning, Mrs Cooper. Quite something, isn't it?'

'Yes, it is,' was all Jenny allowed herself to say. She tried not to let her gaze linger on the messages of love and grief lest she embarrass herself.

'May I ask how long you intend this visit to take?' Sergeant Price asked.

'As long as she likes, but not long. It's a courtesy, really – to tell her what to expect.'

Sergeant Price nodded, then glanced away.

Jenny felt a pang of pity for him. Until this moment she had seen him only as an obstructive functionary. It had hardly occurred to her that the subjects of her inquests were his close friends and comrades.

'Are you all right, Sergeant? I can do this alone, if you prefer.'

'I'll be fine. I should be used to this by now. Funny how it takes you sometimes.'

'Did you know Private Lyons well?'

'Since before he joined up. Probably wasn't even sixteen.' He cut the train of memory short and raised his hand to the doorbell. 'Shall we?'

'Go ahead.'

They ascended the stairs in silence. Jenny noticed the dirty yellow walls and the footworn carpet. The common parts of the building felt lonely and unloved.

Kathleen answered the door already dressed for work with the supermarket's blue tabard pulled on over her cardigan. She gave the instant impression of not wanting them to linger. They exchanged formal greetings on the doorstep and Kathleen led them through to the sitting room.

Taking the lead, Jenny explained that she was intending to consolidate the inquest into her grandson's death with that into the death of Private Green. Her job was to determine the cause of death as precisely as she could. This would involve exploration of all the surrounding circumstances. She hoped to discover how Private Lyons had managed to be separated from the rest of his platoon, but there could be no guarantees. All she could offer was her word that she would pursue every possible avenue of inquiry.

'You should also know that a post-mortem was carried out last night,' Jenny said. 'If you wish, I can forward you a copy of the pathologist's report.'

Kathleen glanced briefly at her flat brown shoes, then looked up, still with her emotions fully in check. 'I suppose I had better see it.'

'Of course. And can I ask if your grandson wrote to you at all during the tour?'

'I had a couple of letters. He wasn't one for writing very much.' She smiled for the first time. 'Took after his mother like that. They weren't allowed to say much, of course, not even where they were.'

'He didn't mention receiving an injury of any sort?'

Kathleen's eyes hardened. 'What kind of injury?'

Jenny glanced at Sergeant Price and saw that her question had caught his attention. 'He had a fractured rib. Not serious, but he'd taken a knock of some sort. It's even possible he was struck by a bullet through his Kevlar vest. It may not be significant, but I have to ask.'

'No. He didn't mention anything.' She turned to Sergeant Price. 'But he wouldn't have been allowed to, would he?'

'Maybe not.'

There was a moment of tense silence. Jenny sensed something passing between Kathleen and Sergeant Price that she didn't understand.

Reacting to Jenny's puzzled glance, Kathleen said, 'I don't suppose you'll be asking whether it's right for sixteen-year-old lads to be sucked into the army and shoved out onto the front line as soon as they turn eighteen?'

'I think that would be considered outside my terms of reference,' Jenny said. She glanced again at Sergeant Price and saw the colour draining from his face. 'Although, he was very young and questions surrounding his experience and training may be relevant.'

'If you get them young enough they're not really making a choice, are they? If you take a kid for rides in a tank and give him a trip to the firing range he's bound to think it's all fun and games, isn't he?' There was no question that her remarks were aimed squarely at Price.

'I was helping with recruitment, Mrs Lyons. I was just doing my job.'

'Tell me you believed he was cut out to be a soldier.'

'He was as good as the next man.'

'He was a scrap of a boy.'

Another, more awkward silence descended. Jenny fought

the urge to smooth things over. She wanted to hear what Kathleen had to say.

The grandmother turned her accusing gaze away from Sergeant Price and spoke in a level voice to Jenny. 'I mostly hold myself responsible, Mrs Cooper. I knew it would be prison or the army, but it was the wrong choice. I was weak. I let him go to save myself the hard work and the heartache. I work on a till where I have to ask anyone who doesn't look twenty-five for ID before I can sell them a bottle of cider. We treat grown men like babies while boys like Pete are expected . . .' The words caught in her throat. She swallowed and managed to recover herself. 'While boys like Pete are expected to fight for their lives in a country he couldn't even find on a map. They call them volunteers. How can you volunteer for something you don't under-stand? And what if you change your mind? What then?'

'I'm sorry for your loss, Mrs Lyons. I truly am,' Sergeant Price said quietly. 'Skip was like a little brother to all of us.'

The silence was broken by the sound of the doorbell. Kathleen looked up in alarm.

'Is that something to do with you?'

'No,' Jenny said.

Kathleen got up from her chair and crossed to the window overlooking the street. 'There's a big black car . . .'

Sergeant Price came to her shoulder and followed her gaze. 'They're lawyers. You don't have to speak to them.'

'What do they want with me?'

'I really shouldn't—'

Jenny cut Sergeant Price off mid-sentence. 'We can't tell you whether to speak to them or not, Mrs Lyons. You're fully entitled to representation at the inquest. It's up to you.' She rose to her feet. 'We should be going.' She handed Kathleen a card as she headed for the door. 'Call my office any time. We'll do our best to help.'

Claydon White and Carrie Rhodes were waiting in the entrance hall. White ignored Sergeant Price's hostile glance and addressed Jenny warmly. 'Good morning, Mrs Cooper. Mrs Lyons mentioned you were on your way down. Could we have a brief word?'

'It's all right, I'll deal with this,' Jenny said to Sergeant Price.

He reluctantly exited the building.

'I was wondering what you intend to do about what happened yesterday?' Claydon White said.

'There's not a lot I can do,' Jenny said, 'except infer that those involved may not be inclined to tell the whole truth.'

'You'll say that in court?'

'I intend to, yes.'

'I call it perverting the course of justice.'

It occurred to Jenny that any operator as sharp as Claydon White would have taken care to have the voice recorder on his phone picking up this off-the-record conversation. If he was hoping to trick her into making a compromising remark, he was out of luck.

'Well, how about locking Norton up for contempt? Show him you mean business,' White goaded.

'If I thought for a moment it would get me closer to the truth, I would give it serious consideration.'

'I'm going to let you in on a secret, Mrs Cooper – in the few short days we've been acting for the fiancée of Private Green, my firm has had its email system go down twice and this morning we've had notice from Revenue and Customs that we're about to be audited. If I were a suspicious man, I might be tempted to think these events were not unconnected.'

'Lawyers owe their clients a duty to be fearless, Mr White – as do coroners.' She turned to the door.

'If we're getting the treatment, I'll have to assume you're getting it too. That has implications.'

Jenny paused and looked back. 'It's a little soon to be attacking my integrity, don't you think?'

Claydon White was unabashed. 'I'm just getting it all out in the open, Mrs Cooper. Less than a week old and this whole thing stinks like a barrel of turds already.'

Jenny kept her cool. 'Then you and I must do our best not to make the smell any worse.' She smiled pleasantly at Carrie Rhodes, thinking that she looked too innocent a young woman to be working for a man like White – which, she guessed, was exactly why he had chosen her. 'I'll see you both later in the week.'

Sarah Tanner lay on the couch in the consulting room and winced at the coldness of the gel Dr Pauline Keller was applying to her midriff.

'When did the cramps start?'

'Sometime in the night,' Sarah said. 'I'm not sure what time.'

'Do they come and go or are they constant?'

'Come and go. It's not so bad now.'

'OK. Hold still.'

Dr Keller switched on the ultrasound scanner and moved the probe slowly over her abdomen. Sarah looked over at the grainy image appearing on the screen. It was a little shadowy at first, but then it became clearer: arms, legs, head. It was all curled up in a ball like it was midway through turning a somersault.

Dr Keller glanced across at Sarah's notes displayed on her laptop. 'You've had no other scan since twelve weeks?'

'No.'

'Any bleeding or spotting?'

Sarah shook her head.

Dr Keller took her time, looking at the baby from every angle. Sarah searched for signs of alarm on her face but didn't spot any.

'I don't know if you want to know if it's a boy or a girl?' the doctor said.

Sarah thought about it. 'Go on, then.'

'It's a boy. And he looks fine.'

A boy. Sarah realized that somehow she already knew this. It's what she had felt all along.

'Are you all right?' Dr Keller asked.

'Just thinking,' Sarah said. 'It suddenly seems real.'

The doctor smiled. 'The baby's heart rate is normal. So is yours. And you've no temperature, so it doesn't look like you've got an infection. We'll take some bloods to double-check, but my guess is that it's nothing serious. Sometimes stress can bring cramps on. That's the most likely cause.' She reached for some antiseptic wipes and started to clean the probe. The baby vanished from the screen. 'How are you feeling otherwise?'

Sarah shrugged. Tears leaked out of the corners of her eyes.

'Silly question, I guess,' the doctor said. She handed Sarah a paper towel to wipe off the remaining gel and glanced at the clock. They had already run five minutes over their allotted time. 'Did I hear that there's an inquest coming up?'

'Later this week,' Sarah said, using a corner of the towel to dry her eyes.

'I don't normally like to give a pregnant woman too many drugs, but I think maybe I ought to give you some-thing to help your mood. Would you like that?'

Sarah nodded. Anything to take away the pain. It seemed to get worse every day, not better. At first she had just felt numb, but now it was gnawing at her constantly, never allowing her a moment to forget.

'Here, I'll get you a picture.' Dr Keller hit some keys on her laptop and as Sarah climbed off the couch, a page emerged from the printer on her desk. She fetched it and handed it to her. 'You can pick the prescription up from the dispensary. It may not feel like it now, but it will get better.' Another glance at the clock. 'Straight on the phone if it gets any worse, all right?'

Sarah walked out of the medical centre clutching her print-out and a paper bag containing her tablets. The sun had come out but it did little to lift her spirits. She felt empty and exhausted and the thought of being cooped up in the house trying to avoid Rachel all day filled her with dread. She decided to head into town and sit in a cafe. Maybe later she would have a look around the shops. If the lawyers were right and she came into some money, she might at least be able to buy the baby some nice things.

She turned left towards the bus stop, barely noticing the three young women, one of them pushing a toddler in a buggy, heading her way. Only when she was a few feet from them did she see them looking at her and exchanging glances.

'Bitch.'

The one with the buggy said it, and then the one nearest her, the girl with the waist-length leather jacket, spat in her face. As Sarah recoiled, bringing her hands up to her face, the one in the middle slopped Coke from an open bottle over her shirt.

'Fucking bitch.'

They walked on, gloating and laughing, leaving Sarah standing bewildered and humiliated at the kerb. She wanted to say, 'What was that for?' but the words wouldn't come. She started to sob. Choking back tears, she stumbled across the road and with her hands crossed over her stained shirt hurried towards home.

She saw the police car immediately as she turned the corner into their road. It was double-parked outside the house with the blue lights still silently flashing. As she drew closer she saw Paul on the front path talking to two constables. He had a hand pressed to his face and blood running between his fingers. He was saying: 'They came out of a van, just came straight at me, didn't say a word . . .' Then, in answer to a question: 'They could have been army. Couldn't tell – they had their faces covered.'

Sarah arrived at the gate. She and Paul looked at each other. A deep purple bruise was spreading from the bridge of his nose outwards to his eyes. The blood was from a gash on his cheekbone. Through the open front door she could see an emotional Rachel being calmed by a young female officer.

'Sarah?' the constable said.

She nodded.

He saw that she'd been crying. 'There's been an incident. We think maybe this isn't the safest place for you to be right now.'

TWENTY-TWO

Colonel Hastings seemed almost pleased at the turn of events. He looked at Jenny from behind his desk with the smiling satisfaction of one who was enjoying the feeling of being truly vindicated.

'I was told you would be especially sensitive to the requirements of a military inquest, but clearly not.'

'Requesting relevant evidence hardly amounts to provocation,' Jenny countered. 'I thought this meeting was to discuss your press release.'

Hastings refused to be deflected. 'Whether you intended it or not, you have given the impression that Private Green was drunk while on guard duty and that it contributed directly to the fate of Private Lyons. Perhaps you don't understand the implications of that among a community of men whose lives depend on absolute mutual trust?'

'I was very clear about the nature of the evidence.'

'Sophistry will get you nowhere, Mrs Cooper. You're dealing with private soldiers, not highly educated lawyers.'

'If you'll pardon me for pointing out the obvious, Colonel, it's my job to unearth the evidence and yours to deal with military discipline.'

'That's one approach, but I'll give you fair warning, the atmosphere in camp is febrile. An eighteen-year-old soldier has been decapitated. There's a natural human desire to take revenge for that sort of thing. And the object of that revenge may not be rationally arrived at.'

'I'll do my best not to be inflammatory,' Jenny said with thinning patience. 'Do you want to discuss the press release or not?'

Hastings pushed a single sheet of paper across the desk. 'I don't like having to do this, but it's better than leaving the press to speculate. It's expressed as coming from Chris Norton. He's agreeable.'

Jenny read through the two paragraphs written as if by the major. They stated that he would be telling the inquest that there were no discipline problems whatever in his platoon and that it enjoyed an unbreakable spirit of comradeship. He was deeply saddened by the circumstances of Private Lyons's death and urged all concerned not to prejudge the findings of the inquest, which, he was sure, would examine every relevant piece of information. With hindsight, he regretted frustrating the coroner's attempt to take hair samples from him and his men. He had done so out of concern that doubtful evidence, which in any other context would be dismissed out of hand, might nevertheless be used to undermine the credibility of young soldiers who had consistently proved their bravery and in whom he had entrusted his life.

'It doesn't meet with your approval?' Colonel Hastings said.

Jenny handed it back across the desk. 'What are you asking me to do?'

'I'm sure you'll be asked to comment.'

'I'll decline.'

Colonel Hastings studied her with his soft, disingenuous eyes. 'I need you to know that Chris Norton is one of the bravest, most committed soldiers I have ever had the pleasure of working with. He will never blow his own trumpet, so I have to do it for him. He is probably responsible for the apprehension of more enemy insurgents in both Iraq and Afghanistan than any other soldier in the British Army. He has not only risked his own life on countless occasions, he has saved thousands, maybe tens of thousands. His behaviour over your order was an error in judgement explicable entirely in terms of the fierce loyalty he has to each and every man under his command.'

'I can't endorse what he did, Colonel.'

'I understand that. I'm just making you aware of who it is you're dealing with. The rest is between you and your conscience.'

Jenny sensed that he was trying to send her a message that she was failing to interpret. Was he issuing a veiled threat? Or was his obliqueness simply a means of maintaining an air of mystery designed to intimidate her? The more time she spent in his presence, the more unsettled she felt. He was a skilful manipulator – of that much she was certain – but of whom or what, she wasn't entirely sure.

She decided it was time for a dose of honesty. 'Colonel, why don't you just tell me what's on your mind? It'll make life easier for all of us.'

He looked at her steadily for a moment. 'Very well, since you asked. What's on my mind is the fact that what holds fighting men together is not the protection of the law, it's their faith in one another. Green and Lyons are dead. We wish they weren't. But the idea that picking over their carcasses and trying to find someone to blame other than the enemy is for the common good, is beyond my comprehension. This country of ours is filled to overflowing with decent, liberal-minded people who don't even begin to comprehend what it takes to protect their freedoms. We live in a world of savagery, brutality and butchery, Mrs Cooper. That's the reality: murderous savages who'd hack your head off in the name of religion as soon as look at you. And the reason you and I inhabit this green and peaceful paradise free from their barbarity, is because we have sufficient numbers of young men and women who don't stand on their rights but go out and fight for them.'

'My partner spent twenty years in the RAF,' Jenny said calmly. 'I do understand the level of sacrifice.'

Hastings shifted back in his chair. She could tell that she had surprised him. It was time to bring the meeting to an end, while he was still on the back foot. She rose to her feet. 'I'll be holding a further preliminary hearing tomorrow. The inquest proper will start on Thursday.'

'I wish you the very best, Mrs Cooper,' Colonel Hastings said. 'A truly unenviable task.'

'I'm sure we'll all be relieved to get it underway.' She smiled politely and made her way out.

Heading back along the long corridor, she found Lieutenant Gallagher hovering by the stairs.

'Been in to see the boss?'

Jenny gave a guarded nod.

'I tried to find you in your office – ran into Sergeant Price. You've got him well trained.'

'Nothing to do with me,' Jenny said. 'He was a political appointment.'

Gallagher glanced both ways along the empty corridor then gave her a look that said he might have something for her if she was interested. He turned back up the stairs. Intrigued, Jenny followed him up.

On the next landing, Gallagher checked again that they couldn't be seen, then beckoned her across the corridor to an office marked, 'Captain Ed Lycett'. He produced a key and unlocked it.

'A friend of mine. He's on leave this week.'

They entered the empty office. Gallagher locked the door from the inside.

'Do you think we got away with it?' he said, with a hint of mischief.

'I think so,' Jenny said, indulging him.

'Are we all right to have another word off the record?'

'It's not my preferred way of doing business.'

'Yes or no?'

Jenny sighed. 'OK. Just this once. But don't hold me to anything.'

'I don't know what Hastings just told you, but he went ballistic over Norton dodging your order. I was in here late the night before last, heard the yelling from two floors up. I'm no great fan of Chris's – far too gung-ho for my liking – but I might've done the same thing in his shoes. Men get hold of a little something and sprinkle it in their tobacco, who does it harm?'

'Does that happen?'

'I don't know if it does or not, still less do I care. You're asking young guys to risk a bullet in the head, you've got to cut them some slack and look the other way sometimes.'

'Why are you telling me this?'

'Because I think you're interested in the truth. Norton ran a tight ship. He's got issues, we all do, but he'd have laid down his life for any one of those boys. I wouldn't say the same of our colonel.'

'We'd probably best leave it there. If you want to speak to his character I'd rather you did it under oath. The other thing, I'll pretend I didn't hear.'

She reached for the key in the lock. Gallagher reached out and put his hand on her wrist. 'Hey – there's something else.'

He said it with an urgency that caused her to look into his eyes.

Gallagher held her gaze. 'The rumours about Kenny Green that are spreading through the regiment – Hastings blames you and Norton equally for providing the ammunition, but if you want my opinion there's something else at work.'

'Like what?' Jenny said, aware of Gallagher's hand still resting lightly on her arm.

'People gossip, but this regiment doesn't turn on itself. It must have taken some serious, orchestrated agitation to wind up guys to go and attack a soldier's family.'

'Who do you suspect?'

'I had a phone call last night,' Gallagher said. 'It was from someone asking if I had anything to say about either of your cases.'

'A lawyer? That wouldn't surprise me.'

'That was my impression – or someone working for one. Fortunately, money isn't my current motivation. No wife or kids and no plans for any.' He finally took his hand away. 'You look perplexed. Don't be – the first step to winning is knowing your enemy. Would you like to meet for lunch?'

Jenny swallowed. She had had an odd feeling about the way he was looking at her but had dismissed it as ridiculous. He was twenty-three years old, for goodness' sake.

'Maybe another day,' Jenny said.

'I'll look forward to it,' Gallagher said.

She attempted to unlock the door with clumsy, nervous fingers.

'Here, let me.' Gallagher stepped forward and turned the key. He held the door open for her. 'See you soon, I hope.'

Detached. Clinical. Forensic. These, Jenny decided, would have to be her watchwords from now on. She'd had her arm twisted into conducting her inquiry from inside Highcliffe Camp, but she would have to rise above the egos and personalities crowding in on her. It was time to assert herself and start issuing orders. She began with Sergeant Price.

'What's the latest on Sarah Tanner?' Jenny asked, having summoned him to her office.

'The police are looking for two attackers and Miss Tanner's been moved to another address.'

'They can't look after her in her own home?'

'It's all about the perceived level of threat. Theoretically, soldiers have access to guns.'

'Have we got contact details for her?'

'Still the same number, as far as I'm aware.'

'What about Private Lyons's personal effects? Any progress?'

'I've emailed the stores. I'll go along shortly and see what they've got.'

'You can leave that to me,' Jenny said. 'You'll be busy taking statements from all those in the platoon who haven't yet been asked about Private Lyons's disappearance. I need them all ready to be disclosed to the interested parties at tomorrow's hearing.'

'I suppose that's achievable.'

'It will have to be. Thank you. That's all. Can you tell Alison I'd like a word?'

'She's not here, ma'am.'

Jenny glanced at her watch. It was nearly nine thirty. 'She's not here yet?'

'She arrived when you were with the colonel. I told her what had happened at the Greens' house and she left again. She seemed a little upset.'

'I'll call her. That's all for now. Thank you.'

Sergeant Price seemed surprised at the brusqueness of her tone, but left without a murmur. She would have to channel her inner Boadicea more often.

Jenny pulled out her phone and dialled Alison's number.

It rang six times before her voicemail kicked in. She left her a message asking her to call straight back. It wasn't like Alison not to answer her phone; Jenny was the one who was always dodging calls. And she didn't like the sound of her being upset. It suggested that there was something she knew but hadn't let Jenny in on. Going her own way had become a bit of a habit recently. It seemed to be Alison's way of proving her worth. The problem was that she wasn't quite as competent or trustworthy as she once was. Perhaps it was hardly surprising, since she had lost a chunk of her brain the size of a golf ball.

Jenny turned her attention to her inbox, in which she could see a recent arrival from Dr Kerr. She clicked it open to find a message saying that no traces of alcohol or narcotics had been found in Private Lyons's blood. A full report would be with her later in the day, but it would largely confirm what he had told her at the mortuary. There was also a message from Simon Moreton saying that he hoped she was bearing up and that he would very much like to take her to dinner in Bristol 'somewhere decadent and expensive' when it was all over. Two offers within minutes of each other. She didn't know if it said more about her or men in general.

Sergeant Price knocked on the door and came back in. 'Stores think they've located it. I really don't mind—'

Jenny cut him off. 'Press on with the statements. We've a lot of ground to cover.'

Armed with directions, Jenny headed across the camp on foot in search of the stores. She had some urgent questions for whoever was in charge there.

'Danny? Danny are you in there?' Alison had managed to slip through the main door of the accommodation when a soldier was exiting and had made her way up to the fourth floor. Music from several different radios leaked through the thin doors and mingled in the narrow corridor of a building that reminded her of a student hall.

Having failed to get an answer, she knocked louder. 'Danny, it's Alison. Please. It's important.'

Eventually, she heard footsteps and the sound of the catch being reluctantly drawn back. Danny opened the door, half-hiding behind it. He looked pale and dishevelled. 'Quick. Don't hang about.'

Alison stepped into the small but tidy bedsitter. She noticed that Danny was moving stiffly, clutching a hand to his middle.

'Are you all right?'

Danny gestured her to a chair and lowered himself onto the little two-seater sofa, grimacing as he did so.

'What happened to you?'

He took a moment for the pain to subside.

'Had a bit of a run-in after I messaged you last night.'

'Not you as well. What's going on? When you said rumours, I had no idea that anyone was going to be hurt.'

'Nor did I.'

'Tell me what's been going on.'

Danny was at first reluctant to speak, but after some gentle prompting said that he had first become aware of the rumours early the previous afternoon. He had started seeing Facebook posts saying that Kenny Green was drunk on watch and let the Tali right in over the wall. He had weighed in along with several others to set the record straight, but to no effect. The story had soon been embellished: Kenny was being protected by Major Norton because his dad knew things from his time in Iraq that he'd kept quiet about. By late evening, it had changed again: Kenny and several others had been smoking weed while out on patrol and managed to lose Skippy. It was crazy stuff, completely off the map. All bullshit. Then someone said that one of the lads in 2 Platoon had given a statement to the coroner saying that Skippy wasn't abducted from the post, but never returned from a foot patrol. The others were meant to have left him behind, let the Tali have him rather than risk their lives on the last day of tour.

'No one's given a statement like that,' Alison said.

'I know. And that's what I said to a couple of blokes at the gym who were repeating it like it was a fact . . . Well, words to that effect.' He allowed himself to laugh, but immediately regretted it. 'Could have been worse. He could've kneed me six inches lower.'

Alison smiled. 'You need some ice on that.'

'I'm OK . . .'

Ignoring his protest, she made her way across the room to the pocket-sized kitchen housed in a recess. She dug around in the freezer compartment of the tiny fridge and found a bag of frozen peas buried in a heap of accumulated ice.

'These'll do.' She dried them off with a tea towel. 'There's not much food in there – don't you look after yourself?'

Danny shrugged as he took the peas from her and slipped them under his shirt. 'Thanks.'

Alison glanced around the room and noticed there were no photographs except for a group shot of soldiers posing next to an armoured vehicle somewhere out in the desert. She remembered him saying in the pub that he didn't have relations to go to during his leave. She imagined that the others in the picture were probably the closest thing to family he had.

'Who do you think started these rumours?' Alison asked.

'Can't figure it out,' Danny said. 'People talk crap some-times, but not like this.'

'So why's anyone taking any notice?'

'Because it's Skip, I guess.'

'What do you mean?'

'He was just a kid, wasn't he? Couldn't even shave. He did OK, but none of the lads really thought he should have been out there. No one said it, but we all thought that if someone wasn't going to make it back, it'd be him.'

Responding to an instinct, Alison said, 'You were close to him, weren't you?'

Danny seemed more than a little surprised by her insight. 'I s'pose.'

'And you've no one to talk to aside from your mates?'

Danny avoided her eyes and gave another shrug. It was a well-practised gesture that she noticed he used to disguise all manner of uncomfortable feelings.

Alison knew she should resist getting too involved, but Danny was lonely and grieving and it made her want to comfort him. Why shouldn't she?

'You never told me how you ended up in the army. Was it what you'd always wanted?'

'It was either that or a room in a B and B. I'd seen what happened to the lads who went down that road.'

'You were in care, were you?'

'Council home. Wouldn't call it care, exactly.'

There. The sadness in his eyes. She wanted to scoop him up and hug him.

Alison felt her phone vibrate silently in her pocket. She pulled it out and glanced at the screen. It was Jenny again. Now wasn't a good moment. She returned it to her pocket unanswered and turned her attention back to Danny.

'I'll bet you haven't had a proper breakfast.'

His eyes tracked mistrustfully towards her. They were those of a small boy gauging a dubious promise.

'Tell you what – why don't I fetch some bacon and eggs

from the shop and cook them up for you? You can make me a cup of tea while I'm gone.'

She didn't wait for his answer. She bustled to the door issuing instructions to make it strong and not too milky. As she left, she caught sight of him from the corner of her eye and saw that he was smiling.

The regimental stores were on the far side of the camp and housed in a warehouse clad with corrugated sheets painted ubiquitous military green. Jenny entered a small reception area with windows that looked into the body of the stores: rows of metal shelves stretching into the distance laden with different-sized crates. She was greeted at a front desk by a cheerful West Indian man with biceps that bulged out from beneath the short sleeves of his camouflage tunic. He had a bright smile and a boxer's flattened nose.

'You must be Mrs Cooper.' He extended a shovel-sized hand. 'Jed Harris, Corporal.'

Jenny felt as small as a child in his huge physical presence. 'Good morning.'

He glanced at a computer monitor sitting on the counter top. 'I've located Private Lyons's kit for you.'

'Does your system tell you when it arrived?'

'Looks like it came back with the rest of the platoon.' He clicked through to another screen. 'That's right.'

'Has it been touched?'

'Haven't got to it yet. Everything we had out there's been shipped back in the last week. Each item has to be cleaned, sorted, logged. It's all gone crazy. What do you want done with it?'

'I was planning to take it with me.'

'A sixty-pound pack? Do you have a car?'

Jenny felt suddenly foolish. 'I walked over.'

Corporal Harris grinned. 'I'll give you a lift, don't worry.'

As an afterthought, Jenny said, 'What about Private Kenny Green's kit?'

Harris looked again at the screen. 'It's in the same place.'

'I suppose I had better take that, too.'

She went with him into the body of the building. They walked between two rows of shelves that rose fifteen feet high. The concrete floor was covered with a thin film of pale sand that crunched beneath her shoes.

'Gets everywhere,' Corporal Harris said. 'Sometimes I think we must've brought half the dirt in Helmand back with us. This section's where we keep all the personal kit – each man has approximately forty-three separate items of standard issue on tour – and at the far end's the armoury. You've got radios and electronics over there and most of the rest of the space is taken up with vehicle parts. You want to know where your taxes go – here it all is.'

They arrived at a section of shelving loaded with assorted crates. 'Anything that doesn't belong anywhere else fetches up here – the orphans' section,' Corporal Harris said, and pulled over a wheeled ladder. He skipped up it as lightly as a dancer and came back down with a bulging rucksack. 'That's Private Lyons's stuff.' He beat it with his palm to knock off the worst of the dust. 'See what I mean?' He went back up the ladder and returned with a second pack. 'This one's not so bad.' He picked one in each hand and set off along the aisle, the thick veins curling around his forearms like angry snakes. 'The vehicle's out the back there.'

Jenny said, 'Have you been out to Helmand?'

'Three tours,' Harris said. 'I wouldn't recommend it for a holiday.'

'Were you stationed to a forward command post?'

'Two out of the three.'

'You've heard about Private Lyons going missing overnight from 2 Platoon's FCP?'

'Yes . . .' A trace of wariness entered his voice.

'It may seem a slightly odd question, but assuming he'd bedded down like everyone else, what would you expect him to have been wearing?'

'In the summer, not much. Underwear. Some guys keep their sandals on. Depends how peaceful things are.'

'You have sandals?'

He nodded. 'You're meant to keep them on at all times – even in the shower. In case you have to run for cover.'

Jenny recalled that Lyons's body was recovered wearing tightly laced boots.

'Will anyone have touched that rucksack before today?'

He shook his head. 'I just fetched it from the crate it flew in on.'

'What about his weapon?'

'Rifle, pistol and ammo will be back in the armoury.'

'I'd like you to check that for me.'

Corporal Harris hesitated.

'Is there a problem? Is there someone you have to refer to – a senior officer? I am in rather a hurry.'

'No, I can do that for you.'

'Thank you.'

They headed on down the row towards the armoury.

Harris said that strictly he shouldn't let her inside, but if she wanted to take a quick look, he couldn't see the harm. Jenny said she would like that – she was curious.

The armoury was a small building within a building: a windowless rectangle of concrete and steel accessed through the kind of door she imagined securing the entrance to a bank vault. It took two separate keys and an electronic swipe card to open. Once inside, Harris locked the door again. It closed with an airtight *thunk*. Jenny tried to ward off a rising sensation of claustrophobia as Corporal Harris flicked on a computer and brought up the inventory lists.

There were guns everywhere: rifles lined upright all along one wall, handguns on rows of smaller shelves and bipod-mounted machine guns and hand-held rocket launchers arranged on the floor. The remaining space was taken up with green plastic boxes loaded with ammunition and cases of rockets and mortar rounds. She became aware of a subtle but potent smell that was new to her: a metallic odour mixed with what she imagined was gunpowder. The weapons looked well used and battle scarred. There was something terrifying but at the same time vaguely thrilling about being in the presence of objects that had so recently seen the heat of battle.

'OK – looks like we've got his rifle, but his sidearm is still entered as not yet returned.'

'What about Private Green's weapons?'

He checked the computer again. 'Both here.'

'So Lyons had a gun that never came back?'

'A pistol. Let me make sure that's right.' He scribbled down a couple of serial numbers on a message pad and went to check the racks. He found the rifle, but like the computer said, the 9mm Glock pistol which had been issued at the start of the tour in February hadn't come back.

'Who would have been responsible for returning his weapons?' Jenny asked.

'There's an official hand-in at Bastion. Doesn't matter if the weapon's broken or in pieces, it comes back whatever the condition. If it was lost in theatre, you'd expect a note on the records.'

'Is there a note?'

'I don't see one,' Harris said. 'I'll drop an email to the platoon sergeant, see what he says.' He flicked off the computer, then stared for a moment at the blank screen before looking back at Jenny. 'Look, I really don't want to get involved in any of this. I'm happy in my work here, keeping my head down – if you know what I'm saying.'

'It's unusual, isn't it – not to have a note?'

'I'm saying nothing more, ma'am. I'm just a corporal who's grateful to see a salary at the end of the month.'

He unlocked the door and stood aside to let Jenny out.

Jenny dealt with Private Lyons's kit first. It had been stowed neatly into the three compartments of the rucksack. Down on her office floor on her hands and knees, she removed the items one by one, beginning with the camouflage helmet, and arranged them in rows on the carpet, scattering more of the Helmand dust. The main thing she noticed was how little clothing there was: one pair of trousers, one pair of underwear, spare socks, an undershirt and a tunic-style shirt. Never mind the danger, Jenny thought, the toughest thing had to be surviving six months in the searing heat with only one change of clothes. She found the body armour: a heavy Kevlar waistcoat designed to protect the torso from bullets and shrapnel. It was surprisingly thick and heavy. She examined it for damage, but saw nothing obvious. Down towards the bottom of the pack, she found a pair of open sandals. They looked well used with worn tread and frayed straps. She printed off the kit list Corporal Harris had emailed through and checked off each item. After she had discounted the clothes and boots Lyons was found in, there were seven missing items: pistol, holster, night-vision goggles, bayonet, scabbard, notebook and cigarettes. She took out her phone and took photographs.

There was a knock at the door.

'Come in.'

Alison entered. 'Sorry I went AWOL, Mrs Cooper.' She glanced at the connecting door and spoke in a whisper. 'I was trying to get to the bottom of the business at Sarah Tanner's place.'

'You could have called.'

'I couldn't, really. I was with one of the lads from the platoon – Danny Marsh. He was a bit upset. Is this Lyons's kit?'

'Yes,' Jenny said impatiently. 'Upset about what?'

'He was a good mate of Pete Lyons.'

Now it was Jenny's turn to glance at the door behind which she couldn't help but imagine Sergeant Price straining to hear every word.

'What does he think happened?'

'He's as clueless as everyone else. They all bedded down for the night and when they woke up he was gone. He found this with his things, though. He was going to give it to his grandmother.' From her coat pocket she produced a small, army-issue notebook with plastic camouflage covers. She handed it over to Jenny. Seven missing items had become six. 'I hope you're feeling strong.'

Jenny turned through the pages. Most were filled with jottings of what looked like briefing notes for patrols: sets of coordinates, landmarks to look out for, radio call signs, warnings of areas that might be mined or booby-trapped. Here and there he had doodled and drawn sketches of faces – some of them not bad – of what looked like members of the platoon. Then, towards the back, she had found the letter he had written. It was dated exactly ten days before he went missing. He had taken care to write it neatly in carefully joined-up writing.

Jenny read it through, then waited for the lump in her throat to subside.

'Does Danny Marsh know why he wrote this?'

'He says a lot of the lads wrote their last letter – just in case. Especially if they've had a few close scrapes. He didn't like to say too much, but I get the feeling Norton was pushing them hard right to the end.'

'We'll have to get a copy sent to his grandmother.'

'I'll do it straight away.'

Jenny looked again at the notebook and turned over the remaining pages. She noticed that several at the very back – four or five – had been crudely ripped out. On the remaining stubs were the odd pencil mark. Lyons had evidently written more.

'There are pages missing.'

Alison nodded. She had noticed that, too. Danny had said that's how he had found it – in amongst his kit.

'What else did he tell you?'

'He mentioned the rumours. Doesn't know where they started. He's not sure anyone does. It's like someone's trying to turn the men against each other.'

'Then we must be on to something,' Jenny said. 'Why else would whoever it is be kicking up so much dust?'

Alison looked troubled. She ran a hand uneasily through her hair.

'What is it?'

'Nothing, really . . . just the atmosphere in the camp. Everything feels so tense . . . The thing is, deep down every last one of them knows they lost this war. They've had friends killed, seen others blown up, and for what? It's human nature, Mrs Cooper – all that anger has to go somewhere.'

Jenny set the notebook on her desk and tried to fight off the vertiginous feeling that had suddenly swept through her. In a few short words Alison had captured what she had vaguely sensed but been unable to articulate since she had first arrived at the camp: behind all the buttoned-up stiffness there was a brooding sense of menace and unfinished business. A dirty secret that it was her rotten luck to have to root out.

She pressed on. 'Let's get this stuff back in the rucksack. I want to have a look at the other one.'

Five minutes later, Kenny Green's kit was laid out on the floor. He had been shot wearing his full combat gear, so there were more missing items, but the absence of one in particular troubled Jenny more than the rest. There was no notebook, but in the pocket of the spare pair of trousers there was a well-used pencil.

She now knew where to begin.

TWENTY-THREE

Jenny and Michael lay with their toes and fingers touching listening to the sound of early-morning birdsong. The dawn chorus was a muted, almost melancholy affair at the end of summer – the odd blackbird, a wood pigeon cooing to its mate – that evoked in Jenny the same feelings that the end of the long school holidays had brought when she was a girl. A sense of things coming to an end, of new and harsher responsibilities about to be loaded onto unwilling shoulders. It was five minutes to seven. Five precious minutes of stillness before the start of a day that carried only the promise of trouble. Her imagination ranged over all the different people and players who would now be rising from their beds to make their way to her courtroom. All of them expecting something of her. She thought of Sarah Tanner, now housed in safe accommodation with a police officer in permanent attendance, and of Paul and Rachel Green and Kathleen Lyons. Each one a human being hollowed out with grief and desperate for answers that she was expected to deliver.

'You'll be all right,' Michael said, as if reading her thoughts. 'You always are.'

'I don't feel like a woman about to hold court. I feel like crawling under the duvet and making it all go away.'

Michael stretched over and gave her a bristly kiss on the cheek.

'You need a shave.'

'You need to wake up.'

He reached under the covers and squeezed her knee.

'Don't!' Jenny objected. 'I've still got two minutes.'

She sank into the pillow, closed her eyes, and within moments was drifting back into a comfortable doze.

It lasted all of seconds. The doorbell sounded and jarred her awake.

'Really? At this time? I swear he gets earlier every day.'

Michael swung out of bed, pulled on his jeans and went down to answer the door to the postman while Jenny forced herself upright a full minute before her alarm was due to sound and staggered to the bathroom. She glanced down the stairs from the landing and saw Michael signing for a registered letter while John, the postman, filled him in on some of the local gossip. There was a newly divorced woman living in a neighbouring hamlet who had set tongues wagging up and down the valley. Jenny could only imagine what rumours had circulated around her when she had first moved in to Melin Bach.

Freshly showered and beginning to feel human again, Jenny chose her most sober outfit – a tailored black suit, black heels, dark tights and a white shirt with a high collar which she wore with a plain silver brooch at her neck. A darker shade than her usual lipstick and a trace of black eyeliner completed the effect of impregnable formality. She stared at her reflection and hardly recognized the figure looking back at her. In her mind's eye she was a gentle, approachable person who had to work hard to hide her feelings. The woman in the mirror had a heart of ice. It made her uncomfortable, but on this occasion she acknowledged to herself that it might prove a useful disguise. In a professional context, she had learned men only truly respect women who give the impression of having stripped their characters of all inward femininity.

Slightly dreading what pointed remarks or ill-judged jokes Michael might aim at her, Jenny made her way downstairs. She had taken so long getting ready she hadn't left herself much time for breakfast. She would have to be quick. There was no sound of the radio coming from the kitchen, nor any smell of coffee. She entered to find the room empty and the door to the garden ajar. As she switched on the kettle she spotted a letter on the table and next to it, Michael's phone. She crossed to the sink and looked out of the window. He was standing at the far end of the lawn, almost hidden in the shadows of the ash trees by the stream. He seemed to be staring out into the meadow beyond.

She went to the table and quickly read through the two terse paragraphs.

Dear Mr Sherman,

Following our recent communication, we have received a formal request from the Foreign Office for all records relating to an incident that took place on Highway 16, thirty miles south-east of the Iraqi city of Amarah on June 8th, 2007. We understand that this is in response to a request made by the government of Denmark.

Having reviewed the video and audio evidence in our possession together with the statements provided by you and other personnel at the time, we have isolated several issues that require urgent clarification. Please telephone the number below on receipt to arrange a meeting with Wing Commander Philip Brammell at your earliest convenience.

Jenny set the letter down and checked Michael's phone. He had already dialled the number. Michael had never mentioned an incident in Amarah. He had spoken of inadvertently causing civilian casualties in the Balkans while carrying out direct orders, and of an incident in Afghanistan, both of which haunted him, but he hardly ever spoke about his tours in Iraq except to recall the intense heat and equally intense boredom of being confined for months on end in a desert airbase. Jenny had never been a conspiracy theorist, but the timing of this letter and the problem with Michael's medical felt more than merely coincidental. And the fact that Colonel Hastings had seemed surprised by the information that Jenny lived with a former fighter pilot made her fear that if moves were being made to destabilize her, they were coming from far higher up. A request like this could only have been made by one of a handful of Whitehall mandarins at the very top of the Ministry of Defence.

If her suspicion was correct, it was intended to send her a message: harm us and we'll harm not you, but the man you love. And it will lie on your conscience.

Her heels sank into the damp grass as she made her way across the lawn, all thought of breakfast now abandoned.

'Michael? I saw the letter.'

He half-turned and made an effort at a smile.

'Do you want to tell me what it's about?'

'Just one of those things.' He shrugged. 'One of many.'

'Denmark?'

'As far as I recall, I was called in to fire on a group of vehicles containing insurgents who'd just shot up a village and were heading for an army checkpoint. The intel was that the lead vehicle was jammed full of explosives. There was another vehicle coming in the opposite direction. It was left to my discretion. There were six guys at a checkpoint half a mile down the road. What do you do? I thought I'd judged it OK, but the blast turned the other vehicle over. We later learned there were two civilian medical staff inside: one British, one Danish.'

'Surely it was investigated at the time?' Jenny said.

'Thoroughly.'

'What happened?'

'I was reprimanded – not officially. These things happened all the time. I never heard another thing about it.'

'You seem very calm.'

'Stamping my feet isn't going to make it go away.'

'If this is anything to do with me, I'm really sorry. I can make some calls, see if I can find out who—'

'No. It'll only aggravate matters. Let it play out. I'm seeing him today. What's the worst that can happen?'

Jenny didn't like to answer that question. She could imagine it only too well: a long drawn-out inquiry; revenge exacted slowly over many years. An exercise in soul-crushing conducted under the guise of due process.

'You've got to get to work. I'll see you later.' He stepped forward as if to kiss her, but stopped himself. 'I daren't. You look too perfect.' He stroked her arm. 'We're not going to let my past affect your present, OK? Don't give it a moment's thought.'

She nodded, grateful for his understanding, but at the same time disconcerted by how unruffled he seemed.

They parted with smiles and a press of hands, but Michael's eyes told a different story. He didn't have to say a word, Jenny knew exactly what he was thinking. They had intended their life together to be a peaceful one; her home, now their home, was to be the place where they finally found the equilibrium that had always eluded them both. It had been a nice dream, but that's all it had ever been, and all it was ever likely to be.

*

Jenny intended the preliminary hearing to be as short as possible. Alison and Sergeant Price had worked late into the previous evening to finish typing up witness statements and had emailed them out to both sets of lawyers along with copies of Dr Kerr's post-mortem reports. On the face of it, the evidence was straightforward and there would be little to argue about. The aim of the exercise was to conduct the basic housekeeping: to make sure that all parties were in possession of the evidence that would be explored in the main hearing and to settle any disputes over its admissibility. Jenny had never relished technical legal argument and prayed the lawyers felt the same way.

Any hope of a quiet and straightforward morning's work were dashed the moment she turned into the staff car park at the side of the old magistrates' court. A cluster of news vans sprouting aerials and satellite dishes were parked in the street. Several reporters with microphones were talking to camera outside the ornate curving stone steps leading up to the main entrance. Others were stopping the soldiers and their family members who were already arriving in a steady trickle a full hour before proceedings were due to commence.

Hoping to avoid being spotted and pursued by the reporters, Jenny kept her head down as she made her way from her car to the side entrance. A sudden flurry of excited voices made her glance up. Claydon White's limousine was sweeping up followed by a police squad car. It came to a halt and White and his colleague, Carrie Rhodes, climbed out. A bemused Sarah Tanner and a female police officer emerged from the car behind as the reporters abandoned what they were doing and headed for the star attractions.

Now in no danger of being noticed, Jenny paused at the corner of the building to listen. Claydon White drew Sarah Tanner alongside him and addressed the microphones with the relaxed confidence of a man sincere in the belief that only he was capable of seeing or speaking the truth.

'We have every faith that the coroner will investigate thoroughly and not shirk in her duty to ask the hard questions the army may not wish to answer. The most important of these is how Private Lyons came to fall into enemy hands. Nothing we have so far heard goes any way to explaining that. We will then need to establish whether the military response which was mounted on the last day of a tour, in the dying hours of a failed campaign, was an appropriate or a lawful one.' He paused briefly and showed the cameras a thoughtful and dignified profile. 'This inquest is an inquiry into the deaths of two brave young men, but we are also mindful of the fact they are only two among many hundreds who have given their lives in this conflict. We, the public, were powerless to prevent this war, but now the guns are silenced we are determined to hold its perpetrators to account. The law of this country allows our leaders to send young men and women to die, but it does not allow them to do so with impunity. In this courtroom, we will ensure that the warmongers answer for their actions.'

It was quite an oration. Prewritten and extensively rehearsed, no doubt, but it had the desired effect. By the time Jenny had arrived in her chambers, Claydon White's last sound bite was making its way across social media and the hashtag *#Helmand2* was already trending. She glanced through the feed on her phone and watched White's statement of intent catch light and spread before her eyes. Very soon, his message was being augmented and refined. The last posting she read before switching off her phone said: *#Helmand2: Afghan war on trial.* She had to admire White: this was precisely the message he wanted the jury who would be sworn in on Thursday morning to receive. His aim was for nine ordinary men and women from north Somerset to feel as if their job was nothing less than to reach a verdict on the justice of a thirteen-year-long war. In one short speech, he had drawn the battle lines and cast himself as the champion of the underdog pitted against the merciless machinery of the state.

Jenny breakfasted on weak coffee and biscuits while she reviewed her file and tried to push aside the nagging sensations of anxiety and self-doubt that had always plagued her before a court appearance. She envied lawyers and judges who were gifted with a sense of their own importance. Ever since the first time she had risen to her feet as a nervous, newly qualified solicitor, she had felt like an imposter. More than twenty years later, the sensation was just as acute and every bit as irrational. There was nothing to worry about in a straightforward preliminary hearing, but still her mind worried over unlikely possibilities and imagined covert plots and conspiracies to subvert her. She fixated on the only likely point of contention: she had emailed Robert Heaton QC late the previous afternoon requesting that Major Norton be made available for this morning's hearing. She had expected a message in return but had heard nothing. As the minutes passed, his continued silence added to her building sense of unease. At the very least, it told her that Heaton and the anonymous suits from the MOD instructing him had no intention of being cooperative. She anticipated a policy of passive resistance designed to frustrate and drain her. If she was pushed to the point of losing her temper so much the better. It would all be ammunition with which to mount an accusation of bias against her if events didn't go their way.

Alison knocked on the door with five minutes to go. She brought the news that Major Norton had arrived along with Sergeant Bryant and most of the platoon. Jenny's worst fears receded: she wouldn't be forced into a confrontation that might have compelled her to have Norton arrested and brought to court in the back of a police car.

Alison's next piece of news wasn't so reassuring: 'Simon Moreton's here, too. He doesn't quite seem his usual self.'

'He's used to being well out of the firing line,' Jenny said. 'This time it's all on his shoulders. He appointed me to this one and the Chief's holding him responsible.'

'Between you and me, I've always thought he was rather in love with you,' Alison said, as casually as if she were commenting on the weather. 'But I think you confuse him – he doesn't understand what it is about you that he's drawn to.'

Jenny checked the time. Two minutes to go. Not the moment to be discussing Simon Moreton's misguided romantic feelings.

Alison persisted nonetheless: 'He's a bit of a coward, isn't he? That's the last thing you are.'

Jenny gave an appreciative smile and thought how far she and Alison had travelled since their first few difficult years, when nothing Jenny did seemed to meet with her officer's approval.

'Forget about him,' Alison said. 'You've got far more important things to worry about. Shall we go?' Without waiting for an answer, she headed out of the door.

The atmosphere in the crowded courtroom was tense and the air muggy with the perspiration from so many tightly packed bodies. The animosity between the two sets of lawyers was palpable. Heaton and the three lawyers from the MOD seated behind him were stony faced. Claydon White had the steely, defiant look of a gladiator about to do combat. Sitting to his left, Carrie Rhodes maintained the elegant poise of a swan. Behind them sat Sarah Tanner and Kathleen Lyons along with the female police officer charged

with ensuring Sarah Tanner's safety. Jenny spotted Paul
Green's bruised and swollen face in the row behind them.
Next to him, Rachel Green was already sobbing into a
handkerchief. Tucked away at the back of the room was the
familiar face of Simon Moreton, only this morning it had a
distinctly grey pallor. Jenny briefly met his eye and sensed
his plea to avoid embarrassments.

Jenny assumed her most businesslike tone and announced
that she proposed to consolidate the inquests of Private
Green and Private Lyons. There were no objections. She
moved swiftly on to inquire if all parties had received the
bundles of witness statements and post-mortem reports
which had been forwarded to them. They had. Next, she
turned to what she had anticipated would be a potentially
thorny issue: the scope of her inquiry.

'My duty is to examine the circumstances of and leading
up to death. I interpret this as meaning that I have to examine all and any events which may have a direct causal
connection with each fatality. Specifically, I propose to
inquire into how and why Private Lyons came to be separated from the rest of the platoon. This will not only include
the physical circumstances, but I will also inquire into Private Lyons's psychological state.' She looked across at the
lawyers, 'Are the interested parties happy with that?'

Robert Heaton rose to his feet. 'We are content with
those parameters, ma'am, but not with any attempt by my
friend Mr White to conflate this very specific inquiry into
some sort of pseudo-trial of wider events in Afghanistan. I
don't know if you are aware of the comments he has made
this morning, ma'am—'

'I've seen them, Mr Heaton,' Jenny interjected, 'and I will
be asking the jury to disregard them.' She addressed herself
directly to White, 'For the avoidance of doubt, Mr White, I
will treat any attempt to distract the jury from their central

task as an abuse of the process of this court. This is an inquiry into the tragic deaths of two soldiers, no more, no less.'

He couldn't resist a response: 'I would be grateful if you would detail exactly what motives you are imputing to me, ma'am. If I, and by extension my clients, are under suspicion from the outset, it would seem that any prospect of a fair hearing has already been cast into doubt.'

Jenny thought better of crossing swords at this early stage. White was desperate to cast her as hostile to his cause and to reinforce the narrative he hoped that prospective jurors would already have ingested before they even came to be sworn in.

'You are not under suspicion, Mr White. Quite the reverse – I anticipate you assisting this inquiry to the best of your ability.' She gave him what she hoped was a charming smile and moved on. 'Now, there is one issue I would like to clarify. Yesterday, the kit belonging to Privates Green and Lyons was examined. I have a few questions I would like to address to Major Norton.' She sought out Norton's face among the sixty or so arranged in front of her. 'If you wouldn't mind coming forward to the witness box, Major, it won't take a moment.'

As Norton stood up from his seat among his men and shuffled along the row, Jenny was aware of anxious discussion taking place between Heaton and the triumvirate of government lawyers. She had deliberately not informed them of the issue she intended to raise with him. This time she wanted to avoid any danger of being outmanoeuvred. Heaton appeared to be telling his colleagues to sit tight, but they weren't having it.

While Norton climbed to the witness box, Heaton politely rose to inquire what the matter was that Jenny intended to raise with the major.

'It's just a small matter regarding items of kit.'

'May I inquire which ones?' Heaton ventured.

'It will become more than clear in a moment, Mr Heaton,' Jenny said briskly, and invited Alison, acting as court usher, to administer the oath.

Heaton reluctantly sat down, but as he did so, Jenny noticed one of the lawyers behind him cast a reproving glance in the direction of Sergeant Price, who had been sitting alongside Alison at the clerk's desk beneath Jenny's. It came as no surprise, but she filed this detail away.

Norton pronounced the oath in clipped tones that excluded any possibility of emotion. His gaunt face and shaved head, now beginning to show the shadow of re-growth, added to the sense of him being not quite fully human. He stood with hands folded, straight-backed and statue-still.

'Am I right in thinking that all men in the platoon were issued with notebooks as part of their standard-issue kit, Major?' Jenny asked.

'That is correct.'

'There was no notebook in either Private Green's kitbag or about his person – do you have any idea why that might be?'

'No, I do not, ma'am.'

His answer came a little too quickly for Jenny's liking, without even the slightest pause for thought.

'Is it usual for soldiers to carry their notebooks while on patrol or on a mission such as the last one you led into Shalan-Gar?'

'They may sometimes carry notebooks. There is no standing order preventing them from doing so.'

'But surely you wouldn't expect them to carry information that may be of assistance to the enemy?'

'That's correct.'

'Do you recall if Private Green's pockets were searched after he was shot?'

'I do not recall that happening, but it would not have been a priority, particularly in the circumstances.'

'Were you aware of his notebook being removed from his kit for whatever reason, after his body was evacuated?'

'His kit would have been packed by one of the men. I couldn't tell you which one.'

'So one of the platoon may have removed it?'

'That is possible.'

'Would you not, as officer in command, specifically have looked for a fallen man's notebook? It might have contained intimate thoughts that loved ones might have appreciated reading.'

'That has not been my practice, no.'

'Your sergeant?'

'You would have to ask him, ma'am.'

'I don't wish to labour the point now, it can wait until the full hearing. One last matter – Private Lyons's notebook appears to have had several pages torn from it. Are you able to cast any light on that?'

'No, ma'am. Again, his kit would have been packed up by one of the men.'

'You didn't at any time see Private Lyons's notebook?'

'No. I did not.'

Jenny realized that she was talking to a stone wall. Now wasn't the time to try to prise him apart, that would have to wait until the main hearing. For the time being, she was quite content to let him think he could get the better of her.

'Thank you, Major Norton. That's all for now.'

'Excuse me, ma'am.' The interjection came from Claydon White. 'While Major Norton is on oath, might I be permitted to raise one brief matter with him?'

Jenny tried to think of a legitimate reason to object, but none came to mind.

'Please be quick, Mr White. And remember this is not an occasion on which to take substantive evidence.'

'I'll be very brief.'

Jenny nodded her assent.

Claydon White turned to the witness with a benign smile. 'Good morning, Major. I wonder, do you have any intention whatever of telling the truth at this inquest, or will you continue to instruct your men to obstruct the course of justice? People have gone to prison for less than what you did last week—'

'Mr White . . .' Jenny objected.

He ignored her and pressed on: 'If members of your platoon weren't drunk or intoxicated with drugs you'd have had nothing at all to hide would you?'

'Mr White!' Jenny's voice resounded around the courtroom. She gathered herself. 'Now is not the time.'

'I beg to differ, ma'am,' Claydon White said. 'Now is precisely the time for me, on behalf of my clients, to mark our outrage at Major Norton's brazen attempt to undermine this inquiry before it has even begun.'

Major Norton stared impassively ahead, as if he were entirely removed from the scene.

Jenny considered her response, careful not to allow herself to glance in Simon Moreton's direction.

'As I have already said, there will be ample opportunity to pursue these issues later this week.'

'Do we have your word on that, ma'am?'

'Mr White, let me make this clear from the outset: there is only one person who sets the agenda for this inquiry and that is me. I will not now, or at any stage, tolerate any attempt to barrack, bully, grandstand or impute false motives. Nor will

I allow any relevant issue to go unexplored. Have I made myself understood?'

'You have, ma'am, but my clients would still like to know what you intend to do about Major Norton's attempt to pervert the course of justice. If it's allowed to pass, what are we to conclude? Will other witnesses be allowed to withhold evidence?'

However Jenny replied, the damage had already been done. Claydon White had embarrassed her: made her look weak as well as biased. She had fully intended to take Norton to task in the main hearing, but in her attempt to catch him unawares over the notebooks, she had blundered straight into a bear trap. The last thing she had wanted was for this morning's hearing to generate headlines, but she had been left with little choice.

'Major Norton, perhaps, on further reflection, now would be an appropriate moment for you to explain why you and your platoon frustrated the process of gathering hair samples.'

'I have nothing to say on the matter,' Norton replied mechanically.

'Are you refusing to answer my question?'

'No, ma'am. I simply have no comment to make.'

'Do you realize that wilfully failing to answer a proper question amounts to contempt in the face of the court?'

'I take full responsibility for my actions.'

'Did you order your men to make the collection of samples impossible?'

'I did.'

'Then I have no option but to fine you five hundred pounds for contempt and to pass details of what has occurred to the Crown Prosecution Service. They may wish to take the matter further.'

Major Norton showed no reaction. He was a more than

willing martyr. Robert Heaton and the three men behind merely stared at their hands. Among the many journalists in attendance there was a murmur of excitement. The hearing Jenny had planned to be a non-event had delivered a story from which Claydon White would emerge as the hero. She would be portrayed as weak, out of her depth and as having been outmanoeuvred. As these thoughts rushed through her head in the space of a second, she also became aware that with the single exception of Alison, she would have lost the respect of every single person in the courtroom.

As the reporters reached for their phones to fire out their first messages onto social media, the sharper ones among them picked up on another item of breaking news that would bring Jenny even more unwelcome attention.

TWENTY-FOUR

Anna Roberts had planned to be at the hearing, but instead found herself in the back of a taxi travelling up the now all too familiar motorway to Selly Oak. The call had woken her shortly after six a.m. The voice at the other end belonged to a male nurse who introduced himself as Jason. No surname. He told Anna that there had been an incident late the previous evening. Lee had become agitated and started raving. Jason had gone to him and found that he had pulled out the intravenous lines trickling fluid and drugs into his body. He was highly distressed and incoherent and appeared to be suffering delusions that were probably flashbacks to the incident in which he was injured.

A psychiatrist was summoned to examine him. He diagnosed a psychotic episode. Shortly afterwards, a second psychiatrist made the same finding. Together they decided that, for his own safety, Lee should be sectioned. Jason tried to reassure her that this would have no practical implications while Lee remained on the ward being treated for his wounds. All it would mean was that he would lose any say in his medical treatment.

'Why did this happen?' Anna had asked. 'Is this normal?'

'It's either the trauma, or the trauma has triggered something underlying. It's hard to say. We'll have to see how he progresses.'

'I need to see him.'

'He's under sedation, Mrs Roberts. You won't get much from him at the moment.'

'He's my husband. I *need* to see him.'

Jason had seemed less than enthusiastic. 'Well, I'll leave that with you.'

Anna had smelt the rat from the moment the call ended. She called Sergeant Price. He was very sympathetic but explained that he was busy at court that morning and wouldn't be able to drive her until later. Anna prepared to make the gruelling round-trip on the bus for the second time that week, but while she was struggling to work out what to do with Leanne while she was away, Sergeant Price called back shortly afterwards to say that Colonel Hastings had authorized him to book her a taxi. He passed on Hastings's good wishes and sympathy and offer to do anything more that he could to help. It was as welcome as it was unexpected.

Anna arrived at the hospital at ten a.m. The four hours since she had received the call felt like four days. She ran through the reception area and up the stairs, in too much of a hurry to wait for the lift. Breathless and perspiring and eaten up with fear, she arrived at the nurses' station and demanded to be allowed to see Lee. This time there was no obstruction. A young nurse named Sandra gave her a kind smile and said that he had been moved to a private room further along the corridor. She led the way.

'He's been quiet since I came on this morning,' Sandra said. 'Don't be too alarmed. I've been here four years. I've seen it many times before. We call it ICU psychosis.' They arrived outside the door of Lee's room and stopped. 'Would you like me to come in?'

Anna shook her head. She wanted to thank the nurse, but it was as much as she could do to stop herself from crying.

Sandra patted her wrist. 'You know where to find me.' She headed off, leaving Anna alone.

A glimpse through the observation pane in the door sent Anna's heart thudding against her ribs. Lee's face was badly bruised. His left eye was swollen to the point that it had nearly closed. Coupled with the strangeness of his shaved head, she barely recognized him. She took a deep breath, told herself to be strong and forced herself to go inside.

Lee's eyes were open but they gazed emptily into space. His wrists were secured by straps to the side of the bed.

She leant over and looked into his eyes. 'Lee? It's me – Anna. Can you hear me?'

She thought she detected a slight movement, but nothing more. His jaw remained slack, his lips slightly parted. She pulled over a chair and placed it at the side of the bed. Squeezing his fingers, she found they were cold and bloodless.

'Lee – if you can hear me, move your eyes.'

She studied them intently. No. She had imagined it. She grabbed his notes that were hooked over the rail at the foot of the bed. The handwriting was hard to decipher, but she made out an entry from ten o'clock the previous evening: *Raving/ shouting incoherently. Flashbacks? Nurse tried to calm – lashed out. Struck himself repeatedly in the face. Restrained & sedated – haloperidol 5mg.* Further entries had been made at hourly intervals throughout the night. From what she could make out, he had been given repeated injections of the same drug.

He had been depressed the last time she had seen him, several days before. She had put it down to the shock of him learning about Pete Lyons, but logically it didn't make sense. Lee must have known that he was most likely dead from the moment they lost him. Even she knew that no soldier could go missing in Taliban country without coming to serious harm. No, it can't have been hearing that his comrade was dead. The desperate slump in his mood had to be something to do with being forcibly shaved – not losing his hair, but what it meant to him.

'Lee – listen to me,' she pleaded. 'I need you to know that you can tell me anything. I'm here for you. Whatever it is, I don't care. I'm here for you.'

The door opened behind her. She turned round to see a doctor, a tall, balding man in his fifties.

'Mrs Roberts?'

She nodded.

'Anthony Conway. I'm the psychiatrist who attended your husband last night.'

'What's happened? What's wrong with him?' Anna demanded.

'Psychotic episodes are fairly common in highly traumatized patients. The causes may be purely psychological or have some physical element. We'll have more insight as we decrease his medication over the next few days.'

'What was he saying? What was he raving about?'

Conway shook his head apologetically. 'I'm afraid he was incoherent, Mrs Roberts. I couldn't make any of it out.'

Something in the doctor's manner made Anna uneasy. 'Did he mention Skippy?'

'I was mostly concerned with making sure he didn't do himself any more harm,' Dr Conway said. 'He really was in quite a distressed state.'

'Why have you put him in here, by himself?' Anna said.

'The room was available. We thought it would be more peaceful for him. Do you understand why he's been sectioned and what it means?'

Anna said she did. It had happened to her best friend after they left school. A bad relationship had led to drugs and a downward spiral that saw her spend six months in a secure unit.

'We hope this condition is temporary, Mrs Roberts. We really do. And if you have any questions you mustn't hesitate to ask me. Email is always good.' He produced a card from his breast pocket and handed it to her. He looked at Lee, then back at Anna as if he were expecting her to go.

'I'm going to sit with him for a while,' she said.

'I really do feel that complete rest is what he needs.'

'I'm his wife,' she answered, with a note of steely defiance that took her by surprise.

'Of course.' Dr Conway nodded and, after a pause, quietly left the room.

Anna sat clasping Lee's hand, and for nearly an hour kept up a constant monologue hoping to see just the faintest flicker of life. She told him about Leanne and about what it had been like while he was away – all the gossip and silly rumours that had circulated amongst the families. She told him about a weekend she had spent in Cornwall and her plans for redecorating the flat, but still he remained in his catatonic state, conscious but seemingly able only to blink.

It was approaching midday. She had to be back in time to collect Leanne, who, in the absence of anyone able to mind her, was booked into the WAGs Club nursery for both the morning and afternoon sessions. Anna kissed Lee on the forehead and told him that she loved him. She felt sure that somewhere, somehow, he would understand. As she stood up to leave, she remembered the picture Leanne had drawn of him which she had brought with her. She fetched it from her handbag. It was nothing more than a crayon scrawl, but there was a face and a smile and 'Daddy' spelled out in big letters. She propped it up at his bedside where he would see it when he came round.

Anna set off along the corridor towards the exit. Up

ahead, Sandra and another nurse were busy talking to one another and hadn't seen her. Anna glanced right, through the door into the ward. A consultant and his registrar were doing their rounds. She continued on several paces and came alongside the entrance to the day room. Inside, a young soldier who was missing a leg beneath the knee was watching television. Unseen by the nurses she slipped in.

The young man looked up at her. He had boyish brown eyes and a ready smile.

'I'm Lee Roberts's wife,' Anna said. 'I've seen you in the ward, haven't I?'

'I think so,' he answered in a soft Welsh accent. 'Gary. Gary Owens.'

Anna noticed his eyes flick to the door behind her.

'You must have been in the ward when Lee flipped last night?'

He nodded, casting another anxious glance to the corridor.

'What was he saying? The psychiatrist is pretending he couldn't make it out.'

'Seemed like he was having a flashback, like . . .' Gary said uncertainly.

'To what? Did he say any names?'

With something approaching panic in his eyes, Gary shook his head.

'What did he say? Please! I need to know.'

'He didn't, love. No one likes to see a lad like that. He's stressed out, that's all. He'll get over it. We all do in the end.'

'What happened when they shaved his head? Who ordered that? Did he talk to you about it?'

'Love, it's the army. You do as you're told.'

Sandra, the nurse, appeared. She smiled awkwardly at Anna. 'You shouldn't really be in here.'

'Why? Because someone might tell me the truth?'

Sandra looked puzzled.

'Forget it.' Anna pushed past her and, feeling as if she were on the brink of losing her own sanity, ran all the way to the exit.

Jenny had hoped to avoid Simon Moreton at the end of the hearing, but he appeared in her chambers less than a minute after she had left the bench. His usual charm deserted him as he asked her acidly if she was feeling all right, and then told her that if she didn't sharpen up she was in danger of letting Claydon White humiliate her.

'Simon, you almost pleaded with me to take these cases.'

'I thought I was offering you the chance to redeem yourself.'

'I beg your pardon?'

'By proving that you're capable of handling a tricky case without making a public exhibition of yourself. Clearly not. Old habits die hard. And as for that bloody boyfriend of yours . . .'

'What are you talking about?'

Simon thrust his phone under her nose. A reporter had posted a photo of Michael punching a photographer in the lane outside Melin Bach along with the message: *#Helmand2 Coroner's partner investigated over war crimes. Assaults reporter.*

The picture took Jenny by surprise. It had clearly been taken that morning while Michael was leaving the house. How had the reporters found out? There had to have been a leak. Jenny struggled to contain her rage. Thus far she had managed to persuade herself that what had happened to Michael was a coincidence. Now she realized with full clarity that she had been guilty of wishful thinking.

'What do you expect him to do?' she retorted. 'You know

as well as I do that this investigation is completely malicious.'

'I've been reliably informed that it's been bubbling for some time.'

'Really? What do you take me for? It's meant to unsettle me, make me fear that if I embarrass the army there will be consequences.'

Her reply silenced him for a moment. His face twitched uncomfortably as he was forced, against all his instincts, to acknowledge that she may have touched on the truth.

'We both know these things happen,' he muttered. 'The way to deal with them is to remain calm and dignified, to let the sensible heads in the press do your talking for you.'

'And quietly steer this inquest through to a non-conclusion? Is that the idea? Take the evidence, keep White on a leash, nudge the jury to an open verdict – would that be sufficient to save you from an early exit?'

Simon met her gaze. She had never before seen the expression with which he looked at her: it was almost pleading. 'Jenny, I'm going to let you into a confidence. Can I trust you?'

'As long as it's not evidence in the case.'

'No, it's not evidence.' He dipped his head as if in shame. 'I committed an indiscretion a little while ago. A junior colleague at the Ministry – before I transferred to the Chief's office. The woman, well, she wasn't much more than a girl really, she kicked up a bit of a fuss when I ended it. All dealt with internally, discreetly, but not strictly according to the rules, if you get my drift.'

'No, I don't.'

'I paid her off. She withdrew her complaint. For the sake of my marriage, my children, everything I've worked for. I didn't see why all that should be ruined as the result of a foolish office . . . dalliance.'

Jenny felt a ridiculous pang of jealousy. Somehow, some egotistical part of her had allowed itself to imagine that she was the only woman Simon had fantasized over. She pushed the unwanted emotion aside and told herself to grow up.

'Let me guess – someone's got hold of it?'

'I've had an indication,' Simon said. 'They must have seen my private emails. It's the only possible way, and in pretty short order, too. Someone in the MOD must have picked up the phone to a trusted friend in GCHQ and gone straight after me.'

'That's a lot of trouble and risk to go to over the deaths of a couple of private soldiers.'

'It's not the ranks who are going to be culled. There's plenty with a shoulder full of pips who'll be pushed out of the door if government gets its way. They want a new order. An army stripped down to its essentials. They've got slick salesmen taking them out to lunch telling them the future's in high-tech weaponry. Drones, robots, all controlled by a bunch of spotty kids from a warehouse somewhere. Politically embarrassing wars with an endless parade of soldiers' coffins appearing on the evening news are meant to become a thing of the past. Meanwhile, plenty in the MOD know the truth – just around the corner there'll be another Middle Eastern war, far worse. We'll need all the men, guns, bullets and boots we can get hold of.' He let out a sigh of despair. 'It's bizarre how such huge issues get tangled with such trivial ones.'

Speech over, he looked at her dejectedly, like a child fishing for sympathy and reassurance. When Jenny remained silent, he said: 'I've been good to you, Jenny. Think how many times I've saved your neck in the last seven years.'

'Alison thinks I act as your conscience.'

'She's a perceptive woman. But do we want to be martyrs? And even if we were to be, would it do any good?'

Jenny would have been more than within her rights to explode and tell Simon that attempting to manipulate her inquest using whining personal appeals was just about the lowest and most unforgiveable thing he had ever done, but she remained patient. Something inside her prompted her to treat him like the wounded little boy he was. 'I'm sorry that your "dalliance" has put you in an awkward situation, but Simon, there is only one way I know how to conduct an inquest – I'll go after the truth, whatever it takes. Even if everyone else deserts you, you've still got to live with yourself.'

'I was very afraid you were going to say that.'

Jenny couldn't raise Michael on the phone and she couldn't face returning to Highcliffe so soon after the hearing. Needing a few moments to herself to clear her head and process the morning's events, she slipped out of the building, and managing to avoid the media scrum still gathered at the front steps, hurried across the road and went in search of a cafe in one of the small side streets between High Street and The Broadway. Although the reporters' attention was on the lawyers and soldiers still emerging from the court, one woman in the crowd spotted Jenny making her getaway and went after her.

Jenny sat at a seat in the window and tried to force down the filled baguette. Mozzarella, avocado and tomato with basil vinaigrette – it should have tasted delicious, but each mouthful was an effort. Besides worrying over Michael's problems and the unwanted pressure from Simon Moreton, she was carrying a burden of guilt for the way in which she had mismanaged the inquest to date. Underneath it all, she realized that she felt intimidated and out of her depth. She was there to help, to root out the truth for the good and benefit of the soldiers still serving and those who would follow, but none of them seemed to want it. It was as if they willingly gave up the normal expectations of justice the moment they stepped into uniform. There was something in the male mind – and despite the odd female face, the British Army was most definitely a male institution – that she couldn't fathom: the willingness to embrace and accept violence as a fact of life. Men seemed to revel in it. To hear Michael talk sometimes, you would think that a man wasn't worthy of his sex unless he had stared death in the face. Perhaps that was just how it was – a primal instinct that could never be expunged?

'Is this seat free?'

Jenny glanced up to see a pleasant, slightly worried look-ing woman in her early thirties carrying a full cup of coffee. She could see that there were plenty of other free seats in the small cafe but to turn her away would have seemed churlish.

'Yes,' Jenny answered, and tried to force down another mouthful of baguette.

She ate in silence, taking occasional sips of the large Americano she had bought to accompany it. She avoided the woman's gaze but quickly became aware that she had sat at the same table for a reason and was struggling for a way to initiate a conversation. Finally, Jenny could bear the tension no longer. She looked up at the woman and offered a smile.

'Have we met?'

'No, I don't think so,' the woman said with obvious relief that Jenny had broken the impasse. 'But I've seen you in court. I was there this morning.'

'Oh,' Jenny said, trying to fathom who she might be. 'Well, obviously I can't discuss anything to do with the case.'

'Of course not.' The woman stared down at the table. She

drew in a breath and spoke in a quiet, but clear and heart-felt voice. 'My husband's in the regiment. I've watched him over the years, seen him change from a bright-eyed young man into one I sometimes feel I hardly know. They do their duty and they do it willingly, but if you're any sort of human being the responsibility of having those young men's lives in your hands . . . Well, it can't help but change you. There's no one for them to turn to. No one to share their feelings with.' She let out a laugh. 'It's an absurd thought really, isn't it – talking about what sending boys to their deaths and killing people makes you feel? I don't suppose there is anything anyone can say to make it better. It has to be done. But it eats away the souls of those who have to do it . . . People talk about the army as if it's a world apart, as if soldiers are nothing to do with them, but they're as much a part of us as anything else. Someone has to clean out the sewers. Who can be surprised if they come back stinking?' She looked up and met Jenny's eyes. 'I'm sorry. I don't know where that came from, I just knew I had to say some-thing . . . I shouldn't have troubled you.' Embarrassed, she rose from her seat.

'You're Mrs Norton, aren't you?' Jenny said, guessing, but at the same time in no doubt who she was.

Melanie looked back and nodded. 'I'll do my best to make sure he cooperates. He's not himself at the moment.' She swallowed a lump in her throat and made for the door.

Jenny watched through the window as Melanie hurried away along the pavement outside. She looked as ordinary and unremarkable as every other woman in the street. She could have been a teacher or an office worker married to someone leading an equally worthy but uneventful life. Nothing about her would have suggested that she shared her life with a man who had spent the last ten years in bloody combat and seen more death than most could ever imagine.

Jenny felt her resolve return. This case wasn't just for the soldiers' benefit, it was for the ones at home who loved them. The invisible casualties of war.

Leanne was sobbing inconsolably when Anna arrived to collect her. It was the first time she had spent the whole day in nursery and the break from her usual routine, coupled with the fact that so many of the other children had been talking about their newly returned fathers, had made her miserable. Anna did her best to console her, but it was as much as she could do to stop herself from crying when Leanne asked when her daddy would be coming home from hospital.

'Soon,' Anna lied. 'We just have to be patient.'

'What's "soon"?'

Anna bundled Leanne into her buggy, trying to ignore the pitying stares of the other mothers who had heard the little girl's pleas. She hurried out of the hall with Leanne still waiting for her answer.

Anna had shopping to do but couldn't face a trip on the bus into town. She made do with walking to the local Co-op, doing her best to reassure Leanne without lying to her. But every word of false optimism only made her feel bleaker and more desperate. She had come away from the hospital that morning with a sense of dread that had grown steadily worse. It loomed like a great black wave drawing inexorably closer. Lee was alive, but only clinging on. She could feel his grip loosening, his will to survive slipping away. They had taken his legs, his mind and his spirit.

She came to the edge of the main road they needed to cross to get to the shops. Traffic rumbled past but Anna couldn't seem to move. Rooted to the spot, she felt warmth on her cheeks and tasted tears. Her body convulsed with sobs that she couldn't control. Passing drivers stared and gawped at her – not that she noticed. The world had narrowed to a tiny point. The light had faded so much that she just couldn't see any more.

From the far side of the road, a woman in a fraying mackintosh, hunched over and with her grey hair flapping in the wind, made her way across. She came face-to-face with Anna at the kerb.

'Oh, love,' was all she said. Her sad eyes were still smarting from tears of her own.

Kathleen Lyons rested a hand on Leanne's buggy and pulled it back safely onto the pavement. She led the mother and child over to a bench and sat Anna down. There were no words she could offer that would make it any better. She simply put her arm around the young woman while she wept and stroked her now silent and puzzled daughter's hand. It hadn't been a good day. She had gone straight from the court to work to find that Phil Peters had discovered that she had made more mistakes. After her last shift, her till had been out by more than eighty pounds. Kathleen felt she had no choice but to resign. Phil didn't voice a word of objection.

Still, there were more important things in the world. When Anna had dried her tears, she would take these two home and make sure they got something to eat.

TWENTY-FIVE

Paul Green had been suffering with a raging headache ever since he had been attacked on his own doorstep by two idiots who thought they were protecting the honour of the regiment. The irony was that he had smelt the booze on their breath as they sunk their blows into him. He couldn't begin to comprehend how two young men who called themselves soldiers had convinced themselves that beating him up was going to help anyone, but he had seen a lot of bad and violent behaviour amongst returning soldiers in recent years. Bar fights were commonplace. Less talked about was what went on behind closed doors. He knew for a fact that Highcliffe was full of young women who had felt the fists of angry, disturbed young men struggling to make the switch from front-line warrior to domesticated male within the space of days. There had been times in the past, he was ashamed to admit, when Rachel had felt the back of his hand.

The one consolation had been the many warm words of condolence he and Rachel had received that morning at the court. He had feared that Kenny's comrades had been turned against him, but he could see from their faces that his close pals remained as true as they ever had been. Alan Bryant, the platoon's sergeant, had been particularly fulsome in his praise. 'A hero. Brave to the last,' is what he had said as he shook Paul's hand and looked him straight in the eye. From a man like Bryant, whom Paul remembered as a truly courageous young corporal from his last tour in Iraq, the words meant a lot. He had no doubt they were the truth.

Dealing with Rachel and Sarah had been the most difficult part of the morning. For reasons he simply couldn't fathom, the two of them had hardly been able to bear the sight of each other since the news of Kenny's death. In his heart of hearts he knew it was Rachel's fault. She had never been able to accept the idea of Kenny loving another woman more than her. Even so, the bitterness he felt in Rachel wasn't rational. It was almost as if she held Sarah responsible for Kenny's death in some way. She hadn't even been able to bring herself to sit next to Sarah in the court. Why? He couldn't begin to understand. He heard the weary voice of his long-dead father talking to him after another run-in with his quick-tempered mother, 'Never try to understand them, son – you'll end up crazier than they are.'

He and Rachel hadn't been back from the court more than half an hour and had barely said a word to one another when there had been a knock at the door. The visitor was an old friend and comrade, Sam Williams. They had served most of their long careers together and Sam now worked for an events security firm based in Bristol. They hadn't seen each other for nearly a year. Sam had put on a few pounds and turned a bit greyer, but he still had the same keen eyes that could spot the first sign of trouble at five hundred yards.

It quickly became apparent that he hadn't come just to offer his condolences. After a few minutes of painful chitchat during which Rachel had wept continually, he confessed that he'd picked up on a few rumours that were circulating in the regiment. He claimed he had heard them from his two nephews, both of whom were currently serving, but Paul sensed that someone had had a word in his ear. Sam was the sort of man the officers would have turned to in a delicate moment like this. The gist of it was that people were saying that the lawyers who had foisted themselves on Sarah Tanner and Kathleen Lyons were after one thing: money. Money for them and for the next-of-kin. And according to the speculation doing the rounds, they were going to do whatever it took to make a court believe the army had ballsed it up and that they, not the Taliban, were responsible for Kenny and Pete's deaths. The idea of rich, pampered lawyers trying to turn soldiers against each other so that they could get even richer was causing a lot of resentment. Everybody in the regiment knew some poor young widow struggling to bring up kids on a tiny pension, and the thought that Sarah might land a windfall wasn't helping matters.

'What do you want me to do?' Paul asked.

'Maybe you should have a word with her,' Sam said, 'tell her that some things are more important than cash.'

'She didn't go out and find these people . . .'

'Still, it might help to put her in the picture. They're working for her, after all. She calls the shots.'

Paul couldn't imagine Sarah giving orders to the man he had seen in court that morning, but he took straight to heart what Sam was saying. The army was a family, and families work on love and loyalty. The bonds which he and his former comrades enjoyed were far more important to him than any financial reward. There was a reason he was content to live in this down-at-heel house and put up with a badly paid job in a delivery firm. He had chosen to make his life among people who respected him for what he was and his years of service. To the world outside Highcliffe he was just another face in the crowd. Here, he was still Sergeant Paul Green. A somebody.

When Sam had left, Paul called Sarah on her mobile. He could hear from the sounds of clinking crockery and civilized conversation in the background that she was in a restaurant. Somewhere expensive, no doubt – a treat from the lawyers. Sarah didn't mention where she was – the Angel Hotel, the only four-star establishment in the town – or that Kathleen Lyons had refused the invitation and advised her to do the same because, as she put it, 'Nothing goes unseen in this town, and you don't want people thinking the worst of you.' Sarah didn't give a damn what people thought of her. She'd lost her fiancée. Her life was in ruins. If the lawyers wanted to buy her lunch, why not?

Paul asked if they could meet later that afternoon. He told her there were a couple of things he would like to discuss before the inquest. When Sarah responded with silence, he reassured her that it would be all right – Rachel was fine. They just wanted everything to be all right between them before they faced what was bound to be a very difficult few days. Sarah had responded to his mollifying tones. Despite her problems with Rachel, Paul was the closest thing to a father that she had. She promised to talk to the policewoman who was following her everywhere and arrange to come over.

By some small miracle, Rachel's mood seemed to lift during the afternoon. It was as if the dark cloud that had hung over the house for the previous week had suddenly dispersed. Paul prayed that it meant that his wife was beginning to move on from the first agonized throes of grief and would be able to keep her emotions in check. The early signs were good. Sarah arrived shortly after four and the three of them sat down to tea in the living room. Rachel asked with concern how it was, staying in a small flat guarded by a policewoman. Sarah confessed that it was lonely and that she really couldn't see the point: why put her in a separate flat? Paul confessed that the police had wanted to move them all out, but that he had insisted on staying at home and Rachel had decided to stick with him.

With the small talk over, they lapsed briefly into silence. Feeling the tension rise, Paul reached over from the sofa to the armchair on which Sarah was sitting and rested his hand on hers.

'Sarah, love, you know we all want to hear the truth about what happened to Kenny and Pete . . .'

Sarah waited for the 'but' that she sensed was coming next.

'But people are worried about these lawyers you've got. They think . . .' He paused to choose his words as carefully as he could. 'People are worried they're going to start slinging mud where it doesn't deserve to be slung. They're all good boys in the platoon. You know that – they're friends of yours. And look what Norton did, for goodness' sake – he may have gone too far, but he was only trying to protect Kenny. There's no way they're going to let him or Pete down.'

Sarah looked from Paul to Rachel with a puzzled expression. 'Claydon wants the same as us – the truth. That's all. The army's said nothing about how Pete went missing – it doesn't make any sense. If they're hiding something, we've got a right to know. We've got a right to know what Kenny died for.' She appealed directly to Rachel, 'You said it yourself last week – a man can't get snatched from a post without someone knowing how.'

Paul sensed Rachel wrestling with all the contradictions that had tormented her for days. Her pride at her brave son in uniform was pitted against a mother's need to know why his life was taken. Her loyalty to the army, and all the community that surrounded it, vied with her suspicion that the life of an individual private soldier counted for little or nothing compared with the careers and reputations of the officers who led them. Part of her was the proud and selfless mother of a fallen warrior; another part was raging at the injustice of losing her only child.

Finally, Rachel spoke, 'I want to hear the truth as much as you do. But I think what you've got to ask yourself, Sarah, is whether that's what your lawyers want. Kenny would have laid down his life for any of the lads in the platoon. That's what he did. Would he have wanted lawyers tearing into them? Calling them liars? Turning them against each other?'

'I know he would have wanted his child provided for.'

Paul stepped in. 'Love, all we're asking is that you let those lawyers know what you think of those boys. They're not the enemy – they're Kenny's mates. They've got families, too.'

'What are you saying – you care about not upsetting anyone more than finding out what happened?'

'No, love. It's just . . . You're going to need all the friends you can get in the next few years.'

Sarah looked at them both, aghast. 'You think this is about me chasing money, don't you? I've been trying to work out what exactly the problem is you've got with me, Rachel – now I know. There's only one thing worse than Kenny dying as far as you're concerned, and that's me and the baby getting compensation for it.'

'It's nothing to do with money,' Paul said calmly, desperate to cool the temperature.

He was already too late.

'How dare you speak to me like that,' Rachel hissed. 'Get out of this house, and don't ever come back.'

'I'm going.'

'Love . . .' Paul protested. He got up and tried to grab her wrist to hold her back, but Sarah shook free and ran to the front door.

Paul stood helpless for a moment, wondering what he had done wrong. He turned to Rachel. 'What did you say that for?'

'I've never trusted that girl,' Rachel said bitterly.

Paul looked at his wife and wondered how the joyful, fresh-faced young woman he married had become so jealous and embittered. If she couldn't have Kenny, she seemed prepared to destroy everything, to spread her misery as far as she was able. He realized in an instant that a life with her was going to prove unbearable.

'I'm going out for a while,' he said, and headed for the front door.

'Where?'

He didn't answer. He didn't know where. All he knew is that he wanted to drink away his pain in a place where she couldn't find him. Somewhere he could be alone.

Jenny made it home by seven. After a tumultuous morning her afternoon had been thankfully uneventful. It had been spent making preparations for Thursday's inquest and issuing a bland sequence of press releases she hoped would quieten down the excitement.

She had also taken the unusual step of writing to both sets of lawyers telling them that she expected them to conform to the highest standards of courtroom decorum and copied it to the office of the Chief Coroner. Neither Robert Heaton nor Claydon White responded but she imagined that they had got the message. Whatever else might happen, she was determined to run a tight ship.

Closing the front door behind her, she set down her briefcase and kicked off her shoes. She heard sounds of movement coming from upstairs.

'Michael?'

He stepped out of the bedroom onto the landing. He was wearing scruffy jeans and a grey T-shirt that hung off his shoulders. 'Oh, hi. I didn't hear you come in.'

There was something evasive in his manner that made Jenny uneasy. Hardly surprising, given the nature of his day.

'Are you OK?'

He shrugged. 'Not bad.'

She noticed the rings beneath his eyes. 'Fancy a drink?'

'Sure. I'll be right down.'

He turned back into the bedroom. Jenny heard more sounds of hurried movement. Something wasn't right and she had a pretty good idea of what she had just heard. She kicked off her shoes and hurried noiselessly up the stairs.

She pushed open the bedroom door to see exactly what she had expected: Michael lifting a fully laden suitcase onto the floor. Drawers were open, as were the wardrobe doors. It had been a hasty packing job. He looked up at her guiltily, but also with a sorrowful air of resignation. He sat heavily on the corner of the bed looking emotionally drained and physically exhausted.

'Where do you think you're going?' Jenny asked, trying to stay as calm as she could in the circumstances.

Michael let out a sigh. 'I thought it was probably better that I move out while you're doing the case. One of the guys at work has got a spare room – he lives in Bristol.'

'Why would it be better?'

'You've got a job to do. The last thing you need is to be worrying about me.'

'What happened today? I mean, not this morning – I know about that. What happened with Bramble, or whatever his name is?'

'Wing Commander Brammell. He was perfectly nice. I remembered him. The story is that the daughter of the

Danish guy in the vehicle started researching what happened when she got to university. She got involved with some anti-war group or other and persuaded her MP to take up the cause. He went to the police in his home town, Odense, and they have requested the cockpit video and full statements explaining what happened.'

'Wasn't this done years ago?'

'Apparently not.'

'What does Brammell expect to happen?'

'He said the MOD could have chosen to reject the request, but apparently there's a policy of cooperation with fellow EU countries. He doesn't think it'll amount to much, but even so, everybody's going to spend the next few months going through the motions.'

'Surely there's no case to answer?'

'That's not the point, is it? It's window dressing. If people see a retired pilot being called to account for something that happened over ten years ago, it gives the impression that we're all operating to the highest ethical standards.'

'The point is they would have stonewalled it if it hadn't been for me. I'm the reason this is happening to you now. Did he say when the Danish police made their request?'

'No,' Michael said.

'You didn't think to ask?'

'What difference does it make? Look, Jenny, this is precisely why we can't be under the same roof at the moment. I'm a distraction. And besides, if I'm no longer living with you, from their end it doesn't have quite the same impact, does it?'

Jenny pressed her hands to her face. 'We can deal with this, Michael. I can lodge a protest. There are journalists who'll take this up. We don't have to take this lying down.'

'One piece of good news – I went to the doctor and got

another ECG. My blood pressure was up but there's nothing whatever wrong with my heart.'

They looked at each other, sharing a sense of weariness and dread that neither had the power to lift.

'Yes, it's best I move out for a while. We're going to stress each other.' He pushed up from the bed. 'I'll get you a drink.' He stroked her arm, kissed her lightly on the cheek, then grabbed the heavy suitcase and lugged it down the stairs.

Jenny changed out of her suit in what felt like a state of semi-detachment. Her mind was so overloaded, her outrage so intense, that her brain seemed to have short-circuited and rendered her temporarily incapable. Ten days ago, she and Michael had been looking forward to a lazy holiday in the sun; now they were being forced apart by events wholly outside their control. She felt like debris caught up in the workings of some huge impersonal machine, and what made it worse was that there was no single person, no identifiable antagonist at whom she could aim her fury. Her only option was to continue down the tunnel in the hope of detecting a speck of light.

She pulled on jeans and a loose shirt and rummaged in an open drawer for a pair of socks to wear inside her canvas pumps. Sharing a sock drawer with a man had been a mistake that she had never found the time to remedy. She delved into the tangle in search of the pair she was after but couldn't locate them. She pulled open the drawer next to it that housed Michael's odds and ends with the thought that they might have gone astray. In amongst the never-worn ties and underwear that had long passed its best she spotted a small blue box. Curious, she took it out and opened it to find a gold ring set with a single diamond. Simple, but elegant. Exactly the sort of ring she would have chosen had the need ever arisen. She studied the box more closely: it was new, the edges crisp and clean.

Michael was standing on the lawn filling two glasses with white wine. Still barefoot, Jenny went out through the kitchen door and joined him.

'I found this.' She placed the box on the table alongside the wine bottle.

'Oh,' was all he said.

She waited for him to explain. Michael took a sip of wine. His eyes were sad, almost desolate. She noticed he had lost weight. She could see all the bones in his face and the muscles and sinews in his suntanned arms. She had been so preoccupied that she hadn't appreciated quite how he had been suffering.

'I bought it a few weeks ago,' he tilted his head as if to indicate he had acted on no more than a passing whim. 'I was thinking of giving it to you on holiday.'

She met his gaze, searching for what he was truly feeling. Whatever it was, he was hiding it well.

'Things haven't worked out like they should have done, have they?' Michael said. 'I can't even fly a plane. I've got the Danish police on my case.' He picked up the box and put it into his jeans pocket. 'Can we agree now isn't the time?'

'If you say so.'

'Look, Jenny . . .' Michael ran out of words. He put down his glass, threw his arms around her and kissed her with a passion that sent her back in time to their first moment as lovers. It was achingly beautiful and she wanted it to go on and on.

It lasted only a matter of seconds. Michael stepped away from her knowing that if they continued a moment longer there would be no going back.

'Don't go,' Jenny said. 'We can manage. It'll be OK.'

Michael shook his head. 'I'll call you when you're done with the inquest. Be brave.'

He smiled, and without touching her again, headed into the house.

Jenny stood looking out over the garden as she listened to him leaving through the front door and loading his case into his car. He drove off down the lane – slightly too fast, as always. As the sound of the engine faded and died away, she caught the faintest scent of bonfire smoke on the breeze. Summer was over, and the one thing in her life that had felt too good to last had proved to be just that.

Alison had spent the early evening delivering formal summonses to the homes of every member of the platoon. Each soldier had already been instructed when and where to present himself by text and email, but she wasn't taking any chances. Her contribution to what she expected to be fraught proceedings was to make sure they ran as close to clockwork as possible. With the last envelope delivered, she headed back to the office to lock up and to double check that there were no urgent emails on the official Courts Service account, which for security reasons, she wasn't able to access from her phone.

It was later than she thought – nearly eight o'clock. The evening was almost gone. She hurried along the empty corridors of the administration block and made her way to the office, where she tidied her desk and checked her computer. Thankfully, there was nothing urgent. She switched off her computer, swept up her few stray papers into a drawer and locked it. She was glad of having put in the extra hours: tomorrow would be an easier day in which she could concentrate on getting the court ready for Thursday's hearing.

Turning to go, Alison heard something – a shuffling noise, a footstep – coming from the adjoining office. Her first instinct was to call through to see if it was Jenny, but she realized it couldn't be. Jenny had called earlier to say she wasn't intending to stay late.

She stepped as quietly as she could to the connecting door, paused briefly, then yanked it open. Sergeant Price was standing awkwardly by the door to the corridor, having evidently found it locked as he attempted to leave.

'Hi, Alison,' he said with an innocent smile. 'I was just checking that the physical evidence was secure.'

Alison glanced at the items of kit which had been bagged and tagged in clear polythene sacks on the office floor. She couldn't tell if they were as she had left them or if they had been disturbed.

'Steve, what were you doing?'

'I told you. Just checking.'

He was a bad liar.

Alison had bitten her tongue for days. She had known exactly what he had been doing – keeping a close eye on everything, glancing over her shoulder at her emails, listening in on her phone conversations – but she had tolerated it on the grounds that there was nothing he was seeing or hearing that wouldn't soon be a matter of public record. But sneaking around in Jenny's office late in the evening was the limit.

Her patience snapped. 'Don't take me for an idiot. You've been looking for something – what?'

'I was just curious. I'm as interested in the case as you are. I knew those boys.'

'I know you did. So why lie to me?'

'I wasn't—'

Alison cut him off short. 'Colonel Hastings ordered you to report everything you see or hear in the office straight along the corridor to him, didn't he?'

Steve looked back at her with something approaching defiance.

'Didn't he?' Alison barked.

Sergeant Price looked startled. He hadn't seen this side of Alison. 'I'm a sergeant. It's the army – you do what an officer orders.'

'If you've interfered with any of this, it's not the army you'll be dealing with, it's the police.'

'I've touched nothing, I swear.'

'I've had enough of this,' Alison said, 'and when Mrs Cooper hears I know she'll feel the same. You're out of here. I don't care what the colonel says. Go. We don't need you here any more. The job's over.'

Sergeant Price didn't bother protesting. He knew there was no way back. Alison stepped aside and waited for him to leave.

When he had gone, she picked up the phone and called Jenny on her home number.

'You did the right thing,' Jenny said, when Alison had explained what had just occurred. 'I'll contact Hastings and tell him what happened. We'll move out of there tomorrow and base ourselves at the court. I've had my fill of that place.'

'Me too,' Alison said. 'They drive you crazy, these young soldiers – you don't know whether to shout at them, fancy them or give them a hug. Goodnight, Mrs Cooper.'

TWENTY-SIX

Jenny knew coroners who endeavoured to remain as lofty and distant as a High Court judge. These men (they were nearly all men) kept their contact with the families of the deceased to an absolute minimum, often only meeting them for the first time in the courtroom itself. For some there may have been an element of pride involved in their desire to keep a distance, but for most it was the fear of appearing too reassuring, of slipping into the trap of making unrealistic promises, that held them back from looking bereaved relatives in the eye. Jenny had never been one of those, but began to have second thoughts as Alison led Kathleen Lyons, Sarah Tanner and Paul and Rachel Green into her chambers at the old magistrates' court on Thursday morning.

All four appeared visibly traumatized and overwhelmed by the occasion. The media circus outside the building and the blanket coverage of what all news outlets had now lapsed into calling the 'Helmand 2 inquiry' would have done nothing to lessen their distress. It took only a few moments watching them settle into the four chairs on the opposite side of the desk to realize that there were even more tensions in play: Paul Green, still sporting black eyes, carefully placed himself between his wife and Sarah, but even so, Sarah dragged her chair two feet to the right before she sat. Rachel Green made eye contact with no one, least of all her husband. The tension between the three of them was palpable. Jenny felt for Kathleen Lyons, being forced into their company. She resolved to keep the meeting brief.

She thanked them for coming and explained that the purpose of the hearing was to gather as much evidence as possible into the circumstances of their loved ones' deaths. She couldn't promise that clear answers would emerge, only that she would do her best to get as close to the truth as possible. An inquest wasn't a trial – there were no parties competing against each other, no individuals in the dock – it was simply an inquiry at the end of which the jury would be asked to return a verdict. As coroner, Jenny would lead the questioning of witnesses, then allow the lawyers for the families and the MOD to ask questions of their own. In anticipation of what she expected would be a theatrical performance from Claydon White (although she was careful not to say anything that might suggest this), she explained that lawyers' questions had to be helpful and relevant – the lawyers' role was to *assist* the inquiry. If they strayed into point-scoring or argument with a witness she would be forced to step in. When she had finished her brief explanation, she asked them if they understood. All four nodded and murmured that they did.

'Does anyone have any questions or requests?'

Sarah glanced across at Rachel. 'Can I sit by myself?'

'Certainly,' Jenny answered, aware of the older woman seething. 'You can all have as much space as you need to make yourselves comfortable.'

Alison assured them that she already had it in hand. They would have a row of seats to themselves and two rooms had been set aside for them to visit in private any time they wished. If Sarah liked, she could see about sorting out a third.

'It's all right,' Kathleen Lyons said, 'I don't mind sharing.'

Rachel turned her glare on the grandmother. If Kathleen

noticed, she didn't let it show. 'It's a difficult time for all of us,' she said, perhaps aiming to apply some balm. 'I'm sure you'll do your best, Mrs Cooper. Thank you.'

Paul Green and Sarah thanked her also. Rachel couldn't bring herself to speak.

Jenny aimed her final remark at her: 'The pathologist's evidence will be the most distressing. If at any time you wish to step outside the court, please, just get up and go. I don't want this to be any more distressing for you than it has to be.'

There was still no flicker of response from Rachel. The poor woman was trapped in her own private hell. There was nothing Jenny could do to help her except get on with the job.

After Alison had showed them out, Jenny made a final phone call to the Selly Oak hospital and asked to be put through to Dr Thurlow, the consultant surgeon overseeing both Lee Roberts and Dale Carter. A secretary connected her to his mobile. She caught him just before he was due in theatre. She asked for confirmation that Private Dale Carter was still unconscious and incapable any time soon of giving evidence.

Thurlow's answer was admirably honest: 'I'm afraid Carter won't ever be capable of giving evidence. He's alive in only a relative sense. If he does regain consciousness, the shrapnel damage to his brain is so extensive that I'm afraid his life will be one of being spoon-fed in a care home.'

From Thurlow's tone, Jenny guessed that he rather thought Dale Carter would have been better off dead than facing whatever awaited him.

'What about Lee Roberts?'

'Still under heavy sedation. My psych colleagues will begin weaning him off shortly, but the short-term prognosis isn't good. Maybe in a few months he might be able to offer something that could be considered reliable, but not now, I'm afraid. As far as I recall, when he was lucid he didn't seem to have much memory.'

'That's right,' Jenny said. She had in front of her the two-paragraph statement Alison had been able to take from him. It said simply that he had no idea how Private Lyons came to be missing and that he volunteered to be one of the party that went into Shalan-Gar village. He remembered a burst of gunfire and a grenade exploding, but nothing more.

Jenny thanked Dr Thurlow for his help and left him to his work. She checked her list of witnesses one last time. There were plenty who might have something to say about Private Lyons, but very few who were present at Private Green's death. Of the five involved in the firefight inside the village compound, one was in a coma and another was in a psychotic torpor. The remaining three were Major Norton, Sergeant Bryant and Lance Corporal Jim Warman, a twenty-year-old soldier who had been on his second tour and whom she had once heard Sergeant Price describe as the quietest and gentlest man in the platoon.

Jenny was still pondering the seemingly contradictory notion of a quiet and gentle soldier when Alison returned, having seated the four relatives, to say she was ready when Jenny was.

'Oh, and one of the young officers gave me this for you.'

She handed Jenny a note. Jenny unfolded it. It was from Lieutenant Gallagher wishing her luck. She didn't know whether to feel touched or uneasy at receiving his continued attentions. She decided to give him the benefit of the doubt. Sometimes, but not often, people genuinely surprised you.

The courtroom was even more crowded than it had been for the preliminary hearing. A narrow gallery which Jenny had barely registered during her previous hearings had been given over to the press. There were thirty or more of them packed in, looking hungrily down at her from a height. The main body of the room was filled with soldiers in uniform and their families. Jenny spotted several senior officers including Colonel Hastings and General Browne. Simon Moreton was lurking somewhere near the back several seats away from Lieutenant Gallagher, who threw her an encouraging smile as she took her seat. Major Norton sat with Sergeant Bryant at the front of two rows containing the shaven-headed members of his platoon. In amongst them, incongruous as the only man with hair, was Sergeant Price, now formally relieved of his responsibilities as liaison officer. Melanie Norton, whom Jenny thought of as the woman from the cafe, was seated alone at the end of a row amongst some other women similarly separated from their menfolk. The four relatives had a row to themselves behind the lawyers. Sitting between Sarah Tanner and the female constable keeping watch over her, was another young woman. Jenny at first assumed she was a friend; only later in the morning would she learn from Alison that she was, in fact, Anna Roberts, the wife of the injured Lee Roberts.

For a brief moment after she had settled into her seat, Jenny felt an almost crippling weight of expectation bear down on her. More than a hundred sets of eyes were trained in her direction. The atmosphere of anticipation was electric. She dealt with her fear the only way she knew how – with the sound of her own voice.

She began her formal introduction: 'Ladies and gentlemen, this is an inquest into the deaths of Privates Peter Lyons, aged eighteen years, and Kenneth Green, aged twenty-one. Both men died whilst on active duty in Helmand Province. We will be hearing from a number of witnesses, most of them soldiers who were serving alongside the deceased, but our first task this morning is to empanel a jury.' She turned to Alison. 'Usher, would you please bring in the members of the jury pool.'

The process consumed the next half hour. Twelve members of the public who had received a summons for jury service were called in from where they had been waiting in the corridor. Immediately a harried-looking woman in her thirties asked to be excused on the grounds that she had an ill child at home. Several others followed suit offering arguments of varying persuasiveness. Jenny released a man who produced a doctor's note testifying to his chronic back pain and a young woman who had just begun a new job as a primary school classroom assistant. Those that remained looked on enviously as their former colleagues made their escape.

The nine remaining jurors were a collection of people unlikely to have been gathered together in any other circumstance. Two of the women were in their late sixties. One was bespectacled and smartly dressed – a retired doctor or academic, perhaps? The other was plump, softly smiling and grandmotherly. The other three women were all in their early twenties. One was a confident young professional wearing a business suit; the remaining two might have been scooped from one of the many bed-and-breakfast hostels in the town that housed the young unemployed.

The four male jurors were an equally eclectic mix: a huge bearded character of indeterminate age with thick tattooed forearms, a young Pakistani man with carefully sculpted hair, a retired blue-collar worker with a wiry frame and a permanently sceptical frown, and lastly a middle-management type in his fifties – the only one among them wearing a jacket and tie.

Jenny stole several glances at the lawyers as each of the jurors read from the oath card of their choice with varying degrees of confidence. She could tell that both sets were having the same thought: who were these small-town non-entities who were being called upon to decide a case of national importance? It was the moment in every inquest that always made her smile. Despite the best efforts of successive governments who had tried in their various ways to wrench this eight-hundred-year-old process out of the hands of local coroners and the ordinary men and women who made up their juries, inquests carried on as they always had. The truth fell to be determined not by trusted judges who had shown career-long loyalty to the Establishment, but by grandmothers, mechanics, young British Asians and unemployed young women struggling to survive on benefits.

The only downside of the jury system was the time it took to explain to complete novices, many of whom would never even have heard of a coroner, what was expected of them. Jenny took her time asking them to put all the courtroom dramas they had ever seen out of their minds and to think of the inquest as a fact-finding exercise. If, when they had heard all the evidence, they felt that they still hadn't sufficient grounds to make any finding as to how Privates Lyons and Green met their fates, they would be obliged to return an open verdict. But were the evidence to paint a clear picture of the causes of death, they would be able to return a verdict that reflected it. Possible verdicts included accident or misadventure, suicide, death by gross negligence or unlawful killing. In order to return a verdict of suicide or unlawful killing, the jury would have to be satisfied beyond reasonable doubt that the evidence justified it. For all other verdicts, they merely had to be sure on the balance of probabilities. A jury in a coroner's court also had the option of making specific findings of fact which they could record as a narrative verdict. The range of options open to them meant that they would have to pay extremely close attention to the evidence. They were about to embark upon one of the most serious tasks they had ever, or would ever, undertake. Lastly, she counselled them to stay away from all news reports and not to read anything about the case, online or otherwise.

'There is nothing that any of those journalists sitting up in the gallery or camped outside this court can add to what you hear for yourselves in this court. You, and only you, are the arbiters of truth in this. Do you all understand?'

Nine heads nodded in unison. Even the two young women, who half an hour before had looked entirely resentful at this intrusion into their lives, were sitting up and taking notice. For once in their lives they were being called upon to do something truly important. Jenny never ceased to be amazed by how even the most unlikely looking jurors invariably rose to the challenge.

Kathleen Lyons and Rachel Green chose to leave the courtroom while Dr Andy Kerr was in the witness box. While Jenny had prearranged with the lawyers that the evidence relating to the deaths of Lyons and Green would be taken in turn, the pathologist would deliver his evidence in a single block.

Over the years Jenny had known him, Dr Kerr, normally a man to avoid speaking in public if he could possibly avoid it, had gradually grown in confidence. He came forward and held himself with an air of quiet authority. His educated Northern Irish accent increased the impression that he was a man who dealt solely in fact, never in groundless theorizing.

His testimony would begin with his findings on examining the body of Private Pete Lyons. Before she started to lead him through his evidence, Jenny asked Alison to distribute bound bundles of photographs to the members of the jury. She warned them that they contained graphic images of the bodies of both soldiers during their post-mortems. If they felt unable to look at them now, they didn't have to. There would be plenty of opportunities for them to do so privately in their own time.

Jenny turned to Dr Kerr and asked him to take the jury through his findings.

There was a gasp from one of the young women and several shocked faces when Dr Kerr referred to the first photograph in the bundle which showed the clothed, partially decomposed body on the autopsy table. Although the head was situated above the shoulders, it was clearly not attached to the torso. Jenny herself felt a sudden and unexpected sensation of physical revulsion. She reached for her glass of water and took a large gulp.

Dr Kerr's even delivery took the worst of the sting out of the grisly evidence. There was no disguising the fact that he had found the examination an ordeal. He explained that the body was that of a slightly built male, five feet six inches tall, who in life would have weighed somewhere in the region of 115lb – a little over eight stone. His best estimate was that death had occurred ten days before the body was recovered and placed in refrigeration. This was consistent with him having gone missing in the early hours of 22 August. According to the official report he had been handed by the army, the body had been found on the roadside at Shalan-Gar following a tip-off and had been dressed in the clothing that it could be seen wearing in the photograph: boots, camouflage trousers and T-shirt. The wrists had been bound behind the lower back.

Cause of death was not hard to ascertain. The head had been separated from the body with a sharp instrument, probably a machete. Three or four points of impact were visible on the vertebrae at the back of the neck. Jenny didn't invite him to enlarge on precisely what this might have

meant. In the circumstances, it would have been an unnecessary detail. There were twenty-three bullet wounds in
the body. All of the rounds had been fired from behind and
had passed through and exited the front of the torso, causing inevitable damage to bones and organs on the way. The
relatively minor blood staining to the T-shirt indicated that
the shooting had occurred after death when the body had
already been emptied of most of its blood. These injuries
were consistent with a burst of automatic gunfire from
short range.

Jenny allowed the jury a short pause in which to recover
before she continued. Most had chosen to look at the
photographs, and most of those who had were wishing they
hadn't. The grandmother in the second row was already
wiping away tears. Paul Green and Sarah Tanner, however,
both remained expressionless. It was the young woman at
Sarah's side who turned a ghostly white.

'Aside from these injuries, did you detect any others,
Dr Kerr?' Jenny asked.

'If you turn to the sixth photograph in the bundle, you
will see a close-up of the fifth rib on the left side of the body.
The thickening around the rib that you're looking at there
is fibrocartilaginous callus – cartilage that bridges the gap
as the bone heals. It was a fracture, not a break, and I estimate it may have occurred three or so weeks before death.'

'What would cause such a fracture?' Jenny asked.

'A blow. I'm unable to say what kind, but it was a significant trauma.'

'And what symptoms might it have produced?'

'It would have been painful, for sure. He wouldn't have
been able to sleep on that side and the area would have remained sensitive. It may even have hurt to breathe deeply
– when running, or carrying a heavy load, for example.'

'More than just a niggle, then?'

'Certainly. I would be most surprised if he didn't complain about it.'

'Would you be surprised that he continued on active duty while carrying an injury like that?'

'All I can say is that it wouldn't have been comfortable. You or I would have spent at least a couple of weeks on painkillers.'

Jenny glanced over at the lawyers for any sign of reaction. There was none. All had their heads down, taking careful notes. Claydon White and Robert Heaton favoured the old-fashioned method and wrote by hand; Carrie Rhodes typed dextrously on a slim, state-of-the-art laptop.

'Lastly, Dr Kerr, can you talk us through the results of the blood and histology tests you ordered?'

'There were no obvious abnormalities in the tests we were able to conduct at this stage of decomposition. There were no signs of disease in the major organs. There was no sign of opiates or other drugs in the tissues, and hair analysis came back negative for alcohol or drugs.'

'He was a fit and healthy young man who was both clean and sober?'

'Yes, ma'am. As you would expect from a young soldier on tour.'

'Thank you, Dr Kerr. Before we move on to Private Green, Mr White or Mr Heaton may have some questions for you.' She turned to the lawyers, 'Gentlemen?'

Robert Heaton rose to his feet and, and assuming the role of a wise old head, peered at Dr Kerr over gold-rimmed reading glasses.

'The fracture you mention, it's the sort of thing sportsmen – rugby players or boxers – live with all the time, isn't it?'

'I suppose it is.'

'Soldiers take all sorts of knocks on active service. This is just run-of-the-mill stuff, surely?'

'It's a minor injury,' Dr Kerr said diplomatically.

'And probably far less serious to a man in his position than, say, a fractured toe?'

'A fractured toe would impede movement far more, yes.'

Heaton nodded. 'Well, we all know the phrase "soldier on" – that's clearly just what he did, isn't it?'

'I presume so, sir.'

Heaton aimed an avuncular smile at the jury, letting them know he was on their side.

'Now the matter of his stomach contents – disregarding the final meal of rice, vegetables and dates, are you able to say when his previous meal was taken?'

'Not exactly. Intestinal transit is a very hard thing to estimate. Typically the stomach takes four or five hours to empty and the small intestine two and a half to three hours. Somewhere between five and eight hours would be a reasonable guess. But it would be a guess.'

'Assuming he died sometime in the morning of the twenty-second, and that is an assumption, could the penultimate meal have been eaten late the previous evening?'

'It's just about possible,' Dr Kerr agreed. 'I would say late in the evening.'

Heaton thanked him politely for his assistance and sat down.

Claydon White took his time standing up. It would be the first time the jury would have heard him speak and he was determined to make an impression. Dressed in a dark navy suit and sombre silk tie, he exuded a glamorous dignity that wouldn't have looked out of place at a mafia funeral. Without saying a word, he already had their attention.

'Private Lyons was crudely and brutally decapitated – is that correct, Dr Kerr?'

'It is.'

'The rough twine around his wrists, the inexpert method of execution, the needless burst of gunfire into his dead body – it feels more like the work of an opportunistic lynch mob than that of professional assassins.'

'I have no way of telling,' Dr Kerr answered.

Jenny let Claydon White's comment, disguised as a question, pass. Having been burned once, the last thing she was intending to do was allow him to paint her as his antagonist so early in the hearing.

'At the time of his death, Peter Lyons weighed barely eight stone and had been on active service for weeks with a fractured rib. He was eighteen years old. What would a healthy weight have been?'

'Yes, he was technically underweight. Another ten or fifteen pounds would have been desirable, but in the intense heat it's not surprising he ate less than he might otherwise have done.'

'Would you agree that he had been allowed to fall into poor physical condition?'

Dr Kerr considered his reply carefully. 'The most I can say is that his weight was at the bottom end of acceptable, but he was about to return home.'

White shot straight back: 'It wouldn't have taken much to overpower a boy in that state, would it? And with a damaged rib, he wouldn't have been able to defend himself in a hand-to-hand situation?'

'I would have to agree that he would not have been particularly strong, though he was undoubtedly very fit.'

Claydon White nodded as if Dr Kerr had answered his question entirely in the affirmative. It was an old advocate's trick that never lost its power. It had worked: the jury's eyes remained trained on him, not the witness.

'And his system was completely clean. No alcohol or

drugs. Not at the time of death or in the weeks before-hand?'

'Correct.'

'Thank you. One last question, Dr Kerr – not very tech-nical, I'm afraid – but would you say that eighteen-year-old, eight stone, Private Pete Lyons, known to his comrades as "Skippy", I believe, was a man or a boy?'

Dr Kerr hesitated for a second or two, which was all Claydon White needed before stepping back in. 'It's not clear, then, I take it? We're talking about a boy not yet a man, aren't we? And a slip of a boy at that?'

'He was a young man,' Dr Kerr said, and left it at that.

Claydon White nodded his thanks and sat down.

In the brief silence that followed their exchange, Jenny found herself looking at the two rows of soldiers from the platoon, most of them barely out of boyhood. Some stared straight ahead, others dipped their heads or glanced uncom-fortably away. All were struggling to contain their emotions. In amongst them she noticed Sergeant Price, his chin resting on his chest. His hand moved to his cheek.

From her seat at the clerks' desk beneath Jenny's, Alison noticed it, too. Could he really have shed a tear? She remembered him saying that he had known Skippy since he was sixteen and found herself softening towards him again. It had been easy to forget that he'd lost two friends, and even if he had been spying on them, he was only a lad fol-lowing orders, and a lad who had been lucky to survive an IED blast with only the loss of an eye. Several seats along from him she could see Major Norton, his face as blank and expressionless as always: he didn't seem quite human. If that's what it took to survive, she thought to herself, a boy like Pete Lyons would never have stood a chance.

TWENTY-SEVEN

Kathleen Lyons returned to her seat but Rachel Green remained absent as Dr Kerr moved on to deal with Private Green's post-mortem. The photographs, at least, were easier to look at: they showed an intact body. Dr Kerr confirmed at the outset that the cause of death was a single bullet wound. The projectile had entered behind the right ear and exited through the left temple. The only other injuries of note were assorted lacerations on his forearms, face and neck. These were consistent with him having been in the proximity of a grenade blast. Although there was no shrapnel embedded in his skin, there had been small stones and grit which had probably been scattered by the force of the explosion. In addition, there were two significant bruises on the side of Private Green's chest and back, likely to have been caused by automatic rifle rounds striking his Kevlar vest. If there was such a thing, his was a typical battlefield death: he had been unlucky enough to catch a bullet beneath the rim of his helmet. An inch higher, and in all likelihood it would have bounced off.

Like Private Lyons, Green was in a depleted physical condition. He was a touch over six feet tall but weighed only 65.2kg or 10st 4lb. Despite his small build, his organs and skeleton were healthy and there was nothing to suggest that he wasn't fit for active service. Dr Kerr re-emphasized that carrying less bodyweight in fact made operating in extreme heat easier. Having dealt with this point, Jenny moved on to the issue she had been dreading. She asked the pathologist to explain the findings gathered from the blood, hair and tissue samples taken from the body.

Knowing exactly what was required of him, Dr Kerr kept his answer as low-key as possible: 'Alcohol was present at a level of fifteen milligrams per hundred millilitres. This is what I would term a trace amount. Cannabinoid THC was detected at three picograms per microgram. Although this is technically a positive test, it is on the margins of reliability.'

Shooting Claydon White a look warning him not to interrupt, Jenny pressed on: 'Are you saying, Dr Kerr, that the cannabis trace in the blood sample was so small that for all practical purposes it can be disregarded?'

'If there was a genuine trace of THC, and I stress *if*, then it was at such an insignificant level that it would have had no effect on Private Green's cognitive function, his reaction times or his ability to perform his duty.'

'Is the same true of the alcohol?'

'It was a negligible amount. I would be surprised if it affected his ability to function in any way.'

Jenny moved on rapidly and ran through the last details. She established that Private Green's helmet and Kevlar vest were not among the items of clothing repatriated along with his body. The clothing that had been returned had been examined but revealed nothing of significance. A tiny amount of broken glass in the left breast pocket of the tunic was consistent with that area having been struck by a round that was repelled by the bulletproof vest worn outside it.

Before inviting cross-examination, Jenny offered an olive branch to the lawyers girding themselves for attack: 'I am prepared to disregard the THC detected in the blood test and to discount it from consideration. I am also prepared to accept that however it got into his system, the trace of alcohol had no material bearing on the immediate cause of Private Green's death. Does this satisfy the interested parties?'

Robert Heaton rose quickly. 'From our point of view that would appear entirely sensible, ma'am.'

Claydon White interrupted. 'Ma'am, this was a soldier on active service. Alcohol and drugs are strictly forbidden by standing order and for good reason – these young men needed their wits about them. There are many reasons he might have had alcohol in his system which would have had a direct bearing on the circumstances of his death. We are not prepared to sideline this issue. We intend to examine closely the culture within this platoon and to get to the bottom of how Private Green was allowed to go into a life-or-death situation with alcohol in his system. You heard it from Dr Kerr's own mouth: a single inch is what separated his life from death.'

Another sound bite deftly delivered.

Jenny had to accept that he had a point. The issue of how Private Green came to have ingested alcohol couldn't be avoided, nor should it be. Nevertheless, she decided to fire a warning shot: 'We will, of course, examine the possible sources of the alcohol. But we will do so forensically, Mr White. I am sure you appreciate what I mean by that.'

'Of course, ma'am.' He was the soul of reason.

Jenny did her best to police scrappy and increasingly tetchy cross-examinations of Dr Kerr by both Robert Heaton and Claydon White. Heaton tried repeatedly to force him to accept that the alcohol in Private Green's blood could have been derived from a purely innocent source such as medicine, fermented fruit or even vinegar, which he was assured was among some of the food items that soldiers from time to time obtained from local residents. Dr Kerr stood his ground:

he was unable to rule such possibilities either in or out. Claydon White took the opposite tack and tried to force an admission that what Green had in his bloodstream was a morning-after residue. He was armed with charts that purported to show the rate of elimination of alcohol from the body of a man of Green's weight and height. According to his calculations, it was obvious that Green had been drunk the night before and may have been nursing a hangover. Jenny began to see where he was going: if he could paint a picture of Major Norton having presided over an end-of-tour party that inadvertently led to two deaths, it would amount to negligence and a large cheque making its way into Claydon White's bank account.

'Mr White, can we just accept that there was alcohol in the body and that Dr Kerr is not able to tell us where it came from?'

'I apologize, ma'am – for doing my best on behalf of my clients in difficult circumstances. It would have been nice to think that Major Norton and the other members of the platoon would have been able to assist on this point, but they have already wilfully obstructed justice by avoiding the tests that would prove whether any of them had taken drugs or not.'

'Let's not rehearse that now, Mr White.'

He wasn't to be deterred. 'It's hardly my or my clients' fault, ma'am. The only reasonable inference we can draw from the evidence so far, is that apart from Private Lyons they all have something to hide.'

'You will have your opportunity, Mr White,' Jenny said wearily. 'Now can we please let Dr Kerr go?'

Jenny's budget didn't extend to high-tech fripperies such as the computers and large flat-screen monitors that had become commonplace in other courtrooms. The large-scale plan of the forward command post which had been the platoon's home for six months was erected on a flip chart stand in front of the jury box. They had also been provided with several photographs of varying quality that showed the post from various angles, both inside and out.

In truth, there wasn't much to see: a rectangular compound roughly forty yards along its east–west axis, and twenty yards wide. Its thick walls were built from earth-filled Hesco bags. At each corner was a sangar tower: a metal framework protected from the outside by more Hesco bags, and with further bags on the tower's roof providing protection from above. The post was located on a slightly raised area, which was the highest point in that part of the Shalan-Gar valley. It was surrounded by mines to a distance of approximately fifty yards, save for the dirt road which led directly from the north to the solid metal gates at its single entrance. Beyond the mined zone were fields and orchards, which in the wet months of the year were irrigated by a series of ditches connected with the naturally occurring wadis that channelled floodwater down from the surrounding mountains. The Shalan-Gar valley was a primitive but productive farming area that produced a wide variety of fruit and vegetables from its silty mineral-rich soil, but its principal product was the opium poppy.

The statements that Alison and Sergeant Price had collected from the twenty-four members of the platoon who were now in the courtroom all had very little to say on the subject of how Private Lyons came to go missing overnight. Most of the men claimed not to have paid much, if any, attention, to his whereabouts on the evening of the twenty-first. Those in his section, who slept under the same tarp, agreed that he was present shortly after midnight when Sergeant Bryant had ordered a routine kit inspection to take place early the following morning. They also agreed that he was missing when they woke at five forty-five a.m.

Jenny had decided in advance to concentrate her attention on the four members of B Section still standing, Sergeant Bryant, Major Norton and the various soldiers who had been on sentry duty throughout the night. She began with the sentries.

Sentries had been on duty in two shifts throughout the night: from ten p.m. until two a.m., and from two a.m. until six a.m. Private Kenny Green had been one of those on the earlier shift and had been manning the sangar at the south-west corner which overlooked an orchard of apricot and almond trees. The remaining seven had little to say for themselves and were in the witness box for only a few minutes each. They all repeated the same line: it had been a clear night, visibility was good, and except for the odd stray dog, nothing had stirred outside the post. Claydon White asked each of them if they had drunk alcohol or consumed cannabis at any time during the tour or if they had seen any other members of the platoon doing so. He was met with uniformly predictable responses: there was no alcohol at the FCP, and if anyone had been caught, there would have been hell to pay, not just from Sergeant Bryant or Major Norton, but from the other men. Their lives depended on one another staying sharp and alert. Claydon White didn't force the point. For now, at least, his aim was to portray himself as a friend of the young soldiers.

The seventh and last of the overnight sentries, Private Liam Todd, entered the witness box and had repeated, almost word for word, the testimony of those who had gone before. He had manned the south-east sangar from two a.m. until six a.m., and had remained alert at all times. His field of vision interlocked with the sentries on the north-east and south-west sangars, leaving no area of ground uncovered.

Robert Heaton asked only a few questions intended to emphasize what each of the preceding sentries had confirmed: that it would have been close to impossible for Private Lyons to have been abducted from inside the compound without being seen or heard. It was incredible even to think that he could have left the post on his own, but if he had, the most likely moment would have been as the sentries changed over, when it was conceivable that, for a period of no more than a minute or two, the outlying ground might have gone unobserved.

Jenny had become curious to know what, if anything, Heaton and his team of MOD lawyers were proposing to put forward as an explanation for Private Lyons's disappearance. Two minutes before the lunch break, she got her answer.

'You and Private Lyons were on friendly terms, were you?'

'Yes, sir. We weren't in the same section, but I knew him well enough.'

'How would you describe his state of mind in the final days of the tour?'

'Same as always. Bit of a joker. Always had a smart reply.'

'In good spirits?'

'Yes, sir.'

Heaton gave another of the innocuous smiles that served as a pat on the head to the witness. 'Cast your mind back to February and March, if you would – the start of the tour. The platoon contained a Lance Corporal Darren Foster, a medic. Can you tell us please what happened to him?'

Private Todd shrugged. 'He went back to Bastion after a couple of weeks.'

'Because?'

The soldier glanced towards Major Norton as if looking

for a steer. Jenny sensed it was an unscripted moment, and purposefully so: Heaton intended it to make an impact.

'I'm sure you remember what happened to Lance Corporal Foster, Private Todd.'

'Yes, sir,' he said hesitantly. 'I understand he froze while out on patrol. His party had come under fire. He refused to run across an area of open ground to where they intended to take cover.'

'And what happened?'

'One of the lads had to give him a punch. Then they had to drag him. Could have got them all killed.'

'He lost his nerve and panicked. And had he remained where he was, he would have been killed?'

'Yes, sir,' Todd said uncomfortably. 'It doesn't happen often.'

'Had he exhibited such tendencies before that day?'

Todd shook his head. 'Not that I remember.'

'In other words, he snapped?'

'Yes, sir.'

From the corner of her eye, Jenny spotted Lieutenant Gallagher giving her a look as if to say, 'I told you so.' In the row behind the lawyers Kathleen Lyons adamantly shook her head. It was the first gesture Jenny had seen her make since her return to the courtroom.

As Heaton returned to his seat, Carrie Rhodes and Claydon White hurriedly conferred. It was she who stood to cross-examine.

Blonde, slim and frankly beautiful in the effortless way that turned men to putty and made otherwise level-headed women furious with jealousy, she smiled sweetly at the young man in the witness box.

'Private Todd, you said you were friendly with Pete Lyons, or "Skippy", as you all called him?'

'Yes, ma'am.'

'We've heard from the pathologist earlier this morning that he was a small lad – not much more than a boy. Did that ever concern you?'

'He was tough. He could carry his kit, do everything everyone else did.'

'Did he ever get picked on for being small?'

Todd shrugged. 'Only a bit of mickey-taking. We all get it for different things.'

'There was no feeling that he was a liability to the rest of the platoon?'

'No. He had it all up here.' He tapped his temple with his finger. 'When you're in a tight spot, that's where it counts.'

'Of course.' She flashed him another smile. Private Todd smiled back. He couldn't have failed to. 'The thing is, we know he had invested everything in the army, in being a soldier – a man. Whether he was mature enough to do the job that was asked of him is another issue, but what I'm interested in, is how you think he thought of himself. Did Private Lyons think he had done a good job?'

Robert Heaton rose to protest, 'Ma'am, this witness can't be expected to have insight into Private Lyons's state of mind . . .'

It was a borderline call. Jenny decided to allow the question.

'I think he was proud of himself, yeah . . .' Todd said.

Carrie Rhodes picked up on the lingering note of uncertainty in his voice. 'You're not sure about that, are you? What are you thinking of?'

She was sharp. Todd had suddenly lost confidence and was glancing anxiously at the rest of the platoon. There was no doubt he was hiding something.

'Please answer the question,' Jenny prompted. 'You really mustn't hold anything back.'

Todd shuffled uneasily, then, turning to Jenny to avoid

the eyes looking at him from the court, said, 'It's nothing, really . . . It's just there was one time when he got left behind out on patrol. His section had gone off across the valley and were going to be picked up by helicopter. He'd lagged a bit behind and they took off without him. They went back for him once one of the lads had spotted it, but it was a hairy moment for him.'

'I can imagine. And whose responsibility was it to make sure he was counted on to the helicopter.'

'Sergeant Bryant, I suppose.'

'You *suppose*?'

'It was a mistake – you know. It happens. He just had a bit of trouble living it down.'

'What was the joke – that it had been deliberate? That the platoon would have been better off without him?'

Todd shook his head. 'Not like you're saying it. It was a laugh. We all had the mickey taken out of us.'

Claydon White tugged his colleague's sleeve and whispered into her ear. Jenny sensed the atmosphere in the courtroom shift. The expressions on the soldiers' faces told her that Carrie Rhodes was finally cutting through to something.

'Tell me,' she continued, 'did you get the impression that Private Lyons felt he had to prove himself after that humiliation?'

'Maybe.'

'Well,' Carrie Rhodes said patiently, 'I think what you might be trying to say is "yes". Am I right?'

Jenny had to hand it to her, she was giving a masterclass in cross-examination technique.

'I suppose . . . Yeah, I guess you could say Skip was trying to prove himself.' He shrugged. 'What's wrong with that?'

Carrie Rhodes and Claydon White exchanged the briefest

glance, as if they were considering a dangerous gamble. His subtle nod gave her the go-ahead.

'Would you say that became his reputation – his source of esteem? A soldier who was constantly trying to prove himself, but who was nevertheless limited by his size and stature?'

Todd looked startled, as if she had stumbled on a sup-posedly unknowable secret. What she was in fact doing was skilfully pursuing a theory which appeared to be skirting close to the truth.

'I'm correct, aren't I?' Carrie Rhodes said when Todd failed to answer.

He nodded mutely.

'Think carefully – did anything happen in the days or hours before he went missing that might have dented his confidence further?'

Backed into a corner, there was no way out. 'I think he might have fainted on patrol.'

'When did he faint while out on patrol?'

'That morning – I mean the morning before he went missing.'

'And were people having a laugh about it?'

'It wasn't anything serious. No harm done. It was forty degrees. Could have happened to any of us.'

'And did it ever happen to anyone else?'

Todd made a show of trawling his memory. 'I can't re-member.'

'So, not that you know of?'

He had to agree.

'In your opinion, was Private Lyons physically and men-tally fit to go on patrol on the twenty-second of August?'

'He seemed well enough, from what I remember.'

Jenny glanced at the clock. It had gone past one. She would have expected a jury to be restless and ready for their lunch by now, but the exchange between Carrie Rhodes and the witness had their rapt attention. She decided to let the cross-examination run its course.

'Tell the court, please, what would happen if a soldier declared that he wasn't fit to go on patrol?'

The question seemed to stump the witness. The expression on his face conveyed an answer with more instant clarity than words could have achieved: the possibility was unthinkable.

'Did it ever happen, Private?' Carrie Rhodes persisted, 'or was that simply not an option in Major Norton's platoon?'

'If a man's not fit, he's not fit,' was the best he could do.

'Private Lyons had been nursing a painful fractured rib for several weeks. Were you aware of him ever having been excused duty because of that injury?'

'I didn't know he was injured.'

'He didn't let it show?'

'No.'

'Do you know how he came by that injury?'

'I don't.'

Carrie Rhodes was silent for a moment. She held Private Todd in a level gaze that was neither friendly nor hostile; it was one which simply expected the truth and nothing less.

'I want you to answer this as honestly as you can, Private. Do you think it was possible that, having endured an injury which you hadn't even noticed for a period of several weeks, that fainting on patrol during the penultimate day of the tour was something Private Lyons would have felt brought disgrace and the potential for ridicule down upon him? After all, there he was, the runt of the litter, so to speak, the one considered so insignificant he was even abandoned out on the field.'

'Ma'am, I really must protest at this emotive speech making.' The angry interjection came from Robert Heaton, whose simmering resentment at his opponents' success had finally boiled over.

His objection and Jenny's censure came too late. Carrie Rhodes had deliberately taken the opportunity to impress her narrative into the jurors' minds and had most likely succeeded.

Jenny then rephrased the question herself: 'Private, perhaps you can tell us what, if anything, you knew of Private Lyons's state of mind following the last fainting incident on patrol?'

'I didn't notice him much that day. I guess that meant he was keeping himself to himself.'

'Was that unusual?'

'I guess.'

'And when was the last time you saw him?'

'When I went up on the sangar. He was still digging a latrine.'

'Digging a latrine,' Jenny repeated. In none of the statements of any of the platoon had there been any mention of Private Lyons digging a latrine late on the evening of his disappearance. She opted for the most open-ended question she could: 'Tell me about that.'

Not for the first time, Private Todd had the look of a man who felt he had said far too much already. He seemed a good-natured young man, well intentioned but not over-endowed with intelligence. He looked over at the poker-faced Major Norton with a mixture of remorse and panic, but received no cue as to how to answer.

'Tell us about this task,' Jenny urged.

'I think it was for what happened on patrol,' Todd muttered eventually.

'Digging the latrine was a punishment for fainting on patrol?'

The soldier nodded.

'If I may? Just a few more questions, ma'am . . .'

Jenny gave way to Carrie Rhodes, already anticipating what was coming.

'While Private Lyons was carrying out this humiliating punishment, what were the rest of the platoon doing?'

'Just getting ready to bed down for the night.'

'The second to last night on tour. Was alcohol being drunk?'

'Yeah, we'd just been to Bargain Booze and picked up some cans.'

Carrie Rhodes turned to ice. 'I'll ask you again – yes or no?'

'No,' Private Todd shot back.

'Were the rest of the platoon passing around whatever it was you were drinking while Private Lyons sweated away his evening digging a latrine?'

'No,' Private Todd answered.

There wasn't a person in the room who believed him.

TWENTY-EIGHT

Jenny resisted checking what the online world was saying about her inquest as she ate her take-out sandwiches in the unnerving quiet of her chambers. Alone in a silent, timeless room, she felt bizarrely distant from what she knew would be scenes of excitement and panic elsewhere in the building, but at the same time she had a growing, ominous sensation, as if what had just occurred in court was merely a gentle precursor to something far bigger, and far more incendiary, which was yet to come.

Whether by accident or design, or more likely a mixture of both, Claydon White and Carrie Rhodes had found in Private Todd just the witness they had been hoping for. Through him, they had woven a convincing story of Private Lyons as a vulnerable boy soldier who, despite his valiant efforts, had suffered repeated humiliation. Although they didn't yet have evidence to prove it, the subtext of their narrative was that he disappeared over the wall in a fit of pique, or even in a self-destructive frenzy. Might it be that he had gone to attempt something foolhardy and heroic on his own – the ultimate proof of his worth? Or perhaps he had simply snapped under a combination of the pressure of his own expectation and that of being a constant butt of ridicule. Whichever route their story ultimately took, if they managed to stand it up, it would allow Claydon White to argue that Private Lyons was unfit for the role he was being asked to perform and that the army was responsible for his fate.

This had not been part of the MOD's plan and Jenny was certain that the witnesses yet to come would not drift so readily from their prepared accounts.

Alison burst in excitedly a few minutes before they were to commence the afternoon session, brimming with gossip. She had overheard an ill-tempered clash in the corridor between Claydon White and Robert Heaton, and while checking on the families had walked in on Paul Green pleading with his wife to make her peace with the soon-to-be mother of their grandchild. She had also seen Simon Moreton pacing agitatedly, relaying every detail of the morning's proceedings over the phone. She presumed he was reporting back to the Chief Coroner and had heard him use the phrase: 'The MOD are going apeshit.' Jenny stopped her there. Tempting as it was to listen to this hearsay, it didn't help. The prospect of returning to court was already causing her heart to pound and her palms to sweat.

'Just give me a moment,' Jenny said. 'I'll be through in a moment.'

'Something I said, Mrs Cooper?'

'No,' Jenny assured her.

She waited for the door to close and addressed the stifling, claustrophobic feeling that had been growing inside her. When it refused to abate, she resorted to desperate measures and said a prayer: 'Please God, please let me hold it together while I sort this mess out.' It wasn't much, but it was the best she could do.

The relentless thump-thump of her heart only grew more rapid as Jenny returned to a courtroom bristling with tension. Everywhere she looked there were either stern, anxious or expectant faces. She took a deep breath and called Sergeant Alan Bryant to the witness box.

Bryant marched smartly forward. Like the other men in the platoon he was severely underweight. Nevertheless, he exuded an aura of invincible physicality. His movements were keen and sharp, and despite his palpable toughness, there was nothing thuggish about him. His deep-brown eyes were intelligent and evaluating. He was polite, well spoken and chose his words carefully. An accent that hovered somewhere between rural Somerset and Bristol lent him a reassuring, homely quality. Above all, he gave the impression of being a man who would remain calm in a crisis.

He had had plenty of practice. As Jenny took him through her opening questions, she established that in twenty years' service, he had served in the NATO Implementation Force in Bosnia, with Operation Palliser in Sierra Leone in 2000, and had completed a total of twelve tours in Afghanistan and Iraq from 2002 onwards. For the previous six years, he and Major Norton had worked alongside each other during nearly every foreign deployment. Although he downplayed the fact, he was unquestionably one of the most battle-hardened soldiers currently serving in the British Army.

Having established Bryant's military record, Jenny took him to the evening of 21 August. But before she could turn to details, Bryant slipped in with a request: 'Ma'am, would you mind if I briefly answered some of what I heard said about Private Lyons this morning?'

'Certainly. Go ahead.'

The sergeant looked straight to Kathleen Lyons. 'That young man was one of the bravest and most dependable soldiers I have had the pleasure to serve alongside. Yes, he wasn't the biggest physical specimen, but size doesn't make a warrior – you only have to look at the Michelin Men the US Army calls soldiers to prove that. Load them with kit, they're all spent after half a mile – that's why they never get out of their vehicles.' His jibe at the Americans' expense drew smiles from the soldiers and officers in the court. 'The only reason I didn't count Private Lyons on to that helicopter back in March is that I assumed he was already on board. I hadn't clocked that he was still thirty yards away covering our backs. Yes, he tried to prove himself, but that's what a good soldier does. Believe me, if I ever thought for a moment he was a liability on patrol, he would've been staying back making breakfast. He did faint on predawn patrol that morning. It was hot. We'd covered five miles in full kit. But the only reason he went down is that he hadn't drunk enough. I fed him some water and electrolytes – he came to without a problem. I gave him the latrine to dig so he wouldn't forget next time. What I saw in Private Lyons was the heart of a lion – still a bit of a cub maybe, but well on his way.'

It was a heartfelt outpouring that flipped the mood in the courtroom. It was hard not to feel warmth and admiration for Bryant. He was the epitome of tough love: a man, one was tempted to believe, with an unnatural gift for transforming troubled and wayward teenagers into professional soldiers.

Jenny steered him back to the events of the evening of the 21st.

Bryant said that everyone had been looking forward to going home. There was an end-of-term feel in the post which he was having to keep an eye on. He and Major Norton were keenly aware that there were still pockets of Taliban active in the area and that they would have liked nothing more than to send the British packing with a bloody nose. There had been no room for complacency.

His job was to maintain discipline, not least because discipline was the greatest guarantee of safety. The main risk they faced in their final twenty-four hours was of an unexpected attack. Later in the evening, they had received intelligence reports that intercepted radio messages passing between the Taliban, who were speaking of a lightning assault on a British post. They knew it was as likely to be bravado and sabre rattling as a genuine threat, but all threats had to be taken seriously. He had wanted the men to be on their mettle, so at about midnight he woke them up and told them there would be a full kit inspection at six a.m. the following morning.

'And was Private Lyons present at that time?' Jenny asked.

'He was,' Bryant answered.

'And when did you become aware that he was missing?'

'I called the men to attention at six a.m. He wasn't there.'

'Had anyone noticed he was gone?'

'I don't think so, ma'am. Most of them had sorted out their kit the night before – they were still half-asleep. We searched the post, which didn't take a moment, and there was no sign of him.'

On closer questioning, Sergeant Bryant revealed that some of the men had been sorting out kit until one a.m. and that others would have been awake from shortly after five. The most likely time for Private Lyons to have gone over the wall would have been at change of sentries while there was movement in the post. If he had done so voluntarily, Bryant had no idea why. It was a complete mystery to him.

Jenny moved tentatively onto more contentious ground. 'Sergeant, you have heard it alleged that some of the men may have been drinking alcohol that night. What do you have to say about that?'

He answered without a moment's hesitation: 'I didn't see

any. I didn't smell any. If someone had managed to make some prison hooch – and I admit, that's possible – we're talking about a tiny amount and no stronger than beer. Each and every one of those men knew I would have blown my top if I'd have found anything of that nature. I don't seek to flatter myself, but not one of them would have risked being intoxicated.'

A quiet and apparently spontaneous murmur of agreement sounded from the soldiers in the courtroom.

Jenny consulted her notes. 'Privates Kenny Green and Dale Carter, both of B Section, of course, were on guard duty on the south-facing sangars that night. Private Green, as we know, had traces of alcohol in his system.'

Sergeant Bryant nodded as if to accept a regrettable fact.

'It's possible, isn't it, that even a mouthful or two of something could have made him less vigilant than usual? He might even have fallen asleep?'

'Knowing Green as I did, ma'am, he would not have fallen asleep.'

'The issue of the sentries aside,' Jenny said, 'is it possible that Private Lyons made his way out from the post by any route other than along the road?'

'There were two escape corridors through the mines, ma'am. Not marked, but we knew more or less where they were. Each about five metres wide. They led out diagonally from each of the south-facing towers.'

The reactions on the lawyers' bench told Jenny that this was as much a revelation to Claydon White and Carrie Rhodes as it was to her. Heaton and his team, however, seemed unsurprised. It made her suspicious. There had been no mention of escape corridors in any of the written statements. She had a feeling that the lawyers for the MOD were about to unveil a narrative of their own.

Jenny leant down towards Alison and issued instructions.

Alison brought out the heavy evidence bags containing both Private Lyons's and Private Green's kit and placed them on the desk. She then handed Sergeant Bryant two lists detailing the items belonging to each soldier that had been returned to stores.

'Let's accept for the moment that it was possible for Private Lyons to make his way unseen from the post,' Jenny said. 'I'd like to see if we can establish what he took with him. Can you first please tell me what happened to his kit after you discovered he had gone missing?'

'I saw his bedroll on the ground and his kitbag next to it. I tipped it out to see what was missing.'

'And did what you saw accord with the list just passed to you?'

He read it through carefully. 'Yes,' Bryant agreed, 'there are seven missing items: pistol, holster, night-vision goggles, bayonet, scabbard, notebook and cigarettes, though Lyons didn't smoke. He'd have given the cigarettes away.'

'We'll hear in due course that the notebook was retrieved by another soldier,' Jenny said, 'so technically, it's not missing.'

Jenny observed Bryant's eyes quickly scanning the members of the platoon in search of who that might have been.

'Do you know anything about his notebook, Sergeant?' Jenny asked.

'I thought I saw it with his kit, that's all. I don't know why anyone would take it.'

'It contained a letter to his grandmother – to be read in the event of his death. I understand a lot of soldiers do that.'

The sergeant put his momentary loss of composure behind him. 'Yes. We do.'

Jenny returned to the main subject. 'Given what we know was missing, it's reasonable to deduce that Private Lyons went out into the night with a handgun, night-vision goggles and a bayonet, which, as I understand it, doubles as a knife.'

'Yes, ma'am.'

'Do you have any idea why?'

Bryant glanced apologetically at Kathleen Lyons. 'I can only hazard a guess based on a few conversations I've had with him.'

'I shan't invite you to guess, but if you could tell us what he said to you?'

'He told me he never knew his dad, that his mum left him with his grandmother when he was a young lad. We get lots like that in the army. It gets to some more than others. I wouldn't say he confided in me exactly, but I got the feeling he was hurting. A lot of the lads would have been talking about going back home to families, wives, girlfriends, kids. He didn't have any of that.'

'Had he shown any signs of being unhappy enough to take his own life?'

'No ma'am . . . But then again, you never know, do you?'

'But he didn't take his own life. He was captured.'

'So it would seem.'

'Can you think of any other possible reason he might have left the post?'

'None at all ma'am,' Bryant said. 'None.'

'One last question on the subject of Lyons: do you know anything about him having a fractured rib?'

'He never let on to me he was carrying an injury,' Bryant said without hesitation. 'He was always right in the mix when the lads were playing football. It could have happened there as easily as anywhere.'

Accepting that Bryant had offered as much insight as he could into the disappearance of Private Lyons, Jenny moved on to the subject of the abortive rescue attempt. Bryant described the arrival of Yusuf, their local interpreter and go-between, and Major Norton's decision to lead a party to the village of Shalan-Gar in an attempt to negotiate their man's release. When Jenny asked if he had considered this a wise response, Bryant replied adamantly that they had no other choice – the alternative was to leave him in the hands of kidnappers.

'Did it occur to you that it might have been a ploy to lure you into an ambush?' Jenny asked.

'That was always a risk. It was one we had to take. When we weighed it up, we thought the most likely scenario was that Private Lyons had fallen into the hands of locals – part-time insurgents who had day jobs as farmers and shepherds. They would have known we had good relations with Musa Sarabi – the senior elder at Shalan-Gar – and that's why they sent his grandson to make contact.'

Bryant then described how Major Norton had gathered a detail to go to Shalan-Gar. They had driven the short distance to the village compound in two armoured Land Rovers. Privates Danny Marsh, Dean Paget and Mike Allerton were left outside with the vehicles, while he and Major Norton went inside together with Privates Lee Roberts, Dale Carter, Kenny Green and Lance Corporal Jim Warman. They found the village to be noticeably quieter than usual. The plan had been for Norton and Bryant to negotiate with Musa Sarabi while the others stood guard outside. But no sooner had the old man come to the door than gunmen opened fire from a nearby rooftop and a grenade exploded in the square behind them.

The firefight lasted probably no more than a minute or two, Bryant said. His memory was more a collection of fragments than a detailed sequence of events. Musa Sarabi's door slammed shut from the inside and they had all dived for cover in different directions. He made it to a gap between buildings from where he opened fire at what appeared to be three gunmen on the rooftops on the far side of the square. Major Norton had ducked behind a low wall twenty yards or so to his left and was also returning fire. Meanwhile, two men were down in the middle of the square – Carter and Roberts. Roberts appeared to have lost his legs – he was screaming. Private Green was pinned down behind the palm tree. He couldn't see Lance Corporal Warman, but would later learn that he had ducked into an alleyway several yards beyond where Major Norton had taken cover.

'I heard the major yell at Green to stay put,' Bryant said. 'I think another grenade went off at that point. There was a lot of dust. Bullets flying everywhere. Eventually, we took out the gunmen who had been up on the roof. The shooting stopped as quickly as it began. When the dust began to settle, I saw Green lying out in the middle of the square halfway to Roberts. A few seconds after that, the three lads who'd been outside were on their way in. I took charge of trying to keep Carter and Roberts alive while we waited for a helicopter to medevac them out. Major Norton searched the village for any remaining enemy. None was found. Nor was there any sign of Lyons.'

'Did you know at that point that Private Green was dead?'

'Yes, ma'am. It was obvious.'

'Had Green stayed behind the palm tree, do you think he would have survived?'

'Probably. But it's hard to stay put when your mates are bleeding out just a few feet away from you.'

'Did you at any point check his clothing?'

'No, ma'am. All we did was stretcher him out to the helicopter when it arrived. There were two lives in the balance. Sadly, there was nothing to be done for Private Green.'

Jenny asked a few further follow-up questions but

learned nothing more of substance. She had got as far as she could with Sergeant Bryant. With the troubling feeling that she had missed something important, she handed the witness over to the lawyers.

TWENTY-NINE

Robert Heaton rose to ask his questions of Sergeant Bryant with the relaxed manner of a man who had escaped unscathed from a tight spot and now saw the end in sight.

'You've been most helpful, Sergeant,' he began. 'And I'm sure we all appreciate that it can't be easy, relating events that are so fresh in your mind.'

Bryant accepted his thanks with a self-deprecating nod. Several of the women in the jury box smiled in sympathy.

'I think we can assume from what you have said that you were fond of Private Lyons?'

'I was very fond of him,' Bryant said. 'He was what I call a proper scrapper. Maybe wasn't the best at getting up in the morning, but put him to a job and he'd get it done.'

His joke raised a smile from Kathleen Lyons. Sarah Tanner reached over and touched her arm.

'He'd told you his family history, but given you no clue that he was deeply troubled?'

'If I had thought that, I'd have got him straight back to Bastion. He'd be a danger to the rest of us.'

'And I'm right in assuming, am I, that far from feeling under huge pressure, the platoon was feeling the pressure lift as the tour entered its final hours?'

'Exactly, sir. My only concern was keeping everybody focused during the last day.'

'Of course,' Heaton said. 'This must have been the very last thing you expected.' He turned back through the pages of his handwritten notes. 'There's one matter I'd like you to enlarge on, if you would – it's correct, isn't it, that all forms of alcohol are strictly prohibited whilst at a forward command post?'

'Yes, sir.'

'In your experience, how common is it for soldiers to brew something up?'

'It hardly ever happens. But even when it does, the most anyone can stomach is a couple of mouthfuls – imagine vinegar stirred up with rotten fruit.'

Heaton smiled. 'In your experience, was Private Green the sort of man who would have done this?'

'No. I would have trusted that young man with my life.'

'So if it did happen, it was out of character, to say the least.'

'Completely. But we're all human. We all make mistakes, especially when you add in a bit of peer pressure. But what I can tell you is that he was sharp as a razor the next morning. No one wanted Private Lyons back more than he did.'

'In your opinion, did he die trying to assist Private Roberts, who had been badly injured in that initial grenade blast?'

'It's not just my opinion, sir. I'm certain of it.'

'Thank you, Sergeant. I'm most grateful.' Robert Heaton settled back in his chair and gave Jenny a look of quiet satisfaction. From his seat at the back of the courtroom, Simon Moreton did the same. Colonel Hastings and his colleagues exchanged glances. She could almost hear their collective sigh of relief.

The lull in tension would last only seconds. Claydon White, until now a virtual spectator, rose to confront the witness with the dead-eyed look of a prize fighter facing-off an opponent in the final seconds before the bell.

'You're something of a bully, aren't you, Sergeant Bryant?'

'I beg your pardon, sir?' Bryant shot back.

'You heard me well enough, Sergeant. It's no secret in the regiment, is it? You pride yourself on taking no prisoners. If a soldier doesn't jump when you issue an order, you let him know about it.'

'Can we stick to questions?' Jenny interjected. 'And try not to be so combative, Mr White. I won't tolerate witnesses being barracked in my courtroom.'

Claydon White looked at Sergeant Bryant wearing something akin to a smirk. 'You're free with your fists and your boots, aren't you, Sergeant? If you think a man's slacking, you'll give him a punch or a kick.'

'I don't know where you're getting this rubbish from . . .' Bryant said, struggling to keep his cool.

'I'll tell you exactly where,' Claydon White said, allowing his gaze to drift across the courtroom before allowing it to settle on the jury. 'My colleague, Miss Rhodes, and a small team of assistants, have been contacting members of the regiment and their families and asking questions. That's our job.'

'Mr White,' Jenny interrupted a second time, 'let me make this clear – I am interested only in specific and reliable facts. Gossip, hearsay and allegations designed only to smear is not evidence and I won't tolerate it.'

'I have a very specific question, ma'am.' He turned to the witness: 'Did you break Private Lyons's rib some weeks ago by kicking him when he didn't jump up quickly enough for your liking from his sleeping mat?'

'No, sir.'

'Do you accept that you frequently do give sleeping men an encouraging kick in the ribs to get them to their feet?'

Sergeant Bryant hesitated for the first time. Robert Heaton shifted uncomfortably in his seat.

'I did not injure Private Lyons.'

'But you admit you kick men in the ribs?'

'The army is a physical environment. Everything I do is proportionate.'

'A proportionate kick in the ribs. That's an interesting concept, Sergeant.' White paused, then refocused his gaze on Bryant. 'Did you or did you not kick Private Lyons?'

'I don't recall,' Bryant answered.

His answer was greeted with raised eyebrows in the jury box and grim expressions among those who only minutes before had been so smug.

'You don't recall,' Claydon White repeated at the jury, and shook his head as if to say that the witness was taking them all for fools. 'Well, unless your memory returns, Sergeant, we'll just have to draw our own conclusions.'

Jenny felt the heat of Simon Moreton's stare across the length of the courtroom. He was pleading with her to rein Claydon White in, but his questions were perfectly proper. White was a grand performer – audacious – but more than bright enough to tread on the right side of the line. She had to admit that she was a little in awe: Sergeant Bryant was an imposing man; Claydon White was treating him with an almost casual contempt.

'Forgive me, Sergeant, I'm about to shoot in the dark here a little. I'm going to accept what you say – that there was nothing in Private Lyons's past to suggest he had depressive or suicidal tendencies. So, accepting for a moment that he was mentally stable, give me your best guess as to why he took the incredible risk of going over the wall.'

'I've already said – there is no credible reason.'

'From your perspective, maybe. Let's look at it from his. The boy had suffered a humiliation at the start of the tour when you left him behind. He got over it, proved himself over many hard months. Then, on the penultimate day, he fainted during a predawn patrol – another humiliation. Back to square one – in his mind, at least. Are you with me so far?'

Sergeant Bryant gave him a cold look.

'He's still nursing a fractured rib. While the others are relaxing, he's digging a latrine as a punishment. When he finally gets to bed down, you wake the platoon up. Please correct me if I'm wrong, but I imagine you screamed at the top of your lungs – and announced a kit inspection for six a.m. the next morning. What do you think Private Lyons would have done at that moment?'

'I imagine he checked his kit,' Bryant said.

'Am I right in thinking that allowing equipment to fall into enemy hands is a serious disciplinary offence?'

'You are, sir.'

'When had Lyons last been outside the post? Was it when he fainted on patrol earlier that morning?'

'Yes, sir.'

'Where was the patrol when it happened?'

'About a kilometre from the post.'

Jenny could have kicked herself. White was doing precisely what she should have done – pursuing the logical line of questioning and coming to an obvious answer. Why hadn't she? Had she really allowed herself to be overawed and intimidated away from doing her job? Clearly she had. This realization brought another: the ominous feeling that had gripped her at the end of the lunch break was nothing but her own cowardice.

'Bayonet and scabbard. Pistol and holster. Night-vision

goggles. Which of these items is he most likely to have left behind while out on patrol?'

There was a brief moment of silence. Then Bryant's shoulders seemed to sag.

'Sergeant?' Jenny prompted.

'We may have taken his goggles off when he fainted. It was getting light, anyway.'

'You took off his goggles and presumably also his pack – while you tried to revive him?'

Bryant nodded. 'He came round pretty quick. He was on his feet again in a couple of minutes.'

'And no doubt you were in a hurry to get back?'

'Yes, sir.'

'Seeing that he was conscious and able to walk, would you have considered it Private Lyons's responsibility to make sure he had all his kit?'

'I suppose so, sir.'

'But in the confusion Lyons might have left his night-vision goggles behind. A valuable piece of equipment that could be of enormous use to the enemy.'

Bryant was forced to agree.

Claydon White exchanged a look with Carrie Rhodes. He seemed surprised at his own success. At the other end of the lawyers' bench, Robert Heaton was whispering reassurances to his solicitors: the evidence was unexpected but didn't harm them. It was premature advice.

'All right,' Claydon White said, pretending to be thinking aloud, 'what it seems we've stumbled on, Sergeant, is the most likely explanation for Private Lyons leaving the post – he wanted to get his goggles back. And if that was the case, he can only have taken such an incredible risk if he feared the alternative was worse.'

'I would have reported him to Major Norton, that's all. He would have dealt with it.'

'Not administered some rough justice of your own? Another dig in the ribs?'

'No, sir.'

'You didn't send him out to get those goggles did you, Sergeant?'

Bryant bristled at the suggestion. 'If I'd known they were missing, I'd have sooner gone myself.'

Claydon White knew when to stop. Jenny reasoned that, having struck paydirt with Bryant, if he managed to persuade a few more soldiers to testify that their sergeant had crossed the line from administering military discipline to violent bullying, he would have all he needed for a verdict that laid the blame for Lyons's death at the army's feet. He would also have a powerful argument that the mission to Shalan-Gar followed as a direct consequence. He was tantalizingly close to establishing a case of gross negligence and was probably already smelling the commission.

White's objective was now to protect what he already had rather than risk too many questions that might have given Bryant an opportunity to rehabilitate himself. He struck a markedly less confrontational tone as he explored the death of Kenny Green.

He began by suggesting that Major Norton had been reckless in leading a party to Shalan-Gar when it would have been open to him to communicate by means of their local interpreter, or even by radio. Bryant dealt with this swiftly: trust and personal contact were everything when dealing with the locals. Nothing would have been achieved by radio contact. And besides, he and Major Norton had sat down with Musa Sarabi more than a dozen times during the course of the tour. He had proved nothing but co-operative.

Realizing that he was on weak ground, White shifted his attack to Bryant's choice of personnel, in particular to his selection of Private Green, a soldier who had been on sentry duty until two a.m. and had had less than four hours' sleep.

'You were leading him into a potentially dangerous situation. One in which life and death might depend on a split-second decision. Surely, given the choice, you want the freshest, most alert men at your disposal?'

'Maybe there were fresher men,' Bryant conceded, 'but when bullets start to fly, an hour or two's sleep won't make a damn of difference. If he hadn't been on guard duty, do I honestly think that Private Green wouldn't have gone to Roberts's aid? You have to be kidding me. I don't think anyone has said it yet, so I'm going to take my chance: Kenny Green died like a hero.'

All across the courtroom heads dipped and eyes lowered in respect. Paul Green finally found himself clutching his wife's hand, and Sarah Tanner, who had retained her composure throughout the afternoon, wiped away tears. Jenny would have shared in the spontaneous moment of emotion had her eye not been caught by a solitary dissenting figure: Lieutenant James Gallagher seemed to pull a face and shake his head slightly. He for one wasn't buying the hero line, and he seemed to want her to know it.

THIRTY

Jenny could have cut the day short when Bryant stepped defiantly down from the witness box, but the faces in the jury box were still alert. She detected an appetite among them to continue. The sense in the courtroom was of a story that remained half-told. She exchanged a glance with Alison, who seemed to be having the same thought: the end of a long and eventful day was when truth was most liable to slip out – when resistance was low and well-laid plans had been ravaged by events.

She called Major Christopher Norton to the witness box.

As Norton left his seat alongside Colonel Hastings, Jenny observed the woman who, since their meeting two days before at the cafe, she knew to be his wife. She was seated at the end of a row by the aisle her husband had to walk along. She looked up at him as if expecting him to glance her way, to acknowledge her and her support. If he saw her, he gave no sign of it. As he passed by, the hope seemed to leave Melanie Norton's face. She watched him go into the box and recite the oath as if he were a stranger.

The tall, angular, stubble-headed figure held the room's attention in an entirely different way from his sergeant. He stood perfectly still. Little or no emotion registered in his polite, measured responses. He didn't merely exhibit the stiff upper lip so beloved of the British Army, Norton transcended stiffness as he seemed to have transcended fear. He managed to be both soft and hard; approachable and unreachable.

Jenny began by trying to establish the nature of the relationship he had enjoyed with his men. He explained that he was on first-name and nickname terms with all the platoon, but operated at more of a distance than his sergeant. He was friendly with the men but not friends. While the men socialized, he would often be engaged in planning and administrative tasks. Although he was embedded with 2 Platoon, he had overall command of the five forward command posts stretched out along a twenty-kilometre stretch of valley. He was in constant radio contact with the other platoon commanders and with HQ in Bastion as they struggled to leave their area of Helmand in a state in which the Afghan National Army could continue to keep the peace after their departure.

On the evening of 21 August he had been working at the fold-up desk in the tarped-off area that served as both his office and his living quarters, 'If you could call them that,' he added with a trace of a smile. His attention that evening had been focused on arrangements for travelling back to the UK. He was also liaising with other platoon commanders over the radio, attempting to finalize inventories of equipment. At the same time, he was compiling a closing report on what he felt their mission had achieved. He judged it a qualified success: while insurgents had been largely but not entirely removed from the valley, he felt there was a sporting chance that, once the British had left, those who remained would be reabsorbed into the local population. There was plenty remaining to deal with – the opium trade, the lack of education for local women – but he and his men had helped deliver Helmand from the grip of ideological extremists. It was, as he had frequently told his platoon, an achievement to be proud of.

Norton confessed that, absorbed in his work, he had been only vaguely aware that Private Lyons was digging a latrine pit. Earlier in the day he had been informed that Lyons had fainted whilst on patrol, but had not regarded it as a major issue. No harm had been done. He had conferred with Sergeant Bryant midway through the evening and they had disagreed over whether to mount a patrol the following morning: their last. Norton had felt it might not be necessary whereas Bryant had been keen to continue with business as usual.

'Sergeant Bryant was right to press the point,' Norton added. 'He was determined to do the job until the last moment.'

Following that discussion, he had continued working late into the evening and had retired shortly before Sergeant Bryant announced his early-morning kit inspection.

'Did you consider that reasonable of him?' Jenny asked.

'If he thought it necessary to ensure discipline and safety, then it was perfectly reasonable.'

'And what of the suggestion that Bryant was, to quote Mr White, "free with his fists and boots"?'

Major Norton gave what Jenny could only interpret as a knowing smile based on long experience. 'A malingering soldier may need some robust encouragement. I have never seen Sergeant Bryant assault a man. There is a line, and he is someone I would trust never to cross it.'

'Was he a bully?'

'No.'

'Do you have any idea how Private Lyons's rib came to be fractured?'

'It could have happened any number of ways. The injury

was never reported, so I had no cause to investigate the circumstances.'

Jenny had no choice but to take his word for it. Unless one of the soldiers testified that they had witnessed Private Lyons being kicked, there was no evidence to prove it.

They turned to the events of the following morning. Major Norton had woken before six to the news that Lyons was missing. He had immediately set about drafting plans to carry out a systematic search of the surrounding area. The first search party was due to leave when Yusuf, their local fixer, arrived with the news that a group of Taliban were holding Lyons and demanding a ransom. They wished to communicate through Yusuf's grandfather, the elder, Musa Sarabi. Norton had weighed the options and decided that negotiation was the best way forward. He didn't assume for a moment that Lyons's captors expected to receive $100,000. The demand was typical Afghan hyperbole. He felt confident of being able to negotiate something far more modest: he had in mind a few rifles.

'You seem to have been placing a lot of trust in a young Afghan fixer, not to mention his family. Might your decision to lead a party into Shalan-Gar have been a little reckless?'

Major Norton bristled. 'There is nothing reckless about trying to save a life,' he said in such a quietly withering tone that Jenny felt her confidence dissolve.

She tried to press on: 'Couldn't you have negotiated through your fixer?'

'And had that failed, would I and my men have been better soldiers? Your question seems to imply that we would.'

'I'm asking what risks you weighed up, Major.'

'There was a risk that Private Lyons would be murdered. My duty was to stop that happening.'

'I am asking about the risk to the men you took with you.'

'We each risked our lives every time we set foot outside the post. That is the nature of war. That is what it means to be a soldier. Civilians will find that hard to understand – they live with the illusion of peace and the values that accompany it.'

Jenny felt crushed by his response. It was impossible not to feel as if one were in the presence of a superior being. Her questions felt spiteful and petty. With each one, she felt as if she were demeaning herself further. Nevertheless, she ploughed on and asked him to describe his recollection of events inside Shalan-Gar.

'I have nothing to add to Sergeant Bryant's account,' Norton said.

'Nevertheless, I am sure the jury would like to hear it in your words.'

'We arrived. We came under fire. The exchange lasted a minute or two. In such a situation the mind, in my experience, concentrates its attention on the task in hand. My focus was on neutralizing our attackers. I was not aware of Private Green's position until the firing ceased.'

'You have no recollection of ordering him to stay where he was, behind a tree?'

'None.'

'Were you aware that two men were brought down by the first grenade?'

'No.'

'What do you recall?'

'Musa Sarabi's eyes. A sense of his panic. An explosion. A burst of gunfire . . .' He stopped and seemed to search his memory, a curious expression on his face. 'No. Nothing. The dust clearing. Bodies on the ground. Women shrieking from inside a building. Then our attempts to keep Carter and Roberts alive . . . And a sense of deep regret that we had lost Green. I knew his father, you see.' He looked across at Paul Green. 'We served together in Iraq. I felt especially responsible.' For a moment the stiff upper lip seemed in danger of quivering. 'If you have to die in combat, then attempting to save a life is the way to do it.'

Norton's final words prompted simultaneous tears from both Sarah Tanner and Rachel Green and yet more in sympathy from the grandmother on the jury.

Responding to the sombre, mawkish mood, neither Robert Heaton nor Claydon White troubled Major Norton with more than a few questions. Jenny assumed that each had their own reasons to leave well alone. Heaton would be more than satisfied that Norton had presented himself in the best possible light, and White would know better than to take on a man who might just get the better of him. Besides, it appeared to be Bryant, not Norton, that he was gunning for.

Jenny ended the day by reminding the jury to avoid news reports and to resist all temptation to conduct any research of their own and adjourned until the following morning. Taking refuge in her chambers, she waited for the building to empty and the journalists to disperse.

She turned through her notebook and looked again at the evidence which had changed the course of the day. Claydon White's cross-examination of Sergeant Bryant had been textbook. Seemingly from nowhere, he had uncovered facts which seemed to unlock the sequence of previously inexplicable events that had led to Private Lyons's disappearance. There was no doubting that he was a skilful advocate, but it was also true that the mark of the very best advocates was that they seldom, if ever, asked a question to which they didn't know the answer. White had admitted in court that his team had been making inquiries and had surfaced with rumours that Sergeant Bryant was a known bully. That was the sort of gossip that was easy to pick up from anyone in the regiment, or even from a family member. But if he had been tipped off about the night-vision goggles, that would have to have come from someone inside the platoon, or at least someone very close to them.

That fact wouldn't be lost on either Heaton and his team or on Colonel Hastings and the faceless powers-that-be he was reporting to. Jenny imagined that a mole hunt would already be in full swing. If Claydon White had a plan to back up his narrative, it would have to involve one or more members of the platoon speaking up against Sergeant Bryant, but the more she thought about it, the less likely that seemed. The men of 2 Platoon were as tightly bound together as a group of soldiers could be. Stepping forward to commit what would be seen by their comrades as an act of the utmost betrayal would take either extreme bravery or a very large inducement. Jenny couldn't imagine that Claydon White, sharp operator as he was, was stupid or criminal enough to buy witnesses.

She took a sip of tea and mentally ran through the members of the platoon waiting to give evidence. There were fifteen soldiers. All had given virtually identical statements. The only one who had shown any signs of independence was Danny Marsh – one of the three from B Section who had been posted outside Shalan-Gar when the ambush took place. Could he have cracked? Jenny put a mark next to his name. She didn't like to think what might happen to him if he did implicate Bryant, but she had no choice. She had to push at the points of weakness. Just as in war, the search for truth inevitably involved collateral damage.

It was with this depressing thought that she scooped her papers into her briefcase and uncovered the good-luck note that Lieutenant Gallagher had sent her that morning. She recalled his expression across the courtroom at the close of Sergeant Bryant's evidence – his refusal to be swayed by the assurance that Green had died a hero's death. Then she remembered their brief meeting in the upstairs office at Highcliffe – he had mentioned a phone call from someone fishing on behalf of Claydon White's team. The detail of what he had said was obscured by the cringeworthy memory of his clumsy pass and her even more awkward response. She looked again at the note. It was written on his regimental headed notepaper, but alongside his office extension he had written his mobile number in neat black print that on first glance had been almost indistinguishable from the type.

She fetched out her phone and switched it on, feeling stupidly self-conscious. Why did there always have to be strings attached?

Gallagher answered on the third ring. 'Jenny! I was hoping you'd call.'

'I was wondering if we might have a quick chat?' she said, trying to sound as businesslike as possible.

'Do you know the Ship Inn, further along the front?'

'I'm sure I can find it.'

'It's got a car park at the back. Pick me up from there in ten minutes and we'll go somewhere. It's probably best if we're not seen together – wouldn't you agree?'

'Yes. Probably.'

She had no sooner rung off than there was a knock at the door. Alison entered.

'All clear, Mrs Cooper. I'm sure you'll be wanting to go home now after such a long day.' Her voice was peculiar and exaggerated and seemed to be trying to convey a warning of some sort.

Simon Moreton stepped in behind her. From his cheerful

expression Jenny could guess that his worst fears about what might emerge in court hadn't come to pass.

'Ah, Jenny. Not a bad day's work.' He waited for Alison to take the hint and leave, but instead she bustled over to Jenny's desk and found something to tidy. 'I thought you might be in the mood for a spot of early dinner. I'm staying at the Angel – know it? Not at all bad for the sticks.'

'Sorry, Simon. I've got to go.'

'Surely you can manage a quick drink?'

'I don't mind keeping you company,' Alison said, flashing Jenny a mischievous smile.

'Oh . . .' Simon said, casting Jenny a desperate, rescue-me look.

'I'll leave you two to it.'

Simon looked at her pleadingly as she stepped past and out of the door.

Jenny smiled, all innocence. 'Another time. Enjoy your drink.'

THIRTY-ONE

Jenny didn't at first recognize the slim, relaxed figure in sunglasses and faded jeans with a crumpled linen jacket slung over his shoulder. From behind the wheel of her car, she scanned the car park of the sea-front pub, looking for a military uniform. Only when the young man started to stroll towards her did she recognize the lazy gait and air of indifference – or was it acceptance? – that accompanied his unhurried movements. He strolled around to the passenger door and climbed in.

'Didn't recognize me in civvies?' He smiled behind the glasses. 'I've got a flat in town – living in camp never agreed with me. Where shall we go?'

'Before we go anywhere I need to know there's no danger of you becoming a witness. It wouldn't be right . . .'

'I'm not a witness. Does anyone know you're meeting me?'

'No.'

He nodded. 'Actually, I know a place – about five miles from here. I'll give you directions. Back out onto the road; turn left.' As she swung the car round, he reached into his jacket and pulled out a baseball cap. 'Sorry about this.' He put it on and pulled the brim down over his glasses. 'It's a small town.'

Jenny followed his directions. They headed inland for a

mile or two, then turned onto a side lane that followed the ancient boundaries between golden brown wheat fields on the cusp of harvest. Satisfied that they were no longer in any danger of being seen, Gallagher was relieved to lose the cap and glasses.

'Not my usual style,' he joked. 'It must suck, being a spy.'

Eventually they crossed a narrow stone bridge over a small river and arrived in a hamlet of a dozen or so sandstone houses arranged around a crossroads. In amongst them was the Sedford Inn. It looked like a place that was hanging on by its fingernails: a faded sign swung from a rusted bracket; the wooden bench tables arranged at the front had been crudely patched up by an amateur carpenter. 'Authentic' was the most generous description Jenny could think of.

'No mineral water. Sorry – too fancy for this place. Got you lime and soda.'

Gallagher set their drinks down on the table in the small, secluded garden at the rear of the pub. The grass was uncut and the beds needed weeding, but it caught the sun and was brought to life by the presence of two talkative hens and an elderly ginger tom, which sat watching them with inscrutable yellow eyes.

Jenny took a sip of her green drink. 'Wow. Fourteen again.'

'The beer's not much better.' Gallagher took a mouthful from a pint glass filled with a dark, cloudy ale. 'But still, it's the sort of thing I was dreaming about a couple of weeks ago. Cheers.' He forced some more down.

Without any alcohol to smooth away her inhibitions, Jenny found herself tongue-tied. As she groped for where to start, an awkward silence opened up.

Gallagher was good enough to save her. 'I found this place when I was out walking one day. I was with a girl, actually – we were engaged for a while, went to university together. We came here a few times one summer. Didn't work out.'

'What happened?'

'She was nice enough, but the kind who wants life to be over before its begun. Job, kids, house, Sunday with the in-laws. I suppose I must have given out that sort of vibe at one time.' He smiled at the absurdity of it.

'You were studying theology, you said?'

He nodded. 'Cambridge. Thought I had a calling.'

'What gave you that idea?'

'I had an identical twin brother, Harry. He died when we were sixteen. Lymphoma. Identical DNA but he was the unlucky one. My parents did their best but they couldn't accept what was happening. They lied to him, and to me, and to themselves. They couldn't tell him he was going to die. No one prepared him. Even when he was in a hospice they kept telling him he'd be coming home soon. It was cowardice – they preferred their version of reality to his . . . In the end, I had to do it. I could see he was scared. Terrified. I could *feel* it. You know they say this peace descends on the dying? Maybe on some – not on him. I mean, he was fighting, and he was furious with me that he was the one who was going, and I just had to tell him to let go and that I'd see him again soon. Something like that . . . It seemed to take those words, from me, for him to die. And so I'm looking at a dead body that's identical to mine – and I feel this thought crystallizing . . . I felt myself thinking that we began as one life that split into two, we're two halves of a whole, so if I'm still here, in some sense the whole must still exist. You can tie yourself in philosophical knots, but you get the idea – I felt a greater power at work, trying to tell me something.'

Gallagher smiled, as if vaguely amused by his teenage self.

'What do you think it was saying?'

'It was saying that life is like invisible water. It gets poured into you and at a certain point it drains away. But like water, it never vanishes. It merely changes form. And that's what we call God – the breath of life and all the unknown rules that govern it.'

'That's quite a thought.'

'It was more a feeling than a thought. A useful one. It carried me through a few tough years.' He took another drink from his glass.

'What ended it?'

Gallagher shrugged. 'I just woke up one day and the fuzzy feeling had gone. I was angry as hell about it. Suddenly I was down there in the pit with everyone else, caught up in the brutal struggle for survival.'

'Angry enough to go to war.'

'I guess.'

'Do you still want it back – the fuzzy feeling?'

'Do I think this is all part of the spiritual journey – the wilderness years?'

'What do you think?'

'Who knows? These days I try to stick with the here and now.'

'I'm not sure what kind of conversation I was expecting, but it wasn't this kind,' Jenny said.

'You asked for it.'

'Only because I got the feeling you were trying to tell me something.' She met Gallagher's gaze, overcoming her earlier embarrassment. 'Was it you who gave Claydon White the idea about the goggles?'

Gallagher glanced away.

'It was, wasn't it?'

'It was just a guess. Happened to be a good one, that's all.'

'Based on Bryant's reputation?'

'I've never worked with him.'

'That's not what I asked.'

'You saw his reaction. He was gobsmacked. He had no idea Lyons might have gone out looking for his bloody goggles. He may be a bastard, but there's no way he would have sent a man over the wall.'

Jenny checked herself. She was in danger of doing just what she had told herself she mustn't – taking evidence by the back door. She proceeded with caution, ready to stop if Gallagher offered any more than an opinion.

'I saw you looking at me when Bryant said Green died like a hero. You were the only one in the room who wasn't buying it.'

Gallagher glanced away. 'Just a feeling, that's all.'

'Based on what?'

'The fact that he had a baby on the way, that he was due to get married in two weeks, that it was the last day of tour, that if you're pinned down in a close-quarters firefight you want to hold on to life with every last fibre of your being.'

'A selfless act of courage? You must have seen them.'

'They're rarer than you'd think, especially from men with as much to lose as he did.'

'Don't people who get decorated for bravery always say they didn't give it a second thought?'

'Jumping out in front of three gunmen goes against the laws of nature, that's all I'm saying. Scratch beneath the surface of a man who does that and in most cases you'll find a death-wish. I'd met Green a few times, and he didn't strike me as that sort. That's just my opinion.'

Jenny was sceptical. 'This is all just instinct?'

'And a measure of suspicion.' His eyes looked directly into hers. There was something about them. Perhaps it was just having heard his story, but he felt like a man with no reason to waste her time with empty theories. 'Think about it, Jenny. What else do you know about him?'

She cast her mind back over the evidence, such as it was. 'Two bullets bounced off his vest . . .' Gallagher shrugged as if to say that was of little significance. 'No notebook, and some fragments of glass in his tunic pocket.'

'There are a lot of hours to kill out there, and not much to fill them with. Guys write things down. In your shoes I'd like to know where it's gone. If he'd left a letter it'd be nice for his family to have it. Personally, I keep mine in that pocket – top left.'

Jenny felt an unwelcome return of the sensation of dread that had ebbed and flowed throughout the day. Gallagher seemed to sense it in her.

'Everything all right?'

'Why are you doing this?' Jenny asked. 'What would Colonel Hastings say if he knew you were here talking to me?'

'I don't have a problem with war,' Gallagher said, 'just with dressing it up as something it isn't. Tell it like it is – blood, shit and pain.' He smiled apologetically. 'Sorry. Is that it? Are we finished with business now?'

'Yes. I'll run you back to Highcliffe.' She took a final gulp of her lime and soda.

'There's no hurry,' Gallagher said. 'Why don't you tell me your story. I'd like to hear it.'

He met her eyes again, and for a moment she forgot they belonged to such a young man. They seemed to see right inside her and Jenny felt that fleeting, dangerous thrill of connection far beyond physical attraction, that could so easily explode into something uncontrollable. He had felt it too. In the space of a second and without any intent, they had touched without touching; kissed without kissing.

She drew back and tried not to let him see how startled she was. 'Maybe after the inquest.'

'I'll look forward to it.' Gallagher smiled. 'It's a date.'

What have you done, Jenny? This, along with many other questions, swirled around her mind as the clock at her bedside moved inexorably towards two a.m. The young officer was missing something in his life. He was still grieving for his brother. He had fixed on her as an older, reassuring presence. It was nothing to do with genuine attraction, and besides, even if she weren't already in a relationship, rocky as it was, she would not under any circumstances be in the market for a twenty-three-year-old soldier. Her rational mind worked hard to assert itself over a confusion of conflicting emotions with only limited success.

Meanwhile, she was agonizing over Kenny Green's notebook and wondering how far to pursue the issue. Should she recall Bryant and Norton to the witness box? Would she be forced to go through every member of the platoon asking the same questions? If she did, it would become the news story of the day. Even if it had simply been lost, it would become the smoking gun, the missing piece that would ensure that neither Kenny Green's parents nor his fiancée would ever know any peace. Sometimes, exposing the whole truth was far from the most desirable outcome. Over the course of the day, this case had developed that smell about it. Now in the small hours, it was becoming a stink.

Two a.m. Jenny climbed out of bed and tramped downstairs to the kitchen in search of the emergency sleeping pills she kept at the back of a drawer. She rifled through and retrieved the packet, but found it empty. Michael. It had to have been. One of his many irritating habits – finishing things and failing to mention it.

She caught her reflection in the uncurtained kitchen window. She looked exhausted. Wrung out. Hardly the stuff of a young man's dreams – or any man's for that matter. This nervous wreck of an insomniac was meant to be holding court in the morning. It would be funny if it wasn't so serious. She grabbed some milk from the fridge, tipped a cupful into a pan and set it on the range to warm. Mixed with some brandy, it might just do the trick.

Waiting for it to heat, she reached for her phone and by force of habit flicked through the emails – all junk – that had accumulated since she'd last checked it at midnight. There was nothing from Michael. There hadn't been a message all day. What was he thinking? In her rundown state her imagination started jumping to conclusions: either he cared so little about her that he hadn't thought to get in touch, or he felt that whatever he did have to say couldn't be said yet. Either way, it was bad news. She put the phone down in disgust and tried to resist the urge to cry. *Pull yourself together, Jenny, for God's sake – people are depending on you.* Easy to say. So hard to do.

She poured the milk into a cup and sat at the table to drink it. Her mind refused to quieten. Her fears and anxieties seemed to accumulate to form an impossible burden from which there was no escape. She searched for points of hope, but one by one they shut off until all she was left with was a series of taunting phrases that endlessly repeated themselves: *You're a failure, Jenny. An imposter. No good to anyone. You used to at least have some guts, but you've even let that go. You deserved this case, it's shown you up for what you are – a sell-out, a disappointment to everyone. The truth will never be heard.*

She felt herself approaching the depths of despair. And then it struck her: the piece that she had been searching for.

She reached hurriedly for the phone and, with no thought

to the fact that it was the middle of the night, dialled Andy Kerr's personal number.

There were nearly a dozen rings before he answered groggily.

'Two thirty in the morning. This is a new one,' he croaked.

'I need something tested for tomorrow.'

There was a pause as Andy Kerr came to terms with the fact that his night's sleep was over.

'Only for you, Jenny.' He gave a sigh of resignation. 'Tell me what you need.'

THIRTY-TWO

No amount of make-up could hide the fact that Jenny had managed only three hours of restless sleep. She was physically drained, jittery from too many cups of coffee and deeply preoccupied with thoughts of what Andy Kerr might deliver later in the day. Most of all, she felt for the relatives. She wished she could tell them to brace themselves for more trauma, but she couldn't afford to give even the merest hint of the line she was pursuing. If she stood any chance of unearthing the whole truth, she would need to retain the element of surprise. Nothing would happen for a few hours yet. Andy hadn't been hopeful of any result before the afternoon. Her principal task for the morning was to stay calm; to keep things on an even keel and to chip away at the remaining witnesses.

Just as Jenny had anticipated, the remaining members of 2 Platoon who passed through the witness box during the morning session were barely more than monosyllabic, and bore all the signs of having been ordered to say the minimum. None of them was going to be tricked or seduced into going off message as Private Todd had the previous morning. Soldier after soldier from A, C and D sections repeated the same line: the first they knew of Private Lyons's disappearance was when they were readying themselves for kit inspection on the morning of the 22nd. None of them would admit to having any idea why he would have left the compound or to ever having witnessed Sergeant Bryant administering brutal discipline. Each time Claydon White suggested that perhaps no one had noticed Lyons climbing over the wall because they had been drinking home-made booze, he was met with blank faces and stubborn denials.

Jenny knew she wasn't hearing the truth. Occasionally she would glance across at Lieutenant Gallagher and see that he was sharing her frustration. A sense of inevitability began to descend. Jenny saw the hope bleeding from the faces of the relatives as satisfied smiles appeared on the faces of the three men in suits behind Robert Heaton. Anna Roberts, who had remained loyally at Sarah Tanner's side, held her friend's hand. Paul and Rachel Green both stared disconsolately into space; Kathleen Lyons seemed to have disconnected altogether and drifted elsewhere.

On meeting the same stone wall for the twelfth time, Claydon White erupted at Private Matt Laws: 'Are you honestly asking me to believe, Private, that for one hundred and eighty days in the searing heat and in fear of your lives, you stayed as clean and sober as a troop of Girl Guides?'

'I wouldn't know, sir,' came the soldier's deadpan response. 'They've never let me go camping with them.'

Laws's joke prompted an outburst of laughter and made Claydon White look ridiculous. The harder he had tried to drive a wedge between the men, the tighter they had locked together. With each new witness, the gains he and Carrie Rhodes had made the previous day were eroded further. Their whispered exchanges grew increasingly agitated as they felt the jury's sympathy slipping away from them. They badly needed to score another point.

Lance Corporal Jim Warman was the only member of the party to have entered Shalan-Gar village who was yet to give evidence. Like the others in B Section, Warman claimed to have been mystified by Lyons's disappearance and had no qualms about helping secure his release. He remembered being with Privates Green, Carter and Roberts in the square when the first grenade hit. He saw Carter and Roberts go down and ran for cover on Sergeant Bryant's order. Mindful of the need to fire at their attackers from a wide angle, he had run past Major Norton and dived into an alleyway between two buildings some fifteen yards from Musa Sarabi's house. He had been seen by one of the gunmen on the roof and had come under repeated fire. Unable to retaliate without risking being shot, he'd set off along the warren of passageways intending to re-emerge on the left side of the square. During the time it took him to work his way back to the square, he heard another grenade explode and multiple bursts of automatic fire. He got an angle on a gunman retreating over rooftops and was able to take him out with a single shot.

When he returned to the scene of the ambush, Privates Paget, Allerton and Marsh had arrived and Sergeant Bryant and Major Norton were taking stock of the three casualties. There wasn't time to think or to be shocked, it was all hands-on. If he felt anything, he admitted, it was relief that he was still standing.

As Robert Heaton asked the lance corporal a few gentle questions designed to cast him and his comrades in an even more heroic light, Jenny watched from the corner of her eye as Claydon White and his assistant argued over tactics. Carrie Rhodes seemed to stand her ground and get her way. It was she who rose to cross-examine the witness.

'Lance Corporal, you're an experienced soldier – if it were your decision, would you have led a party of men straight into the heart of Shalan-Gar village as Major Norton did?'

'Ma'am, really – is this a relevant question?' Robert Heaton objected.

'You can have this one, Miss Rhodes,' Jenny said.

'Would you have, Lance Corporal?' Carrie Rhodes urged.

Warman thought hard about his answer. As the silence stretched on, Jenny saw Claydon White daring to hope that he was finally about to get what he had so desperately wanted: a soldier ready to say that the whole enterprise had been a reckless fool's errand.

'I can't see he had any choice,' Warman pronounced finally.

'It took you a long time to think about it. You don't seem entirely sure,' Carrie Rhodes persisted.

'Well, the way I see it, what you're trying to get me to say is that Private Green was killed because Major Norton led us into the village.'

'No. I'm merely asking—'

'No, you're not,' Warman said, cutting her off and taking her aback. 'I'm sorry we lost Kenny – he was one of my best mates, but he had the wrong head on that morning. He was normally a calm lad, but he was right on edge – I could see it in him.'

'Maybe he had doubts about the wisdom of the mission?'

Warman shook his head. 'We were all angry about Skippy being taken – he was furious.'

'Thank you for your observations,' Carrie Rhodes said, attempting to cut her losses.

Lance Corporal Warman hadn't finished. 'There's no disgrace in it. He cared about his mate. I was standing closer to him than Sergeant Bryant or Major Norton when it all kicked off. The last I saw of Kenny he wasn't hiding behind a tree, he was out in the open giving it everything. It can happen when you're that angry – you think you're invincible.'

Carrie Rhodes tried her best to patch up a fraying case with several follow-up questions casting doubt on the quality of the lance corporal's recollection, but the damage was already done. The jury left for their lunch break picturing Kenny Green standing in the middle of the bullet-riddled square, ignoring Bryant's order to take cover and going berserk. As Jenny stood and made her way out, she saw Claydon White turn to comfort a bewildered Sarah Tanner. She didn't envy him having to explain to her that Warman's evidence might just have destroyed their case.

Had he known what would be sprung on them later that afternoon, his job would have been even more painful.

The three remaining witnesses, Privates Allerton, Paget and Marsh, had all been posted outside the Shalan-Gar village compound while the others went in. Mike Allerton proved the most taciturn and obstructive witness Jenny had encountered that day. When all she managed to elicit from him was a series of grunts and single-word answers, she began to believe that he must just have been as blinkered and unobservant as he claimed to have been. He was the kind of young man who seemed to have joined the army so that he could have all his decisions made for him. There was no danger of him deviating from the official line, and even Claydon White seemed to accept the fact. He offered only a desultory cross-examination during which Jenny began to sense that he had begun to write the case off. He had rolled the dice and come up short. His thoughts were probably already racing on to the next set of clients he would be taking for rides in his limousine and dining in expensive restaurants. The Helmand 2 were not going to buy him a villa in the Algarve after all.

Private Dean Paget was nineteen years old, smooth-skinned, boyish-faced and had a spark of mischief in his clear blue eyes. He struggled not to smirk as he took the oath. Jenny got the impression that he was one of the jokers in the platoon. He did his best to perform like the others had, but it quickly became obvious that he had an engaging, lively spirit that couldn't easily be suppressed. He clearly wasn't a young man who was used to thinking carefully before he spoke.

Jenny tried him with some open questions designed to prompt an unscripted comment or two. He admitted that Sergeant Bryant was prone to fly off the handle and that Private Lyons had incurred his wrath by answering back from time to time, 'But that was just Skip,' Paget said. 'He was like a little terrier – always yapping, even when the sergeant was standing right behind him ready to go off like a bomb.'

'Did you ever see Sergeant Bryant kick or punch him?'

'When you can shout as loud as he can, you don't need to smack anyone,' Paget said.

There was an eruption of laughter from the soldiers in the courtroom and the jurors exchanged glances at what they instinctively felt was a nugget of truth.

It was as much insight as Jenny would get from him. His account of events at Shalan-Gar mirrored Allerton's. They had been guarding the Land Rovers when they heard the first grenade blast and gunfire. They held their position, fully expecting to receive incoming fire themselves, while trying to make contact on the radio. It was Sergeant Bryant who had called them in over the radio about thirty seconds after the action started. They had lost almost a minute trying to beat down the heavy gates at the village entrance. By the time they had made their way through to the square the fighting was over. Through the fog of dust they saw bodies on the ground and Sergeant Bryant and Major Norton crouching over them.

The light left Paget's eyes as he relived the scene. 'Sergeant Bryant yelled at us to call for medevac. I got straight on the radio but it was hard to communicate for all the screaming.'

'Screaming?' Apart from Major Norton's passing reference, it was the first Jenny had heard of it.

Paget nodded. 'Women screaming. It was almost the worst thing about it.'

Jenny made a note of this detail and passed the witness over to the lawyers.

Seizing on a last glimmer of hope, Claydon White rose to cross-examine. He began unconfrontationally, winning Paget's trust with a few easy questions delivered with good-natured bonhomie. He got him to agree that he, along with most of the men in the platoon, was frightened of getting on the wrong side of Sergeant Bryant, and that, for all his bravado, Private Lyons may have been more frightened than most.

'Is Sergeant Bryant the sort of man who keeps soldiers in line by teaching them a lesson?'

'I suppose.'

'Would it have surprised you if he had kicked Lyons so hard he cracked his rib?'

'He was a little lad. Wouldn't have taken much doing,' Paget said with a shrug.

'Why do you think Private Lyons didn't complain about this injury?'

'He wasn't the kind to complain. He just got on with things. Everybody liked Skip, even the kids from the village. They'd all swarm around when they saw him – he'd give them the sweets out of our ration packs. They loved it.'

'Not just his own rations?'

'No, he'd cadge them off us, too – swapped his ciggies for them.'

'You gave away your sweet ration? Didn't you need all the calories you could get?'

'Hearts and minds. We tried to be friends with the locals.'

'And were they friendly?'

'On the whole.'

'I suppose we must be talking about the children and young men? I presume the women stayed well out of your way?'

'They did.'

Claydon White traded a look with Carrie Rhodes. She gave a nod as if to say they had nothing to lose.

'It was these young men you got your cannabis from? What did you give them – sweets? Money?'

'No—'

'You must have given them something in exchange?'

'No, I mean, we didn't—'

'You didn't what? You didn't buy a little hash off the locals and smoke the odd joint to take the edge off before you went out on patrol? Are you putting your hand on your heart and telling me, Private, that never happened? That Major Norton didn't look the other way because he was a commanding officer who pushed his men hard and took them out on patrol more often than any other platoon in that valley?'

Paget took on the look of a startled animal, and Jenny realized that Claydon White had acted his part brilliantly. He had given Allerton a gentle ride to soften Paget up, and he had swallowed the bait.

Robert Heaton turned a deep shade of crimson and was rising to his feet, but Claydon White pressed on.

'I'll bet you all had a slug of something and a smoke before you set out to Shalan-Gar. The ragheads had got hold of your mate. This was showdown time, wasn't it? You were ready to shoot those bastards to pieces, weren't you?'

'Mr White, please!' Jenny interjected.

Claydon White shouted over her. 'Is that or is that not the truth, Private?'

Paget's frightened eyes widened even further. He struggled to find his voice. 'No . . . no, it's not.'

Claydon White turned to the jury with an expression that let them know exactly what he thought of Paget's feeble answer. Keeping his gaze on them, he made his final remark to the witness: 'I admire your loyalty, Private. After all, as we have been repeatedly reminded, it is the most important quality in a soldier.'

Robert Heaton fumed with indignation and demanded that the latter part of Claydon White's cross-examination be scrubbed from the record. Jenny did her best to pacify him and reminded the jury that their only concern was the evidence. Facts and facts alone were all that must concern them. They listened, but with the scepticism of people who suspected she was trying to pull the wool over their eyes. Claydon White had done it again: planted a theory that had captured their imaginations far more dramatically than anything as mundane as facts.

Jenny turned to Alison, 'We'll have the final witness please, usher.'

As Alison stood to call Private Danny Marsh to the witness box, a familiar figure appeared at the back of the court. It was Andy Kerr and he was clutching a document in his hand.

'Actually, usher, I think we have another witness to recall first. Dr Kerr – would you like to come forward, please?'

The lawyers all looked up in alarm.

It was Heaton who got in first, 'Ma'am – we've received no notice of additional evidence—'

'No, Mr Heaton.'

He was momentarily speechless.

Claydon White added his protest: 'All interested parties are entitled to advance disclosure—'

'I'm not even sure what the witness has to say,' she said breezily, 'so, we're all at the same disadvantage.' She turned to Dr Kerr. 'You're still under oath, Doctor. I believe you may have something to add to your earlier evidence.'

'I do, ma'am.'

'Please sit down, gentlemen,' Jenny said to the lawyers, who were both still standing.

Like reluctant schoolboys, Robert Heaton and Claydon White obeyed.

'Carry on, Dr Kerr.'

'At your request, ma'am, I ordered a specialist examination of the glass fragments I had previously detected in the left breast pocket of Private Green's tunic top. Early this morning I personally delivered the tunic and the glass sample to Decon Analytics, a forensic laboratory I have employed on many occasions. A little less than an hour ago, I received this response by email from Dr Susan Adler. I am sure Dr Adler would be prepared to appear in person if required.'

'If necessary, we'll call her. What has she said, please?'

Dr Kerr read out the short email:

'*A small quantity of glass fragments approximately 8.6g in weight was subjected to microscopical examination along with the fabric of a camouflage tunic pocket in which glass fragments were embedded.*
The following findings were made:

1. The sample of glass fragments recovered from the tunic pocket during post-mortem examination were identical in structure to the fragments still embedded in the fabric.

2. The glass was of the alkali-aluminosilicate variety commonly known by its trade name, "Gorilla glass". This

*toughened glass is principally used as cover glass for portable
electronic devices, most often mobile phones.'*

Jenny felt her body greet the evidence with a heart-
stopping dose of adrenalin. She sensed similar reactions
throughout the courtroom. She reached for her glass and
took a large mouthful of water.

'So the upshot is, Dr Kerr, that Private Green may well
have had a mobile phone in his pocket that was shattered
by the impact of one of the bullets that was repelled by his
Kevlar vest?'

'That's certainly how I would interpret it,' Dr Kerr
answered.

'Was there a phone in his tunic pocket?'

'No, ma'am.'

'So from that we can deduce that it was removed at some
stage between his death and the body's arrival at the Severn
Vale District Hospital's mortuary?'

'Yes, ma'am.'

'And am I right in thinking that the body had arrived at
your mortuary having first been examined by a pathologist
at the John Radcliffe Hospital in Oxford?'

'Yes. It was brought by military transport. As I recall the
clothing and effects were contained in a separate bag.'

'Thank you, Dr Kerr. Does anyone have any questions?'

Claydon White and Robert Heaton exchanged a glance.
They'd both been caught badly by surprise. Soldiers at forward command posts were not permitted personal phones.
If Private Green had one, it would have been a serious disciplinary offence and a huge security risk for the platoon.

'No questions at this stage,' Claydon White said cagily.
His face was as pale as Sarah Tanner's behind him.

'Likewise, ma'am,' Robert Heaton said, though with a
degree of calmness that took Jenny by surprise.

'Very well. You can stand down, Dr Kerr.' Jenny sought out the witness she had decided would be next during the sleepless hours of the previous night. 'I would like to hear from Sergeant Steven Price.'

The looks of alarm that appeared on several faces in front of her told Jenny that, for good or ill, she had made the right call.

THIRTY-THREE

Sergeant Price remained composed as he recited the oath promising to tell the whole truth and nothing but the truth.

'You are Notifications Officer, is that correct, Sergeant?'

'Yes, ma'am.'

'And is one of your duties arranging the collection of the bodies of fallen men repatriated to the UK.'

'It is.'

'Did you arrange the transport of Kenny Green's body first from RAF Brize Norton to the John Radcliffe Hospital in Oxford and from there to the Severn Vale mortuary?'

'I did, ma'am.'

'When was the clothing first removed from Private Green's body?'

'At the John Radcliffe, ma'am.'

'By whom?'

'The mortuary technicians, ma'am.'

'Were you present?'

Jenny detected the slightest pause before he answered.

'Yes, ma'am.'

'And was the clothing searched for personal effects?'

'Yes, there would have been a check.'

'Did you witness pockets being searched?'

'Yes. I did, ma'am.'

'And if we call those technicians as witnesses they will confirm everything you say?'

'They will.'

'Sergeant, were you alone with the body at any stage before the clothes were searched by the technicians?'

'Briefly. Private Green's body was in a body bag. The undertakers who brought it to the hospital transferred the bag from the casket to a hospital trolley.'

'Where was this procedure carried out?'

'In the back of their transport.'

'A black van. A private ambulance?'

'Yes, ma'am.'

'Were you in that van?'

'No, I followed in my own vehicle.'

'And then accompanied the body into the mortuary?'

'Yes.'

Jenny tried a change of tack. 'Sergeant, is one of your roles to search the clothes and possessions of fallen soldiers to check for things such as the final letters that I know many men write to be read in the event of their deaths?'

'That would normally happen in theatre, ma'am. Someone would go through a soldier's kit and notify me of anything that should be handed over to the next-of-kin.'

'When Private Green's body was delivered to the Severn Vale his clothing was in a separate bag, but there was no Kevlar jacket or helmet with it. What happened to those items?'

'I took them back with me to Highcliffe.'

'Really? So they were there, in the coffin when it was opened?'

'Yes, ma'am.'

'And he was wearing the Kevlar vest?'

'Yes, ma'am.'

Jenny considered the multiple possibilities. Green's pockets

could have been searched on the ground in Shalan-Gar, in the
medevac helicopter, or at Bastion. There was no point wasting any more time with Price: she cut to the chase.

'Sergeant, did you or did you not recover a phone or any
other items from Private Green's tunic pocket?'

'No, ma'am. I did not.'

'Did you receive any notification that a phone or a notebook had been found in his clothing or in his kit?'

'No, ma'am.'

'Did the absence of a notebook seem odd to you?'

'I didn't give it much thought.'

Jenny looked to the lawyers. 'Any questions for this witness?'

Claydon White was quick to his feet. 'Would some
soldiers have had devices with which to listen to music –
iPods, for example?'

'Yes, sir.'

'Would you agree that Private Green was more likely to
have had an innocent device such as an iPod in his pocket
than a phone?'

'Yes, I would, sir,' Sergeant Price said with evident relief.

He glanced at Sarah Tanner and smiled.

'Thank you, Sergeant.' Claydon White sat, safe again.
Without proof of where it came from, the glass was irrele-
vant.

Jenny had found herself briefly distracted during Claydon
White's short run of questions. She had been watching a
flurry of activity taking place at the other end of the advocates' bench. A note had been passed forward from somewhere in the rows behind and had arrived with Robert
Heaton. Its contents seem to shock him. He turned to the
three behind him for verification then seemed to glance all
the way back to Colonel Hastings, who nodded, like a discreet bidder at an auction.

'Mr Heaton?' Jenny said, as he continued to ponder in silence.

He looked up at her, then at the witness, then over at Sarah Tanner. The aura of unflappable calm and authority had evaporated. As he rose uncertainly to his feet, it was with an expression of genuine shock.

'Sergeant Price, while 2 Platoon was on tour, were you conducting an affair with Private Green's fiancée, Sarah Tanner?'

The question was met with stunned silence. Rachel Green, whose gaze hadn't lifted all afternoon, looked up sharply. Anna Roberts's mouth fell open. Claydon White froze as he tried to compute what was coming next.

'No, sir,' Price said.

'You're absolutely positive about that, Sergeant?'

'Yes, sir.'

'Because, if for example, Private Green and his fiancée had exchanged illicit messages that revealed the fact – well, you would have had every reason to search his clothing.'

'It's not true, sir. They were due to get married.'

'Quite. Sleeping with a colleague's fiancée would, as I understand it, be a disciplinary offence.'

'Yes, sir.'

Heaton nodded regretfully. 'We'll see what Miss Tanner has to say about it, shall we?' He looked to Jenny. 'I think it only right that we call her, ma'am.'

'I agree, Mr Heaton,' Jenny said, feeling herself reeling from the allegation.

Claydon White let out an audible groan of despair as Jenny called Sarah Tanner to the witness box.

She stood up from her seat and looked to her lawyers for help but there was none they could offer. Carrie Rhodes gestured her to comply.

Sarah climbed unsteadily into the box. Heavily pregnant

and ashen, she looked as if she might faint at any moment. All of Jenny's better instincts cried out to her to show compassion, but there was no avoiding what needed to be done.

'I don't, I don't understand what's going on . . .' Sarah said as Alison handed her the oath card.

'Just a few questions, Miss Tanner. Please read the oath.' Jenny tried her best to sound soothing.

Sarah stumbled through it, her voice cracking with emotion. There was little sympathy coming her way from the soldiers in the courtroom. Rachel Green fixed her with a look of pure venom.

'Miss Tanner, please answer my questions truthfully. Failure to do so is a serious matter, do you understand?'

She nodded, sniffing back tears.

'Did your fiancée, Private Green, have a phone with him during the tour?'

'I don't see why this is . . .' She faltered and sobbed.

'Please answer the question, Miss Tanner.'

'He hardly ever . . . he hardly ever used it. Five or six times, that's all . . . Only texts. Just to say he was thinking of me.'

'Do you have the phone on which you received these messages?'

Sarah looked at her with startled, frightened eyes and shook her head.

'What happened to it?'

'I . . .' Her mouth moved noiselessly.

'Did Sergeant Price advise you to get rid of it?'

'I didn't want to get Kenny into trouble . . . What does it matter anyway?' Her desperate plea echoed around a silent courtroom.

Anxious to end Sarah's ordeal as quickly as possible, Jenny followed her instinct: 'Did you send Kenny a message before he died indicating that he might not be getting the homecoming he was expecting?'

Sarah broke down and wept. Jenny waited nearly a minute for her to collect herself.

'All I said . . . All I said, was that we needed to talk.'

'And when did you send this message?'

'About midnight . . . on the twenty-first . . . I shouldn't have. I was feeling . . . It was over with Steve anyway . . . I would have married Kenny. I know I would.'

'So about three thirty a.m. on the night Private Lyons went missing. Did he respond?'

'No.' Sarah broke down again. This time there was no hope of her recovering.

Jenny gestured to Alison to see her out. Sarah's wrenching, painful sobs continued all the way to the back of the courtroom. The female police followed them out. Anna Roberts, Jenny noticed, remained in her seat. There was a moment of silence, then Sergeant Price shot up from his seat and marched out of the courtroom too. The soldiers of 2 Platoon stared contemptuously after him. He had transgressed in one of the most unforgivable ways and compounded it by lying. His career was over, along with any chance of walking safely through Highcliffe again. If Colonel Hastings felt any emotion at having thrown him to the wolves, he didn't let it show. A hint of a smile played across his soft features. Jenny glanced across at Lieutenant Gallagher and remembered what he had told her during their first meeting in the tea room: 'Shit rolls downhill.' She couldn't have put it more succinctly.

It was late in the afternoon at the end of a long week. Everyone in the room was desperate to leave, draw breath and take stock, but Jenny had something to say that couldn't wait. She addressed herself to the rows of soldiers, to Sergeant Bryant and Major Norton and to the wives, girlfriends and family members scattered throughout the room.

'There are many people present who have proved themselves immeasurably brave. They have confronted dangers the rest of us aren't able to comprehend. But I now know that not all of them have told the whole truth. I want all of those people, and those who love them, to ask themselves just who and what it is they are serving. What did those two young men give their lives for? If you have something more to say, it is your duty to say it.' She surveyed the ranks of faces looking back at her. 'We'll resume at ten a.m. on Monday morning. If you have anything you would like to tell me in the meantime, please contact my office over the weekend.'

As Jenny left the courtroom, Anna Roberts jumped up from her seat and caught up with Melanie Norton as she hurried to be one of the first out of the door.

'Melanie. I need to talk to you.'

Melanie kept walking. 'I'm in a hurry.'

Anna grabbed hold of her arm as soldiers pushed past either side of them.

'Anna, please.' She tried to shake free but Anna had a tight grip on her.

'He knows something. Your husband *knows* something. Look at these men. Look at them all – they'll do anything for him.'

Kathleen Lyons appeared at Anna's shoulder. 'We all share some of the blame, Mrs Norton,' she said. 'We've all lived the same lies.'

Cornered, Melanie glanced across the room and saw her husband making his way along the row behind Sergeant Bryant. He looked back and saw her with Anna and Kathleen.

'Leave her,' Kathleen said, and steered Anna towards the exit, leaving Melanie in the emptying aisle.

Major Norton came to the end of the row and sent Bryant on his way. He waited for a while, making no move towards Melanie as the last of his men trickled out of the door.

Melanie opened her mouth to speak.

'Not here,' he said, nodding towards the front of the courtroom, where the lawyers were still in huddles and Claydon White was attempting to console a distraught Rachel Green. 'No need to look so distressed. We'll find somewhere private.' He started towards the door.

'No.'

He turned. Her voice had carried and turned the heads of Carrie Rhodes and one of the MOD lawyers.

'Calm down, Melanie. Please.'

'You can tell the truth or you can say goodbye to me and the girls.'

'I had no idea Green had a phone . . .'

'I mean it, Chris. Cowards lie. You may be many things, but I never thought you were that.'

He looked at her with a shocked, wounded expression, then turned abruptly towards the door and marched out.

Melanie let him go. Finally, she thought, she had got to him.

Jenny had made a swift getaway. Knowing that Simon Moreton would be desperate to collar her, she had dashed straight from the courtroom, down the back stairs and out of the building, pausing only to grab her briefcase from her chambers. Whatever the fallout from the afternoon's revelations, it could wait until tomorrow. It was Friday night and were it not for the adrenalin still coursing through her veins, she would be close to exhaustion. She planned on buying some wine and a takeaway meal and blotting out the world for the rest of the evening.

She was ten miles out of Highcliffe with the stereo turned up loud and the wind blowing through the open window when the music stopped and the ringtone from her phone sounded through the speakers.

She looked at the caller display on the dash, begging for it not to be Simon. It wasn't. It was an unknown number. She resisted the urge to shut the phone off altogether and hit the button on the steering wheel to answer the call.

'Hello? Jenny Cooper.'

'It's Major Norton.' He sounded hesitant. Strangely unsure of himself.

'Major. How can I help you?'

There was a pause. She heard him swallow: every tiny sound was grossly amplified by the six high-quality speakers channelling the call. 'I know it's not the most convenient time, but I wondered if we might meet briefly. I feel I may have something to say.'

THIRTY-FOUR

The windscreen spotted with rain as Jenny pulled over into a lay-by and keyed the location Norton had given her into the satnav. It was a coastal car park, situated several miles outside Highcliffe at the end of a single-track lane that led down to the sand dunes of Whitehorse Bay. She had a vague memory of once having visited there with her parents. Norton had explained the location on the grounds that he needed to be assured he could speak to her privately and that wasn't possible in Highcliffe. Jenny said she understood, but left him in no doubt that anything he told her could potentially be used in evidence. Norton said that he had anticipated that would be so. They had arranged to rendezvous in forty-five minutes.

Jenny started back the way she had come, with her hopes of a relaxing evening dashed.

She tried playing some music – an old Pretenders CD that was usually guaranteed to bathe her in nostalgia – but her emotions refused to stir. She was stubbornly stuck in work mode. She decided that she would make it clear from the outset that this was to be a strictly on-the-record conversation. Norton would be given a choice: she could record their exchange on her phone or write verbatim notes. Either way, she would transcribe the content and turn the parts relevant to the inquest into the form of a witness statement.

She would still be skating dangerously close to the margins of what she could get away with, but on balance she decided that she was better off hearing what he had to say. Jenny had never been inclined to follow protocol for its own sake. The interests of truth, she had always thought, trump those of procedure.

Approaching the outskirts of Highcliffe, she spotted Alison driving from the opposite direction on her way home to Bristol. Alison must have seen her too – she flashed her headlights. Anticipating her inevitable call to see why she was going back, Jenny called her first.

'Alison, hi.'

'I thought that was you. Forgotten something?'

'No. Major Norton called me. He wants to meet – somewhere called Whitehorse Bay, not far out of town. I assume he doesn't want anyone seeing us together.'

'Oh . . .'

'I know what you're thinking, but I've made it clear that this is on a formal basis. If he wants to talk in a car park instead of across a desk, that's fine, but the rules are the same.'

'Do you think it's about the phone business? I heard some of the soldiers talking – they had no idea. It's against standing orders – he'd have been in serious trouble.'

'He was young and in love. It makes people reckless.'

'It's not much better when you're old and in love,' Alison said. 'It's the poor girl I feel sorry for. She won't be able to show her face.'

'Sergeant Price won't find himself very popular either.'

'He should have known better,' Alison said. 'He'll just have to take what's coming.'

'I'll call you later,' Jenny said. 'Thank God this will soon be over.'

The route took Jenny back through the centre of town,

then south along the narrow coast road. A mile and a half out of town she turned right at the sign to Whitehorse Bay. A keen and unpredictable Atlantic breeze had picked up. The low trees either side of the lane were being buffeted this way and that by erratic gusts. The low, darkening clouds promised rainstorms soon. It wasn't an evening that would be tempting many down to the beach. After a further mile without encountering a single vehicle, the lane terminated at a gate to a rough farm track. To the right was an entrance to a car park, which amounted to little more than a levelled-off area of hard-packed sand. She turned in and found it empty – a glance at the clock told her she was five minutes early. She parked facing out to the windswept dunes and the foam-flecked sea beyond.

The last place Gallagher wanted to be on a Friday night was the officers' mess. He was one of a number of young officers who had been asked by Major Norton to join him in entertaining a visiting party from the 1st Kenya Rifles who had spent the week training with B Company on Salisbury Plain. In several weeks' time he was meant to be part of a group led by Norton who would travel back with them to their base at Nanyuki in the shadow of Mount Kenya. There they were to train new recruits in counter-insurgency techniques honed in Helmand. There were far worse jobs in the British Army and he liked what he had seen of the Kenyans, but he knew they liked to drink, and as a junior officer he would be expected to keep them company. He had never been much of a drinker – a beer or two was fine; half a bottle of red was enough to give him a bad head the following morning – so tonight was guaranteed to leave him with a stinking hangover. From the champagne through to the port and brandy, it was his and his fellow lieutenants' duty to get their esteemed guests as drunk as possible and match them glass for glass.

Fully expecting to be close to incapable by the time the last cigars were extinguished, Gallagher had booked a guest room in a neighbouring accommodation block. He lugged his overnight bag upstairs and smartened himself up ready for the evening's onslaught.

He was dressed in his freshly pressed uniform and dabbing at a stubborn shaving cut when he heard the siren. It was an unusual enough sound at this early hour of the evening to make him part the blinds. Gallagher looked out to see a car bearing the insignia of the Royal Military Police, blue lights flashing, race past the block, turn left and head off in the direction of the regimental stores. Thinking nothing more of it, he finally succeeded in staunching the cut and buttoned his jacket. Turning to the door, he heard a second siren, slightly different in tone from the first. He went again to the window and saw a civilian ambulance heading in the same direction as the police car. It crossed his mind that Sergeant Price might have found himself on the end of a few fists after being exposed in court. If so, he only had himself to blame for not steering clear of the camp. *Stupid bastard.* It was almost a rule of army life that you didn't sleep with another man's girl. Gallagher checked himself over in the mirror one last time. Everything was sharp-creased, starched and shining. He looked the part, even if he didn't feel it.

The alcohol was already flowing by the time he entered the mess. Several of the younger officers had evidently arrived early and were already conspicuously well-oiled. A waiter approached bearing a silver tray laden with flutes of champagne. Gallagher politely declined. Drinking could wait until it was strictly necessary.

'Corporal Harris – flat-out, cold.'

Gallagher caught a snatch of conversation from the group to his left. He recognized Corporal Harris's name instantly – he was a quartermaster. Throughout a tedious week of post-tour stock taking, he had had far too much to do with Harris and his colleagues in the stores.

Gallagher stepped into their discussion and quizzed the speaker, a fellow lieutenant, Daniel Francombe. 'What's happened to Harris?'

'He's been found unconscious with a head wound,' Francombe said. 'The MPs are over there trying to work out if someone's broken into the armoury.'

Gallagher couldn't easily picture Corporal Harris being bested by anyone. The man was a wall of muscle and an experienced heavyweight boxer.

'Are they looking for someone?' Gallagher said.

Francombe didn't know. What little information was known had come from a sergeant who'd arrived at the stores at the same time as the MPs.

'If I were you I'd get the drinks in before they lock us all down,' Francombe said, and necked the rest of his glass.

Gallagher smiled and excused himself. He scanned the room looking for Norton. There was no sign of him. He couldn't help feeling that whatever had occurred at the stores might have been connected with the events of that afternoon. He had sensed the darkly restive feeling among the men leaving the court building. He didn't have a solid theory, only an instinct – he felt strongly that someone was in a mood for revenge. He guessed that, if that were the case, Norton would have become involved. He was probably talking to the police already. He checked his watch. The Kenyans were due to arrive in ten minutes. Someone sober would have to be on hand to meet and greet them in the major's absence. He glanced around the room and didn't see any obvious candidates. It would probably have to be him. But what to tell the Kenyans – 'Major Norton sends his apologies. It appears one of our men has run amok'?

Gallagher stepped outside the room and pulled out his phone. At least if he stepped into Norton's shoes he wouldn't be obliged to get quite so drunk. He dialled the major's mobile. It connected straight to a message informing him that the phone he was calling was switched off. He searched his contacts file and found a home number. It was worth a try.

The phone rang only once before Melanie Norton answered with a concerned, 'Hello?'

'It's Lieutenant Gallagher, Mrs Norton. I was wondering if you knew where Chris is at the moment? He's supposed to be hosting a dinner this evening.'

'Where are you?'

'I'm at the mess.'

'And Chris isn't there?'

'No, not yet. Do you know if he's coming?'

There was a brief silence. 'I don't know. He hasn't been home.'

'Right . . . If you don't mind my saying, you sound concerned, Mrs Norton.'

She didn't reply.

'When did you see him last?'

'At court, this afternoon.'

There was more she needed to say. He could hear it in her voice. She was frightened.

'Did something happen?'

Another silence. Gallagher considered mentioning the incident at the stores but didn't want to alarm her any further. He was fond of Melanie. He had been to dinner twice at the Nortons' home and both times she had been more than generous. She was a woman from whom maternal warmth seemed to flow effortlessly.

'I don't know what happened in Helmand,' Melanie said, her voice unsteady now. 'But I know he isn't the same man he was before he went. I told him to tell the truth . . . to tell the truth or . . . I told him I couldn't be with a man who—'

'It's all right. I get the picture,' Gallagher said. 'Look, I'll track him down for you. I'll give you a call. Oh, and if he calls you, call me. All right?'

'Thanks, James. I will. Thank you.'

Gallagher didn't stop to discuss arrangements with his fellow officers. They had commanded platoons in Helmand, they could organize a drunken dinner. He hurried out of the mess and jumped into his car.

There was cordon tape across the approach road to the stores and a redcap standing guard. Gallagher jumped out of his car and approached him. Outside the stores he could see two military police cars and a flurry of activity.

'I'm looking for Major Norton. Do you know if he's here?'

'I've no idea, sir.'

'Could you ask someone? It's urgent.'

The redcap called through on his radio and relayed the query. The answer came back negative. Major Norton wasn't with them.

Gallagher asked him if it was true that Harris had been assaulted and that there had been a break-in at the armoury.

'That's what we're investigating.'

'Well, tell whoever's running things that they should probably start with Major Norton.'

'Sir?'

'Major Christopher Norton. My commanding officer. He's missing.'

Gallagher turned back to his car, not sure what to do or

where to look. He thought back to the last moments in court that afternoon and tried to reason through what it would have meant to Norton. He was a man renowned for running a tight ship. He and Bryant were the most disciplined team in the regiment. It was what they were known for. They were legends. To have all that shattered, to be publicly portrayed as sloppy – to have a man go missing and another one using a smuggled-in phone for six months. It was humiliating, but enough to flip and steal a weapon from the armoury? And who would he shoot – one of his men? No. Gallagher dismissed the thought. They'd all been steadfastly loyal, even the few who'd been tricked by the lawyers.

What had Melanie said? She had told him to tell the truth. Then he remembered Jenny's closing words – her plea to the members of the platoon and their loved ones, and her invitation to contact her office with any further evidence. Norton had held fast until now, but had something changed?

Gallagher dialled Jenny's number. If Norton had tried to make contact with her, at least it would provide a clue. After several rings he reached an automated message: 'The number you are calling is not available.' He brought up his internet browser and searched for 'Severn Vale Coroner'. It led him to an official website and an emergency contact number. A dab of the finger and he was calling it. It rang several times. There followed a click and a different ringing tone as his call was diverted.

It was Alison who answered from her moving car. She had turned off the motorway and was threading through the suburban streets of Stoke Bishop, nearing her home.

'This is Lieutenant James Gallagher. I'm trying to reach Jenny Cooper.'

'You've reached her officer, Alison Trent.'

'I work with Major Norton. I need to know if he's been in contact with you or Mrs Cooper?'

'Right. For any particular reason?'

There was no time to sugar the pill. 'He's missing. He may be armed. I'm concerned for his state of mind.'

'Oh,' Alison said. 'Oh, dear.'

Jenny spotted the army Land Rover, painted desert khaki, in her wing mirror as it turned into the car park. Norton was at the wheel, alone, in the dress uniform and cap he had worn to court. He drove in front of her, then reversed to park alongside her to her left. Jenny reached for the blue legal notebook and pen she had ready on the passenger seat: she wanted it to feel like a formal encounter from the outset.

Norton climbed out of the Land Rover and came to her passenger door. The briskness of his movements was exaggerated by the thinness of his limbs. Stripped of excess flesh, his body had taken on a mechanical, machine-like quality. Jenny gestured to him to climb in. His eyes quickly scanned the surrounding area as if looking for hidden spies, then he joined her.

'Mrs Cooper. Thank you for taking this time.'

'Not a problem. You don't mind if I take notes?'

'Whatever you deem appropriate.'

He sat erect in his seat, staring out through the windscreen at the sea. He made no attempt to connect. All he presented was an outward form. A shell. Jenny searched for signs of the human being beneath but detected none. The emotional man, the father, the lover, all the things he must once have been, were locked away in an unreachable vault.

'You said you might have something to say?' Jenny said.

'Yes . . .'

She waited. His face flickered, not with feeling but with

conflict. She sensed a struggle taking place beneath the surface.

'Yes,' he repeated, seeming to reach a conclusion. 'I wished to tell you something about my career . . . To provide you with some context.'

'Feel free,' Jenny said, in as relaxed a manner as she could manage.

Norton clenched his jaw and breathed deeply through his nose.

'As you may be aware, I have seen many tours of duty over the last dozen or so years. I have served in Afghanistan and Iraq, always under Colonel Hastings's command, and mostly with Sergeant Bryant at my side. In Iraq we worked alongside Special Forces. Our job was to kill or capture insurgents. Post-invasion, the country splintered into fragments. There were more terrorist factions than we could count. Every local gangster and religious maniac had his own armed band looking to carve out a piece of turf. We sniffed them out, recruited informers, kicked down their doors, arrested them, shot them if we had to. On and on it went. Week after week. Month after month. I couldn't tell you how many times a bullet has whistled past my ear or a bomb exploded just around the corner from where I was standing. I shouldn't just be dead, Mrs Cooper, I should be dead twenty times over . . . But it was never me. I had the luck of the devil. It was the men around me who fell.' He paused and glanced across at her. 'You're not taking notes.'

'I only have to record evidence.' She smiled, suddenly feeling more like a therapist than a coroner.

'I hold two records, Mrs Cooper, only one of which I am proud of. Outside of the SAS, over the last decade I have been personally responsible for the apprehension and elimination of more enemy insurgents than any other British officer. But I have also lost the most men under my command. In Iraq we kept score of our successes, it was like a game – who had the highest head count. Richard Hastings was a major at the time – he wanted to win. We were attritional, relentless. He didn't seem to regret the loss of life in quite the same way as I did. Some men seem to have an extra skin; well, that's him. It certainly got results. Promotions. Kudos. Decorations.

'It's a philosophy Hastings carried through to Helmand, only he was behind a desk by then. Like stamping on ants, he said. Kill enough and the colony dies from within. *How many this week? What's the score? Are they still crawling out of their holes?* They never stopped coming. They never would . . . And I kept on scooping up young men and sending them home in pieces. Arms. Legs. Guts by the bloody armful. And for what? . . . I'll tell you something about those goat-fuckers we were meant to be protecting – they hate us. They haven't stopped hating us since 1839. British, American, Russian, it's all the same to them. Foreigners. Devils. They've never heard of the UN or President Bush. They've never seen a map, they don't read or write – the beginning and end of their world is that valley. Ignorance you won't even begin to comprehend . . . And we expect them to learn a lesson and be grateful.'

Norton closed his eyes as if overcome by a sudden weariness; as if the effort of maintaining the buttoned-up front had become too great and crushed his spirit.

'Tell me about Private Lyons,' Jenny prompted. 'Is there anything more I should know?'

'He did his best, but shouldn't have been there. He was just a boy.'

'What about his injury?'

'Sergeant Bryant struggled to keep him in line. Sometimes a young soldier needs a kick. Lyons needed several. You don't have discipline without fear, Mrs Cooper. Fear is necessary.'

Jenny wrote down his reply. 'Did he leave the post to look for his goggles?'

'It's hard to fathom an immature mind . . . But I can't think of any other explanation.'

'It must have taken more than fear to make him do that. He must have been terrified.'

'He probably was. But if you send a boy to war, what can you expect?' Norton let out a sound – a grunt of resignation. He shook his head. 'Skippy, we called him. Skipped like a lamb. Truthfully, I never expected to bring him home.'

Jenny let him have his moment of grief. He turned his face away from her. His jaw clenched tight. She felt an urge to put an arm around him, to let him cry and have it all spill out.

She couldn't, of course. All she could offer was words: 'It's all right, Major. There's no shame in this . . . none at all.'

'I, I don't know what to say about Kenny . . . I don't know how to explain . . .' His face twisted and contorted.

'Take your time.'

'We went into the village . . . it was my fault . . . I should have . . .' He pressed a hand to his face.

'It's OK . . .'

Norton's head whipped round suddenly. He stared at her with wild, demented eyes.

For a moment she held her breath. Her muscles locked. Her body refused to move. She cursed her stupidity at coming to him here. What was she thinking?

And then she noticed that it wasn't her he was looking at. He was staring straight past, and out of the window. She turned to see what looked like a police vehicle approaching along the lane at high speed.

Without another word he jumped out of the car and into the Land Rover. He started the engine and lurched forward as the police car turned into the car park and blocked his path. Norton veered right, catching it with a glancing blow, and barrelled straight towards the gorse hedge that ran along the edge of the farm track.

Two military police officers leapt out of their vehicle, drawing revolvers as the Land Rover ploughed through the hedge and bounced off along the track. Three shots rang out in rapid succession that sent the military policemen diving to the ground. Jenny let out a scream of alarm as one of the shots pierced her windscreen and thumped into the passenger seat. She sat, shaking uncontrollably, as one of the officers scrambled round to her door and hauled it open.

'Are you all right, ma'am?'

Jenny nodded. The wind blowing through the open door felt icy. An odd sensation of warmth travelled down her forehead.

'You're bleeding,' the officer said. 'Must have been a piece of glass. I've got a first-aid kit in the car.'

Meanwhile, the second officer ran forward through the gap in the hedge onto the track. Jenny heard two more shots. Then silence. He came back through a few moments later, shaking his head.

'He got away,' he called to his colleague. 'Where does that track lead?'

'I don't know. Call in air support.'

The first officer returned to Jenny's car with a first-aid kit. He popped open the plastic box and fished out a sterile dressing. 'Do you mind if I ask your name, ma'am?'

'Jenny Cooper. I'm a coroner. I'm holding an inquest . . .'

'Oh, that's you is it?' the officer said suspiciously. 'And Major Norton was here because . . . ?'

'He asked to see me. Whatever it was, he didn't get round

to telling me.' She took the lint dressing from his hand and pressed it to her grazed forehead. 'He's got something important to say.' She didn't know why she was telling the military policeman this. She felt dazed, as if she had suddenly found herself in a waking dream. She looked across at the neat hole in the back of the passenger seat. It occurred to her that if Norton had fired a degree or two to the left the hole would have been through her chest.

Another car, a small dark blue VW hatchback, careered down the lane and swung into the car park. Both redcaps span round, their hands reaching for their guns as Gallagher climbed out. He held up his hands.

'Lieutenant Gallagher. I'm a friend of Mrs Cooper . . .'

Still shaking, Jenny climbed out from her car, dabbing away the last of the blood.

'James?'

He looked at her in alarm, then noticed the snowflake of shattered glass in her windscreen.

'Where's Norton?'

'He took off along there.'

'You've let him go?' Gallagher said to the first officer.

'There's a police helicopter on the way.'

'Colonel Hastings lives the other side of that hill. Somebody warn him.'

Gallagher ran to his car.

'Sir . . .'

'James . . .'

He jumped in, span the VW around in a tight arc, spewing up dust, and aimed it at the hole in the hedge. He smashed through, ripping off half his exhaust in the process. The car thumped and clattered off along the track, the sound of the rasping, unmuffled exhaust splitting the air as he forced it to full revs in second gear.

The two redcaps dived for their car.

'Leave the scene as quickly as possible, ma'am,' the first officer yelled at her. 'Get in your car. Go.'

She did as he asked. She leapt behind the wheel, strapped herself in and clung on to their tail as they sped, siren wailing, back along the lane.

The two part-Arab mares were hungry after their ten-mile hack. They tore impatiently at their hay nets hitched either side of the stable door while Richard and Lizzie Hastings unfastened their girths and removed their bridles.

'Stiff?' Lizzie asked as she observed her husband limping slightly as they carried the saddles into the tack room.

'Only a touch. Nothing a warm bath won't sort out.'

He smiled at his wife as they stowed their equipment away. There had been an awkwardness between them since he had come home that he had felt dissolve during their ride. Until this evening he had been aware that Lizzie had been struggling to adjust to his presence in the house. He seemed to get under her feet and impede her regular routines. She oversaw their home as well as its many animals with remorseless efficiency, rising before six to see to the horses, feed the chickens and exercise their two Labradors before leaving for her part-time job as a secretary in a local primary school. Her life was contained, orderly and ran like clockwork. And always had done. As the years wore on he had seemed to become less and less a part of it. Without children to bind them together, he often wondered what did, exactly.

Lizzie smiled back and touched his arm affectionately. 'I was impressed. If I didn't know different, I'd have thought you'd been riding every day.'

'Thank you,' Hastings said. Compliments from Lizzie were rare, and smiles like the one she had just given him scarcer still. 'Even if I don't quite believe it.'

'No. Honestly.'

She pushed her hair back from her face and gave a quick glance towards the door. She flashed another smile. Hastings read the cue. He stepped forward and slipped his hands around her waist.

'I missed you,' he said.

It wasn't entirely untrue. There had been moments during his last tour when he had felt the odd pang of loneliness and a longing for their three acres on the downs overlooking the sea.

'You, too,' Lizzie said.

She leant forward and kissed him. It was a tentative kiss, but he felt the urgency behind it. As he responded, she stepped in closer, pressing herself against him. Her hands travelled across his back and she pulled him hard against her. The force of her passion took him by surprise. Was she seducing him here in the dusty tack room? Really? Wonders never ceased. He went along with it, sliding his hands under her shirt and feeling the warmth of her soft flesh.

Someone coughed. A man.

Lizzie hurriedly pulled down her top and stepped away as a figure appeared outside the doorway.

'Chris?' Hastings first thought was that there must be some sort of emergency. Norton was meant to be hosting a dinner at the mess. Then he noticed Norton's odd, glazed expression – and then the Glock pistol in his hand.

Lizzie had seen it, too. She backed into the corner, waiting for him to do something.

Hastings stepped forward. 'Chris, what's the matter?' He spread his arms in a trusting gesture of openness.

'Baghdad.'

'What about it?'

Norton squeezed the trigger and shot a hole through

Hastings's thigh. Outside, the mares whinnied and bolted off across the field.

Lizzie let out a stifled scream as Hastings staggered back a step and fell.

'Basra.'

Another shot, this time through the other thigh.

Hastings writhed and thrashed, smearing blood across the bare concrete floor.

'Helmand.'

A shot ripped into Hastings's left shoulder.

'Stop it! Stop it!' Lizzie screamed.

Norton turned the gun on her and she fell silent. Hastings groaned. Blood was pumping hard from all three wounds. He was powerless and he knew it. Fighting back wasn't an option. He was surprised to find himself supine in the face of death. The final instinct was to appeal to human sympathy.

'Please, Chris,' he croaked.

There was no trace of pity in Norton's face. There was nothing. Only blankness. Hastings had never seen a face so devoid of feeling. He waited for the last bullet, feeling surprisingly calm in the circumstances.

He became aware of a sound. An engine. It could have belonged to an old tractor, only it seemed to be moving too quickly. It was approaching from the far side of the field.

Keeping the gun trained on Hastings, Norton glanced over his shoulder as the vehicle came to a halt not far away. A door opened and closed.

'Norton!'

A voice travelled across the field. Through the fog of pain, Hastings vaguely recognized it. 'Norton. Put that down. The MPs will be here any second. There's a helicopter on the way.'

Hastings saw Norton look up at the sky. Then turn his

head at the faint sound of a police siren approaching along the road. It was still a long way distant, perhaps half a mile or more.

Lizzie whimpered. It was a pathetic sound. Hastings longed to tell her to shut up, but he hadn't the strength to speak.

'Toss the gun away, Chris,' the voice outside said.

Gallagher. James Gallagher – that's who it belonged to. What the hell was Gallagher doing here?

That was the last thought Hastings had before he felt the bullet burst through the muscle into his stomach and a sensation like an explosion of fire tear through his body and consume him.

'For all those boys,' Norton said.

But Hastings hadn't heard him.

Jenny skidded to a halt on the gravel driveway outside the Hastings's modest, stone-built farmhouse. As she jumped out, the two military police officers had already spotted something and were running across an area of lawn at the side of the house towards a wooden post-and-rail fence that divided it from a paddock. Following a reckless impulse, she went after them.

'Stay away! Stay away! Get down!' the first officer ordered.

She ducked behind the trunk of a cypress tree that stood in the centre of the lawn and watched the two redcaps throw themselves to the ground by the fence and take aim across the fifty yards that separated them from the two figures in the field. Gallagher was walking very slowly towards Norton, who was standing outside a stable block, aiming the pistol at him.

'Stop! Stop there!'

The shout from the redcap carried across the field.

Gallagher did as he was asked. He stood no more than twenty feet from Norton now. He appeared to be talking. Jenny thought she heard the sound of a woman in distress coming from inside the stable.

Gallagher slowly held up his left hand as if in reassurance to the redcaps and, putting his right hand out in front of him to receive the pistol, walked towards Norton. As the gap between them closed, Norton appeared to raise his hands as if in surrender.

Then, at the very last moment, he changed his mind.

As Gallagher lunged forward to disarm him, Norton dodged sideways, pressed the gun to his temple and pulled the trigger.

THIRTY-FIVE

Anna Roberts had been through every kind of emotion in the day and a half since she had seen Sarah Tanner in the witness box being forced to confess, in front of all those people, that she had been cheating with Steve Price. And while she was pregnant, too. Anna hadn't known whether to feel fury or pity, whether to blame Sarah for being weak or Price for taking advantage of her loneliness. Whoever was to blame, it made her feel sick. It made her remember the few occasions on which, while Lee had been away, she had felt a guilty twinge of desire for another man. Burning with shame, she had fetched the expensive underwear she had bought two weeks before and thrown it out with the rubbish. That part of her life was over. She wanted nothing more to do with it. Not ever.

Then on Saturday she had heard the news about Major Norton and Colonel Hastings: Kathleen Lyons had called and told her before breakfast. Her phone hadn't stopped ringing all morning. Everyone had wanted to know what had happened and why. Claydon White, the lawyer, had called three times asking if she had heard anything more, but she had to tell him that there was no more news. No one had any answers. In the afternoon she had plucked up the courage to phone Melanie, but her sister had answered and said that she wasn't able to talk to anyone at present. She didn't think that she would be ready to speak to anyone for several days. There was a rumour that all the men in the platoon had been called in for a meeting with General Browne and told not to say anything, not even to their wives and families. Anna had tried calling Sergeant Bryant. He sounded as if he'd been drinking and told her that he knew as much as she did. He hadn't been told anything except that Hastings was badly injured and clinging to life in intensive care. Bryant had sounded almost human as he told her this – as shocked and confused as everyone else – and had asked after Lee. He confessed that he had always felt safest when out on patrol with Lee. 'Any problem, your Lee would spot it a mile off. I always said he had two sets of eyes.'

His parting words had turned over and over in her mind all through the night. Two sets of eyes. That was the Lee she knew: sharp, alert. He missed nothing. At five a.m. she gave up trying to sleep and dragged herself out of bed. She knew she had to go and see him straightaway.

Leanne was tired and scratchy, her mood not helped by having been cooped up on buses for most of the morning. Her interest in the handful of books Anna had brought to entertain her during the journey had run out by Bristol bus station along with the cereal bars and three cartons of juice. Anna let her play with her phone, but the battery soon died. Bored, and frightened by the prospect of going to see her dad in a hospital, Leanne started to moan and grizzle. On the last leg of the journey, the local bus to Selly Oak, she had a full-blown tantrum that brought impatient sighs and looks of disapproval from the other passengers. Anna had wanted to slap them. If only they knew where they were going, she thought. Eventually, Anna pacified Leanne with sweets bought from the shop in the hospital reception, but by then her nerves were in pieces and she was fit to drop.

As they set out early that morning, Anna had tried to prepare Leanne for the shock of seeing the man she would probably not recognize as her father. He would be very sleepy, she warned, and the doctors had had to shave off his hair. Leanne had simply listened, or half-listened while pretending to be interested in something else, and to Anna's astonishment didn't ask a single question. The child who, since shortly after her second birthday, couldn't go more than ten minutes without asking 'why?' had simply accepted what she was told. Anna concluded that her infant mind was sharp enough to know that she didn't want to know why. Anna had overheard the talk of bombs and guns among the kids at playgroup enough times to know that Leanne's imagination must be peopled with dark and sinister characters she would rather not think about. She couldn't blame her.

For once, Anna's arrival coincided with official visiting hours. Gently reminding Leanne that her daddy would probably still be asleep, she led her along the corridor to the door of Lee's room. She glanced through the observation pane. He was still as she had left him: propped up on pillows, staring vacantly into space. A feeding tube had been added to the drips and catheter and his cheeks looked even more hollow. She hated the idea of Leanne seeing him like this, but there was no choice.

'Sweetie, Daddy isn't very well,' Anna said. 'But he's OK. The doctors and nurses are looking after him.'

Leanne glanced up at her with a sad, serious face, but said nothing. Anna pushed open the door.

'Lee? It's me, Anna. Look who I've got with me.'

She lifted Leanne up and carried her towards the bed.

'There's Daddy, look. I told you he'd be sleepy.' She reached out and stroked Lee's arm. 'Do you want to hold Daddy's hand?'

Leanne shook her head and buried her face in Anna's shoulder.

'OK. I'm just going to sit you down over there with one of your books.' Anna carried Leanne over to the chair in the corner, trying hard not to cry. A foolish part of her had expected Leanne's presence to work a miracle and wake him from his torpor. She sat her on the chair and hurriedly fetched out the handful of books. 'Here we go. I just need to talk to Daddy for a minute.'

'But he can't talk,' Leanne said with brutal honesty.

'Well,' Anna said, 'I can still talk to him.'

She went and sat on the side of the bed and took hold of Lee's hand. She spoke to him in a whisper, although she was aware that Leanne would hear every word.

'Something happened, Lee – the day before yesterday. Major Norton went crazy. No one knows why, but he went to Colonel Hastings's place and shot him . . . Then he shot himself.'

She studied his face. It remained a blank.

'Norton's dead, Lee. It's to do with Kenny and Pete, isn't it? . . . I think you know why he did it . . . Lee? It turned out Kenny had a phone. He was sending texts to Sarah. She sent one to him saying they needed to talk the night before he was killed. She'd been sleeping with Steve Price. There was something different about him that morning, wasn't there? . . . You were with him, Lee. You must have seen it.'

Lee's eyes seemed to come into focus. Anna felt tension return to the slack muscles in his hand.

'Norton's gone. Couldn't live with himself. Whatever's happened, you can tell me now. It's safe, babe. You're home now. You've got me and Leanne. You're safe.'

Very slowly, but with strength that surprised her, Lee's fingers curled themselves around Anna's and he squeezed them tight.

THIRTY-SIX

There were no officers in the court and only a very few other ranks. The men of C Company had finished their post-tour leave and the order had evidently been given that the conclusion of Jenny's reconvened inquest was to be kept as low-key as possible. A police inquiry was underway into the circumstances of the incident at Colonel Hastings's home and Jenny had not been asked to deal with the inquest into Major Norton's death. In the little over two weeks since it had happened, the press had largely lost interest and moved on to more current and thrilling stories. There was only a scattering of reporters present, whom Jenny assumed from their yawns and bored expressions were expecting to hear nothing more than her closing remarks followed swiftly by open verdicts. This, too, was what Simon Moreton was expecting. From his usual seat at the back of the court, he listened to the evidence of the penultimate witness, Private Danny Marsh, with evident impatience. He had had his fill of the north Somerset coast and was anxious to be back in the thick of the action shuttling between Whitehall and the offices of the Chief Coroner in the Royal Courts of Justice.

The intervening fortnight had taken its toll on the relatives. Sarah Tanner, now even more visibly pregnant, looked to have aged ten years. Sitting next to the female police constable who during her weeks of isolation had become her only companion, her eyes stared out from above dark shadows. Paul and Rachel Green appeared no longer to be on speaking terms. They sat two seats apart and barely exchanged a glance. Kathleen Lyons was composed as always, but somehow cut a more diminished figure. Her defiant dignity had given way to weary resignation. She seemed more caught up with her own downcast thoughts than with what was going on around her.

Claydon White and Carrie Rhodes did their best to give an impression of optimism, but the smiles were forced. They had read the public mood and could feel it magnified inside the courtroom. Even in the space of seventeen days there had been an imperceptible turning of the page. The war was over. The social media storm over the *#Helmand2* was a distant memory. The wave of outrage had crashed on the shore. There would be no emotional verdict, no headline moment. If there was anything to be milked from the case, it would most likely entail a long and costly slog through the civil courts which they would have no appetite for. The relatives behind them would be palmed off with vague promises and the money spent on dining and driving them written off as a business expense.

At the other end of the lawyers' bench, Robert Heaton radiated quiet, understated confidence. He had been given the job of steering the ship safely home and the harbour was in sight. In the face of all of his opponents' bluster, he had already proved beyond doubt that Private Green had been the author of his own misfortune. There were many reasons that front-line soldiers weren't permitted personal phones, and the dangers posed by unfaithful partners were high among them. He had lost his head and had only himself to blame for it.

Despite assurances from Alison that Private Marsh was a

disaffected, spirited young man who wouldn't shy from telling the truth, he had followed his colleagues in saying as little as possible. Jenny could understand why. With no qualifications and no immediate family to fall back on, the army, for all its faults, was all Danny Marsh had. Everyone has to belong somewhere and Danny clung to his sliver of security.

At the end of his brief spell in the witness box, Jenny turned to the final matter she wished to raise with him.

'You took Private Lyons's notebook from his belongings, didn't you?'

'Yes,' Danny said.

'Why did you do that?'

'I wanted his nan to have it.'

'And you didn't think it would get to her otherwise?'

'I don't know . . . I suppose I was worried it wouldn't.'

'Because it contained a letter he'd written to her to be read in the event of his death?'

Danny nodded. 'Yeah.'

Jenny motioned to Alison who passed the notebook up to Danny.

'Look at the letter. You'll see that several pages have been torn out after it.' She paused while he turned through the notebook. 'What was on them?'

'Nothing . . . I don't know.'

'That's not an answer, Private Marsh. I'll make it simple: did you tear out those pages?'

It was Alison to whom Danny's eyes turned. From her elevated position, Jenny couldn't see her expression, but she could guess it. Danny found himself paralysed and tongue-tied. He shifted uncomfortably from foot to foot.

'Try again, Private,' Jenny said. 'Did you tear out those pages?'

Danny nodded.

'What was on them?'

He squirmed with embarrassment. 'Nothing. Just stupid stuff . . . Stuff the other lads had written – messing around. It was just mickey-taking. We all got it . . .'

'When did they write this?'

Jenny could see Danny's mind groping for any way out, but there was none. He was cornered.

'When he was digging the latrine.'

'So this was, what – teasing? Bullying?'

'No. Just banter.'

'And had you been drinking?'

'Not much. Hardly anything . . . A couple of the lads just brewed some stuff in their canteens because it was the end of the tour.'

Jenny felt the atmosphere in the court turn. All attention was suddenly focused on Danny's every twitch and gesture. Robert Heaton stiffened and leaned forward.

'And did this "banter" have anything to do with what happened later that night?'

Danny Marsh's lip began to tremble. Alison fixed him with a stern, maternal look.

'It was just meant to be a joke,' Danny said. 'We hid his goggles . . . And when the sergeant ordered kit inspection we wound him up a bit – told him he'd be court martialled for letting his equipment fall into the hands of the enemy. It was just a joke. A stupid joke. No one thought he'd take it seriously.'

'But you did know he'd take it seriously, didn't you?' Jenny said, 'Because he was just a boy, wasn't he? Was that part of the joke – the fact that there was so much he didn't know or understand?'

Danny couldn't deny it. 'No one thought he'd go over the wall. You'd have to be crazy.'

Or young, or very frightened, or both, Jenny thought to herself.

'Thank you, Private Marsh.'

She handed Private Marsh over to the lawyers and watched the faces of the jury as Danny was forced to accept that Lyons suffered more than his share of teasing and was the frequent butt of Sergeant Bryant's temper.

'You make it sound like we had it in for him,' Danny objected loudly to Claydon White. 'That's not how it was. We loved that lad. Skippy was a mate. We all loved him like a brother.'

'You had a funny way of showing it. The sergeant cracking his rib and the rest of you pushing him to the point where he gave his life for a pair of goggles.'

'That's the army,' Danny said. 'That's how it is. That's just how it is.'

'I'm sure. I don't doubt it for a minute.'

White looked gravely at the jury and sat back down in his seat.

'Any questions, Mr Heaton?' Jenny asked.

'No questions, ma'am.' Heaton politely shook his head in the hope that appearing unfazed was the best way to dampen the effect of Private Marsh's evidence. 'I'm sure the jury wouldn't appreciate my delaying them from their deliberations a moment more than necessary.'

'Well, they'll have to wait a short while longer, Mr Heaton. I have one further witness I wish to hear from.'

'Ma'am?'

On Jenny's cue, Alison went to the door at the back of the court and called for Private Lee Roberts.

From the back of the courtroom, Simon Moreton fixed Jenny with an accusing stare. She ignored him.

Seconds later, the two male nurses Jenny had employed to transport him from hospital brought his wheelchair down to the front of the courtroom followed by Anna. Private Roberts was dressed in uniform. The empty bottom halves of his dress trousers were carefully folded and pinned. He looked far from healthy, but following Jenny's intervention a fortnight before, he had been weaned off his medication and on examination by independent psychiatrists was declared to be perfectly sane. The ICU psychosis was explained away as a symptom of an infection. Jenny had her suspicions over whether he had genuinely suffered a psychotic episode, but had put them to one side. All that mattered was that he was recovering and here to tell his story.

Anticipating Heaton's protest at another unannounced witness, Jenny headed him off: 'Do you have an objection to hearing from this witness, Mr Heaton?'

Ignoring the urgent whispers from the MOD lawyers behind him, Heaton glanced at the jury then at Private Roberts and decided that any attempt to block the witness would be counter-productive.

Private Roberts's voice was weak and his delivery shaky, but he was determined to be heard. When he had sworn on the Bible to tell the truth and nothing but the truth, Jenny asked him for his version of the story. Without further prompting, he repeated to the court what he had told her in the hospital canteen the previous afternoon.

His final posting had been his third tour of duty, but his first under the direct command of Major Norton. It had become clear that things would be different from the moment of their arrival. Norton didn't let a day go by without mounting a patrol, and often more than one. While other officers he had served under kept their men within the safe confines of the post for as long as possible, sometimes for days at a stretch, Norton believed in maintaining a near constant and visible presence in the valley. This required the platoon to operate at the outer limits of its abilities. A seven-mile foot patrol in full kit in forty degrees of heat with the constant threat of IEDs, sniper fire or ambush, sapped the energy from bodies and minds. If anyone dared question the need to patrol as often or in such exposed positions, Major Norton would always answer that he was operating on the direct orders of HQ. Colonel Hastings expected nothing less of them. Norton never mentioned his legendary record of killing and capturing enemy insurgents, but Sergeant Bryant reminded them of it frequently: they were working for the best and the bravest, and he expected them to step up their game accordingly.

The remorseless routine took its toll. They had two men seriously injured and one killed in the first three months of the tour. By a quirk of fate, both Kenny Green and Pete Lyons had been on the patrol in which Private Dalton had been killed in an ambush which resulted in them being pinned down for three hours. Dalton took two of those hours to die in writhing agony, in the middle of a dirt road. The incident hit morale hard. Norton responded not by easing back but by stepping up activity. Sensing that the men were becoming restive, Sergeant Bryant became even more ferocious in his discipline. Most were smart enough to keep their heads down, but Pete Lyons couldn't help himself – he'd answer back, then get the rough side of the sergeant's tongue or worse. Roberts wasn't in the least surprised that Lyons had a cracked rib – Bryant's boot seemed to be his regular alarm clock.

Somehow the men got through the rest of the tour without further loss of life, although they had more close shaves than he cared to remember. As the weeks passed they seemed to degrade the local Taliban to the point where the local villagers claimed that they had retreated from the valley altogether, making only the occasional forays from the surrounding mountains. For a while it felt as if they had won the war and that it had all been worthwhile. Then, a month from the end, and with the approach of the opium-growing season, Taliban had reappeared to assert them-selves and let the farmers know they would be expecting a cut of their business. Norton increased the frequency of their patrols still further. An exhausted platoon started to fray at the edges. Discipline suffered. Some of the men cadged small amounts of hashish from the locals and brewed up hooch.

'You couldn't help but think that someone was going to get killed before we got home,' Roberts said. 'We didn't talk about it, it was just a feeling in the platoon – that Major Norton would rather die than take a single backward step.'

The night of the 21st had been particularly edgy. The 22nd was to be their last day of operations. There would be a dawn patrol and one later in the evening. No one wanted to catch a bullet on their last outing. The bottles of hooch had been passed round. There was dark talk of refusing to leave the post the following day. It had seemed like a good idea for a while, but then someone came up with the idea of playing a prank on Pete Lyons. Skippy was all too easy to wind up. Roberts hadn't been one of the ring leaders, but he had heard some of the boys trying to convince him that courts martial could still sentence a soldier to the firing squad.

Lyons had pretended to tough it out as he always did. He certainly gave no clue that he was scared enough to go looking for his missing goggles. Looking back, Roberts guessed it was probably as much to do with his pride as anything else. Skippy had wanted to go home a man, a hero, not in disgrace as a loser who had fainted on patrol and earned himself a serious charge.

They had all felt sick with guilt the next morning when

they realized he was gone. They were all waiting for someone to blurt out what had happened, but no one did. Major Norton became more and more agitated. He had been showing serious signs of strain for weeks – sudden mood swings, outbursts of anger – but Lyons's disappearance pushed him to the edge. Before Yusuf arrived with the news that the Taliban were holding him and demanding $100,000, he was pacing like a caged animal. There had been no question of sending Yusuf back with a counter offer. Norton wanted to resolve the situation immediately. He didn't want to be the officer who had been humiliated by kidnappers on his last day of tour.

Roberts hadn't noticed that Kenny Green was particularly quiet that morning because they all were. They hardly spoke a word to one another. Everyone was dealing with his own private guilt. When the chance came to go to Shalan-Gar, they were almost relieved. Kenny had thrown his kit on. He couldn't get there fast enough.

All Roberts remembered of the short journey along the dirt road to the village compound was the atmosphere in the Land Rover in which he was travelling. Major Norton had been deathly silent, but it was obvious to everyone that his silence was masking his rage. He had owned that stretch of valley for six months. He had earned the trust of the locals. He had led a platoon that had eliminated more than one hundred of the enemy. And here he was on the last day having the Taliban stick two fingers up to him. Even Bryant felt it. Roberts remembered glancing over at Norton in the Land Rover with concern. The two of them had always operated as a single unit. That morning, Bryant looked like a man who had been cut adrift. He couldn't seem to read Norton's intentions, and his uncertainty was picked up by the men. By the time they walked through the heavy gates into the silent village, they could smell each other's fear.

Soldiers have a sixth sense: each one of them knew something bad was about to happen.

Roberts, Green and Carter watched the backs of Bryant and Norton as they crossed the square to Musa Sarabi's house. The compound was often bustling and full of noise, but that morning there was precious little sign of life except the odd chicken scratching in the dust. The Taliban were in the village – they could feel it. Norton knocked on the door of Musa Sarabi's house and Roberts had seen it open and the panicked look on the old man's face. He knew in that moment that the village elder had sent Yusuf to lead them into a trap. Almost immediately a grenade exploded on the far side of the square.

They dived for cover behind the low wall that ran along the perimeter of Musa Sarabi's property as a burst of gunfire issued from a rooftop some thirty or forty yards away on the far side of the square. They returned fire as it became clear that there were two or three gunmen firing from separate positions. Then they heard screams and gunfire coming from behind them inside Musa Sarabi's house. It was a big house that stretched over two floors. Sarabi inhabited it with his extended family – brothers, wives, cousins, children. Roberts heard Kenny say, 'It's Norton – he's gone crazy.'

'I didn't register what was going on at first, but Kenny clocked it. Before I knew what he was doing, he'd shot through the door into the house. I heard shouting – Kenny yelling at Norton to stop or he'd shoot. There were more screams, more gunfire from inside, and more incoming from across the square . . . It was all over in seconds – Sergeant Bryant went in after them. There was a shot. He came out seconds later and took off across the square firing up at the rooftop and ordered us to follow. He took one of the gunmen out. Private Carter and I broke cover. We were firing up at the roof thinking we'd taken the enemy out when another grenade came in. I saw it coming in to land about ten feet in front of us . . . I blacked out . . . Then all I've got is snatches of memory. I saw Bryant dragging Kenny's body across the dirt, Norton following behind . . . I heard voices – Danny Marsh and the others. That's it. That's all . . . I've got a picture in my mind of the helicopter – the female medic sticking a needle in my arm – then nothing till Bastion.'

'What do you think happened to Private Green?' Jenny asked.

'I think he was trying to stop Norton murdering women and children. He was going to shoot him, but Sergeant Bryant shot Kenny first.'

'But you didn't see it?'

'No. Only Sergeant Bryant knows for certain.'

There were only two further questions for the witness. Both came from Claydon White: 'Private Roberts, would you agree with one thing that Sergeant Bryant told this court – that Private Kenny Green died a hero's death?'

'He did.'

'Would you have shot Major Norton if you had witnessed him murdering women and children?'

Roberts took a while to consider his answer. 'I don't know, sir. Loyalty's powerful, but not always a good thing . . . No, I'm not sure I'd have been brave enough.'

Sergeant Bryant arrived in court later that morning flanked by two hefty military police officers. He did as Jenny had suspected he would and refused to answer any further questions on the grounds that he was entitled not to incriminate himself.

As she summed up the evidence to the jury, Jenny stressed that Bryant's refusal to answer the allegations Private

Roberts had made against him was not to be considered as evidence. They had heard his account of the events in Shalan-Gar and they had heard that of Private Roberts. It was up to them to weigh these accounts together with all the surrounding evidence and to decide, if they were able, how Private Green met his death. Likewise, they had to balance what Privates Danny Marsh and Lee Roberts had told them about the circumstances of Private Lyons's disappearance against what all the other members of the platoon had said. Did the others have a motive to lie? Were Marsh and Roberts the only ones telling the truth? These were key questions they would have to answer. That was a matter entirely for them to decide. They had a grave responsibility to discharge, and they must take as long as they needed to arrive at their verdicts. If, having arrived at verdicts, they felt that one or either needed further explanation, they were entitled to include a short narrative. Their task was nothing more or less than to determine the truth insofar as they were able on the evidence they had heard. If they couldn't be sure of the truth then they must return an open verdict; they must not, on any account, feel obliged to reach a decision of which they were not certain.

The knock on Jenny's chambers door came at four thirty that afternoon.

'They're ready, Mrs Cooper,' Alison said.

Jenny looked for any sign or indication of what the verdicts might be, but Alison shook her head. They had gone about their business quietly and deliberately and were holding their cards close to their chests.

The courtroom was heavy with anticipation. The absolute quiet was disturbed only by the sound of the jury's shuffling feet as they returned to their chairs.

'Would the foreman or woman please stand?' Jenny said.

To her surprise, it was the large, tattooed and bearded man who rose. It occurred to her for the very first time that he might have been a retired soldier. The confidence with which he delivered his answers confirmed her suspicion that this was probably so.

'Mr Foreman, in the case of Private Peter Lyons, have you reached a unanimous decision to all the questions on the form of inquisition and have you put your signatures to the same?'

'We have.'

'Can you please state your finding on the injury causing his death?'

'Decapitation.'

'Time and place in which the injury was sustained.'

'The early hours of August the twenty-second in the Shalan-Gar valley, Helmand Province, Afghanistan.'

'Your conclusions as to the cause of death.'

Jenny broke one of her cardinal rules and glanced at Kathleen Lyons as the foreman read out their finding. 'Private Lyons was kidnapped and unlawfully killed by Taliban insurgents. We do not find that anyone in his platoon was individually to blame. We do, however, find that Private Lyons was not yet mature enough for the role he was expected to fulfil and should not have been placed on front-line duty.'

Kathleen's face barely showed a flicker of emotion, though inside she was dying with grief and guilt and shame. The jury had told her what she already knew: the blame was hers as much as the army's. She had known he was still just a boy. She should never have let him go.

Jenny pressed on to the second verdict. The foreman again confirmed that they were unanimously agreed and had signed the form of inquisition.

'Can you please state your finding on the injury causing his death?'

'A bullet wound to the back of the head.'

'Time and place in which the injury was sustained.'

'At approximately seven forty-five a.m. in the village of Shalan-Gar, Helmand Province, Afghanistan.'

'Your conclusions as to the cause of death.'

'Private Green was unlawfully killed by Sergeant Alan Bryant whilst trying to prevent Major Christopher Norton from shooting unarmed and defenceless civilians. We also find that as a result of extreme stress causing mental illness, Major Norton was, in all likelihood, not in control of his actions.'

As Claydon White folded a tearful Sarah Tanner in a hug and Rachel Green sobbed into her husband's shoulder, Jenny thanked the jury for their efforts and told them that in the light of their verdicts she would be passing the file in Private Green's case to the prosecuting authorities with a recommendation that Sergeant Bryant be charged with his murder. She would also be writing to the Ministry of Defence informing them of their verdict in the case of Private Lyons and asking them to act to prevent the deaths of more boy soldiers. She hoped they would respond, but feared they would not.

Jenny turned to Robert Heaton and the lawyers sitting uncomfortably behind him for her final remark: 'Thank you for your assistance, gentlemen – you have reminded me of all the reasons I became a coroner.'

THIRTY-SEVEN

Jenny made her way along the gravel path through the churchyard. There was a snap in the morning air and the first fallen leaves crunched underfoot. She wasn't an official guest but had nevertheless come to pay her respects at the joint funerals taking place at the small church on the outskirts of Highcliffe on this, the last Saturday in September. She stayed away from the main party already gathered at the graveside, and watched from a distance as the minister intoned, 'Man that is born of a woman hath but a short time to live . . .' His voice carried clearly through the stillness, competing with the raucous song of an irreverent blackbird. In amongst the mourners she spotted Melanie Norton, her face covered by a black lace veil. Standing alongside her was Anna Roberts. Lee Roberts was seated in a wheelchair next to his wife with his daughter on his lap. As Melanie cried, Anna touched a hand to her back in sympathy. There had been no military honours for Major Christopher Norton. His passing had been marked only by the briefest unannounced service at the local crematorium. There would be no headstone or name carved into a list of the fallen. Over years to come, he would be quietly erased from the records. A forgotten casualty of a dubious war.

Paul and Rachel Green, surrounded by extended family, were still keeping their distance from the now extremely pregnant Sarah Tanner, who, like Kathleen Lyons, was bearing her grief alone. Thanks to the jury's verdicts the two of them would be well compensated by means of discreet and confidential out-of-court settlements wrung out of the MOD by Claydon White. Money would help, but would do little to ease the pain of loss and the nagging guilt at the small parts they had played in the extinguishing of two young lives. Any comfort, if comfort was to be had, would come from these solemn ceremonial moments that would remain scored forever in their memories: ranks of soldiers standing to attention, saluting the descending coffins and honouring their fallen comrades with that strangely moving inward gaze that men in uniform adopt when fending off emotion.

A military funeral was like no other. Jenny watched, captivated, consumed by alternate waves of pride and sadness.

The orderly progress of the service stood in stark contrast to the uncertainty that had raged since Jenny's jury had delivered their verdicts. The Defence Chiefs had spun the outcome as proof that their overstretched personnel had been pushed beyond endurance by tight-fisted politicians. Their detractors claimed it as evidence that the army really was as barbaric and archaic as they had feared. The government seized the opportunity to wield the knife and weeded out their most entrenched opponents in the MOD. Closer to home, Simon Moreton had been furious with the outcome. 'Heads will roll, Jenny. And if mine's one of them, yours will be, too,' he had threatened ominously before disappearing behind the tinted windows of his government car.

Alison had phoned early that morning with the news that Simon's name was all across the papers. His twenty-six-year-old former lover had broken cover and spilled her story to a tabloid. Passionate encounters in civil service

offices and taxpayer-funded trysts in smart hotels were set
out in toe-curling detail. His career lay in tatters and no
doubt his marriage, too. Jenny had tried to call him but he
didn't pick up. Instead, he had replied with a text that she
was left free to interpret: *'Thank you for your loyalty.'* It
was very Simon. How deep his bitterness would run,
whether he would turn the page or choose instead to make
good on his threat, she couldn't say. There was no predict-
ing how a man whose thirty-five years of public service was
ending in ignominy would respond.

The minister recited the closing grace and uttered the final
'Amen'. There was a pause; a moment of terrible silence
before the regimental bugler sounded 'The Last Post'. Its
haunting notes travelled up to a brightening sky. Jenny
listened with new ears. The simple melody captured both the
depth of loss and, in its final two ascending notes, the pin-
nacle of hope. For a passing moment she glimpsed what led
young men to offer their lives in wars the reasons for which
they could not possibly understand. Then, as with a fleeting
glimpse of sunlight between clouds, she lost sight of it again.

Drifting back to her car some distance ahead of the mourners, Jenny felt a tap on her shoulder.

'Sorry. I didn't mean to startle you.' It was Gallagher. She
hadn't spotted him among the identically dressed officers at
the graveside. 'How are things?'

'Only a little crazier than usual,' Jenny said, sparing him
the details. 'You must be off to Kenya soon?'

'Monday. Can't wait. Any news on Hastings – is he out
of the woods?'

'So my officer tells me,' Jenny said, 'but he suffered a lot
of damage. He probably won't walk again. I wouldn't count
on him ever coming back.'

'I would. He's lucky and a bastard – the perfect com-bination.' He glanced over his shoulder. They were still out of earshot of their nearest followers. 'What about Bryant? Are they really going to court martial him for murder?'

'They'll go through the motions.'

'He should have put his bullet in Norton. Still, I can't say I wouldn't have done the same in his shoes.'

Jenny looked at him. 'You play the part well.'

'What part's that?'

'The tough-guy soldier.'

'Maybe that's what I am.'

'Maybe.'

They passed the crooked lychgate and emerged onto the pavement, where they stopped and faced each other for the awkward moment of goodbye.

'Well, good luck,' Jenny said. 'Look after yourself.' She offered him her hand.

Gallagher took it and pressed it between his. 'I really hoped you'd call me, Jenny. There's just something about you . . .'

Before she could reply he leaned forward and kissed her softly on the mouth. It was so sudden and unexpected that it took her breath away.

'I'm sorry,' Gallagher said, 'I had to kiss you once.'

Jenny shook her head. 'There's no need to be sorry . . .'

'Thank you.' He smiled into her eyes. 'I'll take it with me. Goodbye, Jenny.'

And then, as if deliberately saving her from what she might so easily have done, he turned and went.

Jenny returned home to an empty house. She had agreed with Michael that it would be best if he were to collect his belongings while she was out, and he had done as he had promised. His key lay on the doormat and he had left a note on the kitchen table. The inquiry into the incident in Iraq looked like clearing him of all blame, he assured her, and a second consultant had declared him fit to fly. He would soon be getting his pilot's licence back. There was light at the end of the tunnel, but even so, and as much as he had loved her, he felt that the time was right for them both to move on.

As hard as she tried, Jenny couldn't find it in herself to disagree. Two complicated souls under one roof had, in the end, proved one too many. They had seen too deeply into each other – that was their problem. Sometimes life was better lived closer to the surface and away from the things that haunt us. She drifted around the newly uncluttered rooms and began to find her sadness at his going giving way to the possibility of new beginnings. She hoped that he felt the same.

Jenny changed out of her funeral clothes and went outside into her garden. Untended for weeks, it had grown as unruly as the rest of her life, but the bolting grass and overgrown borders had become a haven for butterflies and were humming with bees and overhead, the last remaining swallows swooped and dived, enjoying the feast of insects her neglect had unwittingly provided for them.

She was alone again, but not unhappy. It was a beautiful Indian summer's afternoon, her long-delayed holiday beckoned and a young man's kiss still lingered on her lips. It would be selfish to wish for anything more.

THIRTY-EIGHT

A week before Christmas, Kathleen Lyons set eyes on her daughter, Holly, for the first time in more than three years. With her lawyers' help, she had finally tracked her down to an address in south London. They arranged to meet in a cafe on the concourse at Paddington station. Holly was sketchy on the details of where she had been and what she had been doing, but her shabby appearance told a story of hard times and disappointed dreams. If Kathleen hadn't initiated the encounter, she doubted if she would ever have seen her daughter again.

Reading between the lines, it soon became clear that Holly had somehow managed neither to read nor hear about her son's death. A crowded railway station was no place to break such news but Kathleen found herself with little choice. She did what she could to lessen the blow. She had brought two envelopes. Before she had mentioned Pete's fate, she passed her daughter the first. Holly opened it with a suspicious expression which turned to one of disbelief as she saw that it contained a cheque made out in her name for £50,000.

'What's this for?' Holly said. 'Is it a joke?'

Kathleen shook her head and asked her to open the second.

It contained a photocopy of a letter written on two small sheets of lined notepaper.

Dear Nan,

It's not long now till we'll be on our way home. We'll be the last lads out of here, which is something to be proud of. But if you're reading this, well, I guess I haven't made it.

Please don't waste your time crying. Ever since Mum went, you did your best for me. I know I caused you heartache, especially when I joined up, but never, ever blame yourself – being a soldier was all I ever wanted and no one could have stopped me.

My only regret is that you've worked so hard to bring me up and you'll think it was all for nothing. Believe me, it wasn't. It doesn't matter how long you live, it's how you live.

The other lads will tell you how I've done out here and I hope it makes you proud.

If you ever see Mum again, and I pray that you do, I want you to show her this and to let her know that I forgive her for everything and that I'll always love her and you, from wherever I am.

Be happy and remember the good times.

Love you always,

Pete

ACKNOWLEDGEMENTS

A little under two years ago I was due to give a talk at the Bookmark bookshop in Spalding, Lincolnshire, a town on the far side of the country from my home. It involved such a long drive for a brief appearance (and I was to be only one of three writers speaking that evening) that I almost cancelled, but thankfully I stuck to my maxim of 'turn no opportunity down'.

When I arrived, late and saucer-eyed from many hours at the wheel, the owner of the shop handed me a note. It had been left for me by one of her customers – someone I hadn't seen in over twenty years. His name is Frank Ledwidge. In the academic year 1989–90 we had been at Bar School together in Gray's Inn, London. I remembered Frank as a friendly and irreverent young man with the stubborn and tenacious streak that all good advocates require. After being called to the Bar he went to practise law in Liverpool, and that is where I assumed he had spent his career.

Frank's note, apologizing for not being able to attend my talk, included his phone number and an invitation to get in touch. I called him the very next day, eager for two decades' worth of news. It turned out that, like me, he had dabbled in the law for a few years before wondering if there was more to life. Unlike me, he had been a member of the Naval Reserve and in the late 1990s spent some time as an observer during the conflict in the Balkans. The experience seemed to light a spark in him. He turned his part-time military career into a permanent one. Soon afterwards he became part of the futile and evidently often comical effort to detect weapons of mass destruction in Iraq.

Following Iraq, Frank was deployed to Afghanistan, where he ended up in charge of justice in the British-occupied territory of Helmand. To say that his experiences left him less than impressed with the effects of British and US foreign policy would be an understatement. He emerged disillusioned and critical of politicians and military leaders who failed to understand the complex consequences of their actions on the ground. It would have helped, for example, to understand that many Afghans still bear the British a deep grudge dating back to their previous occupation of that country in the late nineteenth century. To such people, all foreign occupiers, whether British, American or Russian, are one and the same. Frank has written three seminal works of non-fiction based on his personal knowledge and experience, each of which I recommend. They are: *Losing Small Wars: British Military Failure in Iraq and Afghanistan*; *Punching Above Our Weight: How Inter-Service Rivalry Has Damaged the British Armed Forces* and *Investment in Blood: The True Cost of Britain's Afghan War*.

Frank also introduced me to a young man called Ed, who had recently returned from commanding a platoon in Helmand. Ed gave me a very detailed and candid account of day-to-day life in a forward command post. Much of what he told me was revelatory. What struck me most powerfully was just how young our front-line soldiers are. Our wars are being fought by teenagers and very young men who, while they may be technically described as volunteers, are in reality just ordinary lads often from the most challenging and deprived of backgrounds. The officers who command them can be as young as twenty-one.

After a few conversations with Frank and Ed, I knew I had the subject for the next Jenny Cooper novel. Huge thanks to both of them and whoever or whatever brought us together.

Heartfelt thanks also go to the many readers who have written and emailed and pestered me to hurry up and finish writing. I would like to extend particularly warm wishes to Sarah Hunt, a lady whom I have never met, who recently wrote to say that reading Jenny Cooper's adventures had helped her through her convalescence from a serious illness. Sarah, I hope you are feeling much better.

Lastly, I would like to thank my editor, Maria Rejt, for the invaluable guidance she gave me before I started this book and for her patience in waiting for it.